CW00520664

# Trembleath

## Ruth Shedwick

Chiselbury

First published 2019
Second edition Copyright 2023 © Ruth Shedwick

Published by Chiselbury Publishing, a division of Woodstock Leasor
Limited
14 Devonia Road, London N1 8JH, United Kingdom

www.chiselbury.com

ISBN: 978-1-916556-27-0

The moral right of Ruth Shedwick to be identified as the author of this
work is asserted.

Edited by Alex Stacey
Cover Artwork by Vivian Lally
Graphic Design & Typesetting by RS Graphic Design
Illustration by Harriet Hallam

*To Dad,*
*- my rock, my hero -*
*thank you for encouraging me to dream*

# a-dgerag

A s she ran down the cobbled street into misty darkness, clouds consumed light cast out from the waning moon into the night sky. Her ragged breathing filled the air, her heartbeat pounded in her ears and her panic filled their nostrils; they were hungry for the kill. The slapping of their large feet against the cold wet stone echoed around her. She tried to ignore the sound and focused on making it to the village, where she knew she'd be safe. The pounding continued from her pursuers bringing new life to her tired legs, humming from the pain now fuelled with adrenaline. She could make out a light in the distance, and another, and another; the village she grew up in, people she called friends, family, loved ones were just within reach. The thought of being in the warm embrace of her parent's arms spurred her on.

She didn't see the pothole beneath her feet, she sprawled forwards tumbling hard onto the cobbles, her kneecap shattered on impact sending waves of agony down her leg. The girl howled, as pain coursed through her body, muscles convulsing tightening her limbs; she rolled on the ground in foetal position panting out the pain. Tears ran down her cheeks. The rain hadn't registered until she saw the ripples in the puddle beside her. With a sigh she raised her head skywards watching the drops descend. She knew she had to keep moving, had to get away, put some distance between her and…

Silence, deathly silence. Like someone had clicked the mute button on life. And then she felt it. The hairs all over her body stood to attention; a tingling sensation ran up her spine, rising up the back of her neck; she shuddered as a breath of cold air passed over her, she could smell the stench of death in its wake.

Death was coming for her and there was nothing she could do about it. She thought of her mum and dad at home with her little sister, waiting for her bedtime story. But there would be no story. Not tonight. Not any night. She knew she would not survive. She hung her head low in submission and waited for death's grip, a prayer forming on her lips,

*"Bless me father for I have sinned…"*

# *chaptra onan*

I dyllic coastal life is how he sold it to her, '*Come with me to Cornwall,*' he said, '*it's a great opportunity to make a new start. No one will know us, we can put the past behind us.*'

Amelia sat on the bench staring out to the raging sea. The roaring of the ocean filled the air as waves crashed against the boulders; vision steadily blurred with salty tears, her mobile phone lay in her hand displaying Tatem's last message, '*Sorry, I can't go through with this.*' Those seven words had brought her life to a standstill. As she watched the waves pounding against the rocks she felt her stomach tighten and prayed the heartache would go away. Hypnotised by the rhythmic flow of the ocean, she wondered how it would feel to slip away and let the current take her, hold her, love her. A dark shape in the water caught her attention, she blinked away the tears to see more clearly; it wasn't driftwood or seaweed and was quite sure it wasn't a seal, she was certain it must be a person, an insane one at that.

The seething white water crashed down in huge waves, battering everything in its way and dragging it back into the ocean. As Amelia stood to get a better look, she saw the swimmer go under as another enormous wave hit. She closed the text message and dialled 999, she held the phone tight listening to the ring tone, after a few moments a woman's voice answered asking which service she required.

"I'm at Creek Bay and someone is drowning. You need to send help."

"You need the Coastguard. Can you tell me your location?" the calm voice replied.

"I don't know. Someone! Out in the water!"

"Okay. What is your name?"

"Amelia."

"Look around Amelia, can you tell me where you are? Can you see any distinguishing features?"

Amelia looked up and down the narrow road where she stood and spotted a road sign. "Cliff Mount. I'm by a bench on Cliff Mount Road looking down at the water and they are right down…" she gasped trying to locate the swimmer but they had vanished. "Oh my god! I can't see them anymore. Please hurry."

Ending the call, she stuffed the phone into her back pocket and clambered down the rock face to get a better look. The waves were relentless and she was sure the swimmer had perished. As she inched down the jagged rocks she scraped her leg, cursing her clumsiness as she continued her descent clinging to the heather. The sound of sirens in the distance brought some relief, but she was determined to see if the swimmer was okay. Nearing the bottom of the cliff she saw an old yellow camper van with open side-doors, footprints in the wet sand leading from the van towards the sea.

As she made her way onto the beach her feet sank deep into the soft wet sand, swearing to herself as a shock of cold sand breached the cuff of her boot. Someone shouting in the distance drew her attention; a man wearing a wetsuit was running towards her from the camper van waving his arms shouting, "Stop!"

The young man said something else, but Amelia couldn't hear him over the sound of the waves. As she took another step, the sand refused to stay solid under foot and she sank further down.

"Stop!" the man shouted again.

Panic set in as the sand reached her knees. She tried to lie forward, clawing at the sand around her, but it only made her sink further down.

"I wouldn't struggle if I were you." He sounded closer this time. She looked up at the owner of the voice now standing above her. "You have been lucky enough to encounter a spot of what we like to call lenki treth, more commonly known as quicksand." The young man said with a wide smile.

Amelia didn't feel especially lucky. "No shit," she retorted.

The sirens sounded closer now and she felt safe in the knowledge that help wasn't too far away.

She looked at the young man; it appeared the swimmer was more than okay. It was then that she took in the appearance of her would-be rescuer; tall, slender, athletic young man with dark brown wavy hair. His wetsuit pulled down to the waist revealing a toned midriff.

"At least help is on the way," he said.

"I know. It was me who called them."

"Wow, that's some sixth sense you have."

She couldn't help but laugh at the irony. "Actually, I called them out to rescue someone I thought was drowning."

The man looked back to the water. "Out there?" Amelia nodded. "No-one out there today except me."

"Yeah, kinda gathered that."

"Wait here, I'll be back."

He was already running towards the van before she could call him back. Looking down at her waist she muttered. "Yeah, where else would I go?"

The man returned with a rope and flung one end towards her, making sure to keep his distance. "I want you to put the rope around your torso like this." He showed her with the other end of the rope a step-by-step approach and she mimicked his actions. "Make sure it's tight under your armpits and hold the rope in front of the knot. When you're ready, I'll pull you out."

The sand had a firm grip; she could feel it tightening around her waist pinching at the belt buckle digging into her skin. Grabbing the rope with both hands she held on tight, her knuckles turning white, as he started to walk backwards she felt the sand give, but it didn't want to let go just yet; it pulled her in deeper up to her chest, the cold shock taking her breath away. The man dug his heels into the sand and gritted his teeth as he got purchase to pull once more.

"Relax your body!" he shouted. "Trust me."

As there was still no sign of the coastguard he was the closest thing to salvation, she had no other choice *but* to trust him. Amelia took deep breaths and let her limbs go free. The sand was quick to accept the invitation and she sank again, then suddenly she felt cold damp air against her skin as she was slowly dragged out of the hole, her fingers tightened around the rope as the top of her jeans appeared from the sandy grave. She was almost horizontal as he pulled her free along the sandy beach to a safe distance. Exhausted, she rolled onto her back looking up at the sky watching the gulls circle above. Salty water dripped off his wet hair as he leant over her.

"Feeling okay?" he asked.

A smile crept across her face as he offered his hand, which she gratefully accepted. The coastguard truck thundered across the sand towards them, when it ground to a halt a middle-aged man jumped out.

"Everything okay here Seth? We got a call, swimmer in trouble." The coastguard looked at Amelia, she didn't look like a swimmer, with her bedraggled appearance and wet clothing, and he concluded she might have been a potential suicide.

"Yeah, nothing hurt here but pride," he shouted back. Amelia felt her cheeks flush, "…and wardrobe by the looks of it."

It was then that she realised she did look a bit worse for wear; her jeans were ruined and the suede boots, oh those beautiful boots - totally trashed. She had spent a week's wages on those bloody boots! The two men laughed making her want to sink back into the quicksand in embarrassment.

"I called. I saw someone out there in trouble." Amelia said nodding to the water.

The coastguard turned to Seth. "Just you?" the young man nodded. "Seth's one of our strongest swimmers. If it was anyone else down here I would be worried."

"Strongest swimmer?" she asked.

"I'm a volunteer with the coastguard." Seth offered by way of explanation. "I help Ned when I can."

"Speaking of which, how you fixed this weekend?" asked Ned.

"Sure. Just let me know."

"Aye, will do." Ned turned to Amelia. "Nice to meet you, Miss?"

"Amelia."

"Ned." He said tilting his cap. "Glad to see you are safe and well Amelia. Sorry I can't stay Seth, I was on my way to pick up Jessica from her music lesson when the call came in." He jumped back into the truck and wound down his window. "Remember to take notice of those warning signs in future." He winked at Seth before driving off.

Amelia looked over her shoulder to see that there were in fact several signs dotted along the foot of the cliff, which, unfortunately she hadn't noticed having taken the scenic route down the cliff face.

"Seth." The young man said as he held out his hand, with what could only be described as the cheekiest smile she had ever seen. It had her momentarily forgetting why she was there in the first place.

She shook his hand.

"Give you a lift?" he asked pointing to his van.

She was grateful for the offer; almost certain she wouldn't be able to walk back to her car in the state she was in. "Sure. I'm parked up there."

Seth switched on the heater when he noticed his passenger shivering. "Are you visiting?"

"No, just moved here."

"Where are you staying?"

She hesitated for a moment before answering. "I'm moving into Lowe Cottage, do you know it?"

"I know it."

They continued driving with the sound of the engine filling the awkward silence until they reached her car at the top of the hill.

"This is me," she said.

Seth pulled up behind the lonely vehicle on the country lane. "You know how to get there?"

"I have directions." She jumped out of the van, her limbs still aching from her ordeal.

"You sure you're okay?" He looked concerned.

"Sure. Thanks again for rescuing me. I don't know what I would have done if you weren't there."

"Nah, Ned would have been there if I wasn't. Besides, you called *him* remember and if you hadn't tried to rescue *me* you wouldn't have been on the beach in the first place."

Amelia smiled, "Yeah."

"Stay safe." He flashed her that smile and rolled up his window.

As she watched him drive away she stood by the roadside looking at her tiny Golf packed with all her belongings and then remembered that her mum was expecting a call when she arrived in Cornwall. Amelia frantically patted down her jeans and checking pockets for her phone, stopping when she realised it was now most likely buried in the sand. There was only one number she wanted to remember, and that was mum, the one person she couldn't tell what had happened today, about Tate, about the sand, about her failure. Not that mum was one to actually say 'I told you so', but she knew she would be thinking it. This was a new start, only now she was doing it on her own.

# chaptra dew

Lowe Cottage was proving more difficult to find than she anticipated. The instructions were vague and her SatNav was on the blink again. When the device finally rebooted and eventually found a satellite connection, it proudly informed her that her current location was… in the middle of a field. Amelia switched off the SatNav and threw it into the passenger foot well. "Technology!" she proclaimed throwing her arms in the air. "How can something have so much promise and yet end up being so utterly bloody frustrating?"

After driving up and down what seemed like the same stretch of road she finally came to a stop. Idyllic country life presented itself in the form of Lowe Cottage, a beautiful, traditional two-bed stone cottage, thatched roof, sash windows and lychgate garden entrance surrounded by a mass of scented clematis.

As she took in her surroundings she remembered why she was there. *His* job had been the reason for the relocation from the North West of England whilst the company undertakes a major excavation project, but what if *he* had decided to continue the new life without her? Would he be sitting by a roaring fire toasting his newfound freedom with some new woman on his arm? Amelia started to hyperventilate, but there was no sign of life inside the cottage from where she stood. She walked down the lavender lined path and looked at the plant pot on the top step, hoping the keys would be under the flowerpot as previously agreed. Tatem had been working night shifts to get the project moving during the first couple of months, he had assured her Creek Bay was a 'safe village' with 'very little crime' and that the keys would be fine. She tilted the pot to reveal her set of house keys attached to a Charizard Pokémon keyring; Tate's nickname for his feisty girlfriend. Standing, she fumbled one of the keys into the lock before she could change her mind. Relieved to find the cottage empty and void of confrontation, she dumped her rucksack on the floor and slammed the door shut.

Glad to be out of her filthy wet clothes, she lay back in the warm water allowing the tension to ease from her limbs; Amelia closed her eyes and relaxed. As she began to slide further down under the warm water the unexpected loud ringing of the landline made her jump. She grabbed a towel and ran downstairs "who the hell can this be" she muttered under her breath picking up the receiver.

"Hello?"

There was no reply, but she could tell there was someone on the other end. "Hello? Who is this?"

Still nothing. She couldn't think who might have the number, other than Tate, a wrong number perhaps, or maybe they were looking for the previous owner. Amelia bit her lip; after all, this was the kind of childish behaviour she would expect from her ex.

"Tate, is that you?" she said between gritted teeth. The line went dead leaving the monotone ringing out. She slammed the receiver down onto its cradle. "Asshole!"

As she looked down at her feet, she noticed a puddle had formed on the wooden floor where she stood; angry at the caller's intrusion Amelia stormed upstairs to finish getting dried.

By the time she had finished unpacking the essentials and made her way downstairs, the fire was blazing making the lounge feel cosy and welcoming. Ignoring the boxes of books, DVDs and clothing she had brought inside from her car, Amelia lay on the rug in front of the fire and began reading her journal in the flickering light sipping a glass of ruby Cabernet Sauvignon. The wine was supposed to have been a celebration of their new life together and she should have been sitting there sharing it with her boyfriend, strike that, lousy boyfriend, no strike that, totally hopelessly lousy boyfriend - a complete and total fuckwit; but she told herself she had no regrets. The flames gave ample light for reading as she thumbed through some of the entries in her journal. They brought with them memories she wanted dead and buried:

> *3rd August: He called me again today, I'm pretty sure he will ask me tonight. Tate. My love, my soulmate. Why have I taken so long to say yes to his persistence? Yes Tatem. Yes and yes one hundred times yes!!!!!*

Amelia ripped out the page and threw it on the fire watching the ball of paper unfold and disappear into the flames. She continued to flick through the pages...

> *25th October: He will be back from his trip soon. I can't bear being apart from him. They work him far too hard, he's long overdue on that promotion! If Sarah was here we could hang out and take my mind off him. Go shopping, catch a film, anything to make this week more bearable. Then I wouldn't be so lonely.*

She tore out the page and it met the same fate as the last, a few pages further and her heartbeat started to quicken as she read the next entry, all of the painful emotions she thought were buried came flooding back.

> *2nd December: The heartless cow! How blind must I have been to miss the signs! My best friend… and Tate. I just don't understand. I will <u>NEVER</u> put my trust in anyone ever again!*

Amelia let out a sigh as the memories and heartache flowed through her veins. It was a bad idea to pick this thing up, but she had to find closure, draw a line under this period; she turned to one of the later entries.

> *23rd May: We will make a fresh start. Tate and I. Mum is not best pleased, but we were both naive to even think we knew what love is. In the time spent apart, we have both grown. This time will be different.*

"But it wasn't, was it Tatem?" she muttered throwing the entire journal into the flames.

The journal lay on the fire, edges curling and blackening, the smoke thickened as it filled the chimney. She closed her eyes, tears stinging behind closed lids, Amelia convinced herself it was just the smoke. The phone rang again and this time she was certain she would get an answer. She ran and picked it up within two rings.

"Hello?"

Silence.

"Look. I don't know who you are but—" her words stopped abruptly as an awful gut wrenching sound rang out, the most haunting and terrifying sound she had ever heard. Amelia slammed the phone down, but it hadn't come from the receiver, it was close by, outside in the darkness. She ran to the door and shot the door bolts in panic, closed the curtains and crouched down next to the fire. Again, the horrific sound rang out; it seemed to reverberate through the cottage. She grabbed the poker by the side of the fire and sat holding it close to her chest and waited. She stayed there frozen for what felt like hours; finally she fought with her stiff legs to move again.

Morning crept through the thin curtains rousing her from the limited sleep she had managed. Her stomach growled and thoughts of a full English breakfast was far too tempting, but it wouldn't be a full English, it would be two Jaffa cakes and a cup of black coffee knowing full well the cupboards were empty. She desperately needed to get some groceries, but that meant going outside. Gingerly pulling back the curtains Amelia peered outside, not sure what she was expecting to see, there was nothing sinister out there; it was a bright crisp day, birds full of song, nothing in the immediate vicinity, just her car parked outside. She told herself it must have been her mind playing tricks on her; it was probably foxes or some other unfamiliar country noise, with her emotional state following yesterday's events combined with being alone in a strange place, her imagination had been running wild.

As she switched on the kettle a knock at the front door startled her. She could hear loud voices outside above the sound of a large vehicle, opening the door she was met with a tall man in overalls with clipboard in his hand, his nametag read 'George'. Hambleton Removals was embroidered on his overalls matching the company name on the van, behind him three men wearing the same uniform were busy carry boxes and stacking them beside the lychgate.

"Amelia Scott?" she nodded. "We have your delivery."

"I wasn't expecting you until tomorrow."

He looked down at his paperwork. "According to our records, Tatem London signed for the delivery insisting it had to be today, paid extra for us to travel overnight so we could get here early."

Amelia tutted. "Sounds like the kind of thing he'd do." She opened the door wider for him to come inside.

"Where would you like everything to go?"

She showed him the kitchen and spare bedroom with instructions of what would be best suited to which location and then stopped when she saw a young man enter with a box labeled Tate.

Amelia turned to George. "How many boxes have you got with Tate or Russells Construction on?"

George looked down his consignment list. "Three."

"Would you mind putting those by the back door for me." George nodded. "Fancy a cuppa?"

He graciously gave her the drinks order before leaving to instruct his team about the box locations.

Hambleton's were highly professional and courteous, making light work of the delivery. George mentioned they were going to spend the day in town before heading back North, making the most of their time on the road. When they left, Amelia quickly changed ready to drive into the village where she located the convenience store and stocked up on essentials - bread, tea, coffee, bacon and eggs and a few other emergency rations - wine, ice cream, beer. Putting her groceries away in the boot of the car she felt an uneasy notion that someone was watching her. She looked up where a man across the street in long black coat stood staring, his intense eyes never leaving her; unblinking dark eyes framed by his black wavy hair and pale skin. Amelia was fixated unable to break her gaze from his. A tractor thundered by, momentarily blocking her view; in the seconds it took to pass the man had vanished. She involuntarily shuddered, her skin exploding into Goosebumps. A soft female voice interrupted her thoughts.

"Good morning. You must be the young lady renting Lowe Cottage."

Amelia turned to an old woman whom she guessed to be in her late eighties but had aged well. Her smile put her at ease and she returned the pleasantries. "I'm Amelia." She held out her hand after she closed the boot of the car.

"Miss Chandler, but please call me Lois. Did you get here last night?"

"Yes, a little after six."

The old woman's eyebrows slowly rose, "You haven't heard then?"

Amelia inched closer to the old woman, concern filling her voice, "Heard what?"

A young couple came out of the store speaking to one another in hushed tones. Miss Chandler leant towards Amelia.

"A young girl is missing. Valerie, the Temple girl, she hasn't been seen since last night. The rumour is she ran off with a college boy, but I think something terrible happened to the poor child, she was too sensible to run off with a boy."

Amelia's intrigue went up a notch noticing the people around her were behaving rather strangely. She wasn't one for listening to idle gossip but was starting to doubt Tate's words about the village being safe. "What do you think happened?"

A man with a stern expression appeared from the shop behind the old woman. "Lois! That'll do!" he said. "We can well do without gossip, think of Jean and Tom, they're out of their minds with worry."

"Come now detective, we all know what has happened to that poor girl."

"Lois Chandler, we know nothing of the sort. We'll find Valerie Temple. Mark my words. For all we know, she was most probably at a party last night and lost track of time."

The old woman tutted and ignored the policeman; reaching over to Amelia she whispered, "Be safe Amelia, don't hang around after dark on your own!"

The detective nodded to Amelia as he gently pulled the old woman to one side, linking his arm through hers he led her away. "Come on Lois, let's have a little chat."

"Great, I moved to crazy town," Amelia muttered, as she watched the old lady being escorted down the street.

Turning to her car, Amelia opened the driver's door when a sign reflected in the window caught her attention, 'The Bay Book Shop'. Amelia was a self confessed bibliophile and she would need new reading material now she would be spending the evenings alone.

She made her way over to the bookshop where a small sign in the shop window brought a smile to her face. 'Staff required – enquire within'. The whole point of the move to Cornwall was for Tate's new job, they had planned to live off his wages whilst she found her feet. There was no chance of that happening now, and her savings would hardly last any time at all, she needed some income and sharpish. Amelia couldn't help acknowledging the lucky coincidence. "Excellent, must be fate," she said under her breath as she entered the store.

The bookshop was crammed to the rafters with an eclectic mix of second-hand, antique and new books. She could see that the mezzanine floor had even more books filling the bulging shelves. A group of teenagers sat on two of the four sofas in the middle of the ground floor and chatted to friends working at the computers along the wall nearby. She approached the counter welcomed by the smell of freshly ground coffee.

"Get you anything?"

It was a familiar voice in an unfamiliar setting.

"Seth." The surprise in her voice betrayed her. "Do you work here?"

"I own here," he said with a smile.

She watched him wiping down the counter, hoping she hadn't sounded condescending. "A drink would be great. What do you have?"

"Tea, coffee, water… beer."

"Beer?"

"Yep. Licensed." He continued wiping down the counter. "We have acoustic nights too and nothing goes together better than music and beer."

"Wow, a licensed bookshop. I think I've died and gone to heaven," she said with a nervous laugh. Amelia glanced at the wall clock. "Well, seeing as it is only ten-thirty, I'll have a glass of still water please."

Sitting down on the bar stool she watched Seth as he poured her drink into a tall glass, the ice cubes clinking as they rose bobbing to the surface.

"The notice out front, you still looking for help?" she asked sipping her drink and enjoying the cool liquid roll down her throat.

"You interested?" he asked.

"I'll be honest. I wasn't, but it seems like my plans have changed."

Seth looked her over and smiled appreciatively. "Well, you're young and pretty enough to keep attention of the teenage boys and old enough for the rest of us, I guess you'll do."

"Erm, thanks, I think?" She wasn't altogether sure if she should be flattered or insulted.

"I'm kidding." He gave a chortle. "If you can read and count, then that is fine with me. Hours are nine-thirty 'til two-thirty Monday to Friday plus some weekends and I may need extra help on music nights. Pay is nine-fifty per hour. How does that sound?"

Amelia was counting quickly in her head to make sure it would definitely cover the rental costs, and a little extra on top wouldn't go amiss. "Fantastic, when do I start?" she asked enthusiastically.

"No time like the present. We will see how you go on the weekdays before doing any weekends. Different crowd and you'll need to be on the ball."

Amelia couldn't believe her luck - a new job, a new home, and a new friend all within 24 hours; granted, he was the only one in the village she had really met, who happened to be her saviour for the second time. As cheesy as she knew it sounded, it felt like destiny kept bringing them together at the right time.

Seth showed Amelia around the shelves to familiarise herself with the categories, and to the storeroom for additional stock, publicity material, food and snacks. The mezzanine floor was filled with more specialist books, scatter cushions littered the floor and there was a two-seated sofa, smaller than those downstairs, posing more of a loveseat.

"You have to make sure the kids behave when they come up here," he said when they reached the top step.

"I bet." Amelia looked at the sofa and then to Seth who was observing her, she wondered how many nights he had been up here with someone special. "Seen some action has it Seth?" she asked, immediately regretting her words. He didn't respond but she was certain there was a twinkle in his eye. They were suddenly distracted by raised voices downstairs; the teenagers became amplified during a heated debate. Seth stepped up to the balcony.

"School time guys," he said in an authoritative voice.

One of the teenagers shrugged, "Free period Seth."

"Matthew, you know Mrs Nolan sends me the timetable."

"Arh, fair dos, can't blame a guy for trying." The irked shaggy-haired youth replied.

The sullen teenagers proceeded to pack their papers and books leaving in frustrated chatter and clomping boots before banging the door behind them and then all was silent.

Amelia sighed. "This is the sound of a bookshop."

"Not this one." Seth leapt down the stairs and flicked a switch behind the counter. Pearl Jam's '*Garden*' flowed through the speakers around the store. He nodded to Amelia to join him. "Come on, I'll show you how to operate the coffee machine."

"How hard can it be?" she asked as she made her way down the stairs.

Seth smirked. "Make me a tall frappe choco chino latte."

Amelia frowned. "A what now?" She wasn't one for those poncey drinks and had no idea what he just asked for, he could have been speaking a foreign language for all she knew.

He pointed to the blackboard menu on the wall behind the counter. "I'll go through the drinks, hope you've got a good memory."

She looked over the alien words. "So do I," she muttered.

It took Amelia the best part of two hours to master the menu and machine. As her thoughts wondered, she noticed the doughnuts sitting underneath the glass cloche, taunting her with their jammy goodness.

"You can have one you know, staff privilege," he said, catching her eying the doughnuts.

"I wish. They'll go straight to my thighs, no thanks."

"You certainly don't need to worry about that."

Butterflies swirled around her stomach as she stared at the floor avoiding eye contact; unaccustomed to compliments Amelia wasn't sure whether she was supposed to reciprocate, all she did know is that she was determined not the turn her usual shade of pink when in his company.

"Cold one?" he asked holding up a bottle of beer. "Think you deserve it."

Gratefully she accepted the drink, took a long gulp, and relaxed. Seth motioned for her to join him at the sofa in front of the window. Sitting with his leg crossed over his knee and arm stretching along the back within an inch of her shoulder, he looked at her with a pensive expression, as though he was trying to access her thoughts.

"So," he said finally. "You think you can come to love this place?"

She looked around the store, "It's a lovely bookshop."

"…and the village?"

Placing her beer on the table she smiled. "Quiet, just what I wanted."

He paused while he gave her that look again, "…and the people?"

Uncertain where he was taking his line of questions she tried to keep it as vague as possible, avoiding any mention of a significant other. "I've only met a couple so far. I bumped into Miss Chandler this morning."

"Oh?" He dropped his leg from his knee placing his foot onto the floor and leant forward over the table towards her. "What did she have to say?"

"She was talking about a young girl who's gone missing."

The old-fashioned brass bell clanged against the top of the door and three teenagers entered, nodding to Seth before taking their seats next to the computers.

When Amelia turned back to Seth he was closer to her, an intense look crossed his features as he whispered, "Missing?"

Amelia lowered her voice so the teenagers wouldn't hear. "Yes, I think her name is Valerie." Seth leant back into the sofa, lowering his gaze. "You know her?" she asked. He nodded. "The policeman sounded optimistic about finding her."

He sat upright. "Policeman?"

Amelia nodded. "He was passing when he overheard our conversation." She frowned. "Don't you need to be missing twenty-four hours before the police say you're officially missing?"

There was no response from Seth so she sat back and took another sip of her beer thinking perhaps Valerie was a close friend, a girlfriend even.

His voice was sombre when he finally spoke. "It's out of character for Valerie. She's by the book, sweet kid, only sixteen. And this is a small village, we tend to look after our own, you know? If the police were suspicious they'd act regardless of the rules."

Amelia rested easier believing he would never have relations with such a young person, and then she was racked with guilt; a young woman was missing and she was worried about the competition.

She cleared her throat. "Like I said, the detective was optimistic that she would be found. Guess it's just a—"

There was a loud bang as a young boy burst through the door.

"Jason, have you heard?" he shouted to the other teenagers.

The young boy being addressed momentarily looked up from the computer screen. "What?"

"Valerie!" he managed to get out trying to catch his breath. Everyone in the shop turned their attention to the sweaty out of breath boy. He edged towards his friend. "They found Valerie," he said softly but loud enough for the audience craning to hear. The room filled with gasps as they waited with bated breath… "What's left of her!"

Amelia's gut tightened. "What?" she whispered.

His eyes widened. "Yeah, police are everywhere. Found her an hour ago on Trembleath Moor."

The teenagers all darted out of the shop in a great hurry leaving Amelia standing by the door, she turned to Seth but the sofa was empty.

"Seth?" she called out, but there was no answer. She walked through the store to the back room. "Seth? Did you hear? They've found Valerie."

The bell above the door chimed announcing the arrival of a new customer. Amelia quickly made her way to the counter when she saw a tall man standing with his back to her. The long coat looked familiar, even his hair, then he turned to face her; there was no mistaking it was the man who had been staring at her from across the road earlier that morning. His gaze was intense; dark brown eyes stirred her blood.

Amelia cleared her throat and spoke in the best sales-woman voice she could muster. "Hello. Can I help you?" He continued to stare at her for an uncomfortable length of time. Her throat became dry. "If you're after Seth I'm afraid he just left."

A grin tugged at the corner of his lips. "You're new." His voice was velvety soft, sounding more like a purr. She nodded. "Been here long?" he asked. She shook her head and his grin reappeared. "Well, I know you're not mute because I swear I heard you form words into a sentence just now."

Amelia cleared her throat, the confidence edging away. "I… I started today," she stammered.

He walked to the other end of the counter his hand trailing along the top. "Your name?"

"Amelia." She didn't know why she offered it, if anything he was rude and obnoxious, so why would she have done anything he asked? "Amelia Scott."

The back door banged shut drawing her attention away from the man, she hoped Seth was back. With her gaze still fixed on the corridor she asked, "And you are?" When he didn't answer she turned around, to find he had gone again.

She heard hurried footsteps from the rear of the shop. "You okay?" Seth asked rushing past her and standing by the window.

"Of course, why shouldn't I be?" she said, eyeing him suspiciously.

His stance was rigid as he looked out searching the streets, but for what she didn't know. Amelia walked away from the counter and put her hand on his arm. He felt solid, hot, clammy and muscular… definitely muscular. His gaze never faltered, never left the street.

"Did you hear?" she asked. "Valerie has been found."

"I heard," he muttered between clenched teeth.

"Do you want me to get you a cuppa?" she asked. It seemed silly really, but her mother always made tea when something horrible happened, like that makes it all better.

Without turning away from the window he said, "No. I think we are done for the day."

Amelia was taken aback; she blinked, trying to work out if she had done something wrong, why he was behaving in such peculiar manner. She assumed he must be upset about Valerie, he did know her after all, and perhaps he had been closer to Valerie than she thought. Realising she was still holding his arm she let go. Picking up her bag, she walked past the statue that was Seth pausing as she opened the door.

"See you tomorrow?"

When he didn't answer her, she left the store hoping it hadn't been her first and last day.

# *chaptra trí*

I t had been a productive day for Amelia, fortuitous even, but it had been a sad day too. Poor Valerie, what had happened to the young girl? Amelia snuggled under her fleece blanket on the sofa with a hot mug of tea and pulled a book from her bag. She had always intended to read the Belgariad series but had never got round to it. After recent events it was time to immerse herself into a fantasy world, far away from reality.

She settled into the 'Pawn of Prophecy,' first book in the Eddings series. After an hour she became restless, unable to concentrate, thoughts from her day were running through her mind; Seth standing by the window, the peculiar man who came into the bookshop, the warning from Miss Chandler and her cryptic comments about strange happenings. It was all too much to think about. She went into the kitchen and switched on the kettle, glancing at the time on the microwave. Amelia contemplated popping into the village for a drink to help take her mind off things and found herself wondering if anything actually happens in Creek Bay at six-thirty on a Monday night. Seth had mentioned music nights, or maybe that was just at weekends. Curiosity getting the better of her she decided to take a stroll into the village regardless to find out.

It was a pleasant evening, no need for a coat at this time of year. The sky had turned a mix of burnt orange with a red hue and she was reminded of the saying her mother always recited, 'red sky at night shepherd's delight, red sky in the morning shepherd's warning.' She smiled and picked up her pace down the winding lane. Apart from Lowe Cottage there were only three other cottages along the main road until the paddock, where set amongst the gardens the Kings Arms pub was a welcome sight. She noticed quite a few of the villagers sat outside in the warm evening, recognising a few faces from her short time in Creek Bay; the store-owner and his wife, the postman who sat with two young men of similar age and a couple of teenagers from the bookshop. They nodded to Amelia as she walked by and made her way inside to the bar placing her order. The man at the bar with his back to her turned in his seat upon hearing her voice.

"Managed to dry yourself I see." A large grin and knowing smile formed on his lips.

Her heart sank; it was the coastguard from yesterday and she had to think quickly to remember his name… Ted, Zed, Ned? She blushed remembering how embarrassing it had been to be rescued from the quicksand. The landlord smiled knowingly as he handed her a large glass of red wine, no doubt her escapade had been talk of the village. She quickly looked around searching for the best seat to hide her face and her embarrassment when Ned leaned towards her.

"If you're looking for Seth he's at the bookshop."

Amelia almost jumped out of her skin from his close proximity. "It's a bit late isn't it?"

"Book Worm Club tonight. Every Monday," he said, matter of fact. "Did he not say?" There was slight mocking behind his voice.

"Erm, I don't think so, and I'm sure I didn't see a sign in the shop, I would have remembered."

Ned leant backwards against the bar. "Won't be, he reads for the primary school kids to get them interested, you know?"

Amelia looked at Ned. "In books?"

Ned turned back and continued chatting with the landlord regaling him with an outlandish footballing anecdote.

Ned's laughter became distant once Amelia made her way outside into the beer garden, as she scanned the seating arrangement her gaze fell to a free seat where Miss Chandler waved her over.

"Terrible business isn't it," the old woman said as Amelia took the seat opposite her.

"Valerie you mean?" asked Amelia.

"Poor child. Poor, poor child," she said shaking her head.

Amelia placed her glass on the weathered wooden bench. "What happened to her?"

The locals sat across from their table stared at the old woman but she ignored their silent scorn. "Torn apart she was."

Amelia's eyebrows rose with intrigue. "What? How?"

"Leave it be, Lois!" warned the stocky man sitting nearest to them.

"Shush Harold. The young woman deserves to know," the old woman said gesturing to Amelia.

"It's none of her business," he said glancing at Amelia. "Or yours."

Miss Chandler waved him away and turned back to Amelia. "Be careful who you talk to my dear."

Amelia scanned the garden, locals young and old were staring at her, being new to the village she didn't want to alienate herself from everyone, but her association with the old woman wasn't helping. "I'll do that."

She quickly drank the rest of her wine and left Lois sitting alone. Feeling the eyes of everyone burning into the back of her head she retreated towards the relative security of the bookshop.

It was a short walk from the pub and she was thankful not to meet anyone along the way, especially with everyone knowing about her rescue from the quicksand and the crazy old lady talking to her. She needed to make a better impression on these people.

Table lamps illuminated the inside of the bookshop, she wasn't sure if she was too late. Peering through the window she saw a group of young children sitting on the floor listening intently to Seth. He was sat on one of the bar stools, book in hand, reading to them with animated passion.

She watched him as he played different characters from the book making the children gasp and laugh. Seth looked up from his book and waved her in; the children were so engrossed in the story that they paid no attention to the newcomer. Amelia stood behind a sofa occupied by three middle-aged women; each one turned and nodded her arrival before returning their attention to Seth and the fairytale. He was a gifted storyteller, she could listen to his voice all day, and Amelia wasn't the only one.

Seth's whole demeanor lifted as he read. "Now, they were all three merry. The huntsman took off the wolf's skin; granny ate the cake and drank the wine which little Red Hood had brought, and became strong and well again; and little Red Hood thought to herself, 'As long as I live, I won't go out of the road into the forest, when mother has forbidden me.'"

"Yeah!" the children shouted, clapping their hands together.

"Again, again," shouted the little girl with blonde pigtails.

The three ladies rose to collect their children, one of them stood with arms folded across her chest.

"Now Lydia, what do we say to Seth for his time?"

Lydia's smile beamed as she turned to Seth, "Thank you Seth."

The other children joined in the praise as the women gathered their young, putting on their coats and bags, making their way to the door.

The last lady to depart gave Seth a wink. "Always a pleasure."

"Thank you Mina," he replied closing the door behind them, sliding the deadbolt into place.

When it was just the two of them, Amelia moved out from behind the sofa while Seth started to pick up the floor cushions the children had been sat on. "So. Red Riding Hood?"

"Yeah, it's one of my favourites." He moved the cushions to the side of the room, piling them high.

"Gotta love the Brothers Grimm?" She wasn't sure if he was still in a mood from earlier.

Seth huffed. "Yeah, albeit the censored version, still a good story though." He turned and walked towards the counter.

Amelia watched as he switched off the coffee machine and locked the till. "You never mentioned Book Worm Club."

"Sorry, I thought I had." He sounded distant again like there was something on his mind.

"No." Amelia was beginning to worry she had done something wrong. Maybe he wasn't happy with her performance at the shop today; she started to fidget with her hands. "Not that it's a problem or anything. I was surprised when Ned mentioned it earlier."

"Ned?" He finally turned towards her.

"Yeah, saw him at the pub."

Seth carried on with his duties seemingly ignoring her presence.

Change the subject she thought, and whatever you do, do not mention Valerie. "So, why Book Worm then?"

Seth shrugged. "Not sure, probably a childhood kickback. Just wish we had something like that when I was younger."

"You tell the story very well."

He put the last of the glasses on top of the counter and turned to her. "Thanks." His usual grin was back, and she was grateful.

"If you ever need a hand at Book Worm Club, you can always ask," she said hopeful.

"Are you offering to read for them?"

"Good god no! I wouldn't like to step on your toes. They look like a scary bunch, besides I think Lydia would prefer you to do it."

He laughed a deep throaty laugh she hadn't heard from him before and it suited him, she wished he was like this more often.

"They're a good bunch really... You eaten?" he asked.

With all that had happened today she hadn't thought about food, in fact she didn't even feel hungry until he mentioned it. She had been looking forward to digging into the ice cream when she got home earlier but it had melted having been left in the car all day. She had attempted to salvage it putting the carton straight into the freezer to solidify for later, however, a dinner invitation from Seth far outweighed sitting home alone with a tub of refrozen strawberry vanilla delight.

"No, I haven't, have you?"

He smiled. "We could go to the Kings Arms if you like."

"No." It came out before she realised and was met with highbrow surprise from Seth. "I mean... I was there earlier and well..." Seth waited. Running into the old woman wouldn't be a good idea, not while she was still raving about Valerie, and then there were the locals who all knew about what happened to her on the beach and she couldn't look any of them in the eye, not just yet. "I think they all know about what happened on the beach and I would like to retain some dignity."

Seth laughed. "Oh, that. It'll be yesterday's news before you know it."

"I guess." She watched him lock the front door. "I guess everyone is more interested in what happened to Valerie."

Seth clenched his teeth. "Like I said, yesterday's news."

Instant regret, without engaging her brain before opening her mouth, she had put her foot in it again. Note to self, don't mention Valerie he gets really pissy. "Sorry."

"I'm afraid we're limited on the food front then. The Italian is undergoing a refurb and the Bistro shuts at six." Her heart sank. "We could go to mine if you like," he said.

Her ears pricked up, "Yours?" surprise in her voice.

"Sure. I *can* cook you know," he replied.

She laughed. "I don't doubt that. I mean. I owe you one remember? You saved my life yesterday."

"Oh yeah, you *do* owe me. I forgot about that."

She shook her head. "I would cook for you, but I'm afraid I don't have anything in."

"Then mine it is."

After setting the alarm they walked down the side of the shop that opened out to the yard behind. A black custom chopper sat waiting patiently. "Jump on." Amelia stood motionless looking at the beast, her mouth agape. "You ride?" he asked.

"Erm, no. That would be a definite no."

Seth straddled the motorbike and looked at her expectantly. "Trust me, you'll be grateful we're on the bike, wouldn't recommend we walk it." She slipped on behind him. "Hold on," he said over his shoulder, a grin plucking at the corner of his mouth.

The machine roared to life, the vibration ran through her thighs and up through her arms as her entire body hummed from the power. Seth kicked it into gear and revved the engine, the bike swayed, thankful to be free from its prison. Instinctively her arms shot around his waist, holding on tight. He was solid all right, and warm, and smelt delicious; like the outside, like the ocean, like the beach. She closed her eyes as they rode out of the village.

Every time the bike accelerated adrenaline rushed through her body; she felt truly free. The scenery was passing by through a mix of colours blending into one another, the wind rushing through her hair; Amelia allowed her body to lean into his, her thighs tightened around him, like they belonged there, like they had always belonged there. She wished she could stay like that forever, close to Seth, letting the world pass them by.

As she focussed on the landscape she realized Seth didn't live close to Creek Bay, he lived much further than Lowe Cottage and she estimated it had taken them at least twenty minutes to reach the winding track which led to a lone cottage tucked away in dense woodland.

Night had crept up on them, the headlight shone the way down the dark lane lighting up the humble residence before them. They came to a stop, Seth switched off the engine and the bike came to a spluttering halt.

"Wow, you weren't kidding about the hike." Amelia said as she slid off the bike, her legs numb from the ride. "I take it my legs will eventually feel normal again."

He laughed. "First time?"

"First time," she said apologetically.

"Last time?" he asked pensively.

She laughed nervously. "I hope not. I have to get back remember."

He led the way into the cottage, warmth from the fire in the large open grate was the first thing that hit her making her cold cheeks tingle. She looked around the lounge with two large sofas, laptop on the small dining table with four chairs and large speakers on one side of the room.

Watching the embers gently glow in the hearth she frowned. "You left the fire burning?"

"That will be one of the guys," he said closing the door behind her.

Surprise entered her voice. "Friends?"

Seth put the sound system on before continuing through the lounge switching on the kitchen lights. "More like brothers."

She wasn't sure why it mattered, there was nothing wrong with friends living together. Maybe subconsciously she didn't want their evening together to be disturbed, not that it should matter, it was just a meal between friends, or was that work colleagues? He was her boss after all and it could be awkward if anything happened between them. She stopped herself from over-thinking the situation, she needed this job, she needed stability and she needed to stop thinking about Seth like that.

'*Black Hole Sun*' flowed through the speakers reminding her of a time during her youth she missed terribly. Taking a seat nearest the fire, she listened to him opening and closing cupboards. The heat was welcoming after the ride, Amelia started to feel sensation return to her legs as they warmed.

"Spaghetti and Meatballs OK?" Seth shouted from the kitchen.

"Sure." So he said he could cook, but a frozen ready-meal in the microwave wasn't her idea of cooking.

"Wanna give me a hand?" he called out.

Amelia sighed, was he taking the piss? Did he want her to take off the plastic sheet and put it into the microwave for him? Entering the kitchen she stopped mid-stride surprised to see that he had set out a bowl, bag of flour, rolling pin, and huge pile of fresh mince. "Oh."

Seth smiled. "What did you expect? A microwave meal?"

In her embarrassment Amelia flushed crimson, silently accusing him of being a mind reader having underestimated him for the second time. Or was she just comparing everyone to Tate. Arh! Tatem, get that man out of your vocabulary!

When she didn't answer him Seth looked concerned. "Amelia?"

Stepping towards the kitchen counter she smiled, "Sure. What do you want me to do?"

"Chop the onions and grind the spices in the mortar, while I make a start on the spaghetti."

They worked around each other in relative silence except for the music coming from the lounge. As she watched him, Amelia thought about how generous he was with his free time, whether he had a significant other, and whom he usually cooked for. Feeling self-conscious, she had to break the awkward silence.

"Who taught you how to cook?" That was a safe enough question.

Seth grinned. "I would love to say my mother, but actually, I watch people and learn."

She studied him, his movements, how he fed the sheet of pasta through the mill to thin out. Each time the pasta grew longer, no match for his large hands; his hands, his arms - she had to stop thinking of him like that.

"Me too," she said tearing her gaze from him. "Would you believe I learned to skate by watching my friends?"

"I do." He bent down under the kitchen cupboard and produced a bottle of wine. "Red?"

Amelia smiled appreciatively. "I thought you'd never ask!"

They sat down to an enormous plate of spaghetti and meatballs covered in a handful of freshly grated Parmesan, her taste buds sang when she took her first bite.

"This is delicious." Her nerves got the better of her, talking with her mouth full was impolite; something frowned upon at the dinner table in her family. In fact, being in his house alone would be frowned upon.

"I'm glad you're enjoying it," he chuckled.

Seth stoked the fire making the flames dance and crackle; whenever she tried to stoke a fire, she ended up smothering it more often than not. Amelia was quite impressed; he can cook, has his own business, and is generous with his free time for others at the book club and for the coastguard. The man was too good to be true. There had to be a catch. Was there a catch? She didn't know, was it all an act? Would he turn out to be a serial womanizer preying on the weak? She shook her head; she was over-thinking the situation again and chastised herself for it.

The music continued to flow throughout the evening, an eclectic mix of Seattle grunge meets English 60s rock. When 'Hey Jude' started to play Amelia fell silent. She hadn't listened to this song in years, for it always brought back memories of her little sister, Jude.

The song was playing at Jude's thirteenth birthday party. Although three years younger than Amelia, they were best friends. Sweet Jude.

Everything had happened in seconds, seconds to erase a life. A life of opportunity, a life that should still be living, a life that would have made a difference. But it had made a difference, it made Amelia hard, it made her tougher, if only it hadn't been at the expense of Jude. What she would give to laugh with her again, hold her, braid her hair, tell her how proud she was of her, how much she loved her. Amelia's expression glazed as she drifted into the painful memory of that fateful day…

The fast food restaurant her sister had chosen to celebrate her birthday with family and friends was painted in bright colours, the smell of grease and sweet milkshakes hung in the air. It was a big deal turning thirteen, her little sister was now officially a teenager and she had started to take an interest in boys, but there was one boy that she particularly liked. Ian Jenkins, a tall boy for his age, taller than the rest, he was sports captain and had all the girls' attention. Amelia laughed when Jude instructed her to sit with her own friends so as not to cramp her style. The restaurant had agreed to play music from her CD collection, mostly upbeat songs that had them all dancing, boys on one side, girls on the other giggling amongst themselves, but when a slow song came on, the dance floor emptied. 'Hey Jude' played on the stereo, dad always sang it to her when she was a little girl and Jude fancied this to be her song. Amelia watched on with pride as Ian Jenkins asked her to dance. He led her to the dance floor and they started to sway in time with the music while her classmates looked on, some wolf whistling, others simply watching, and some girls sulking because it wasn't them up there.

Raised voices from behind the serving counter drew her attention to a commotion at the drive thru. Amelia edged towards the sound while her sister, lost in her moment, remained oblivious to everything going on around her. When Amelia neared the counter she saw a man with black mask pointing a gun at the server. The masked man seemed impatient and nervous; without warning a loud crack rang out, Amelia watched as the stray bullet embedded itself into Jude's shoulder. As it hit, the impact sent Jude flying against the wall, she fell in a heap on the floor, her blood pooling around her. Amelia had never seen so much blood.

She ran to her sister and knelt down beside her. All she could hear was muffled screaming in the background as people fled the restaurant, her ears still ringing from the gunshot. Ian Jenkins lay on the floor crying, soaked in blood, but it wasn't his blood, the bullet had missed him by inches. Amelia put pressure on the wound praying it would be all right, she spoke softly to her barely conscious sister. "It's going to be alright, please let it be alright…" But it wasn't alright, the bullet, a .45 calibre (they found out later), far too large for a dainty young lady, had severed the subclavian artery. Her blood pumped through Amelia's fingers as she tried to stem the bleeding. The screaming in the background faded as she concentrated on the slow rhythm of her sister's heartbeat.

Jude opened her eyes. "Am I dying Millie?"

Tears filled Amelia's eyes. "No, you're fine; everything is going to be okay." She couldn't bear the thought of losing her, saying it out loud made it sound real.

"Ok." Jude smiled at her sister. "I can hear them Millie. Hear them calling my name."

"Who Jude? Who can you hear?"

Jude fell silent.

"Jude… Jude! Stay with me." Amelia pleaded. Jude's eyes glazed over as her shallow breathing stopped. "No, no, no, no, no. No!" screamed Amelia. "No!" Her tears streamed down her face landing on her sister's cheek.

Eventually the police found the man responsible, his body was discovered in a squalid bedsit after neighbours complained about the stench, he had OD'd on heroin bought from the money stolen at the drive thru. Even the discovery of his bloated decomposing body didn't give Amelia closure. Jude had died so a bloody junkie could get his next fix, and for what? The life of an innocent.

"Are you okay Amelia?" asked Seth snapping her out of the painful memory she has fought so hard to control.

"I'm sorry. Do you mind if we put another song on?"

Without asking why, Seth changed tracks and started a fresh conversation to lighten the mood.

"Tell you what. Why don't we move closer to the fire," he said holding up his glass and wine bottle.

Amelia followed him, grateful for the distraction; he always seemed to know what to say. After a few minutes staring into the flames, she finally asked the question that had been bugging her.

"Why do you live all the way out here?"

"That's the one question you want to ask?"

"I didn't know I only had one question, I would have chosen more carefully had I known. May I change it?" she asked.

He smiled and poured more wine into both glasses. "If you insist, but choose wisely."

"Who are you?" she said with a smile.

Seth's eyes widened. "Now, that's a question."

He lay back propping himself up with his elbow on the arm rest, a fluid movement he had done countless times before, no doubt, when he was busy flirting with all the women he brought back to his home. The firelight danced across his features, shadows highlighting his chiseled good looks.

"Who do you think I am?" he asked playfully.

"Oh no, you can't do that. You can't answer a question with a question. Besides, I have been proven wrong at least twice already."

"Really?" he asked in jest.

"And you know it. Who is Seth?"

"Indeed," he muttered.

"Oh come on. You are too good to be true. The coastguard volunteering, Book Worm Club, you can make an amazing meal from scratch. You're Mr. Squeaky Clean."

He spat some wine out upon that last reference, coughing as the liquid went down the wrong way. "I've never been called *that* before."

Amelia sat watching him, idly stroking her glass. He *was* too good to be true. "Okay my one question."

"Technically it's your third."

She smiled. "Was there actually a job at the bookshop or did you make it up?"

Seth paused while he thought about his answer. "You want me to say I manufactured the job for you, don't you? That I took pity on you, that I realized you needed a job because your boyfriend bailed."

"I never said anything about—"

"The truth is Amelia." He interrupted. "Yes, I needed some help at the store and you needed a job, and I like you Amelia, so why not offer the job to you?"

Dumbstruck, she pointed to herself. "Me?"

"Besides, having someone look after the store means I can spend more time on the surf."

"Now I'm confused. Are you saying there wasn't a job?"

"No."

"Then there was a job?"

"Of course."

"Then why me?" she wondered whether the liking her comment was just politeness.

He leant forward and looked her in the eye. "You need to find your feet, get settled. When you're ready to move on, I'll understand. But in the meantime I can enjoy my hobby knowing the store is in safe hands. Besides, you were the only one who applied," he added with a smile.

Amelia frowned, rejection and pity all in the same sentence? He had given her help, but the downside for her was that they wouldn't be spending time together at the store after all; maybe that's why he only wanted her to work until half-past two in the afternoon. Oh god. She had been a fool again. She stood from the sofa.

"I think I better be making tracks," she said solemnly.

Seth stood beside her. "I'd happily ride you home, but I have had a bit to drink."

"Then I'll call a taxi. Do you know the number?"

Seth pinched the inside of his mouth with his teeth. "Well. Yeah. I should have said, taxis don't come out here."

Frowning, she said, "Why the hell not?"

"It's a long story." He said as Amelia slumped down on the sofa. "But you are more than welcome to stay here. I have a spare room." He offered, taking another sip of his wine as he sat beside her.

"I really shouldn't." And she knew she shouldn't.

"Truly, I insist. Oh, and I apologise in advance."

"In advance of what?" She said with panic in her voice.

The front door burst open and a young man staggered in.

"For that," he said cringing.

"Hey! Seth, my man. I didn't know you were entertaining!"

The young man's mannerisms suggested he was very drunk. Keeping out of his way Amelia stood by the fire as the intoxicated man stumbled into the lounge.

"You old dog!" The young man flopped down on the sofa next to Seth. "You don't hang about," he said patting his friends back.

"It's not like that Daniel," Seth scorned.

Watching the two men on the sofa, Amelia became increasingly uncomfortable; rejection had a funny way of following her around. The door opened again as another young man entered and she tensed wondering what state this one would be in, but he seemed to be able to stand upright. He had waist length dirty-blonde dreadlocks pulled loosely off his face with a blue bandanna, dark green eyes and a sun-kissed complexion.

"Hey Seth." He turned and noticed Amelia. "Oh, hey, sorry. We didn't know you had company."

"No. It's okay." Amelia interrupted. "We're not... Its just dinner."

The blonde man walked towards her, hand outstretched. "I'm Sonny and this piss-head is Daniel." He said nodding to the semi-conscious man on the sofa. "Are you from round here? Don't think I've seen you before."

"Amelia." She said shaking his hand. "No, just moved here."

"Amelia is staying at Lowe Cottage," Seth said as he came to stand by his friend. "You been drinking tonight Sonny?"

"Nope, why?"

"Would you mind taking Amelia home?"

"Sure thing," he said nodding to Seth and then Amelia. "Are you okay with that?"

"Yes, thank you." She looked to Seth. "Thank you for the meal. I'll see you at the store tomorrow?" she said hoping she hadn't blown it.

The men looked at one another, a silent conversation passed between them, Seth sheepishly turned to Amelia. "Actually, we're off on a trip tomorrow. I guess I forgot to mention it. Sorry. I'm going to be away for a couple of days, normally Mrs Bateman from the corner shop runs things, but she is unavailable. I know its last minute but I was going to close up while we were away. Unless…" he started.

"I could open up for you, erm, if that's Ok." Amelia offered.

Seth thought for a moment. "Will you be okay on your own at the store?"

Amelia nodded, shocked at her boldness, and worried and excited all at the same time. A tremendous responsibility having only just started, she could mess everything up; and then there was the little matter that she wouldn't be seeing Seth.

"If you run into trouble, just give Mr Bateman at the shop a shout." Seth said reassuringly as he handed her the shop key.

"No. No. I'm sure everything will be fine," she said picking up her bag. "I hope you have a good trip."

He wrote something down and handed her a business card for the bookshop. "This is the alarm code and you can reach me on this number while I'm away. Just in case."

Amelia quickly left the lounge and went out into the cold night with Sonny just behind her. He opened the passenger door to the black Jeep parked next to Seth's motorbike, then walked around to the driver's side. She stood by the opened door looking at the footrest; the Jeep had been raised like one of those monster truck types and she wasn't entirely certain if she could get in and retain her dignity. A quick glance behind to check no one was watching she quickly stepped up and bounced onto the seat.

Sonny leant over the passenger seat to steady her. "Sorry, should have asked if you were okay getting in."

Amelia smiled as she closed the door. "That's okay. You go off-road in this then?"

He put his foot on the clutch and started the engine. "Yeah, take her to one of those man-made tracks in the middle of nowhere, it's awesome."

She smiled at his enthusiasm. "I bet."

The stereo kicked in on full volume, just catching the bass riff at the start of Chili Peppers 'Higher Ground' somehow fitting with his chilled surfer attitude and long dreads; as Sonny pulled away from the house and down the lane the uneven surface was no match for the large all-terrain tyres.

"Sorry 'bout that," he said turning the volume down. "How you liking Creek Bay? Life slow enough for you?" He said making idle conversation.

Amelia laughed. "Yeah, just what I need. You lived here long?"

"All my life." Sonny took a sharp right turn onto rougher ground sending Amelia slamming into the door. "Sorry, force of habit. You okay?"

Amelia nodded, discreetly rubbing her outer thigh stinging from the impact of her soft tissue on the door handle. "All your life?"

"Yep. It's a really nice place, once you see past the grumpy oldies and twee cottages."

"And Seth?" she asked as nonchalantly as possible.

"I've known the guys all my life. I can't think of a life without them to be honest. I'd do anything for them."

"So you're pretty close then?" she asked watching his reaction. "The three of you?"

Sonny nodded. "Like brothers."

"Don't you have any family here?" Amelia asked trying to keep the conversations going.

Sonny stared off into the night, his face illuminated by the lights on the dashboard, a soft expression formed across his youthful features when he said quietly. "We used to be a big family, but not anymore."

Amelia wanted to push and ask more questions, but was interrupted by Sonny's mobile ringing.

"Yo!" he answered flipping his phone open. "No. No. I haven't." He looked at Amelia, and then turned his attention back to the road. "Of course not... No... I." The conversation sounded fraught, she could tell the person on the other end was very demanding. "Yeah, sure." He turned again to Amelia and then turned his head and muttered something into the receiver. "I'll make sure. You have my word." Then he closed the phone shut.

"Everything okay Sonny?" she asked.

"Yeah, big bro and all that," he said with a shrug.

They were both silent for the rest of the journey as they listened to the radio and the hum of the engine. Amelia had left the lamp on in the lounge and the heating on low, taking the chill out of the early summer night. Sonny parked the Jeep outside Lowe Cottage, jumping out of his seat he made his way to the passenger side, opening the door as he helped Amelia out of the cab.

"Milady," he jested with a mocking bow.

"Why thank you, young Sir." She said with a curtsey. He was still by her side when she reached the front door. "Thanks for the lift Sonny, I really appreciate it."

"No problem. Are you going to be okay? Do you need me to check the house first?"

She laughed. "For what? What do you think you'll find?"

Then she frowned as she thought about it. The noise she heard last night when Valerie had gone missing, that was not imaginary, and the phone calls, they too, were pretty creepy. Maybe she should let him check out the place after all.

He started walking back to the Jeep. "Okay. I'll see you around."

Amelia called out to him. "Actually Sonny, would you mind?"

She hated coming across as feeble, but there had been some pretty strange things going on, and he could easily see off any kids messing about.

Sonny gave her the sweetest of smiles. "No worries."

Amelia decided Sonny was the nicest, sweetest guy she had ever met. He checked every room and declared Lowe Cottage a safe haven before returning to his Jeep and taking off.

She made sure to lock the doors front and back and turned the lights to low before running a hot bath.

As she lay back, she went through the day's events. Seth and his charitable work with the children and the amazing meal they shared together, the old woman hinting at strange goings on, how odd it was that Sonny would offer to check the house for her. Amelia figured he was just being kind to a lone woman new to the village, a noble gesture. Her thoughts drifted to the man who came into the store, the one who was staring from across the street. She slipped lower beneath the warm water exhaling deeply and closed her eyes.

# *chaptra peder*

T he woman's scream turned into the high-pitched whistling from the
steam wand on the coffee machine. Seth poured a drink and left it on
the counter. Amelia took the glass; the smell reminded her of Uncle
Bob's old change jar that he kept in the window of his study. She took a
closer look at the deep crimson liquid and then at Seth as he uttered, "A
pound for a pound." As she turned around, the bookshop had transformed
into the fast food restaurant. Jude was waiting by the food counter waving
to her, Amelia waved back, happy to see her alive, then movement over
Jude's shoulder made her blood run cold. Amelia saw the man with his gun
pointing the barrel through the drive-in window at Jude, a wicked smile
spread wide on the Junkie's face. "A pound for a pound," he growled and
pulled the trigger. The bullet erupted from the barrel moving as in slow
motion, she could see it propelled through the air towards her sister. Amelia
knew it would hit Jude and ran towards her, desperate to push her out of
its path. Amelia lunged forward, but her movements were also slow. "Jude!"
she screamed in desperation.

Amelia woke in the bathtub panting heavily, her hair plastered to her face.
She hadn't dreamt about Jude in such a long time, certain the nightmares
were behind her. The phone ringing downstairs was a welcomed
distraction. She clambered out of the tub, and frantically wrapping the
nearest towel around her body, ran downstairs picking up the receiver
before it had chance to ring off.

"Hello?"

Silence.

"Look. I don't appreciate this harassment, stop phoning me!"

"Amelia?"

"Yes. Who is this?"

"Lois. Lois Chandler."

She felt stupid for not recognizing her voice. "Hi Lois. Hey, you didn't
try ringing yesterday did you?"

The woman was brusque in her reply. "No. I'm ringing to see if you are
okay," she added quickly.

"Thank you. Yes. I'm fine. Why do you ask?"

"I had a dream about you." The old woman hung up and the phone
line went dead.

"Hello? Lois? Hello?"

Amelia clicked the flash button on the phone a couple of times but was unable to reconnect the call. She concluded that Lois was a sweet old lady, albeit a little peculiar. A sudden loud bang and clattering sound came from the back garden making her jump. She cautiously walked to the kitchen and gently pulled the curtain aside. The old metal bin was rocking from side to side, straining her eyes against the darkness she saw nothing out of the ordinary and told herself that it was probably a neighbour's cat or a fox trying to get at some scraps. Then suddenly frenzied banging started, firstly on the front door, Amelia cowered under the kitchen window the phone still clutched in her hand. The banging stopped as abruptly as it started. She slowly stood trying to make sense of what had just happened when an almighty pounding started on the back door making her shriek; it was so powerful it shook the door in its frame. She ran into the lounge and picked up the piece of paper Seth had given her earlier, punched in the numbers and waited eagerly for a reply. When he didn't answer she assumed he must have already set off for his trip.

"Shit!" she whispered.

The pounding was so forceful it seemed to shake even the stonework; it was so loud she was certain her nearest neighbour could hear. Amelia put her hands over her ears and shut her eyes tight praying for the noise to stop, and then… silence. She slowly let her hands down and crept under the window ledge peering outside, but she couldn't see anything. If it was teenagers' idea of a joke, she didn't share their sentiments. Amelia was just about to dial 999 when there was a banging at the front door. This time she was calling the police but she stopped when she heard someone shouting her name.

She froze, thinking it was her imagination wishing it to be him. Amelia stood beside the front door, her hand poised on the deadlock. "Seth?"

"It's me, are you okay?" She quickly unbolted the locks. Seth rushed in, his eyes wide, searching the living room. "Are you okay?" he asked again.

Stepping back, she didn't quite know how to take in his reaction. "Yes, but how did you—"

"We were driving past and I heard banging, so I stopped to check in on you." All the while his eyes darted over the room towards the kitchen and back door. His nostrils flared when he looked at Amelia stood clutching the towel tight to her chest. "I'm sorry, you were in the middle of something."

"Oh, no, please don't be. I'm grateful you came by. It appears the teenagers have found a new game. Terrorize the lonely newcomer." She tried to laugh, but it was strained, then she saw the yellow camper van outside. "Did you say you guys were heading off tonight?"

"Yeah," he said forcing a smile. "Sonny and Daniel are just ahead of me on their bikes. We're going camping."

"Camping? It sounded like something illegal the way you were acting earlier. You all fit in there?" she said pointing to his camper van.

"God no, they have their own tents, we share the cooker and TV though." She noticed him flinch. "Something wrong?" she asked.

"Are you sure you're all right?" he asked concerned.

"Just kids with nothing better to do, trying to put the frighteners on me."

Seth looked out to the heathland, he could sense them watching in the distance. "All the same I'd rather stay, make sure you are okay."

"I'm fine," she lied. "Besides, the police are just a phone call away if they come back."

"Tell you what," he said forcing a smile to put her at ease. "I'll stay outside in the van, and if I see anything I'll sort them out. How about that?"

"You really don't have to—"

"I insist. Besides, I know the teenagers round here, if it is them they'll listen to me."

The youngsters in the village did seem to respect Seth she told herself; and if they knew he was in the area they'd think twice about messing around. Amelia was grateful he had insisted.

"Okay. Having my own personal security wouldn't hurt."

She left Seth to his duty outside while she finished getting changed out of the wet towel and into comfortable loungewear. By the time she had read a couple of chapters she was certain he would become bored and leave, that way she wouldn't feel guilty keeping him from his trip. She was well into the book when she glanced up at the clock. He had been out there in his van on sentry duty for nearly three hours. Amelia put her book down and opened the front door; cold night air stung her face, she quickly made her way to the driver side window and tapped on the glass. Seth was deep in thought looking out to the heathland. "All quiet on the Western front?" she asked.

He nodded sombrely. "Get back inside where it's warm," he said.

"You want to come in for a cuppa? I feel just awful that you've sat out here all this time and missing your fun. Was sure you'd give up and go by now."

"Nonsense. But a cuppa sounds great."

He followed her inside with one last glance to the distant tree line.

Amelia handed him the mug of steaming cocoa. "This will warm you up. Where you heading anyway?"

"Oh, erm. Just a little north of here."

Amelia noticed his eyes looking a little blood shot. "You know, if you're tired you can stop in the spare room."

"What? No, I'm not tired." He tried his usual smile, but she could tell there was something niggling at him. It was the same look he had when she had mentioned Valerie at the bookshop.

"Well, your eyes say otherwise," she said taking the seat next to him on the sofa. Seth looked forlornly into his mug. "Don't you like hot chocolate? I can make you something else if you'd prefer, a tea or coffee?"

"It's fine, really." He pushed for a smile.

"When was the last time you went camping?" she asked.

"Seems like forever," he sighed.

"Mmm. I remember camping with my dad. Betws-y-Coed was our usual haunt, have you been there?" He shook his head. "It's lovely. One time Dad surprised me by taking us to Silverdale."

"Been there," he said.

There was a notable awkwardness so she changed the subject again. "Any bands playing this weekend at the store?"

"Mmm?"

Amelia raised her eyebrows. He truly wasn't on this planet, wherever his mind was it wasn't there with her. "Go. Please. You'll be able to catch up with your friends and get settled before the morning."

"I really—"

"You really can," she insisted.

He looked out the window towards the trees. The clouds were breaking and faint light of dawn had begun to peep through. "If you're sure?"

"I'm sure."

"You've got my number, anything odd happens again, ring me… anything," his tone sincere.

"I will, I promise."

Amelia locked and bolted the door when Seth left and breathed a sigh of relief. If he had stayed any longer she would be tempted, and that wasn't going to help anyone. She put the business card he wrote his number on back next to the phone.

At the end of the lane two bikes came into view, their riders stood patiently beside them. Seth pulled up alongside his friends and wound down the window. "Well?" asked Daniel.

Seth gritted his teeth. "Kept their distance."

"For now." Sonny spat.

The young men were silent listening to the distant chirping of birds. Daniel looked up at the sky and grimaced. "Come on man, I'm dying here, can we step on it and get there while we're still young?"

Sonny and Seth both smiled. "I can not deny, it's been a while," Seth agreed.

"Yeah, and you look like shit," Sonny jested to Seth.

Daniel made a humph sound. "You sure the shop will be standing when we get back?"

"I didn't know you cared?" Seth laughed.

"I don't. I don't trust her."

"Dan, you don't *trust* anyone," Sonny said putting his hand on his shoulder. "Come on, I'll race you down to the quarry."

# chaptra pymp

The next morning Amelia woke with a start, she looked to the alarm clock and immediately regretted finishing the bottle of wine; it had helped her sleep too well. The glowing bright red numbers on the clock mocked her tired hung-over brain, which struggled to comprehend the significance of the time, through the haze the slow realisation hit her, she had overslept. She flung the bed sheets back and hurried into the bathroom for the quickest shower in history. Still wet, she threw on a pair of jeans and long sweater before heading out to the store. As she past the bakery her stomach growled, the smell of cooked bacon taunting her, but she couldn't stop, she noticed an elderly couple outside the bookshop waiting for it to open, that was all she needed this morning, she was hoping for a quiet start so she could find her feet.

"Morning. Sorry I'm late." She panted trying to catch her breath. The old couple looked at Amelia; finally people who didn't know who she was. "I'm new here, covering for Seth while he—"

"Goes camping." The old man said finishing her sentence.

She frowned. "Yes. How did you know?"

"If Seth isn't here, he will be camping. But he usually leaves someone more… punctual in charge."

Strike one; she had upset her first customers. Amelia sheepishly opened the door and the old couple wandered in, taking their seats on the sofa nearest the window. "Two coffees, white no sugar," was the instruction as they laid out their newspapers on the table.

Amelia clicked on the power to the till, coffee machine and the lamps around the shop and then proceeded into the storeroom to fill the water jugs for the filter coffee. The place smelt of Seth and the ocean, she looked around the small room while the jugs were filling. His coats and leathers hung by the back door. In a daze, she looked beyond the room and into the corridor where there was a notice board hung on the wall. On it were photos from past events that had taken place there. The obligatory pictures of teenagers pulling faces, some of the musicians, a couple of the youngsters from Book Worm Club dressed in Halloween costumes and then she saw one of Seth, with Sonny and Daniel. Try as she might, she couldn't locate pictures of Seth with a woman, but there was one picture with an obscured face out of focus behind him. She stood closer to get a better look. Amelia recognised the person in the background; it was that strange man who came into the store, the man who was staring at her in the street.

The door chimed as someone entered the shop making Amelia jump back to reality. Looking down she realised that the water jug was overflowing; cursing under her breath she quickly wiped down the kitchenette draining board and chastised herself for forgetting the old couple's coffee - strike two, failure to be attentive. She hurried behind the store counter and started the coffee percolating.

"Morning Roy, Mary," the man said as he walked by the old couple.

"Detective Cooke, how lovely to see you," answered Mary. Her husband offered a nod and carried on reading his paper, his attention elsewhere; he shook his head and tutted, mumbling the main headline to himself 'New Road worries for Residents.'

"No Seth today?" he asked of Amelia.

"No, he's—"

"Camping," Mary interrupted.

The detective smiled at the mature lady and took a seat next to the counter. Amelia recognised him from yesterday, he had led Lois Chandler away before she could say anything more about Valerie. He seemed young for a detective probably in his early thirties, but had an authority and maturity about him in the way he spoke and carried himself. He wore his blazer jacket open, white shirt unbuttoned at the top and looking like he had slept in it recently, the day-old stubble confirmed he had been too busy for rest during the recent investigation. Running a hand through his short light brown hair he took a black notebook out of his pocket.

"Amelia Scott?" he asked, Amelia nodded. "I am Detective Inspector Cooke." He showed her his warrant card, and then put it back inside his jacket. "I am conducting routine enquiries, and speaking to all the shopkeepers in the village about the recent..." He paused when he caught Mary eavesdropping. "Is there somewhere private we could go?" he asked.

Amelia looked around the shop, she really didn't fancy taking him through to the claustrophobic storeroom, but the mezzanine would be out of earshot.

"We could go up there," she said pointing upwards.

The detective nodded and followed her up the stairs taking a seat on the small sofa, Amelia opted for the floor cushion opposite.

The policeman looked at her for a long while before opening his notebook again. "I realise you're new here," he said in hushed tone so no one else could hear him. "But I wanted to ask if you had seen or heard anything about the recent tragedy."

"You mean Valerie Temple?"

He nodded. "Yes."

"Nothing more than the gossip in the village, I guess."

"Which is?"

"That poor Valerie had been attacked and found on the moor. Trem... something or other."

He wrote something down in his book. "Anything else?"

Amelia shrugged. "What else is there to say? Everyone seems to have their theories about what happened, whether there is any truth to that I don't know, I don't bother myself with idle gossip, detective. I can form my own opinions."

He briefly looked up from his notes. "Which are?"

As Amelia shifted on the cushion the detective was aware of how uncomfortable she had become with his questions.

"Limited. I moved here on Sunday evening and from what I hear, Valerie was attacked that night. So I neither know anyone's movements that day nor ever met Valerie."

His eyes narrowed as he leant forward. "But you met Seth and Ned on the beach did you not?"

She squirmed again, embarrassed that everyone knew about the quicksand incident. "Oh. Yes. I did." Amelia watched as he wrote something in his notepad. "What is this all about exactly?"

"I explained," he said not looking up from his note taking.

"No you didn't. Not really."

The detective stopped writing and sat back staring at her. "This is a murder enquiry."

"Murder?!" she shrieked.

"...and I am simply asking questions to ascertain the victims movements and you seem overly defensive, almost obstructive. Are you hiding something Miss Scott? Maybe covering for someone?"

"Are you serious?" Amelia scoffed.

He looked around the shop. "You got this job very quickly considering you only just moved here two days ago, or rather a day and a half ago."

Amelia stood. "Can I ask what you are implying?"

"I wouldn't presume anything but I can't discount anything either."

Folding her arms she frowned. "Are we done here?"

The detective slowly stood and met her gaze; he was a foot taller than her and she felt quite intimidated by him. Show no fear, she told herself, and whatever you do, don't look away.

He smiled at her before he turned towards the stairs. "I'll be seeing you around Miss Scott." When he got to the bottom of the steps Mary waved him goodbye.

"Routine questions my arse!" she muttered.

"Smells like that coffee is ready," the old man shouted.

After four cups of coffee and a morning of evil looks thrown her way, the old couple eventually left and she could finally relax, she put on some music and sat down with a glass of beer.

"Drinking on the job?" the gravelly voice behind her rang out.

The shock made her spill part of her drink. "You'd be needing a stiff drink too if you'd had a day like mine; I've had the morning from hell."

Ned smiled as he took a seat at the counter. "Roy and Mary right?"

"How did you know?"

"It's Tuesday."

"Of course," she muttered. Like that was explanation enough. "Well, the old couple and that bloody detective. He came round asking questions."

Ned leant forward and whispered, "About?"

"Valerie. Routine questions he said."

"Mmm, well, tell you what. As Seth is away, why don't you come to the pub tonight and let your hair down? It's quiz night."

"Oh, I don't know."

He tilted his head. "You can win a bottle of champagne."

"I was looking forward to a quiet night in."

"Oh trust me, there are plenty of those in this village. Come on. Meet some people, get out, and stop moping. Besides," he nodded to her drink. "Better to drink with company than alone."

She smiled. Maybe it would be good to get out. "Okay. You've twisted my arm. What time does it start?"

"Seven."

"Meet you there then."

"I'll come and pick you up."

"No need."

"Nah, I'll be going that way anyway."

"And you know where I live because…"

"Small village."

She clicked her tongue. "You're telling me!"

Ned made his way to the door as two teenagers entered. "See you tonight," he called out and left the shop.

The two teenagers made an 'ooh' sound and quickly took their seats by the computers. It would seem studies were best done at the store rather than home, but at least it kept them out of trouble and money in the till.

"You guys okay while I go refill the machine?" she called out.

"Sure thing," one of them answered.

When she walked past them into the corridor one of the teenagers whispered to the other, "Thought she was going out with Seth?"

"Obviously not," the other concluded.

Amelia sighed. She had no idea where the notion of her dating Seth had come from; living here was going to be harder than she realised. Village life was lovely, but the gossips sure do have a field day when you're new. The only way she could think best to quash all rumours was to make it quite clear that she is very much single and enjoying being single, but was she just lying to herself? Having refilled the machine she was grateful for the steady stream of customers and students using the computers to take her mind off what the detective had insinuated earlier. Besides, what did that detective know anyway? When there was a lull she went upstairs and sat on the loveseat watching the youngsters downstairs deep in conversation happy and carefree, when the shop phone rang. Luckily she had the foresight to take it upstairs with her.

"Hello?"

"Hey it's me. Can you do me a favour?"

Seth. Her heart started to beat a little faster. "Sure."

"Can you pick up some flyers from the printers for me?"

"Of course."

"You'll find the details in the diary under the counter. Check with Stu if they are ready first."

"Okay. Will do. Everything okay up there?"

The phone line went dead. At first she frowned, then remembered they were camping and probably in a bad reception area. Making her way downstairs to the counter Amelia fished out the diary. Thumbing through the pages she saw today's entry, 'Fortune Flyer, 1,000' she looked at the contact details, 'Stu: Mayflower Print 01208 864989' dialled the number and waited. "Mayflower Print, Stu speaking."

"I'm calling on behalf of Seth at The Bay Book Shop. Do you know if the Fortune flyers are ready?"

"Right. Yes, they are. I've got them with me, but the thing is I have to dash off. I'll be working down at The Manor later, any chance you can come by for them? It's much closer than the print room."

"Yes, of course. Where exactly is The Manor?"

She repeated the directions making notes and put the phone down. When she looked up there was a young boy stood in front of her.

"The Manor?" he asked.

"Yes. Do you know it?"

"I'll say. Well, I don't know it, I've never been, but I know *of* it. The Manor is really, really posh. People who go there have *way* too much money."

"But is it easy to get to?"

"I guess so. Take the road straight out of the village, it's in the middle of nowhere." The other youths began to leave and called for their friend to join them.

When she arrived at The Manor, Amelia stood back and looked at the huge building surrounded by beautifully manicured gardens. She parked her car as far away as possible; her old banger would stick out like a sore thumb amongst the Porsches and Aston Martins. Amelia ascended the stone steps where a large board was propped up against one of the pillars 'Congratulations, Mr and Mrs Dolan.' She could hear the clanking of glasses and murmuring voices of wedding guests behind the large doors, making her way through the extensive lobby Amelia looked around for the receptionist and spotted a young woman behind the front desk.

"Hello, I'm looking for Stu."

The young lady made a phone call and within a couple of minutes a young man came running down the winding staircase dressed in a smart maroon and grey concierge uniform.

"Amelia?" he asked, she nodded. "Stu." They shook hands. "Come this way." Stu gestured to the doors in front of them as the young lady from reception piped up.

"I hope you're not going through there. You know what happened last time." The receptionist warned.

But it was too late. Stu had opened the doors and was leading Amelia through the wedding reception with unbelievably bad timing, just as the best man stood delivering his speech from the top table. Amelia tried to make herself invisible, glancing over her shoulder she was certain he was the strange man who came into the shop the other day, although he looked different dressed in a morning suit. She hurried after Stu into another room adjacent to the wedding party.

"They are just in here," said Stu. He bent down and pulled a few boxes out from the store cupboard.

Amelia knelt down next to him as he checked the boxes. "I can't believe we went through the reception," she whispered.

"Nonsense, they're too busy enjoying themselves to ever notice us. Believe me. When you wear this uniform they only notice you when they want something."

He handed her a small box, which was heavier than she expected. "Here, I'll get the other one, then we'll be off."

Mortified, she had hoped there was another way other than going back the way they came. "You can't be serious. I can't go back out there," she whispered.

"Relax."

"No chance. I'm waiting here until they finish the speeches at least."

"Suit yourself." He reached for the handle and then turned to her.

"Are you leaving me here?" she asked, eyes wide.

"You're the one who wants to stay." He looked around the small room. "Unless you had other ideas?" he said winking at her.

"Behave," she said trying to put some distance between them.

He was out of the room with the other box before she knew it and now she was trapped in a cupboard.

Amelia sighed heavily and put the box back down, she laid her ear to the side of the door straining to hear how long it would take for the speeches to be over with and then she could make her getaway. After ten minutes she sat down, another five minutes and she got bored enough to open the cardboard box and look at the flyer, when the door opened. In her shock, Amelia's heart stumbled to a regular beat when she realised the dark shape standing above her was the best man. She quickly stood, knocking the box of flyers off her knee and onto the floor, spilling the contents at his feet.

"I'm sorry, I didn't mean to—"

"Crash the party?" he offered.

She was at a loss for words, his presence captivating and stares intense, then he stepped in closer and shut the door behind him. "Drink?" he held out two glasses of champagne.

"Erm, no, I should really be on my way."

He came closer still, his brown eyes burnt into her soul. "One drink. A toast to the happy couple?"

His voice was raspy yet velvety smooth, she surprised even herself when the words came easily to her and accepted the glass. "Thank you."

She gently sipped the bubbly liquid; dainty wet sparkles tickled her nose she was certain she was going to sneeze. The man looked down at the floor noticing the flyers and bent down to pick them up. As he placed them back into the box he came to stand with one in his hand. "Fortune."

"Yes. Do you know them? They are playing at—"

"I know where they are playing." He interrupted folding the flyer in half and stuffing it into his back pocket. "My name is William. You are?"

At last a name, a name she can give him when she says that creepy hot guy William was staring again. She cleared her throat. "We met at the bookshop yesterday. I'm Amelia. Amelia Scott."

"Do you often hide in cupboards, Amelia Scott?"

"Only on Tuesdays."

He laughed and smiled at her, for the first time he smiled and he was… gorgeous. "Of course, Tuesday." His arm rubbed against hers, being so close together was fast becoming a problem as the heat from his skin started to crawl all over her. "I think it's safe to go now," he said. "That is if you actually want to go."

She gulped and asked herself whether she did want to leave. He was starting to look every bit like someone she could spend time with; his beautiful deep brown eyes, the curve of his full lips, his dark curly hair, his smell… Amelia mentally shook herself.

"I have to get these back." It was a lame excuse and she hated herself for it, but she knew she wouldn't have been able to control herself in the cupboard with him.

"Certainly," he said with a smile.

William bent down and handed the box of flyers to Amelia, she quickly gulped down the rest of the drink and exchanged her empty glass for the cardboard box. When he opened the door, she noticed that the guests had all left and she felt an eerie sense of abandonment.

"Where is everyone?" she asked following him out of the small room.

"Outside."

She looked out towards the patio doors but still couldn't see anyone beyond the glass. When he made no attempt to leave she asked, "Aren't you going to join your party?"

"Soon."

He kept staring at her, that same look he gave her in the street the other day. She couldn't put her finger on it, but it was the same way a lion sizes up its prey, waiting for the right moment to pounce, and now they were alone and she had been separated from the herd, a shiver ran through her. She had to get away from him before she did something she would regret, or not regret exactly, she didn't know how she would feel, but she knew it would be amazing…

"Well," she said moving away from him. "Nice to have met you William."

He watched her leave at a hurried pace, exiting through the main doors leading to reception. "See you around Amelia Scott," he said softly.

Stu sat manning reception and called her over. "Thought you'd never leave that room."

Relieved to see the young man again she nodded to the box in her arms, which were starting to ache with the weight. "Give me a lift to my car?"

Thankful to be away from The Manor she couldn't stop thinking about William; his eyes, his shoulders, his smell, his smile, his laugh. But there was something about him that scared her, something that she couldn't quite put her finger on. He was no Boy Scout, that she was certain of. When she pulled up to Lowe Cottage she left the flyers in the car ready for the morning and went to change for quiz night. It was generous of Ned to ask her, but she wasn't exactly a genius when it came to hot topics and politics, she didn't bother herself with those things, and if they had a specialist round she was hoping it contained entertainment, ancient history or literature.

Ned was on time and had changed into something casual, the first time she had seen him without his usual coastguard apparel. To the untrained eye he was smart casual, but everything screamed he had made a special effort dressing to impress, the exaggerated over-powering cologne a dead giveaway. He was nothing but courteous, opening doors for her, buying her the first drink, engaging in conversations she was comfortable with. He was an all-round genuinely nice bloke. Not to be one for letting a man pay for everything, she insisted on getting alternate rounds of drink and made sure he knew that their relationship was just friends, no flirting, no contact, just enjoying one another's company. Ned was quite knowledgeable on the general questions section, she felt awkward about her less than forthcoming contributions, but proved her worth during the movie questions. Although they didn't win any champagne, they both had a very pleasant evening.

"I don't see a lot of the younger ones in here tonight. Not their thing?" she asked.

Ned didn't have to look up. "Curfew."

"Curfew?" she asked surprised. She hadn't heard anything of a curfew; the teenagers at the bookshop certainly hadn't mentioned anything either. Then again, the detective had been particularly insistent. "What do you mean curfew?"

"Our friendly neighbourhood policeman has issued a curfew, everyone to be home by eleven tonight." Amelia frowned. "I know. I know," he said shaking his head. "It's something quite unprecedented but the law take matters into their own hands around here. You either go along with it or get incarcerated."

"Incarcerated? I didn't realise we were living in a totalitarian state. Who the hell does he think he is?"

"Someone who is trying to save your life!" The room fell silent as DI Cooke approached the bar. "All of your lives." The detective looked around the pub, most people kept their heads down, but Amelia was new, she didn't know what the rules were, nor did she know when to stay silent.

"And what if we don't? What if we don't play along with your rules?" she demanded.

The policeman turned to face Amelia with his blood-shot eyes, his voice turning sombre. "Then I would say to you Miss Scott, I pray that you stay safe."

She had readied herself for a fight but he didn't deliver; she really had landed in Bizarro Land. What she would give right now to hear the sanity of her mother's words, it would bring her back to earth with a thud, and a thud she would be grateful for.

"I'm sorry?" she said standing. "But I really don't see why we have a curfew. Sure, there has been a most unfortunate incident, but to put the whole village under house arrest, without telling us why, I don't buy it. What is going on here?"

The detective grabbed her arm pulling her from the table and led her outside away from prying eyes. Amelia was about to find out the price for questioning his authority, but she could handle herself and she wasn't one to shy away like a meek little girl.

DI Cooke led her to the gardens at the side of the pub, out of view of the windows and let go of her arm. He turned, eyes blazing and hands on hips. "You're new around here, so I will give you benefit of the doubt."

"Am I supposed to be grateful?"

The detective leant forward and spoke quietly so as not to be overheard. "What you don't know won't hurt you. And believe me when I say you don't want to know."

"What the hell are you talking about?" Amelia took a step back. "You're just as crazy as the rest of them."

The detective sighed. "Miss Scott," he pleaded.

"Don't," she said holding up her hand to silence him. "Don't come all holier than thou. Not now. Not after all the questions, accusations and being so evasive. If you have something to tell me, tell me now." She was stood with her arms crossed and hips to one side, her body language screamed defiance, she wasn't going to back down any time soon and the detective knew it.

He wanted to tell her, wanted to tell her everything, every last detail, but he couldn't. As he opened his mouth to talk a howl broke the silence and she sidled up to the detective, her eyes wide looking out to the village garden. Memories of the previous night came flooding back as she recalled the same horrifying sound she had encountered on her first night in the cottage.

"What was that?" she asked in a whisper.

His arm caught around her waist and he pulled her close, "Come with me now!"

He dragged her into the pub, locking the door behind them. The regulars sat with their drinks each one silently watching.

"Collette." The barmaid turned to the detective. "Make sure the other doors and windows are bolted."

The young lady nodded and disappeared through the door behind the bar at a quick pace.

Amelia turned to the detective, "What on earth is going on?" she asked.

The rest of the congregation sat in silence ignoring her. Ned came to her side and patted her on the back gently.

"Why don't you come and sit down, finish your drink."

"Finish my drink? What's going on? What was that outside?" she turned to Ned, the villagers and then finally to the detective.

"We need to talk," he said.

# chaptra hwegh

**"I**'m sorry, what did you say?" Amelia shook her head in disbelief. "Say that again, because I'm sure you just said wild dog attack. In fact, I'm pretty sure that's what you said."

The detective took a swig of whisky and slammed the glass down on the bar. "As I said, preliminary findings at the coroner's office state the evidence points to a wild animal attack, probably canine. I wouldn't lie to you."

"Are you sure about that? Because I think you've been lying to me from the start." She turned her back on him, unable to look him in the eye. Everything he had told her had been a cover story. Her shoulders slumped. "Besides," she said half-turning towards him, "I dated a zoologist for a few years, and I can tell you that there have been no substantiated reports of wild dogs in England, and this type of attack on a human by a pack of domestic or feral dogs is very unlikely, besides the press would have a field day with this story!"

"There have been no public reports," he said quietly into his drink.

"So what are you saying then? The authorities are covering up the fact wild animals are prowling the streets of Cornwall at night? Like some 'Beast of Bodmin' type creature?"

The room fell uncomfortably silent; everyone averted their eyes avoiding her as she gazed across the faces of the locals huddled in groups around the pub. She had heard the stories of big cats roaming the countryside; exotic pets released into the wild following the change in law in the 70s, but most of those stories had been dismissed as urban myths.

"Is it real?" she whispered.

A mournful cry could be heard from outside.

Amelia shuddered. "I guess that means we have to go."

"On the contrary," the detective declared, "we stay exactly where we are."

There was a loud banging noise at the front door, it brought back memories of the last couple of nights at the cottage, but this door was solid oak and would surely withstand the scare tactics of a few teenagers messing around. The banging on the door continued but no one moved. Then someone shouted from outside.

"Please! Let me in!"

Amelia looked at the detective. "Are you going to let them in?"

The banging continued. "Let me in."

Amelia frowned at the detective. "Well?"

His blank stare mirrored that of the locals sat around the pub; Amelia stood scraping her chair back against the stone floor. "I'll do it then."

The detective put his hand on her shoulder and shook his head as the banging continued.

"Let me in." The voice outside became muffled as though they were too close to the door, then there was another howl.

"If whatever killed Valerie is out there, then it's your duty to help them."

When he didn't answer she stormed over to the door. Reaching out to the lock she could hear heavy breathing from the other side and when her fingers touched the lock there was a whisper.

"Let me in."

There was something in the tone that made her hesitate, and then the banging continued. She slowly backed away from the door when she bumped into the detective making her shriek.

"Come and sit down, drink your tea," he said.

She looked back at the table where Collette was busy setting out pots of tea; guess she wasn't the only one to think of tea in a crisis. Whist everyone silently prepared their drinks, the detective looked at his watch.

"What is it?" she asked.

"It looks like we are going to be here for the night."

"What are you talking about?" There were murmurs around the pub but she couldn't make out what people were saying, just that they were in agreement and accepted their fate for the evening. "Stay here? Are you quite mad?" she protested.

Ignoring her, the detective turned to the barmaid. "Collette, do you have some blankets to hand out?" Collette nodded. "Good." He turned to Amelia. "Make yourself useful, go and help Collette." She opened her mouth to protest, but the detective cut her off. "It will give you something to do, take your mind off things."

With a heavy sigh, she followed Collette through the bar and upstairs to the living quarters. The barmaid stopped when she reached a cupboard on the landing and began handing blankets down to Amelia.

"Here, hold these." The young woman continued to fill her arms full of the dusty woollen blankets, making her sneeze. "Sorry. They've been in storage a while."

When she had finished, Collette shut the door and turned to Amelia, taking half of the pile and proceeded to walk back the way they came.

"Collette?" Amelia began.

"Mmm?"

"What's going on?"

"It's a lock-in," she said innocently.

"Lock-in. I get that. What is it with all the banging and the noises? Is it a gang or something?"

Collette stopped and turned quickly. "What do you mean?"

"It's just kids, isn't it? Surely the police can handle a few delinquents." Amelia adjusted the blankets in her arms as she continued to follow the barmaid down the stairs. "You know, the same thing happened to me back at the cottage."

The young girls eyes widened. "It happened at your cottage?" Amelia nodded and was perplexed by the strange look Collette was giving her. "Come on," she said changing the subject. "We need to get these to everyone." She pushed her way past Amelia, quickening her pace.

By the time they got downstairs, everyone had arranged themselves along benches and made makeshift beds by pulling chairs together. Collette was whispering to the ashen-faced policeman, he glanced up at Amelia then whispered something to the young girl, who nodded and left. When Amelia had finished handing out the rest of the blankets to appreciative villagers, she walked back to her seat.

"Here," she said holding out a blanket for the detective.

He took the blanket and placed it over the back of his chair. "Thanks. Collette tells me you experienced something similar at Lowe Cottage. Is that true?"

"It's probably just a gang of kids trying the scare the crap out of the outsider, which is why all the theatrics here tonight are uncalled for."

"I don't know what to believe anymore," he said with a heavy sigh and sat down. "When did it happen?"

She took a seat and neatly folded the remaining blanket, placing it on the table. "Sunday night, my first night. And then it happened again last night. Seth came and—"

"Seth?"

She nodded. "Yes, before he left for his camping trip."

"Did you see anyone? Anything?"

She shook her head. "No. Just a lot of banging and…"

"Yes?" he said leaning forward.

"The little bastards must have my number because I've had a few funny phone calls."

"What kind of calls?"

"You know, you answer and there's no one there."

"This may be difficult," he muttered. He pulled his phone from his inside jacket pocket.

"What's wrong?" she asked.

"I need to make a phone call." He quickly left heading towards the room behind the bar.

As she watched him leave Ned took his seat. "What was that all about?" he asked.

"Wish I knew."

Ned sighed. "Did Seth say when he'd be back?"

She shook her head. "No. Why?"

The coastguard shrugged. "He agreed to help out on Sunday. I was going to ask if he could do Friday as well."

"No. I'm sorry, he never said when he'd be back."

After a few moments the inspector appeared, he had a look of dread on his face as he looked around the room. Then he spotted a middle-aged man in the corner with his friends, when he approached the men stopped talking. Amelia couldn't hear what they were talking about but it didn't look good. One of the men, balding, quite stocky, started to rise out of his seat, the colour slowly draining from his face.

"No, no, no!" the man shouted. His companions and the detective tried to console him, but the man became agitated, and after they wrestled him back into his chair he began to sob. The room fell silent.

Mark composed himself. "I've got to tell my wife, she needs to know."

Inspector Cook shook his head. "My patrol are seeing to that, but I'm afraid we stay where we are."

Ned nodded to Collette who came round to escort the man into the back room away from everyone. Once he was out of earshot the detective banged three times on the bar.

"May I have your attention? I'm sorry to report that Mark and Nuala's daughter, Julia, has gone missing this evening. If anyone saw Julia in the last twenty-four hours, please come forward so that I can take an account of her movements. Ask your family and friends when last they saw Julia."

Amelia leaned in to Ned and whispered, "Who is Julia?"

"Valerie's best friend, they were like two peas in a pod."

There was a clanking noise from the corner of the pub when a teacup rolled off its saucer and onto the floor. Miss Chandler stood and addressed the detective and the room. "Another lost soul Detective Inspector, when will this end?"

"Not now Lois, let's stay calm. We do not know where Julia is and until we do, I'd appreciate it if you would stop speculating. Is there anyone here who saw Julia recently?"

Mr Bateman, the corner-shop owner, stood up. "She came in with Brendan and Shaun just before I closed for the evening."

"What time would that have been?"

"Around five-thirty."

The detective addressed the rest of the group, "Does anyone have Brendan or Shaun's telephone number?"

A teenager sat close to the bar with apron around his waist slowly raised his hand.

"Justin?"

"I spoke with them before I came to work. They were winding me up about my job."

The detective raised his eyebrow. "Winding you up?"

"Yeah, they call me Tinkerbell… you know, fairy liquid…"

The detective shook his head. "When did you last speak to them Justin? Try to remember, it is very important."

"That was at ten to six, I remember because I needed to be here at six."

"Did they say where they were going? What they were doing?" Justin was silent. "May I remind you that withholding evidence is an offence."

The young boy gulped. "It wasn't my idea." Panic filled his voice.

"No one is in trouble Justin. Just tell me what you know."

"Julia was really upset about Valerie, she said that her life was empty without her. Brendan said that he knew where she had been found and that…" he paused.

"And?"

The villagers listened with bated breath as the young boy nervously wet his lips. "And that he knew how to bring her back."

There were gasps of horror around the room as people started to talk amongst themselves.

"Hush people." The officer walked over to Justin. "Go on."

"Well. He and Shaun have been delving, you know, into the occult on the web, and he said he found a ritual that would bring her back."

"This is all nonsense," said Lois. "This is the devil's work!" The old woman was ignored whilst the villagers were all intrigued to hear what the young boy had to say.

"Well, I said it was all bullshit," continued Justin. "I said you would need the body to do that, but he insisted her soul was still where it happened."

"And *where* do they think it happened?"

"They were going to the woods, out near Malloy's."

Ned groaned.

"What's Malloy's?" asked Amelia.

Ned ducked his head and whispered to her, "Old Man Malloy's is a run-down shack in the woods. It's rumoured to be haunted and there have been lots of reports of strange things going on up there. But I reckon Wilbur St. Clemins started those rumours, doesn't want anyone finding out about his dodgy dealings."

The detective continued. "Do you have Brendan's number, Justin?"

"Yes."

The inspector held out his hand, took the boy's phone and quickly left to make the call that would put an end to speculation. The room was awash with people muttering, each one with their own theories. Justin sank back into his seat, trying to be as invisible as possible.

"You did the right thing lad," said Ned.

Miss Chandler stood by one of the windows looking out across the village, her arms folded and stern expression made her look hardened. After a few moments the detective emerged and went into the back room where Collette had taken Mark. Moans, groans and more weeping could be heard from behind the closed door, after a few moments the inspector appeared and walked into the bar.

"Collette, double whisky for Mark." The barmaid poured an oversized measure and left.

"Well, any news?" asked Amelia.

The detective stared at her, and then his expression softened. "Brendan and Shaun played a prank of sorts on poor Julia. She ran away upset, but they couldn't find her. Come first light I want to search those woods and I need volunteers." Hands around the bar were raised. "Good. I have my patrol out there now who will keep me informed. I suggest you all get some rest now, we leave at dawn."

There was a gentle hum of murmurs amongst the villagers. Amelia looked over to Miss Chandler who hadn't left the window; she walked over to the old woman feeling sorry for her alienation.

"Will you be coming with us Lois?" she asked.

"What's the point? They've got what they wanted."

She was about to ask the old woman what she meant when the detective called out to her.

"Amelia," he waved her over. "Over here, we need a plan of action." She sat with the policeman and Ned. "Got a map Ned?" he asked.

Ned went to the leaflet display beside the front entrance; a vast array of booklets for circular walks, wildlife, historical places of interest within the local area targeted at the tourist industry.

"You'll need to familiarise yourself with the surroundings, and seeing as you are new here, you don't have the advantage as the rest of us. I want you to be looking for clues, not worrying about falling over and taking a wrong turn."

Ned returned with an ordnance survey map of Trembleath Moor and unfolded it across the table, pinning it down with empty glasses. The table was far enough away from anyone else so they could talk without interruption. The other villagers had begun to settle down for the night, some laying down, eyes closed, to get what sleep they could before embarking on the search.

"So we are here," the detective said pointing to the village, "And to get your bearings, here is Lowe Cottage." Amelia nodded. He turned around to make sure no one else was listening and then turned back. "Here," he said, pointing to a dark green patch, "is where we found Valerie."

"But that's not Old Man Malloy's place," said Ned.

"No it isn't."

"So, Julia should be okay then?" the coastguard suggested. "If Valerie was attacked and killed somewhere else, then Julia will be fine."

"What's out there?" asked Amelia, looking at the map.

"Nothing. The nearest habitable place is Holly Cottage." The inspector looked over at Ned.

"And who lives there?" she asked.

"Seth," Ned whispered.

Her heart was quickening, thoughts racing. She had been to Seth's house recently and wondered if he knew Valerie had been found not far from there, that could explain why he was being cagey about her disappearance, about her attack?

"Something wrong Amelia?" asked the detective.

"I was there on Monday evening."

"At Seth's?" asked Ned. "He doesn't waste any time."

"It's not like that. I went for dinner. I owed him for, you know, saving me and all, but I didn't have any food in, so we went to his."

"I thought you said you had a youth problem Monday night?" asked the detective suspiciously.

"I did."

"So… you didn't stay the night at Seth's then?" asked Ned.

"What? No! Not that it is any of your bloody business anyway."

Although Ned looked relieved, he was worried.

"When was the last time you spoke to Seth?" asked the detective.

"You don't think he had anything to do with it do you?" she said with a frown.

"Just answer the question." He had turned into hardened policeman within seconds.

"It was today. He rang asking me to pick up some flyers from the printers."

"Which printer?"

"Mayflower I think they're called. But I didn't pick them up from the printer direct, I picked them up from The Manor. Stu, who sorted the print job, works there and he said it would have been closer for me to pick them up from there."

The detective looked at the map with a frown.

"What is it? What's wrong?" she asked.

"The Manor is a few miles out past Old Man Malloy's, here," he said, pointing to the map.

"I remember driving through woodland to get there, seemed to go on forever, and I thought I was lost at one point."

"And did you see anyone? Anything out of the ordinary?" he asked.

"No," she said shaking her head. "I didn't pass anyone on the road but when I got there a wedding reception was in full swing."

"I don't suppose you overheard whose reception it was? It's okay if you don't, I can ring The Manor and find out."

"Actually, there was one of those signs in the foyer." Amelia scrunched up her nose aiding concentration. "It began with a D... Dolan! That's it." She was overjoyed she had remembered, otherwise it would have bugged her all night and she wouldn't have been able to relax. A few of the villagers turned in their sleep. "Sorry, was I a bit loud?" she whispered.

"Thank you." The detective made a note and put his pad away in his jacket pocket and sighed. "Fancy a drink?" he asked nodding towards the bar.

"Not for me thanks," said Ned. "I'm going to get some shut eye before we head out." He left to find a free space on one of the booths leaving Amelia and the detective.

"Aren't you on duty?" she mused.

"I won't tell if you don't," he smiled.

"Then a whisky please."

He came back from the bar with a bottle and two glasses, poured their drinks and sat.

"What is your name? I can't keep calling you detective."

He smiled into his glass. "Stephen."

"Well, Stephen," she said raising her glass. "Here's to finding Julia."

They clinked glasses and downed the warming liquid.

"I'm sorry for my outburst earlier," she said.

"It's okay. You don't need to apologise."

"Yes I do. It was rude of me."

He leant back in his chair. "Well Amelia Scott. I accept your apology.

May we move on?"

He poured another finger of whisky into their glasses.

"Are you trying to get me drunk officer?" she laughed.

"Certainly not," he said with a chuckle. "This stuff will keep you warm and rested."

"And horizontal," she laughed.

He smiled and continued to watch her.

"You're staring," she said without looking up.

"Sorry. Laughter suits you."

"Now, that's a line I haven't heard before," she said taking another swig.

"It's not a line Amelia, just an observation. That is my job. To observe and conclude."

"And what do you conclude?" she asked.

He narrowed his eyes. "That you came to Creek Bay alone, but you were to come here with another. That you struck a fortunate friendship with someone who saved your bacon on your first day here, who also gave you a job and I think you are very grateful for that."

"Grateful enough to lie to the police about what I know?"

He leant forward and looked into her eyes without blinking, without looking away. "No, I don't believe it's in your nature to lie."

"Carry on," she said taking another sip. "You're on a roll."

"I also detect some resistance to authority. I know you apologised, but I sense you were rebellious in your teenage years and fought back, maybe because you lost an authority figure in your life when you were younger."

"Anyone can use a computer to do a background check."

"No. I never checked on you Amelia, like I said, I'm good at my job."

"Anything else?"

"I know that you're modest in your appearance, educated and like a good whisky," he said swishing the liquid in his glass. "And…"

"And?" she pressed.

"And I think you look adorable when you scrunch your nose when you're thinking."

That last comment took her by surprise; she wasn't quite sure what to say. She was grateful for the interruption when Collette entered the bar from the side room.

"Well?" asked Stephen.

"He's finally gone to sleep," she said quietly. "Speaking of which, I'm going now. There's a spare room if you want it."

Stephen turned to Amelia and then looked around the room. "No, thank you, I'll be fine here. Thank you Collette for seeing to Mark."

"No problem. Good night." The barmaid flicked a few switches behind the bar, lights went off around the room leaving just the emergency lighting illuminating the fridges and bar top. She closed the door, her footsteps growing distant as she took the stairs to the living quarters.

"What time is it now?" asked Amelia.

The detective looked at his watch. "One o'clock."

"Guess we should get some sleep too."

"You go ahead," he said. "I'll make sure the place is secure."

While he was checking the building was locked tight, Amelia pulled the blanket off the back of her chair and lay down on the booth behind the table. It wasn't the most comfortable of beds, but it would do. She could hear the policeman doing his rounds rattling doors and windows, the rustle of blankets as villagers turned in their sleep, and someone had even started snoring. As her eyes started to close, weariness came upon her and she slipped into oblivion.

*Amelia ran through the deserted village, sirens blared in the distance. The fog was closing in around her, a thick blanket reducing visibility to near zero. A scraping sound echoed behind her, like someone raking clawed nails down a backboard. It made her shudder; she held her hands over her ears blocking the noise and prayed it would stop. As quickly as it came, the sound vanished, leaving nothing but the eerie sound of wind whistling through the streets.*

*"Hello?" she called out, but there was no reply. "Hello."*

*"Amelia." It sounded like a little girl's voice, but with a chilling mocking after tone, haunting and breathless from a disembodied voice.*

*"Who's there?"*

*"Am-eeeeee-leeeeeaaaaah."*

*Laughter sounded.*

*She spun around but there was no one around. The bin by the store toppled over onto its side. Her heartbeat was racing. "Shit," she exclaimed. She told herself it was just the wind. When she turned back a young girl with long red hair stood in front of her, the horrendous sight alone made her scream out. The skin on her face was torn away, Amelia could clearly see the bone tissue where the bloodied flesh was ripped away from the girl's skull.*

*The girl reached out to her. "Amelia."*

Amelia screamed and felt her body connect. She bolted upright opening her eyes.

"Ow!" The detective sat on the floor next to her nursing the back of his head, her knee inches away.

"God, I'm sorry, was that me?"

"Bad dream?" he asked still rubbing his head.

"You could say that. Are you sure you're okay?"

"I'll survive," he turned and smiled at her. "Must have been a good one."

"What?"

"The dream." He stood and arched his back, cracking the bones in his spine. "Remind me again to take the offer of a soft bed next time."

"You were being human, roughing it with the rest of us mere mortals, and I truly hope there is not a next time my neck is killing me." The detective chuckled. "Besides, what time is it?" she asked.

He turned his watchstrap to read the time. "A little before three-thirty."

"May as well get up then." She looked across the pub littered with bodies huddled under blankets. "Time to feed the troops. I'll check the kitchen and find something suitable."

"I'll give you a hand," he said following her.

Amelia looked through the food cupboards and fridge; eggs, bacon, bread, tomatoes. Not quite enough for a full English, but bacon butties and a mug of tea would be perfect.

"Need a hand?" he asked as she started to switch on the appliances.

"I've got this, you go sort out the tables, then come and help me take them out."

The smell of bacon cooking roused most of the villagers, some of them needed a little more persuasion. Ned rose from the depths of sleep with a loud yawn.

"Is it really morning already?" he asked.

"I've never seen this side of the day before," said someone else wincing from the pain in his lower back.

Amelia filled all the pots she could find with tea and the frying pans were at capacity; turning the slices of bacon, she felt an odd sense of belonging. They needed her, needed her to get them on their journey.

"You've done this before," he said stood in the doorway.

She turned to Stephen, his grin wide and mischievous. "My parents sent me to a summer holiday retreat in the woods once. I hated them for it. All that open space, new people and those mundane tasks they made you do to fill the day." She shook her head remembering the ordeal. "So I struck a friendship with the chef, spent most of my time hiding away, helping him prepare food. Catering for the masses is about timing. I like that. It's a discipline."

"Are you sure you've not been in the employ of Her Majesty's service?"

She turned with a scowl. "No, I have not. I don't think me and Her Majesty's service would get along much."

"How so?" he asked.

"Let's just say everyone has a little something they like to keep buried."

Mark stumbled through to the kitchen. "Bacon?" he croaked.

"Whoa, easy Mark." The detective struggled to keep him upright, he was certainly worse for wear, making him wonder just how much alcohol Collette had given him last night. "Easy, why don't we get you a seat and a cup of tea?"

"Tea! Tea! You think that will make everything all right?"

Clearly Mark was not of the opinion that you can solve the world's problems with a nice cuppa.

Amelia stepped forward. "Hello, Mark, isn't it? We haven't met, I'm Amelia." She placed a hot mug of instant coffee on the table in front of him. "Here, help yourself to milk and sugar. I'll get you a bacon butty." Mark looked down at the mug of hot liquid. "Unless you'd prefer something a little stronger?" The detective flashed her a look of disapproval. "My dad would drink coffee with a splash of brandy to take the edge off. Would you like me to fix you one?"

Mark stopped struggling under the policeman's grip. "No." he said quietly and took a seat at the kitchen table. "This will do fine. Thank you."

Stephen joined Amelia at the cooker where she was tending to the large stack of toast and sizzling bacon. "Thanks."

"I didn't do anything," she said with a shrug. "Could you take out the pots of tea? Careful they're hot."

"Yes ma'am," he said with a smile.

The villagers were appreciative when the first pots arrived. Stephen made several more trips - more tea, milk and sugar and then helped Amelia with the two large plates of hot bacon sandwiches. The villagers dug into the food, a gentle hum of chatter over clinking crockery. It was a sorrowful day, one that worst case could end with them discovering another body; all in all a pretty grim way to start the day.

The detective thumbed through his notebook.

"Anything stand out for you?" asked Amelia.

"A few things," he said without looking up.

Amelia and Ned looked at one another, wondering who would be the first to ask the question, the question everyone was dying to know. A voice broke the silence.

"What about the similarities with poor Valerie's case, detective." Lois Chandler, conspiracy theory expert, made her presence known.

"Lois, this is neither the time nor the place."

"I think you should answer the lady Detective Inspector Cooke." Mark stood behind the bar, his red-rimmed puffy eyes bloodshot from lack of sleep and crying. He raised his eyebrows expecting an answer.

Stephen sighed and looked around the table of expectant faces. "There are some—" people groaned, Mark physically heaved, "but these are not the same circumstances. The similarities are purely coincidental." The murmuring began to rise. "Enough!" Stephen shouted and slammed down his notebook. The room fell silent. "We go out today as planned. If you need stout footwear, go home now and meet back here in twenty minutes. If anyone asks, tell them there was a leak at the pub and you are helping out."

"My wife won't believe me," said one villager.

"Then don't wake her. I'm sure you've rolled in past midnight before now. Go! Everyone! Time is of the essence."

The villagers started to gather their belongings and filtered out of the pub one by one, some taking bacon sandwiches with them.

"Justin," the detective shouted. "Start clearing the tables."

The boy picked up his apron and started collecting dishes. Stephen turned to Amelia and looked her up and down.

"Will you be warm enough?" he asked.

Amelia looked down at her feet. She was sure her Doc Martens would be okay in any terrain, she looked at the coat slung over the arm chair, it was a good job she had brought that after all.

"Sure, I'll be okay."

"If you need a warmer jacket, I have one in the boot of my car."

"Thank you. I'll be fine."

Justin had cleared most of the dishes when the detective laid out the map on the tables.

"So, we're going to Seth's then?" asked Ned.

"We'll start here," he said pointing at the map. "We'll convene on the access road to Holly Cottage, make sure everyone fans out from there, then do a sweep all the way down to Old Man Malloy's, then back again."

Amelia examined the map more closely. "What's here?" she asked pointing to a small blob on the map.

The detective and Ned both leaned in closer. "Not sure what that is," said Stephen.

"I do." Ned said rising up. "That's Solomon's place."

"Who is Solomon?" asked Amelia.

Ned sat down. "Solomon is, was… I'm not sure," he said shaking his head, "Seth's father."

"Was? You mean?" Stephen mumbled.

Ned shrugged, "No one knows what became of Solomon."

"I heard about that case," said Stephen. "Before my time; he disappeared. Is that correct?"

Ned sighed, "Right."

"And there has been no word of him since?" asked Amelia.

The old woman sat in the corner tutted. "He's still around all right." She rose slowly from her seat. "You mark my words." As she approached the table she had turned a deathly white colour. "You find Julia, and you find Solomon." She clutched at her chest and started coughing.

Amelia rushed to her side. "Oh goodness Lois, are you okay?"

Lois took a seat. "I'm just old and weary child."

The old lady had aged that night; Amelia noticed that she looked more fragile, like she had given up the fight. She sat comforting the old woman for a few moments when the first of the villagers returned dressed in walking boots, thermal trousers and waterproofs, which, Amelia thought was a little over the top, but when the next villager emerged similarly dressed, she wondered if they knew something she didn't. Perhaps she should take up the offer of a warmer coat after all and she was praying that her Doc Martens were up for the challenge. Ten minutes later and the eight volunteers had congregated at the pub's entrance.

"Looks like this is it then," Stephen said addressing the group. "I've called for a couple of officers who will be here in a few minutes, so split yourselves into groups of four because you will be travelling in the police Land Rover units. Mark, Ned, Amelia you're with me. Justin, make sure to give Collette a hand when she wakes up."

The boy nodded.

# chaptra seyth

The detective led the convoy to Holly Cottage. Mark sat in the front passenger seat with Ned and Amelia sat in the back; as she looked out the window, she couldn't help but think how different it was compared to when she was riding on the back of Seth's bike. Stephen parked on the access track and got out of the vehicle. Pulling the map from his back pocket he spread it on top of the bonnet, his two officers pulled up behind them and the volunteers clambered out.

"Gather round people. PC Jones, you will lead B Team, fanning North East." He pointed to an area on the map and the officer nodded. "PC Halliwell, take C Team South East. We will take the East. Everyone check your watches. I make it four twenty-nine, so we have two hours until the first check in, unless you find anything before then of course. Make sure you travel in pairs and give the officers your mobile numbers in case you get separated. Let's not have anyone else go missing." The officers led their teams to the side and synchronized watches, took each others details and made sure their torches were in working order before setting off to their designated areas.

Ned leant down to Amelia, "Guess that makes us the A Team."

Amelia smacked him playfully on the arm before standing next to Stephen still poring over the map, frowning. "East takes us out past Solomon's, is that right?" she said.

"Yes it does." He handed the map to Amelia and walked off depressing the power button on the torch a couple of times and the others fell in line behind him.

Amelia had to quicken her pace to keep up. "So, what do you expect to find there?" she asked.

"I don't know, but we're going to find out."

Amelia followed Ned and the detective through the dense woodland. Ned had grabbed flashlights and a first aid kit from his truck before they left the pub; the coastguard seemed fully prepared. She kept the light trained on the ground looking for clues, footprints, clothing, belongings; anything that would suggest Julia had been there. The silence was interrupted when Stephen's radio buzzed; Mark, who had been a few paces behind rushed to his side.

"Okay, make a note of where you found it and we'll deal with it back at the station."

"What was that?" asked Mark.

"Looks like someone has been doing some illegal hunting, nothing for you to worry about."

They continued in silence. Amelia walked over to Mark.

"I don't suppose you have a picture of Julia on you Mark. It's just that I don't know what she looks like."

"Of course," he patted his jacket and then pulled out his wallet. In the front was a picture of Mark, his wife and daughter, Julia; a pretty young blonde with blue eyes who most definitely took after her mother.

"She's beautiful."

Tears welled in his eyes. "She is."

The radio buzzed again; Mark, Amelia and Ned watched the detective expectantly.

"What?" There was a long pause. "I don't understand. How old?"

"What is it?" asked a worried Mark.

The detective held up his hand to silence him so he could listen to the officer speaking on the radio. "How many? Shit! Phone the National Wildlife Crime Unit, get them to come out and survey the area. If someone has been dumping carcasses, it needs to be dealt with immediately."

"What is it Stephen? What have they found?" asked Amelia.

"C Team found an animal graveyard."

"A what? Out here?" asked Ned.

"Are you sure it is animal?" Mark asked, a lump in his throat.

"My officers can tell the difference between human and animal remains Mark, I assure you. Looks like our illegal hunting problem just got more serious. We continue our search for Julia as planned. Come on."

He led them on through the woodland, it wasn't long until the trees thinned out and they were now heading into a clearing.

"I can hear water," said Ned. "Don't remember seeing that on the map."

"Maybe it's an underground spring or stream?" offered Amelia.

In the clearing, the ground underfoot felt waterlogged and bouncy, a blanket of soft sponge.

"This is weird," Mark announced.

"How so?" asked Amelia.

Mark looked up and Amelia followed his gaze upwards. "Right up to the clearing the ground was firm and with the surrounding tree cover, the ground shouldn't be this wet and we haven't had enough significant rainfall to explain this."

"He's right," Ned agreed.

The detective stepped forward and knelt down, picking at the forest floor. The damp earth and forest debris smelt disgusting; he lifted a handful to his nose and heaved from the smell. "Jesus!"

Amelia stumbled over to the detective, her heavy boots disturbing the surface, the foul fetid stench hit her nose, it was so bad she could taste it. "Holy shit!" she said holding her nose and mouth. "What is that?"

"Smells like a bloody sewer." He heaved some more, desperate to clear the smell from his senses.

"What could be being pumped out here?" Ned asked. He walked around the perimeter searching for a pipe, anything that would suggest cause for foul odor or sound of water, but he found nothing.

A twig snapped behind them. They spun round pointing their torches towards the sound, but there was nothing. Then a rustling sound came from the other side.

"One of your team, detective?" asked a worried Ned.

"No, they're not in this area, you know that." Stephen kept his flashlight trained on the area where the noise came from.

Amelia gulped then whispered, "Maybe one of them veered off the path and got disorientated, ended up heading back this way?" She was hoping that was the case, kept telling herself that was the most logical explanation.

The detective walked towards the sound.

"Be careful," whispered Amelia.

They all kept their flashlights aimed in his direction aiding him when a sudden explosion of noise made them jump. Amelia screamed and Stephen fell backwards clutching his chest; a murder of crows took off, wings flapping, cawing loudly, annoyed at having their early morning forage disturbed.

Amelia rushed to his side, knelt down and held her hand on his. "Are you okay?" she asked.

Stephen smiled and shook his head. "I'm fine. Bloody birds gave me a heart attack," he said patting his chest.

"Me too," she laughed. The laughter dispelled any thoughts of sinister activities taking place so close to them. Stephen stood up and brushed his clothing free of leaves, when Amelia noticed his notebook had fallen onto the ground. As she picked up the book, a photo fell out from the back page.

"Here, let me," he said trying to grab his notebook from her. But Amelia ignored him, she held on to the picture examining it closely. Her throat tightened as she looked at the pretty young redhead.

"Something wrong Amelia?" asked the detective.

Amelia frowned. "I know her."

Stephen took the picture from her. "Who? This girl?"

"Well. I dreamt about her last night."

"Really? Are you sure?"

"Positive. Gave me the heebie jeebies." The detective placed the picture back inside his notebook and then stuffed it into his jacket pocket. "Who is she?" asked Amelia.

There was sadness in his voice when Stephen finally answered her question. "Valerie."

Amelia's stomach tightened. "But that's impossible. I never even met Valerie. How on earth could I have dreamt about her? I don't understand!"

"Nor do I."

Ned walked towards the undergrowth where the birds had vacated. He pulled back the foliage and winced. "They were feeding on a dog."

"Oh no. Really?" Amelia's voice cracked as she thought of someone at home missing their pet.

"Bloody carrion birds." Ned said walking back to the group. "They'll pick at anything given half the chance. Farmer Brian said they've attacked his new born lambs before now, made an awful mess. God damn shame it was."

After two hours in the woods and no evidence linked to Julia, the teams convened back at the vehicles, everyone looking defeated and glum. The two police Land Rovers departed leaving the detective, Ned, Mark and Amelia. The depressed silence was broken when Stephen's phone rang, he continued the call sat in his vehicle for privacy, the three volunteers stepped forward trying to eavesdrop on the conversation. When he finished his call he stepped out of the vehicle.

"Well?" asked Mark expectantly.

"A young girl matching Julia's description has been found and taken to hospital," he said sombrely.

Mark held his breath. "Is she?"

He nodded. "She is alive, a little shaken up, hasn't spoken a word since her arrival. She was carrying Julia's purse, so we will need to make a positive ID. Would you mind?"

Mark pushed past the detective. "Yes, what are we waiting for? Let's go." He took the passenger seat, fastened his seat belt, making hand gestures for Stephen and the others to hurry along.

"Looks like we're going to Treliske General," muttered Ned.

"I can drop you two off on the way, you should get some rest, no point in all of us ending up like zombies."

Amelia was relieved. Her eyes were starting to sting, that was often the first sign she was ready for closing them and drifting off to sleep.

Stephen drove to the Kings Arms where Ned had parked his truck, and dropped Amelia at Lowe Cottage before continuing to the hospital. It was odd being back at the cottage again. With one thing or another, she had spent very little time there; it didn't feel like her own, and looking at the boxes stacked in the corner, she wondered if it ever would. It was cold and empty, especially without Seth. Weary and tired, her eyes began to close, but it was coming up for eight o'clock and she would need to open the bookshop, she couldn't let Seth down. Maybe she could shut her eyes for five minutes, just a little a catnap; that will make her feel refreshed. Her eyelids felt so heavy it was hard not to give in; sitting on the bottom step she untied her boots, kicking them off and then leant back. When she opened her eyes again she felt disorientated when the first thing she saw was the front door and a rolled up newspaper sticking through the letterbox.

"Oh crap!" She quickly pulled herself up with the aid of the wall and ran to the kitchen, the clock on the cooker read nine o'clock. Running back to the hallway she took the stairs two steps at a time, ran to the bathroom and splashed her face with cold water then put on fresh clothing before running downstairs to put on her boots. The phone rang while she was balancing on one leg to get the clumpy article on.

"Hello?"

"Finally, where have you been?" his voice sounding distant.

"Seth? Is that you?" she asked not sure if it was her imagination.

"I've been trying to get hold of you all night and this morning. Where have you been?" The line was crackling making his voice break up.

"Lock-in at the local."

"And this morning?"

"Arh, yes, we're not supposed—" She stopped herself. The detective had insisted they not to tell anyone about the search party, but seeming as it looked like Julia had been found Amelia decided that it wouldn't hurt after all. "I volunteered for a search party." There was a long pause on the other end and she was sure the connection had been lost altogether. "Hello? You still there?" she asked.

"Yeah." Seth didn't sound like his usual self, if anything she would have thought he was upset. "Searching for what?"

"*Who* you mean. We were searching for a missing girl, who has now been found. She's been taken to hospital for the all clear."

A long drawn out breath sounded down the phone. "Good, I'm glad."

"Listen, I was just about to set off to open up—"

"Did you pick up the flyers?" he asked cutting her off.

"Yes. They are in my car."

"Good, Mr Bateman will be putting some in the paper deliveries for me this week, will you be able to get there before half past?"

"Yes, if you stop talking to me," she said fumbling with her boot.

Seth chuckled sounding more like the Seth she knew. "Okay, I'll let you get off, see you around noon okay?"

Amelia's voice betrayed her when she enthusiastically said, "Great!" She put the phone down. "God, you moron," she said shaking her head, and mocking her own voice picked up her keys and hurried out to her car.

# *chaptra eth*

She opted for parking at the rear of the store and used the back door key, the alarm emitting bleeps when she pushed the door. Putting the box of flyers onto a shelf in the storeroom, she carefully punched in the numbers silencing the alarm and then went back outside for the other box before locking the door behind her. The shop was eerie when it was in darkness, the stale smell of coffee hung in the air mixed with the smells of musty books and fragrant candles. He was coming back and that made her smile as she switched on the lamps and coffee machine and unlocked the bolt to the front door. As she turned the sign to read open she was relieved no-one was waiting outside this morning. Amelia busied herself plumping up the cushions on the sofas, when an overwhelming notion of being watched came over her and she looked up to the mezzanine.

"Good morning Amelia Scott." His velvety voice, as smooth as milky chocolate, floated towards her.

Her heart thudded against her chest. "William! How did you—"

"I was hoping to have some quiet time with you before you opened," he said looking to the front door.

She turned to the front door and then looked up at him. He patted the loveseat inviting her to join him. "I have to get everything ready, but you're welcome to join me down here if you like."

It would be difficult for her to resist him if she went up there to that confined comfort zone. Talking to him downstairs, where she had two escape routes seemed much safer.

"Would you like a drink?" she asked turning her back on him to fill the grinder with coffee beans.

His expression faded from seduction to annoyance. He stood and forced a smile. "Very well, I see you are busy Miss Scott. Perhaps I shall see you tonight?" He started walking down the steps slowly, deliberately, never taking his eyes off her.

"Tonight?" she asked in surprise, but when she turned he was nowhere to be seen, she looked around the store but he had vanished, and yet she never heard the doorbell chime.

Amelia carried on with her routine, setting up the coffee machine, logging on the computers and sorting out the till when the door opened and the detective walked in.

"Morning Stephen, would you like a coffee?"

He was still wearing the same clothes from last night, only now they were creased and worn. "Thank you. A strong one, extra shot please." He said taking a seat on the nearest barstool.

"Why don't you take a more comfortable seat on the sofa over there," she said pointing to the sofa in front of the window. "And I'll bring your drink over."

"Thanks," he said with a heavy sigh. "But if I sit down there I'll never get back up again."

"You look shattered, have you been at the hospital all this time?" He nodded. "So, the girl *was* Julia?" He nodded again. "How is she?"

"Shaken up, still not talking. The doctors have performed all the routine checks, she wasn't harmed, just a few minor scratches. They seem to think she has been subject to trauma, which might explain why she hasn't spoken yet, so they have called for a psychological evaluation."

"What a shame." Amelia poured coffee into a large mug for the detective and set it down. "Help yourself to cream and sugar. Mark and his wife must be overjoyed to have her back."

He took a large gulp of the hot liquid. "Yeah, they are, but they are also concerned at the same time."

"I can understand that."

Two students entered and proceeded to the computers. The detective hung his head and closed his eyes.

"Why don't you get some shut eye, you'll be grateful for it."

"I can't. Gotta get back to the station and make a start on my notes."

"Aren't you able to access your system remotely?" she asked nodding to the computers.

"Yes."

"Then I suggest you take it easy, make a start on your notes here, but after you've had a wash and drunk your coffee."

"Florence Nightingale had nothing on you Miss Scott," he said with a weary smile.

"Go on through to the back, there is a washroom down there you can use," she said with a smile.

The detective left with a grateful smile while she pulled the laptop out of her bag and booted it up. Amelia took it upstairs to the mezzanine so he would have privacy while he worked and then left it on a small table by the loveseat, along with his coffee and a warm bun. Stephen emerged with wet hair and stood by the counter when he saw Amelia coming down the steps.

"I've set my laptop up there for you, so you won't be interrupted."

"Thank you Amelia." He slowly went upstairs, fatigue setting in, whilst events were still fresh in his mind he'd start his notes and then make his way back to the station.

Amelia made a start on tidying the bookshelves and took delivery of a large box containing several books from pre-orders. Looking through the list, one of the books had been ordered by V. Temple, the title *People of History and Influence* was not at all what she had expected. Pulling out the store laptop from under the counter she logged onto the reference system and looked under books ordered and bought by V. Temple. A selection of young adult titles, mixed with twentieth century history, geography and science books, which Amelia assumed were part of Valerie's school curriculum, but there were a couple of books that stood out. There was the note for pre-order of *People of History and Influence by Charles Lane* and there were also a couple of other titles: *From whence they came: A chronological account of shape-shifters in the modern world*; and *Myths and Legends Exposed*. It would appear Valerie was doing research of some sort. Then she scrolled down to Julia's account; she had similar school reference books to Valerie, which was understandable, but there was one book title that made Amelia frown, *Once bitten: Survival 101*.

"What the hell were these girls up to?" she whispered.

"Excuse me."

"Christ," she exclaimed with her hand to her chest calming her nerves while her heartbeat regained its regular rhythm. "You made me jump."

"Sorry." The young boy put his books on the counter. "I wanted to ask if you had a title that has been out-of-print for a while, could you see if you could get hold of it for me?"

"Sure, which title?"

"*People of History and Influence.*"

Amelia's fingers poised over the keypad and she looked over the laptop lid at him. "What?"

"*People of History—*"

"I heard you. Why do you want that book?"

The young boy shifted from one foot to the other. "Erm, I er." Her eyebrow rose while she waited for him to answer; nerves getting the better of him, the young boy dropped his bag. "It's okay. I'll look myself." He bent down to pick up his bag and then ran out of the store so fast she thought he would go through the glass.

Two youths sat at the computers looked up at the commotion and then back to their screens.

"Who was that?" she called out to the youngsters.

One of them turned around and muttered, "Brendan."

There was a shuffle noise from upstairs and heavy footsteps as the detective ran to the railings. "Brendan?" he called out.

The young girl nodded. Amelia recalled Brendan was the name of the young boy who had been playing a prank on Julia, according to the detective.

"What did he want?" he asked Amelia.

"A book."

"What type of book?"

"Out-of-print." She looked down at the open box that had just been delivered. Mindful that the two youngsters were listening to the conversation Amelia waved up to the detective.

"I'll get you another drink."

She carried the drink on the book and sat down on a floor cushion next to the loveseat. The detective was hunched over the laptop typing at a frantic speed, a scowl on his face.

"Here," she said holding out the drink. "Take a break, you look like you need it."

"I've got to get this done." When she didn't move he knew it was an order rather than a suggestion and closed the lid. "Okay. I'll take a break." He took a sip and watched her examining the book in her hand. "What's that?"

"The book Brendan was after."

"I thought you said—"

"It was."

The detective looked at the book on her lap, "Doesn't look out-of-print to me."

"Valerie ordered it before—"

The detective put his mug down. "Valerie? Let me see that," he said holding out his hand.

Amelia handed him the book. He studied the back cover and then opened to the contents page. *People of History and Influence*. He continued to thumb through the pages. "Well?" asked Amelia.

"Well what?" he said, still flicking through the book hoping something would jump out at him, give him a clue as to why Valerie and Brendan would have been interested in it.

Amelia asked expectantly, "What is it about?"

The detective frowned. "I don't know." His eyes were stinging from lack of sleep and he found the words on the pages blurring into one another.

"Would you like me to..." She paused when he gave her a quizzical look. "I mean, I could read it for you and give you an overview if you like."

He looked at her for what seemed an eternity. "Why would you do that?"

"To help you. I can see you're busy and the last thing you need is research on top, so I am offering to do that for you."

"You would do that?" he asked quietly.

"Of course. Besides, will take my mind off things."

"Such as?"

Amelia shrugged. "Just things."

The detective gratefully accepted her offer.

Amelia watched the seconds hand slowly moving around the large clock face on the wall opposite the counter; ten past twelve and Seth should have arrived by now. She tried to keep herself busy notifying customers that their orders had arrived and when she finished the last call she looked at Valerie's book she had put under the counter. Sitting on the sofa next to the window Amelia opened the cover. It had been a long time since she read a title like that, and wondered if her offer was more than she could deliver. She was halfway through the first chapter when someone pulled the book away from her. His wide grin and floppy brown locks were a welcome sight.

"Seth. When did you get back?" she asked, her enthusiasm betraying her desire to remain dignified.

"Just now. Thought I'd check in and see if the store was still standing before we went home."

She closed the book and left it on the table. "Nice to see your confidence in me hasn't wavered." Her beaming smile was reciprocated.

"Any chance of a cold one?" Sonny shouted from the back.

"You brought the crew with you." She jested.

Seth took the seat next to her, his arm draped along the top. "Well, you know, they were pestering to meet you again. Especially Daniel, he was too drunk to remember you last time."

"I heard that," said Daniel as he came into view.

He was wearing his leathers and looking very different from the last time she saw him. Sonny wore his dreadlocks down instead of up, each of them looked refreshed and had a certain glow about them.

"If camping makes you guys look that good, I think I'll be coming with you next time."

"It's a blokes only thing," said Daniel in monotone.

Amelia nodded. "Riiiiiight, and women would *so* cramp your style."

Sonny reached behind the counter and pulled out three beers opening them one at a time. "You want one too Amelia?" he asked.

She looked at Seth who nodded his approval. "Sure, why not."

Seth was idly stroking the back of the sofa inches from her shoulder, she looked at him, her complexion clashing with the claret coloured fabric. He leant closer and she caught her breath as he grazed her leg when he reached to pick up the book on the table.

"What are you reading?" he asked turning the book over, then his smile faded and was replaced with a frown. "This title was—"

"Ordered, I know. I'm sorry I was just—"

"Reading it for me," the detective said, as he walked down the steps.

Sonny and Daniel stood by the counter sipping their beers watching him descend while Seth's expression didn't falter.

"Research. I understand Miss Temple ordered that book and someone else has been in requesting it, someone of interest to us, I have no option but to commandeer the book and find out what's so fascinating about it."

"Nothing, I assure you," Seth said coolly.

The detective stood by the bottom step, laptop in his hand. "I've finished with this, thank you Amelia. I'll be heading back to the station to continue the investigation." He turned to the two men at the counter. "I don't suppose you can tell me where you were last night gentlemen."

Daniel slammed his drink down on the counter. "None of your damn business," he cursed.

"Failure to answer my questions will result in a trip down to the station for obstruction. Again, where were you last night?"

Sonny turned to the detective forcing a smile. "We were camping. All three of us."

"Where?"

"Not here," said Daniel.

The detective narrowed his eyes, "Where exactly did you camp? Specifics, and map coordinates if you please."

Seth stood, his full height was impressive from her viewpoint, but

Stephen stood his ground.

"Kil Margh Tor. Look it up on the computer," Seth said as he took another step towards the detective.

Amelia stood putting herself between the two of them. "I told you they were camping Stephen, why do you need to ask?" she said surprised at her own tone.

The detective handed her the laptop and muttered, "Routine." Before pushing his way past Seth to the door. "I'll be in touch."

When the door closed behind him Seth turned to Amelia. "Stephen?"

She shrugged. "I spent all night and early morning with him, couldn't keep calling him detective all the time."

"Why not," said Daniel, "that's what he is."

"Have I done something wrong?" she asked Seth.

Seth closed his eyes. "No. I'm sorry." He exchanged looks with Sonny and Daniel before taking the two remaining bottles on top of the counter and handing one to her. "They give us grief." He shrugged. "I don't know why. We're just sick and tired of it to be honest."

"Why would they harass you?" she said taking the beer offered. "The police I mean?"

Seth took his seat and picked up the book with his free hand. "Some things never change." He put the book down and patted the seat for her to join him. "Come on, sit down, Sonny and Daniel can look after everything here while you tell me all about what has been going on."

Amelia sat down, happy to be near him, though frustrated at the lack of two-way communication, but he was here now, and she felt safe. She gave him an overview of Tuesday night, going to the quiz with Ned, about the lock-in, about the search party.

"Old Man Malloy's? That's where Valerie's body was found?" asked Seth.

Amelia nodded and drank the last of her beer. "Yes. The police didn't want anyone to know where it was because they didn't want anyone looking up there."

"And for good reason," said Daniel from the counter.

Sonny shot him a look and Seth interrupted her before she could ask any more questions. "Well, it sounds like you've had a very active twenty-four hours. You must be exhausted."

She didn't realise how tired she actually was, and what she wanted more than anything right now was the comfort of her own bed.

Amelia yawned. "Yeah. Sorry," she said putting her hand over her mouth. "I am quite tired to be truthful."

"Why don't you head home, get some rest, I'm sorted here."

"But you've just got back and—"

"Don't worry," he said touching her shoulder. "We can cope."

When she started to get up, he stood and walked her to the back door, his hand gently resting in the small of her back. The heat from his hand sent a wave of excitement through her body. When she got to the door she turned, he was inches from her, kissably close. Amelia looked at his lips and wondered what they would taste like. He bent closer and turned the handle, she stood to one side as he opened the door, when daylight flooded into the corridor she saw his van parked next to her car and the two bikes rested behind.

"Would you like to go to the Italian restaurant tonight?" he whispered. "They are reopening after the refurb."

She would love nothing more than to spend the evening with him, but her body would have other ideas, and she had visions of herself falling asleep at the table, not the best impression to give someone you were trying to impress.

"I am quite tired Seth. Do you mind if we go another night?"

He smiled at her. "Sure, it was rude of me to assume."

"No. I would love to, but I have been up all night and I am just beat. How about Friday?"

"Friday." He smiled.

She turned to leave. "Oh, the flyers are under the counter, Mr Bateman came in for them, they'll go out tomorrow morning, but Mrs Nolan from the school hasn't been in yet."

"No problem, I'll get that sorted."

She waved him goodbye as she reversed out of the parking space and drove away.

Seth closed the door with a thud.

"Well?" asked Daniel stood behind him.

"We need to keep tabs on them," he said with a scowl.

Daniel sighed. "What are they playing at?"

Seth turned. "I don't know, but I'm going to find out." He turned to his friend who joined them. "Dan, you're at Lowe Cottage, Sonny you're with me. We're going to Old Man Malloy's."

# *chaptra naw*

Amelia ran herself a hot bath, unplugged the phone and put on some music, determined no one would be interrupting her peaceful time. She lay back in the bubbles and closed her eyes, it was good to be warm again; her spine settled allowing the heat to penetrate her bones, the water gently caressing her like tiny massaging hands. An hour later when the water had gone cold she begrudgingly pulled herself out, put on her dressing gown and lay down on her bed. She felt like she had spent barely any time in it since she arrived, but it was soft and comfortable unlike the booth at The Kings Arms last night. Amelia curled herself into a ball and drifted into sleep.

*She found herself gliding around the ballroom as she danced at the masquerade ball, the room familiar to her yet she couldn't place it. It was architecturally stunning, with large chandeliers hanging from the high ceiling and an abundance of floral woodland decorations adorning the expansive winding staircase. The guests were elegantly dressed, laughing as they sipped their expensive drinks and ate their way through delicate canapés, the whole affair seemed opulent and excessively decadent. She was being spun around and around by the man whose face was covered by a black wolf mask. Her head was swimming with dreams, wishes and hopes, love and lust. She wanted him to take her, kiss her, run away into the gardens and hold her. The music grew louder as the tempo rapidly increased; it coursed through her body with exquisite temptation, thump thump, thump and then it abruptly stopped. The dance floor emptied but she barely noticed, all she saw were his deep brown eyes through the small holes in his mask. He whispered to her, "Come with me." And she let him lead her, away from the ball until they were alone in the garden and then she became afraid.*

*"Please. Take me back," she said.*

*But the man did not listen. He pulled her closer, crushing her body to his. "My love," he said caressing her hair and face. "We are to be, you and I. Give in to me."*

*He bent down to kiss her, when he opened his mouth his teeth became longer, and sharper. Amelia screamed.*

She pushed the pillows to one side thumping them into submission and then settled back down; she caught a glimpse of the clock on the nightstand, four-thirty pm. Her thoughts drifted to how she would spend her evening, she could have been getting ready for a meal with Seth right now. She felt refreshed enough to go and have a meal with him, engage in conversation, she could string a sentence together even in the most dire of circumstances. Thumping the pillow again she wondered if she had missed her chance.

Amelia looked to the wicker chair where she had left Valerie's book. She started flicking through the first few pages to a point she could remember; this would be the key to finding out what the kids had found so fascinating, she wondered what mysteries it held that captivated them. Amelia began to read on…

*'The two families were now joined by their love and it was to be a joyous occasion worth more than any land title, for it was a union like no other. Through their sustained notoriety over the years, they had become known as 'Krev Arv' (Strong Arm), their victories in battle were unprecedented. They would be the heart of the town, and everyone would bask in their excellence and the freedom they brought to the townsfolk. But it would be a turn of events in the latter years when the young brood would fight and tear the two families apart.'*

Amelia stopped reading and frowned. It was no coincidence that the two family names, Solomon and Malloy, kept coming up in conversation. Old Man Malloy's place had been the focus of both the killing of Valerie and disappearance of Julia and Solomon's cottage had also been mentioned, which, according to Lois, was still occupied by Seth's father whom she claimed had not left the village. She couldn't fathom the connection the families had with the young girls.

Amelia dragged the laptop towards her and switched on the power, when it finished booting up she clicked on Skype. There were only two people listed under her contacts, her mother and Tatem, she really should remove that bastard when she got a chance. Seeing her mother online she clicked on call, it had been too long since she had spoken with her.

"Hey, how are you?" she asked when they were connected.

"Good god, I thought you had been abducted. I've been ringing and ringing you. Why have you not called before now? What has happened?" her mother tried to look over her daughters shoulder, "I cannot see Tatem. Is he there?" then she shifted in her seat. "Goodness, why are you not at work, have you been fired? Was it the move? Have they not seen you at your best? Is it Tatem? Has he been—"

"Mum," Amelia exclaimed. "If you must know, Tatem and I are—"

"I knew it, I knew it wouldn't—"

"Mother," she interrupted. "I appreciate that you did not approve, and believe me, I am living with that pain right now, but I have a job, thank you. I am working at a local bookshop, and the cottage is absolutely gorgeous."

"I heard something on the news about a young girl who has been attacked."

"Animal attack Mum."

"All the same, do you have your pepper spray?"

Amelia sighed. "Yes. Somewhere. I've not unpacked everything yet."

"And you remember the self-defence classes?"

She remembered the self-defence classes, it was called High School - being an outcast, being different, not really fitting in, it meant mental and physical torture on a daily basis. When Jude died she turned into a different person, the meek little girl who always followed the rules was gone.

"Listen, Mum, I need to ask a huge favour."

"Yes, of course, what do you need?"

"I need you to be online between six and eight every evening. If I don't log on, can you please ring my mobile number? No. Wait. I lost it. I need to get another phone. I will ring with my new number. Is that okay?"

"Poppet." She knew her mother was concerned when she called her by that name. "Are you sure you are okay, because I can send Malcolm if you like, it would be no trouble."

Malcolm, her mother's confidant, always there to help her when she needed it, no more so than when Father died. She wasn't adverse to her mother having company, especially now she was on her own.

"Mum, please. Don't bother Malcolm, I'm fine, honestly. I lost my phone when I got here, so I need to get another one, I'll go into town to buy a new one and give you my new number, okay? Nothing sinister I assure you."

She threw the book onto the bed, as it toppled over the dust cover unravelled revealing a photograph; she let out a sharp breath.

"Everything okay love?" her mother asked.

Amelia looked down at the black and white photograph obviously taken in the early twentieth century, but there was no mistaking that face, Lois Chandler, walking through a garden maze. Had Lois written that book under a pen name? It was no wonder she seemed to know so much about the village if she had written a book about its history and the two families. Maybe she had been driven mad by it? Amelia had to find out more, meet with the old woman and quickly before anyone else made the connection. After she said her goodbyes to her mother, she shut down the laptop and made her way down to the village pub.

The A-board outside the pub advertised tapas night; Amelia stood reading the sign when she saw Justin clearing dishes from the outside tables and decided to follow him through to the garden.

"Hello, Justin?" Amelia called out.

"Gosh, Miss Scott, you startled me!"

"I'm sorry Justin. I didn't mean to sneak up on you. Why are you not at college today?"

"They said it was burst pipes, part of the building and grounds have flooded so they sent us all home, thought I'd get some extra money."

"I wanted to ask you a question, something you said the other night, about Brendan."

The young boy stepped back up against the wall. "I can't help you, sorry."

As he turned to walk away Amelia took hold of his arm, "Please, just one question?"

He looked down at her hand then up to her eyes; she didn't look like she would tell, and the guilt, oh, the guilt he had to tell someone. "What do you want to know?"

"The book Valerie ordered, the one about the two families, do you know anything about that?"

Justin kicked a stone from under foot and shrugged. "Maybe, what of it?"

"This is no time to play coy with me Justin. Do you know anything about it or not?"

Her eyes burrowed into him, he turned his head avoiding her stare. "Yes Valerie ordered that book, she and Julia wanted to know what was so special about Old Man Malloy's and—"

"Solomon?"

"Yes."

"You mentioned Brendan had been delving into the occult. What exactly was he getting into Justin?"

He pulled his arm free and sat down on the bench. "He wanted to know if there was life after death. When his dad died Brendan became obsessed with it and he started reading all these books on bringing back the dead, spending loads of time at this strange herb place in town. It freaked us out, freaked us all out."

"But you became curious too didn't you?" asked Amelia.

Justin bowed his head. "Yes. But we didn't do anything," he was quick to add. "We only read about the hypothetical stuff, we didn't practice, we would never do that."

When he didn't meet her eyes Amelia pulled his head towards her. "But someone else did?"

Justin nodded. "Brendan and Shaun, they were teasing Julia about Valerie, about bringing her back."

"Did she believe they could?"

He nodded again. "But I told her there was no way, not without the body. I have read a lot of books about it, I mean a lot, and what Brendan was talking about, really couldn't have helped."

Amelia frowned.

"See." Justin stood and threw his dishtowel down on the bench. "You don't believe me either. None of them believe me."

"I do believe you," Amelia said putting her hand on his. "I do, I just want to know what happened to Valerie and Julia. I want to know about Malloy and Solomon, I want to know everything."

"Why?" he asked.

Collette bellowing from the kitchen window interrupted them. "Justin, will you get in here and see to the tables, we need them clearing before the mains go out!"

He pulled his hand from under hers. "Guess I have to be going now."

When he was nearing the corner Amelia shouted to him. "Justin, meet me at the bookshop tomorrow, please."

The young boy turned to the back door and then paused with a heavy sigh. "I'll see what I can do."

Then he was gone.

Amelia sat at one of the picnic tables in the pub garden musing over her conversation with Justin, what the youngsters were into and what had them all so worried; about what had happened to Valerie, whether her knowledge had been her doom and would the same fate befall Julia? It didn't bear thinking about.

"Penny for them," said Ned as he entered the garden.

"Hey. Sorry, lost to them." She pulled her knees up. "Do you ever work Ned?" she asked.

"I," he said with hand on chest and beaming smile, "have just been granted extra staff, so I won't be putting all the hours in down there."

"But I thought you loved your job."

He took a seat opposite her. "I do, don't get me wrong, but I've been working nearly every day for what seems like forever and believe me it can get to you after a while." Amelia nodded. "Besides, what about you? Pot calling the kettle. How come you aren't at the bookshop?"

"Seth came back."

"Seth's back? When did he get back?"

"About lunchtime. He and his mates are watching the store, told me to go home and rest after, you know, being up all night."

"He knows about that?"

"I told him," she said with a shrug.

"Thought Stephen asked us to keep quiet about it?"

Amelia shook her head. "Julia is out of harms way, why shouldn't he know. Besides, gave me a chance to get some shut eye, I was exhausted."

Ned nodded. "Me too." He turned looking around the garden and noticed the A-board. "Tapas tonight, you game?"

"I'd love to, but I am going into town to get a new phone and then I'm having an early night, I need a change of scenery. Don't forget how long we were holed up in here last night," she said looking back at the pub.

"True. Why do you need a new phone?"

"Lost mine the day I arrived, I fear it's in the belly of the beast." Ned frowned. "You know, in the quicksand, I haven't seen it since."

"I'll keep a look out for it." He rose from his seat. "Have fun in town. Don't go spending all your money."

He left whistling a tune that wasn't actually a tune, just a high pitch noise. She wondered if perhaps she should have taken him up on his offer, maybe Ned was as lonely as she was. Amelia made a mental note to make an effort to invite him round for drinks and a natter. Across the village green the bus air brakes hissed loudly when it came to stop. Amelia quickly gathered her bag and coat as she ran with her hand outstretched to attract the driver's attention.

The journey seemed to take forever, but she was happy to just take in the scenery along the way. When the bus stopped and the driver got out of his cab she was in the heart of the nearest town. She thanked the driver as he lit up his cigarette and asked when the last bus would be to Creek Bay, making a note to be there at least ten minutes beforehand so that she wouldn't miss it.

It seemed odd being in a street with more than five people walking about, a little too overcrowded, she kept her head down and eyes low. She came to a precinct where she recognised the sign for her mobile provider and headed in that direction. It took her the best part of an hour to decide on the handset and mull over the different contracts on offer. When she finally made her purchase she headed for a café and took out her laptop. She sent her mother a message with her new phone number and ended up chatting for a while when she overheard someone at the next table mention the time; she had exactly fifteen minutes to be at the bus stop or she risked missing the last bus. She gave her excuses and shut down the computer before bolting blindly out of the café colliding with someone as she turned the corner.

"Hey, what's the rush?" he said holding her at arm's length. Daniel was the last person she thought she would see again today.

"Sorry, I didn't see you there."

"Well you wouldn't unless you opened your eyes."

"I'm sorry, in a rush, got to get the last bus back." She slid between Daniel and the doorway when he turned and grabbed her elbow.

"Nonsense, I'll give you a lift." His grip was hard enough to stop her, but not enough to hurt or to keep her there.

"No, really, its okay, I have a return ticket."

He bent down so close that his fringe brushed her cheek, she could see faint freckles on the bridge of his nose and his dark brown eyes sparkled when he smiled. "I insist."

"You're not on your bike are you?" she asked with a slight hint of apprehension.

"Yes, why?" His grin widened. "Did Seth take you on his bike?" She nodded. "Don't worry, I'll take it slow."

He turned to leave when Amelia called out, "Didn't you need something from the café?" she asked pointing over her shoulder.

Daniel stopped and half turned with a shrug. "It can wait."

The ride back to the village was surprisingly smoother than she had anticipated, and like he promised, he did take it slow, though she could tell that he took pleasure as she grabbed his waist when he sped off from the traffic lights. He smelt like Seth, the leathers, the ocean, and something else, something that she couldn't quite pin point. He dropped her off at the cottage where she was grateful to have two feet on the ground again, she couldn't remember what time curfew was, but was certain that she wouldn't be going out tonight. What she needed more than anything was to charge up the phone and get connected to the world again, she didn't realise how lost she was without it. First thing was to go through her contacts and make sure she had everyone's number. She started up the laptop and as promised her mother was online, opting for an uncomplicated text conversation stating 'thanks for being online, all is well' and to 'say Hi to Malcolm,' then excusing herself and closing down the computer. She sat watching the low flames in the fire remembering how Seth had looked that night he stopped to check in on her. Amelia ensured the phone battery was fully charged and started her list of contacts - Mum, Malcolm, Bookshop, Seth. A strange feeling came over her when she put the landline entry for Lowe Cottage, *Home*, would she get used to that? Her mother had encouraged her to go through with the move, even though she wasn't Tatem's number one fan, she wanted her daughter to start afresh, get out into the world and enjoy life, perhaps regretting not doing that herself. Tatem (a name she really had to forget) would not make an appearance in her contacts list, of that she was certain. Perhaps he would try and contact her? Would she bother if he did? She opened her purse and pulled out the number for the bookshop, on the reverse was Seth's personal mobile number. Then she found the card Stephen had given her where he had put a separate number alongside his office and work mobile; Amelia guessed it wouldn't hurt to have it just in case the youths come back.

After she had sorted her phone, Amelia settled down with a glass of wine and pulled the book from the table, turning it over to look at the black and white photograph of Lois. She had to find out what the book was about; going back to the beginning she started to make notes. There were references to local monuments, churches, cottages and the two family names that came up time and time again, Solomon and Malloy. Ned had mentioned Seth's father lived at Solomon's, but did he mean it was named Solomon or that it belonged to Solomon? She made a note to ask him, but of the small circle of people she had become close to at Creek Bay, Ned's was one number she didn't have. Cursing, she dialled the operator asking for the number for the local coastguard station, hoping that he would be on duty. When she was connected a young man answered.

"Hi, is Ned there?"

"Ned Kelley?" the young man asked.

Amelia stopped herself from sniggering. "Yes. It's Amelia. Is he there?"

"He is, just a sec."

There was a pause.

"Amelia?"

She fought to compose herself, "Ned, Hi. I was wondering if you could pop round tonight. There was something that I wanted to discuss with you, something about the search the other night. Are you free, or have you been roped into duty?"

"No, no, I'm free. I was just dropping off some gear. I'll finish here then come round."

Somehow she felt a sense of relief. Ned wouldn't hold out on her, she was sure of that, he would answer her questions and offer his take on the mystery. Half-hour later, there was a knock on the door, expecting to find Ned she was surprised to see there was no one there. She slammed the door shut and stormed back to the sofa cursing the teenagers for playing their stupid games when there was another knock at the door. She quickly turned and opened the door ready to give them a piece of her mind, when she came face to face with Ned who had a worried expression.

"What's wrong?" she asked.

"Did you see that?" he said looking down the lane.

"See what?" she said peering around the doorframe.

"Some sort of animal I think."

"No, I didn't, what was it?" she stepped out of the cottage and joined him at the side of his car.

"Don't know, but it was fast."

She felt a sudden cold embrace her. "Come on, get in before it comes back," she said ushering him inside.

Amelia handed Ned a glass of wine and they both settled on the sofa.

"So, what was it that you wanted to talk about?" he asked.

"You remember what Justin said the other night, about the kids getting involved in the occult and stuff." He nodded. "Well, I had a book delivery today and there was a book reserved for Valerie. Brendan came in asking for the same title, so I thought I'd have a look at it, see what was so special."

Ned took a sip of wine. "What kind of book is it?"

Amelia pulled out the book and showed him the picture on the back. "This is Lois Chandler isn't it?"

He took the book for a closer inspection. "Yes, that's Lois. I had no idea she had written a book." He turned it over to read the title. "*People of History and Influence*. Never heard of it. What's it about?"

"That's what I am trying to figure out."

"You don't need to ask me, you need to ask Lois."

Amelia sat back. "I don't think she would be forthcoming with information, do you? Besides—," she took the book from his lap, "—the answers are in here somewhere, I just need to look in the right places."

Ned smiled and poured some more wine into Amelia's glass. "Here let me give you some encouragement. So what do you know so far?"

Amelia gratefully accepted the refilled glass. "Well. I know that the kids are into some shit that they wish they had never laid eyes on. Whatever it is, appears to be the very thing that caused the death of poor Valerie and possibly the attempted murder of Julia too. I also know that whoever you talk to around here either has some kind of crazy conspiracy theory or knows nothing at all, and forgive me when I say this." She took another gulp of wine for courage. "But I fear you may well be as tight-lipped as the rest of them."

"Now hold on a minute. You asked me here. You asked for answers—"

"And you've not given them to me." She sighed heavily. "Please. Ned. What do you know about Solomon and Malloy?"

The colour drained quickly from Ned's face and he fumbled when he tried to put his glass down. "I'm sure I don't know anything more than you."

Amelia touched his arm. "Funny, I know fuck all and if you do know something you must tell me."

Her eyes locked onto his, determination written over her face, he knew he wasn't going to be able to pull the wool over her eyes for much longer.

"Okay, okay," he said sitting forward putting his head in his hands. "I know a little, happened *way* before my time, only hearsay and village gossip mind you."

Amelia sat closer, waiting to hear the truth at long last.

"Well, from what I hear, the Solomon's and Malloy's were close. I mean really close families. They were said to be the power in these parts, had the money and ruled the roost so to speak and from what I can gather there was an uprising during the Civil War. I'm not the best person to speak to about history, you really should speak to Lois about that."

"Gosh, they've been here that long? Sorry, go on."

"Well, just that really. They had the money, the power, everything. Then something happened and whatever it was tore the families apart. I believe there has been some sort of power struggle ever since. Over time the two have grown distant and they no longer reside here."

"Apart from Seth, right?"

Ned nodded. "After his father disappeared, Seth left for a few years. When he came back, it was like he held a heavy burden. I can't tell you what it was, but there was something different in him."

Amelia watched him lie back into the cushions and close his eyes. She had made him reveal something he wasn't supposed to, something he probably said he would never tell.

"I'm sorry Ned. I had to ask," she whispered.

Ned sat up and took another sip of his drink.

"So, who is William?" she finally asked.

He almost choked. "William?"

"Yes. Do you know him?" At last she would find out more about the mysterious man who she found both frightening and fascinating.

There was a howl outside, a long and pitiful cry of the night that sent shivers down Ned's body, but for Amelia it called to her, a heartache waiting to be held. She stood and walked to the window.

"What are you doing, stay back," he pleaded.

Amelia ignored him; she looked out to the trees in the distance, and was sure she saw eyes gleaming in the night, but dismissed it as nothing more than her overactive imagination.

"What is that?" she whispered.

By the time Ned got to the window they had disappeared.

"I think I best be off," he said putting his glass down.

"But we've not—"

"We're done here," he interrupted.

"I'm sorry Ned, if I made you uncomfortable." She followed him to the front door. "It's just this crazy book, and Stephen asked if I—"

Ned spun round. "The detective? What's he got to do with it?"

"He asked me to read through the book, see if it related to what happened to the girls, any subtext that the kids may have picked up on. I had offered really. Considering."

"Considering what?" he whispered. "Considering the book was ordered through your place of employment. Considering the young girl who ordered it is now dead. Considering her best friend is now in hospital because of it. And considering the young boy who possibly put her there has been into the store asking for a copy?"

Amelia stood there watching his crazed expression for a moment. It did sound ridiculous and she asked herself why she got involved in the first place, she didn't know these people, she should just walk away and no one would be any the wiser. But there was something here that reminded her of Jude. If she had seen that man at the drive thru, Jude would still be here today and she will be able to take care of her.

"I care. Okay. I care that poor girl was killed. I care that she could have been so much more. I care that she and her friend were misunderstood and I care that whatever Lois Chandler knows is the very thing that has brought all this about. I think you should too!"

Ned looked like he was going to explode, but rather than say anything else he opened the door and stormed out. That was not how she envisaged the evening would end, and the one person she thought she could depend on had just left in a strop; she thought he had become a mate, a confidant even, perhaps she had gone about this the wrong way. Time for Plan B, find Lois and pin her down about the history.

She heard a banging noise outside and thought Ned had a change of heart, or maybe he had forgotten something, maybe he was even going to apologise. Whatever it was, she was thankful he was back. She opened the door and found Daniel crouching by the flowerpot, which had rolled onto its side. He stood up with a guilty expression.

"Hi, sorry, I was leaving a note, and I accidentally knocked over your pot." He looked down at the miserable pot on the ground; several shards of terracotta had broken free from the rim where soil had spilled out onto the doorstep.

"It's okay, really. It wasn't mine, just inherited it."

Daniel stood with the pot still in his hand. "Well that's a relief, I thought I might have to replace it or something."

She looked at the poor state of flower heads that were not long for this world. "Well, you could buy me a shrub, as compensation."

"But you said it—"

"Compensation for you sneaking around here and for pretending to accidentally bump into me at the café, and then bumping into my plant on the doorstep!"

"Listen, it wasn't my idea, honestly."

Amelia turned away leaving the front door open. Daniel followed her inside. "Don't tell me, Seth had you keeping watch."

"No. What makes you think that?" He had the stench of lie all over him.

"Your poker face is terrible by the way. Besides, Seth has already tried on numerous occasions to protect me. What I don't know is… why." She sat down in a huff on the sofa, the door was still open behind him.

Daniel considered for a moment if he should stay or flee and keep his promise to Seth; don't interfere, keep a distance, and just make sure she is safe. He was breaking every one of those rules. "Amelia. I am sorry I upset you. I'll be on my way." He bowed and turned to leave.

She couldn't understand why Seth thought she needed a bodyguard; there was definitely something he wasn't letting on, something that she should know about. She wondered if he was related to the Solomon in the story, but that meant there had to be a Malloy, maybe it was the Malloy's who had been plaguing her since she arrived. She shook her head thinking she really should stop watching those crime thrillers late at night.

Amelia called him back. "Wait, I'm sorry. I've had a long day, not slept very much. Can you thank Seth for looking out for me and that I will see him tomorrow at the bookshop?"

Daniel smiled. "Of course."

# *chaptra deg*

She woke to her landline ringing and mentally kicked herself for not leaving it upstairs like she intended. Amelia ran downstairs and grabbed the phone before it rang off.

"Hello? Morning detective, what can I do for you?… No, no I haven't, but I may have some interesting ideas for you if you want to discuss them, maybe meet me at the bookshop later on today?… Great. See you then."

She put the phone down with a satisfied grin. First off, she needed to see Lois, make sure she was in possession of all the facts. The old woman passed the shop every day, so why should today be any different. It would just be a chance meeting, Lois would never suspect.

Ten-thirty and Lois had not been past to collect her morning paper from the corner shop, eleven-fifteen and still no sign of her. When the clock registered one o'clock, Amelia started biting her fingernails wondering if something had happened to poor old Lois. Please god no she thought, not now, especially when she was getting somewhere.

"Morning. Or is it afternoon, I forget." Stephen strolled into the shop and took the seat next to the window. He sat with one leg atop the other and an assured expression.

"Afternoon," she mumbled bringing him a cup of tea.

"Well, you're not as bright as you were earlier this morning."

"Sorry, I was expecting Lois to—"

"Lois? Why would you be expecting Lois?" he said sounding surprised as he took the cup from her.

"Well, you know that book," she said taking the seat next to him. He nodded as he took a sip. "She wrote it."

The detective spat out his tea knocking the remainder of the drink all over Amelia's skirt. "God, I'm sorry," he said trying to mop it up with the sleeve of his jacket.

Amelia stood pushing his hand away, before it was ground into the fabric. "It's okay, really." She went to the back room to wet and blow-dry the stain when there was a knock at the back door. She wasn't expecting a delivery and Seth had keys.

"Hello?" she called through the door.

"William."

She dabbed her skirt desperate to make the stain disappear, but was making it worse as it spread into a large wet blob. She calmed herself with a deep breath, adjusting her skirt and hair before opening the door to him.

His wide grin was enough to melt the coldest of ice. "Caught you at a bad time?" he asked looking down at her skirt. His gaze wandered over her thighs and waist for far too long, like he was mentally undressing her.

She shifted on her heel trying to act coy. "No. I was just tightening the tap and got a little wet that's all."

"A woman who is handy around the house, I like that." He leant against the doorframe; his arms crossed over his chest and gave her that piercing look again. "I was wondering…"

Her heartbeat quickened with the sound of promise. "Yes?"

A loud clattering noise came from inside the store, when Amelia turned back to William he had gone. She looked around the small car park, but he was nowhere to be seen, closing the door she made her way back to the shop. A row of books had fallen from the top shelf and a young girl was busy trying to pick them up from the floor.

"Sorry, I didn't mean to," she stammered.

Amelia bent down to help pick them up. "It's okay, really. You go and sit down I'll sort these out."

The young girl rose slowly, her face turning pale.

"Something wrong?" asked Amelia.

"No," the young girl said and turned, running past customers and bursting through to the door almost knocking Lois out of the way.

"Goodness child, please slow down." Lois called after her.

Amelia had the pile of books in her arms when Lois came towards her. She was relieved to see the old woman, relieved nothing had happened to her and relieved she didn't have to go looking for Lois in order to ask questions about the book.

"Lois, lovely to see you." Amelia started to refill the shelving, stepping on her tiptoes to reach the top shelf.

"Here, let me sort that," the detective said taking the remaining books from Amelia.

"Thank you Stephen," she said with a grateful smile, knowing he was probably guilty for spilling his drink on her earlier.

"What happened to you?" asked Lois pointing to the wet patch.

Amelia and Stephen looked at one another. "Don't ask." Leaving Stephen to fill the shelves she turned to the old woman. "Lois, I'm glad you came by I wanted to ask you something, do you mind if we sit a while?" she said leading her to the bottom of the stairs pointing up to the mezzanine floor.

"Of course. I take my coffee strong and black," she said mounting the steps.

Amelia began preparing her drink when the detective came to the counter. "Sorry about earlier."

"Don't be. I've made some notes about you know what," she said whispering so Lois couldn't overhear. "And when I've asked a few questions, I'll give you a call and we can go over things, okay?"

He smiled. "Playing detective?"

She shrugged and then a smile presented itself, "Someone's got to do it."

Lois was settled on the loveseat placing a few cushions behind her back. Today she looked her usual self, confident and strong, unlike the other night when she looked old and fragile. Amelia handed Lois her drink and then took a seat next to her.

"Lois, I wanted to ask you something about the history of this place."

"The bookshop?" she asked innocently sipping her drink.

"No, about the village, about the people here."

The old woman seemed to stop breathing, her eyes narrowed when she said, "Why do you want to know?"

"Curious," Amelia said with a shrug.

"You know what curiosity did to the cat," Lois said pointedly.

"Quite," she mumbled. "Well, I found a rather interesting book the other day, and what made it more interesting was the author."

"Oh?"

"Charles Lane." Amelia braced herself not knowing what reception she would get.

The old woman's eyes glistened and a thin smile spread on her lips. "My, my, I didn't know they were still around. Where did you find one?"

"Special order came in yesterday."

The old woman put the drink down on the small table.

"Oh? Who ordered it?"

Amelia coughed; she didn't want her getting upset or start with the conspiracy theories again. "I don't have the manifest, the paperwork wasn't completed, so I have to wait for Seth." The old woman looked at her, she wasn't sure if she believed her so she carried on with her questions. "The picture on the back, the picture of you in the gardens. Did you write the book under Charles Lane?"

The old woman laughed. "You could say that." A mischievous grin appeared on her aged face and then faded. "Charles was a friend, a very dear friend. We met many, many years ago, he was twenty and I was eighteen." She picked up her drink and took another sip. "It was a lovely summer, I remember because we spent most of our days on the beach. One day, he decided to take me for a picnic in the woods, I remember it so vividly, it was such a beautiful day, bright blue sky, birds singing, trees full of colour. We set our picnic down in an open area and spent the day getting to know one another better." Lois blushed. The images held a special memory for her there was no mistaking that. "We lost track of time, and before we knew it, darkness was upon us. Of course, we had not planned being out so late, so we didn't have lanterns with us, seemed as though we were walking around in circles, trying to find our way, when we happened upon a cottage. Neither of us had been there before, and have not been since."

Amelia stiffened. "Why?"

Lois turned to her with a sad expression. "What we saw that day would haunt me for the rest of my life," she muttered.

The hairs on the back of Amelia's neck stood to attention, "What did you see?" she whispered.

"Anyone serving?" came a voice from downstairs. "Hello?"

Amelia made a clucking noise with her tongue and turned to Lois, "Wait here, I won't be a minute." She ran downstairs and found she had quite the queue waiting to be served.

She looked at the disgruntled faces. "I'm sorry, please, who is first?"

After serving her last customer she leant over the counter to see if Lois was still upstairs, looking through the banisters she was grateful to see her feet in view, and was assured she hadn't gone anywhere. Putting more beans into the machine for a fresh batch of coffee, Amelia poured herself a glass of water and went upstairs to continue her conversation with Lois.

"Sorry about that Lois, there were a few customers to serve." Amelia dropped the glass when she reached the top step.

Lois lay back over the seat, her mouth open and hand clutching her chest. "Lois? Lois? Can you hear me?" Panic filled her. "Call an ambulance," she screamed, hoping someone downstairs would take the initiative. She began checking for a pulse, having seen it done in the films many times; she was certain you were supposed to check the neck and the wrist with two fingers, but she felt no pulse. She sat holding Lois' hand as the tears slowly blurred the old woman's features.

A crowd had gathered outside the shop when the ambulance came to take poor old Lois away. The medics had tried reviving her but she was declared dead at the scene; they said her heart simply gave up. Detective Inspector Cooke walked into the store holding his notepad.

"I'm so sorry Amelia," he said reaching out to her shoulder.

She had kept it together until now, but she couldn't help the tears as they ran freely down her cheeks.

The detective locked the door and turned the sign to closed watching the ambulance leave. His officers dispersed the crowd and moved them along, when he turned to Amelia she was physically shaking, pulling her close he embraced her. "It's okay," he said gently patting her back. "It's okay."

She buried her face in his shoulder, he was warm and soft and smelt of cologne, he wasn't Seth, but it was soothing all the same. He pulled away searching her red eyes.

"Feel up to answering some questions?" he asked quietly.

She nodded as he motioned her to sit on the sofa. He returned with a box of tissues he found under the counter and two bottles of water from the cooler, handing one of the bottles to her as he placed the other on the table and sat down.

Wiping her tears she took a long drink and then sat back with a heavy sigh. "She was fine, we were talking, I went down stairs to serve a few customers, and when I got back... by the time I got back, she was..."

The tears started to well up in her eyes again, memories of Jude laid on the floor came back to haunt her. Her sister's eyes, the old woman's eyes, open and vacant; she closed her own trying to erase the agonizing memory.

"I know this is hard, but I just need to get all the details before we can finish up." She agreed. "What time did Lois come in?" he asked.

Amelia frowned, "You were here when she came in."

"Of course, was that the first time you had seen her today?" She nodded. "And that is when she went upstairs to chat with you about the book, is that correct?" She nodded again. "Did she have a drink while she was here, anything to eat?"

"What do you want to know that for?"

"Covering all possibilities."

"I thought she died of a heart attack." Amelia began.

"We'll know more when we get the lab results back. Lois was not currently under the care of a doctor, nor was she on any medication so without that background, we have to make sure there was no foul play."

"Great, you think I murdered her?" her voice wavered.

He stepped forward putting his hand on hers. "No. I don't think you murdered Lois. I just need to know what she did in the last moments before she passed away."

Amelia moved her hand away and drank the remainder of her water. "Well," she sighed. "She was upstairs waiting for me, when you left I took her a black coffee, and we sat and talked about the book. She was telling me about Charles Lane."

"The name she used to write the book?" he said writing his notes.

"He was her… lover I think. Her 'very good friend' she called him. They met when she was eighteen. How old is… was she?"

The detective looked back over his notes. "Lois Chandler was ninety-five years old."

"Ninety-five. And she wasn't under the care of a doctor? Had no medical condition? I find that extraordinary."

"I call it convenient," he said without looking up from his notes.

Amelia looked at him with a frown. "What ever happened to innocent until proven guilty?"

"I don't work that way," he said looking up at her.

"Just how do you work?"

"Everyone is guilty, that way there are no surprises." He opened his bottle of water and took a sip.

Amelia shook her head. "Anyway, she was talking about this bloke Charles and taking a picnic in the wood when they lost track of time, lost their way in the dark and happened upon a cottage."

Stephen stopped writing. "Is that it?"

"She was reminiscing. What did you want? Chapter and verse?"

"No, but, is that all she said?" he asked.

Amelia wondered if she should reveal her last words. After all, everyone thought she was a nut, but Amelia didn't want people's lasting memory of the old woman to be a nutcase.

"Well?" prompted Stephen.

Amelia closed her eyes. "She did say something a little odd. The last thing she said was that they saw something, something that terrified her."

He turned to her now. "Which was?"

Amelia shrugged. "I don't know, a customer shouted to be served, and when I got down here there were a few people waiting by the counter."

"So Lois was alone during that time?"

"Yes."

"How long do you think you were away from her?"

Amelia shrugged her shoulders. "I can't be certain."

"Try." His voice had turned steely again; he was back to policeman mode. "Five, ten, fifteen minutes?"

She became flustered under the pressure. "I don't know. Fifteen?"

He continued to scribble in his notepad.

"I don't recall anyone going up there though," she said trying to remember if anyone could have slipped past.

"But you can't be certain?"

She shook her head. "No. I'm sorry. I can't."

"And where was Seth while all this was going on?" he asked.

"I haven't seen Seth today."

"Is that usual?"

"I don't know what usual is, I've not been in the job long, remember." It was her turn to be steely.

"Sorry," he said smiling over his notepad. "Checking all possibilities."

Amelia sighed. "Are we done now?"

He took another sip of his water. "I'll need to see a receipt of transactions from today, and if you do know the names of people you were serving, that would be advantageous in my questioning."

"Well, there were only a few I remember seeing before, those that used the computer will be on the systems log in, and there was just one young girl I hadn't seen before, she was the one who knocked over the books."

"I remember," he said taking more notes. "Did you see anyone else in the store, other than those you served?"

She scrunched her nose and frowned. "No. Wait. Yes."

"Who?"

"William." The detective looked up from his notes with a dead expression. "He was at the back door when I went to dry my skirt, but he didn't come in."

"What did he want?" asked Stephen.

"I don't know, he left."

"So he was loitering?"

"He started to ask me something when that girl dropped the books. When I looked for him again, he had gone."

Stephen frowned. "Strange. Think I will have to pay him a visit."

"Is that it Stephen?" she said with heavy sigh. "I am really exhausted."

"Of course." He stood and put his notes away. "If you think of anything else, please let me know. You've got my number."

Amelia locked the door behind him and glanced at the clock; three in the afternoon and no sign of Seth. Taking the phone from her pocket she sent him a text message, '*Give me a ring when you get this, sad news. Amelia.*' She put the phone in her pocket and then closed her eyes wondering what had happened to poor Lois. It had to be natural causes she kept telling herself, and couldn't for the world wonder why Stephen had to look for the bad all the time. She would have given anything to have her back, claiming this or that, Lois was just an old lady with a different outlook. Amelia took a couple of beers from the fridge leaving money in the till, double checked the front door was locked, and setting the alarm, left by the rear entrance.

Amelia made her way to Creek Bay, to the very seat she had sat on the first day she arrived. She looked out to the waters, watching them flow in and out rhythmically. Opening her bag she pulled out one of the beers unscrewed the cap and lifted to toast.

"Here's to you Lois. I hope you have found happiness at last."

Amelia took a long drink. Lois' last words fresh in her mind, she wondered what she had seen that day, what it was that had made her question everything about the village, about what had been going on. Had Lois tied the two families together? Had the kids made the connection from the book? She pulled the book out from her bag and looked at the front cover, her fingers ran over the name Charles Lane. If Lois were ninety-five then that would put Charles Lane at ninety-seven, but the odds on him still being alive were somewhat slim. She considered checking the Internet later, do some digging around, maybe he could answer some questions about the history. The faint noise of a motorbike roared in the distance, thoughts of Seth immediately sprung to mind; she was looking forward to seeing him again. As she looked out towards the hill she waited to see if the bike would come her way, the noise grew louder and she grew expectant, but then the roar of the engine drifted away and she found herself disappointed.

"Often duck out of work do you?" His velvety voice whispered into her ear, his lips touching her hair.

"William." Her heart began to patter quickly, not only from the shock, but his closeness, his eyes, his voice, his warmth as he sat next to her. "What are you doing here?" she asked turning her head to one side so she could see him properly.

"What are *you* doing here? I thought you had a bookshop to run?" His smile was like sunshine making her melt under his spell.

"I was just taking a breather." She put the cool bottle between her legs.

"And a few drinks," he said nodding to her beer.

"Would you like one?" she offered.

A half smile crossed his face while he focused on her drink. "Yes."

Turning to get the other bottle from her bag, he took the one from her thighs and lifting to his lips, drank. She watched him as he knocked it back, then he handed her the bottle with a sparkle in his eyes.

"No, no, you carry on, I have another," she said pulling a fresh bottle out of her bag.

They sat together watching the ocean when Amelia finally spoke. "Lois Chandler died today." William didn't respond, he simply looked out to the waters, his expression unmoving when she continued. "She died. Today. In the bookshop." Watching him closely she wondered if he had known the old woman. "Did you know Lois?" she asked.

William took a large sip of the drink and turned to her. "Yes."

"Are you not upset?"

He shrugged. "Didn't know her that well."

Amelia looked down at her bottle; she had been fiddling with the paper label that it was now hanging off on one end. "I did, sort of. She was the only one here in the village nice to me. Apart from Seth."

His eyes narrowed when he muttered, "And the detective."

Amelia looked up at him. "What do you mean?"

"He's always hanging around you, don't you notice?"

"No, I haven't noticed and how would you know?" Suspicion filling her voice.

"I see things others do not."

Amelia laughed. "Next you'll be telling me you see dead people." When his expression didn't falter she continued. "You know that film with Bruce Willis, and the kid he sees... oh, never mind."

"Amelia?"

She gulped her drink down; she couldn't begin to wonder what he was going to ask. "Yes?"

When he looked at her she hoped he was going to explain everything, but there was something holding him back, something he wasn't prepared to talk about.

"What is it William?" she asked when he sat back with a smile. "What's funny?" she was becoming irritated. Today was not a day to be jovial. Lois Chandler died today; today was a day to mourn.

"I like the way you say my name."

She didn't know what to say to that. William was something of a conundrum, something she had to break, find out more about him. He was the one thing that kept her from second guessing herself.

William looked up to the sky. "I've got to go," he said with a sigh.

"So soon? But you haven't finished your drink," she said watching him down the last remnants of his bottle. He had finished his drink too soon, she needed to know more about him, she had to find a way to make him stay longer.

"How? I mean..." She was starting to get flustered over her own awkwardness. "What I meant to say was, will I see you again?"

William turned to her, "Indeed you will Amelia Scott."

He left with a confident swagger, which she both hated and adored. There was something about William, something she wanted to hold on to, but then there was also Seth and whenever she spent time with either of them, she felt she was betraying the other.

Amelia made her way home, few cars passed her along the way which she was grateful for, she didn't want to run into anyone asking about Lois. Her lonely night consisted of a microwave meal, bottle of wine and TV programme she had never heard of. She switched off the television set and opened the book, her thoughts turning once again to Lois. The old woman had known something was suspicious about the death of Valerie and Julia's disappearance and her subsequent psychotic state, yet no one had bothered to say anything, only Lois had made the connection. The teenagers were also onto something, what with Valerie ordering the book and Brendan coming into the shop asking for a copy, there was something in that book that could explain the strange goings on in the village; she had to get to the bottom of it. Amelia sat on the sofa, going through looking for clues, anything that would stand out, when she found something interesting in one of the margins — faint pencil marks, where someone had written something previously and rubbed out; perhaps Seth had found it in a second-hand bookshop. Amelia was determined to finish the book and find the answers. She pulled out a notepad and began a chronological account...

*NOTES FOR STEPHEN:*

*Solomon: The family were strong at the time of the English Civil War. They had the power, were the main landowners, had many servants and controlled the politicians.*

*Malloy: This family owned half of the land in the area, more woodland than farmland, unlike Solomon.*

*The Malloy's had other interests rather than wealth and money, yet they kept their stakehold in land and property.*

*Master Solomon pushed his brethren away, ostracising any of his siblings who didn't follow his rules. But there was one who stood against him at the most critical time, his nephew Setali, who betrayed his uncle. He betrayed his family. Master Solomon betrayed his friend and decreed that all the land jointly owned with Malloy would be foreclosed.*

*This greatly angered the Malloy's, in a battle of wills to prove that he was no push over, especially with the Civil War looming; they both had something to lose. But it was Master Malloy who had a champion, someone who would destroy their rival, make sure they paid for their betrayal.*

*The book goes on to say that records ceased and facts based on hearsay after that time. Those accounts were thus; the two families, Solomon and Malloy, went to war with one another, regardless of the war spilling around them, it would end with one of them being victorious and then facing the consequences.*

When Amelia got to the end of the seventh chapter, her phone rang. The name DI Cooke flashed on the screen. Amelia couldn't handle more questions about Lois.

"Hello?"

"Hi, sorry to bother you, but have you seen Seth?"

Amelia closed her eyes. "This again? I told you I haven't—"

"Listen," he interrupted. "Have you seen him today? Since I saw you at the bookshop?

She frowned, "No. I haven't why?"

There was a long pause and a heavy sigh from the detective. "Well. I shouldn't be telling you this, but Julia is missing from hospital."

"Julia?" she raised her voice an octave and was quite aware of how unattractive it was.

The detective banged the dashboard to his car. "God damn it!"

"Why are you asking about Seth?"

"He was the last person on the hospital visitor register to see her."

Amelia felt a cold sensation flood her veins. "Why would Seth take Julia? It doesn't make sense."

"Doesn't it? He knew both Valerie and Julia. Makes sense to me."

"You can't blame Seth just because he knew them, the whole village knew them. Besides, if he did take Julia, would he have signed his name in that visitors book like a calling card?"

The detective huffed. "It may be his way of sticking two fingers up at us. A testament to his arrogance to prove he can't be touched."

Amelia shook her head, "That sounds far-fetched to me."

"You'd be surprised," he mumbled. "Anyway, I've been trying to get hold of William, he's the illusive pimpernel."

"William? I saw him earlier this afternoon, up at Creek Bay."

There was a pause on the other end of the phone then he spoke softly. "What time was that?"

"About three thirty, maybe three forty-five. I shut the store when you left. Couldn't stand to be there after… you know, and then made my way down to Creek Bay, bumped into him there."

"Was he there long? What time did he leave?"

"Gosh I can't remember, we were just talking."

"What did you talk about?" he asked.

"Stephen! Where are you going with this exactly?" her voice started rising again.

"Sorry, just seeing who I can cross off my list."

"And Seth is at the top of it I presume. No, William was with me, so he couldn't have taken Julia, and I truly doubt that Seth would have done such a thing either. You need to widen your search. Besides, she may have discharged herself, maybe her parents took her home." If he wasn't for looking at alternatives she would certainly offer them to him.

"No," he sighed, "they were heading in to see her when they found her bed empty."

"Surely someone saw something, what about the psychiatrist?"

"He's next on my list." He gave a heavy sigh.

"I'm sure you'll get to the bottom of it." She paused while she looked at the book. "I've made some headway with the book."

"Oh?"

"Yeah, these two families, Solomon and Malloy. They were best of friends until something happened, just before the Civil War, since then they've been at each other over something or nothing. Land mostly I think, it's all a bit vague, the accounts are just hearsay, no actual official records. I can check into that if you like."

She was enjoying her project, maybe a little too much.

"No, that's okay Amelia, you've helped by going through the book. Solomon and Malloy you say?"

"Yes."

"Seth Solomon, William Malloy?" he asked.

The penny finally dropped, Amelia couldn't breathe. "What? His surname is Malloy?"

"Looks like I will have to find William after all, see what he knows about Valerie and Julia. Thank you Amelia, I'll leave you to your evening."

The phone went dead. Amelia couldn't believe it. William and Seth, Malloy and Solomon; adversaries for years. The families would surely have grown apart; no one could hold a grudge that long, the people who started it were long gone. She decided it was time to look through official records, find out more about these two families.

Opening her laptop she typed the names into the online search engine, several accounts came up, none of which gave her information she didn't already know from reading Lois' book. After sifting through parish records for births and deaths she noted an anomaly, there was no record of Seth. Opening the census records she went through them meticulously, still no mention of Seth. Going back to the book, she looked at the chapter about the uprising to the one name that stood out, Setali; she typed the name into the search and what surprised her more than anything was the reference 'often referred to as Seth.' Her hands poised over the keyboard. Maybe he had been named after his relative because she was sure it couldn't be one in the same. The Civil War was way back in the mid seventeenth century so that meant Setali Solomon was born in the sixteen hundreds sometime. Amelia went back to the records again and to her surprise there was an entry for Setali Solomon registered born in 1620, which meant he was twenty-two when the Civil War broke out in 1642, but try as she might, she could not find a date of death. She kept going through the records, cross checking them, but nothing came up. Tapping the keyboard she wondered whether there was a connection with William, she typed in his name and felt a lump rise in her throat when she saw the birth entry flash across her screen 'William Henry Malloy born 1618.'

"Holy shit," she exclaimed.

A coincidence, it couldn't be *her* William. Scrolling through the names and dates she hoped she would find his death date; that would tie up so many loose ends and would make sense, but she couldn't find it, she double-checked, checked again and crossed references, but nothing.

"Who are you?" she whispered.

Her thoughts turned to Charles Lane. The records showed his death registered as 1940. He had died in the war, one of His Majesty's casualties missing in action, poor Lois; she had found and lost the love of her life, Charles was just twenty-six when he died. Amelia looked up his service records; Charles had been called up in 1939, she did her maths that was two years after he and Lois were together. She picked up the book and looked at the publishing mark, first published in 1950.

"The little minx," she whispered with a smile.

Lois *had* written that book under the name of Charles Lane after all, her one last salute to immortalize his name. It was clear that she had loved him dearly; the two years they had spent together must have been magical for the old woman. The bouncing Skype icon at the bottom of her screen showed a new conversation from her mother; seven forty-five and she had forgotten to log in and check everything was okay. Amelia responded with the usual 'I'm fine' message and added she was upset an old woman she had become fond of had passed away so she was having an early night. Her mother's response was sweet and soothing, she knew just what to say to make everything seem much better.

Closing down her computer, Amelia poured herself a large glass of wine. She sat looking at the book wondering about the kids and their connection to the occult that Justin had mentioned. Her mind was throbbing with all the new information, at least she knew to ask Seth a few questions when he turned up. When she was offered the job, he gave her the impression he was out surfing, but he wasn't at Creek Bay today, assuming that was his local spot. He was a mystery to her, but he was so good to everyone, giving his time for free, there was no way that he would be involved in anything sinister. Distracted by the roaring sound of motorbikes outside she rushed to the window and peered out through the curtains; two bikes flashed by, one of them had a distinctive yellow stripe down the side which she recognised as belonging to Sonny. Amelia watched them disappear over the hill wondering where they were going at that time of night and checked her mobile for a text or missed call from Seth. Sending Daniel to check up on her seemed overkill, or was there something she wasn't getting? She hoped it was he who stayed with her to keep her safe, from what, she didn't know, but she had more questions for Seth Solomon when she saw him again.

The ringing of her phone made her jump.

"Seth?" she asked expectantly.

There was a pause. "It's Stephen."

"Sorry, I was expecting a call. Have you found Julia?"

"No. I wanted to ring before you heard it from anyone else."

"Heard what?"

"Seth is in custody."

"What! What for?"

"He is being questioned about the kidnap of Julia Bent."

"Kidnap. I don't understand, I thought you just wanted to ask him some questions about his visit to hospital."

There was another pause before he said, "Myself and a couple of officers went down to the cottage and found... evidence that Julia had been there."

"What kind of evidence?" she asked.

"Sorry, Amelia, you know I can't tell you that. I've told you too much already."

"Why are you telling me anyway?"

"Because I thought you should know."

"This is bullshit Stephen and you know it. Whatever flimsy evidence you've found can't be right, it just can't!"

The detective continued walking down the corridor of the station towards interrogation when he heard a commotion from inside one of the rooms. "Sorry, Amelia, I've got to go."

The line went dead. Frustrated and annoyed, she threw the phone onto the sofa. It bounced off the cushion and onto the floor with a thud. She winced with the sound of impact, when it buzzed with a new text message, she opened it up, thankful that it hadn't broken. The message was from Seth, and by the looks of the date stamp had been sent earlier that evening. *'I heard about Lois. Is everything okay? Are you okay? Let me know if you need anything, S.'* Not the words of a would-be kidnapper she thought. Amelia decided to ring Stephen and present the message as evidence, when the phone rang out she cursed the detective and sent a screenshot of Seth's text message to Detective Inspector Cooke via whatsapp. She couldn't help but wonder what Stephen had found at his cottage that would result in an arrest. Climbing the stairs, she decided to call it a night and phone the detective again first thing in the morning.

# chaptra unnek

S tephen ran to the aid of his colleagues. "Hold him down."
Two police officers held Seth in a headlock on the floor whilst trying
to restrain him, the table in the interview room lay in pieces across
the floor, and the metal leg of a chair halfway embedded into the door.
The officers struggled to keep him down while Stephen handcuffed Seth.
Now secured in his restraints, the officers managed to get him standing
upright, Seth looked at the detective, his expression hard and determined.

"Take him to the other room, this one is out of commission." Stephen said
to his officers, and then turned to Seth. "You'll be paying for the damage."

Seth curled his lip. "Bill me."

The officers moved him to the adjoining room and sat him down on
the chair, Stephen entered with a folder in his hand motioning to one
officer to stay and the other to wait outside.

"Bit over the top wouldn't you say?" said Seth.

"After the stunt you just pulled, I don't think so." The detective said
with a frown. "I knew you'd slip up and show your true colours eventually,
was just a matter of time."

"Your officers provoked me," Seth said between gritted teeth.

"You can file a complaint when we're done."

Seth huffed. "Yeah, I know what will happen to that!"

The detective laid out the paperwork in front of him scanning over
the notes. "So, do you care to tell me your whereabouts this afternoon
between two-thirty and five."

"I was down in the surf."

"Any witnesses?"

"Unless you count a bunch of seagulls as witnesses, no."

Stephen raised his eyebrow. "How convenient." He began sifting
through the various reports. "And where were you on Tuesday evening?"

"Camping."

"Where did you camp and with whom?"

Seth sat back in the chair. "Is this really necessary?"

"Yes it is bloody necessary. A young girl is missing, for Pete's sake, we
take these things very seriously. So, tell me, where did you go camping
and with whom?"

Seth sighed. "We've been through this already."

"For the recording if you will be so kind Mr Solomon," Stephen said
nodding to the electronic devices on the wall.

"We— myself, Sonny and Dan, went to Diggory's Island."

"In a previous statement you said you had gone to Kil Margh Tor."

"Yes, that's right, we did. We had stopped off at Bedruthan Steps for a bit of surf."

Stephen made a note and then narrowed his eyes looking at the time-frame. "When did you leave and when did you get back?"

"Left Monday night, came back Wednesday morning."

"But you didn't leave straight away did you?" The detective pushed.

Seth frowned. "What do you mean?"

"You stayed at Miss Scott's place, is that correct?"

Seth sat forward, his eyes filled with rage. "I don't see how that is any of your business Detective Inspector Cooke."

The detective put both elbows on the table and leaned forward. "I'm afraid when I'm gathering information it most certainly *is* my business. What were you doing at Amelia Scott's home before embarking on your camping trip?"

Seth laughed. "Wouldn't you like to know."

Stephen stood, the high pitched sound of the chair scraping on the tiled floor filled the room; the officer by the door took a step forward, eager to help his superior if needed. "Listen, you little shit! A young girl is dead, and another missing. You'll tell me everything I want to know or I'll lock you up and you'll never see daylight again."

"Inspector Cooke, I see you are under a lot of pressure to get to the bottom of the situation, and I truly hope you do. But I assure you, I had nothing to do with Valerie and Julia."

Stephen walked to the other side of the table and gestured to his officer. "Take him to the cell, we'll deal with him later."

The officer pulled Seth out of the chair leading by the handcuffs and escorted him out of the room. Stephen picked up the paperwork and followed them down the corridor; as the officer and Seth took a left into the cells, he continued into reception. Sonny and Daniel stood by the duty officer; a heated conversation was in full swing.

"What do you mean we can't see him?" demanded Daniel.

The duty officer held up both hands. "Listen lads, all I can say is that your friend Mr Solomon is in questioning."

"He's our brother," sneered Daniel. "Now you're going to tell me where he is, right now."

"Easy boys," said Stephen as he walked in. "There's a couple more cells with your names on them if you continue."

Sonny stepped around Daniel with a worried expression. "What has he been charged with?"

The detective put the paperwork down on the counter. "You know I can not divulge that information. Seth is helping us with our enquiries."

"What enquiries?" Sonny asked.

Stephen and the duty officer exchanged looks, knowing the young men weren't going away unless they gave them something. "Regarding the disappearance of Julia Bent."

"This is bullshit," exclaimed Daniel.

"You can't detain him for more than 24 hours without charging him with something," Sonny interrupted.

"We're aware of the law sunshine," spat the detective.

"Has Seth requested his lawyer?" Sonny inquired, not rising to the officers condescension.

"No, he hasn't requested legal representation," the duty officer replied.

"Like I said," growled Daniel. "Bullshit!"

Sonny flipped his phone open. "This interview is bogus." He dialled a number and spoke into the receiver. "Hey, its me. Could you come down to the station? It's about Seth. Excellent." Sonny put his phone away and turned back to the police officers. "You can't talk to him again, Seth's lawyer is on his way."

The detective narrowed his eyes. "Get out of my station."

"Looks like our work here is done," said Daniel, pulling Sonny back to the door with him. "We'll be seeing you again Detective Inspector Cooke."

Stephen shook his head as he heard them revving their bikes loudly before speeding off. "Cocky little shits." He mumbled.

The duty officer shook his head. "Never had any trouble with those lads before. I wonder what this is all about?"

"Beats me, but I sure as hell am going to find out." He turned taking the file with him. "Let me know when that lawyer turns up. Oh, and there is a bit of a mess in Interview Room 1, make sure you get that cleaned up."

The duty officer had just finished gathering the shards of wood when he returned to see a tall thin man stood at his desk. "Can I help you?"

"Nigel Pemberton, I'm here to see my client, Mr Solomon."

"Blimey, that was quick."

"Can you arrange for a meeting with the arresting officer."

The duty officer knocked on the door behind his desk.

"Boss, that lawyer has arrived."

"Come in," Stephen finished his phone call and writing a note before sighing heavily. "That was Brian up at Nabbs Farm. He's had some livestock go missing."

"That's odd. I've had a couple come in about missing pets too in the last couple of weeks. Do you want me to notify the wildlife department? Might be connected to that illegal poaching case?"

"Mmm, maybe. But they wouldn't take pets and livestock, would they?"

The duty sergeant shrugged. "Who knows, we've had sheep rustling on and off here over the years, I've given up trying to assume to be honest. People do the strangest of things." As he walked back to the door he smiled. "Hey, maybe it's 'the beast'," he said with a hearty laugh.

Stephen looked up at him with a wry grin. "Get Solomon a room with his lawyer."

# chaptra dewdhek

Amelia had a restless night. Her thoughts were consumed with images of Seth when he came back from his camping trip; how he glowed, looking more rested and radiant, to now being questioned over Julia. Why William showed up at the bookshop again today and then just disappear? She concluded that he was a peculiar person, with his intense stares which made her wonder what he found so interesting in her, whether he would turn out to be a true gentleman like Seth, or whether she was just a conquest to be had, or would he prove her wrong… was Seth truly a gentleman?

She rose earlier than the alarm and took a hot shower, when she stepped out, she heard bikes again roaring down the lane; looking out of her window she couldn't make out any distinguishing features which would tell her who it was, maybe just a couple of bikers passing through. When she finished getting ready, Amelia went into the kitchen, switched on the toaster and bent down to the cupboard for the bread when she felt a cold breeze brush her face; she looked up to see the back door ajar. Amelia was positive that she had locked the back door, especially after Valerie and Julia. She walked to the door and pulled it open, nothing looked out of place outside, and there was no evidence that the door had been forced. Slamming it shut, she bolted the door leaving the large iron key in its lock and returned to making her breakfast. Amelia decided to get to the bookshop and tidy up after what had happened to poor Lois. She shut her eyes to erase the memory, wondering if the place would ever feel the same again.

When she opened the bookshop door, she was concerned that she didn't hear the alarm bleep. Walking through the shop she checked nothing was missing; computers, till, Seth's leathers, they were all there, she felt relieved everything was how she had left it. Amelia was hanging her cardigan on the coat rack when she heard a rustling sound from the mezzanine floor.

"Hello?" she called out.

"Hey, it's only me." Seth replied.

"Seth? What are you doing here?" she said running to the bottom of the stairs peering upwards.

"I own the place?" he said chuckling.

She ran halfway up the steps, when he came into view she saw that he was down on all fours washing the floor, had stripped the loveseat cover and removed the cushions. "What are you doing?" she asked.

"Nice to see you too," he said carrying on with his cleaning.

"No, I mean. I thought you had been arrested."

Seth stopped cleaning and slowly stood, dropping the rag into the foamy water bowl. "Detective Inspector Cooke couldn't wait to gloat hey?"

"What? No, I don't think it's like that." She walked up to the top step. "What happened?"

"They released me. Lack of evidence."

"So it was flimsy," she mumbled to herself.

"What?" he asked.

"Nothing." She stood by the banister and looked down at the seat remembering how poor Lois looked. "What's with the clean-up?"

"I couldn't stand to leave the place like that. Not after Lois…" He turned to Amelia and put both hands on her shoulders. "I heard that you found her. Are you okay?" his eyes were soft and caring, and the warmth from his hands made her bones soften under his touch.

"Yes, I'm fine. It was a shock."

"I understand."

He kept his hands in place and leant forward, his fringe touching her forehead. Amelia looked into his eyes; the weariness an indication he hadn't slept all night.

"Did you get my message?" he asked stepping away from her.

"I did, thank you. It took a while for it to come through though."

"Arh, could have been lack of reception when I sent it, bit hit and miss down the coast." Amelia picked up the loveseat cover. "Its okay, I'll sort this," he said taking the cover from her.

She walked back to the banister. "Are you sure? That's why I came in early, to clear up."

"Why don't you get the machine going, make us both a brew, I could do with it after that awful stuff they serve down the station."

She smiled glad to have her Seth back. "Sure, I'll go fix us both a cuppa."

When she left, Seth turned and frowned looking at the pile of covers on the floor, the old woman's scent mixed with another.

Pouring their drinks, she pictured the old woman sitting on the seat. There was still the faint smell of her rose perfume lingering, and she was glad Seth was dealing with the cleaning. Amelia called out, handing him a hot steaming mug of tea, "Here you go, get that down you."

Seth took the mug with both hands, ignoring the growing pile of cotton beside him.

"So," Amelia began. "What happened down at the station?"

He took a sip of his tea. "Where do I begin?" he mumbled.

"From the beginning?"

Seth sighed, as he sat down on the top step. "Well. I went out, to catch some waves early yesterday and I bumped into an old friend. We got chatting and before I knew it the day had flown by. I should have been back at the store I know, and I am sorry for that. If I had been here, maybe Lois—"

"That's okay," she said with a shrug. "You weren't to know. Who was the old friend?"

Seth gave a short laugh. "You playing detective Amelia?"

She sat on the step below him. "If that's what it takes."

He stretched his left leg and frowned. "That's how I found out about Julia, so I went down to the hospital to see how she was. I signed in." He shook his head, "thinking back that was stupid of me, and then I sat by her bed."

Amelia looked for the obvious sign that he was lying, she was finding it hard to pinpoint when it occurred. "So, you just sat by her bed?" she asked.

"Yes. I did. She never opened her eyes." He took a sip of his drink.

"Then why would the police suspect you had anything to do with her disappearance?" she asked.

"From what my lawyer said, they found Julia's scarf close to Holly Cottage, and, that is how they are linking her to me." He stared into his mug. "Its not true. What they are saying," he whispered.

"I didn't think that it was. Besides. There is one key factor in all of this that you are missing out."

"Which is?" he asked with raised eyebrow.

"William."

His breathing stopped, time stopped, Amelia wished she could take it back. "William?" he asked between clenched teeth.

"Yes. Do you know him?" she asked innocently.

"You are not to speak to William, do you understand." He was standing now, looming over her, which she didn't much care for.

"I'll be friendly with whomsoever I please, thank you very much," she said standing, meeting his stare. "And if you don't like it, then you'd better leave. And while we're on the subject, stop sending people round to check up on me."

They looked at one another for what seemed to be a lifetime, and then he kissed her hard on the lips without warning.

"What on earth are you doing?" she said pushing him away.

He answered by pulling her towards him, holding her body tight to his, and he breathed her in, breathed her scent. He kissed her again, harder this time, she tried to resist but was finding it increasingly difficult, and finally she accepted his caress, his softening kiss, when she was pulled back to reality with the door chime ringing. As they pulled apart from one another Daniel and Sonny entered the shop.

"Oh hey man." Sonny started. "Didn't mean to interrupt. We were just wondering how it went down at the you know where."

"It's okay," said Seth moving away from Amelia and putting his hands on the banister addressing his friends. "She knows," he half turned to Amelia. "She knows about last night."

Sonny and Daniel exchanged looks and then continued to the counter, Daniel taking a seat on one of the bar stools while Sonny pulled out two bottles of water from the fridge. Seth and Amelia joined them.

"So, Amelia, you know everything huh?" said Daniel.

The door chimed again and Detective Inspector Cooke walked in. "Must be my lucky day, all the people I want to talk to in one place," he said walking towards the counter.

Daniel spun around in his seat. "What are you talking about?"

Amelia coughed loudly. "Inspector Cooke, may I have a word please," she called out from behind the three men.

The detective made his way through the muscle into the back room where Amelia pulled the door shut behind him.

"What are you doing here?" she whispered.

"I'm doing my job Amelia. It's about time you left the police work to the professionals."

Amelia snorted. "From where I'm standing you're framing innocent people." She came close to him to avoid her voice travelling, "Why can't you let it go? What is it you think they've done?"

Stephen spoke softly, "Amelia. I've seen a lot of crap in my time, you'd be surprised whom the guilty turn out to be. Then you have to mop up the mess while everyone is left saying '*he was such a lovely man*' or '*they were a lovely couple what could have possessed her to kill them all.*' My personal favourite is '*such a pleasant fellow, would never harm a fly.*' So you'll have to excuse me if I seem a little testy about it."

Amelia backed down. He was right. He was the police officer, he had seen more than she, but she couldn't give up on Seth. "I get it," she said. "I do, truly, but—"

"But nothing," he interrupted. "Do you know the statistics for this sort of thing? It's always the closest people that are to blame, so why would I be looking elsewhere?"

"What? How does Seth figure then? Shouldn't you be checking out her parents? Her family?"

"What do you think I've been doing? They were with my officer when Julia disappeared. The next possibility is your darling Seth here, who, from what I hear, has been tutoring both girls privately."

Amelia felt wounded; he had ample opportunity to mention the tuition, he just said he knew them from the bookshop.

There was a knock on the door. "You okay in there Amelia?" Seth sounded like he was ready for breaking down the door.

She looked at the detective and gave him the 'zip it' mime. "Sure, be out in a sec," she shouted. When she heard his footsteps grow fainter she leaned in to Stephen and whispered. "Right, you'd better go, but don't be back unless you have evidence, *real* evidence. You can't just go blaming the most convenient, it doesn't work that way. And I know you have this whole, 'everyone's guilty until proven innocent," she said mockingly. "But I have a feeling about this, trust me. It isn't Seth."

The detective narrowed his eyes. "Anything happens, then this is on you."

Stephen left the bookshop by the back door.

"Good day detective," Daniel called out to him sarcastically.

Amelia joined them at the counter.

"What did tall and grumpy want with you?" asked Sonny.

She shrugged. "Nothing, just more questions about Lois."

They had heard the conversation, heard it all, they all looked at her with disbelieving expressions when she walked past them and started to log on the computers ready for opening.

Sonny turned to Seth who was still watching Amelia. "What are we going to do?" he whispered quietly, barely audible to the human ear.

"We strike tonight, we end this," he said solemnly.

The other two nodded.

Amelia continued her morning routine, blushing when she caught Seth's eye, the touch of his lips playing on her thoughts.

"Sonny," Seth whispered. "The covers upstairs, take them back to the Cottage." Sonny nodded, "I'm staying here today."

"So you're not—" Daniel began.

"No, I'm not."

Sonny collected the covers and left through the back door, closely followed by Daniel.

The day passed slowly as Seth and Amelia watched the hour hand on the clock go round at a snail's pace. Awkward moments became unbearable as they worked around each other. She wondered if he was regretting the kiss, whether she should have let him, and decided to put some distance between them by cataloging the books on the mezzanine floor. The loveseat looked naked without its covers and cushions, the image of Lois still fresh in her memory; she collected her thoughts and settled down to the task. It was monotonous but kept her away from temptation, she could hear Seth downstairs chatting with the customers and the school children doing their homework and it seemed obvious to her that they all liked Seth and she couldn't understand why the detective would think he was involved. When she looked up, she saw Seth sat on the top step holding out a hot cup of tea.

"Peace offering," he said with a smile.

She returned his smile and put down the book she was working on, and crawled on her hands and knees to meet him at the top of the steps.

"You didn't have to," she said, taking the mug. "But thank you."

She sat back on her knees sipping her drink, watching him over the rim of the mug; he was studying her closely again, as though he expected her to do something.

"What?" she asked.

He smiled again. "Nothing." Looking down at the shop he turned to her. "Everyone's gone, I was wondering about shutting up early and spending some time with you."

Amelia choked on her tea. "What? Why? I mean—" She looked over at the clock registering half-past three. "Gosh, is that the time?"

"That's if you want to spend time with me," he asked quietly.

"I do, yes, that would be lovely. What did you have in mind?"

Seth stood holding out his hand to help her up, "Well, I thought we could go down to the beach today. It's a lovely day, and I think we both deserve a break."

She took his hand as he escorted her down the steps. "Sure."

He pulled his backpack from under the counter and threw in bottles of water and croissants ready for the outing.

# chaptra trydhek

I t felt good to be riding in the daytime, the sun on her face, and wind in her hair, holding on to Seth. Parking at the cliff face north of Creek Bay, he walked her out to the furthermost point and sat down on the ground, his legs dangling free. Amelia looked down at the cavernous drop and gulped.

"It's okay, it's safe," he said holding out his arm to steady her as she sat next to him.

The water was calm today, a turquoise blanket. She breathed in the sea air.

"Too calm to surf today," he said breaking the silence.

Amelia nodded. Looking back towards Creek Bay she could see a few tourists further down the beach in the distance riding the smallest of waves on body boards. "Some people are surfing."

"Phfft, if you call it that."

Seth opened one of the water bottles and took a sip before holding the bottle out to Amelia, she took it with a smile and sipped the refreshingly cool liquid. Seth lay backwards on the grass, hands behind his head, and closed his eyes. She watched him unwind, the first time he had truly relaxed today. It didn't escape her how golden brown he looked under the sunlight, like golden caramel.

"Seth?" she asked.

"Mmm?"

Amelia lay down beside to him, propping herself up by her elbow so she could see him properly. "What the detective said."

He opened his eyes and put one finger to her lips. "Lets not talk about that now."

He moved towards her, his finger trailing across her cheek as he gently wrapped the loose strand of hair around her ear. His fingers rested at the base of her neck as he leaned in, slowly pulling her towards his lips. Soft, full lips still chilled from the drink. He tasted of summer, of honey, so gentle and loving she was lost to him. When he pulled away, his brown eyes sparkled in the sunlight, his long lashes shading them from the brightness.

"That should have been our first kiss," he said softly.

Amelia leant down and kissed him back, he lay down against the ground still holding the kiss. Her thoughts raced about what she was doing, that she needed to keep their friendship professional and being with him, kissing him, was the last thing she told herself she would do, but she couldn't stop herself. He was pulling her in with his intoxicating warmth and sweetness; it took all her strength to pull away from him. She sat back looking down at him, his smile creasing the sides of his mouth.

"I'm sorry, I didn't mean to."

"I'm not sorry Amelia. And you shouldn't be either."

She turned to sit, watching the waves in the distance.

"The day I arrived, I was meant to meet someone. I mean… it was a new start, you know, but he got cold feet and decided he couldn't go through with it." She wasn't sure why she was telling him.

"Is that what you were doing on the beach, ending it all?" Seth said with a smile.

She rolled her eyes, "No man is worth dying over. No. I told you, I thought you were in trouble, so I headed straight for you, the shortest route possible. I just didn't see that bloody quicksand sign."

"Lucky for me you thought I needed rescuing." He held out his hand and swirled a piece of her hair between his finger and thumb.

"Lucky me more like, or I could be under that beach right now."

Seth shook his head. "I beg to differ. We wouldn't have met otherwise."

Amelia frowned, "We would have bumped into each other in the village." A small village like this, there was no way their paths would not have crossed.

He took the bottle from her and drank. "Possibly not. The guys and I were looking to move on, but when you arrived, I thought I might as well stay around a little longer."

She turned to him. "So you're leaving, you were leaving. How long are you staying?"

He chuckled. "Questions, questions, questions, Amelia Scott, I don't know who is more scary, you or that detective."

"Sorry, I didn't mean to pry."

"Don't be sorry, don't ever be sorry."

Seth leaned in again, touching her bottom lip with his thumb, his eyes focused on her pink lips; she anticipated the touch of his lips on hers, when his phone rang. Seth closed his eyes in displeasure.

"Excuse me," he said pulling the phone from his jacket. "What?" he barked into the phone. "Then leave it. It won't work. Try later." He turned away from her and continued talking into the receiver. "I told you it won't work. Leave it for me when I get back." He paused. "No! It is. I'm telling you." There was a low rumble noise in the back of his throat. "That's an order." As he closed down the phone, his face was thunder.

"Something wrong? Do you need to get back?" she asked concerned.

He half smiled. "Nah. Just some problems with… the washing machine, Sonny and Dan are not exactly domesticated."

Amelia pulled out a croissant from the backpack, breaking it in half offering the rest to Seth, as she took her first bite her stomach growled. Looking at the sorry piece of flaking pastry she sucked her bottom lip. "Fancy going to the Italian tonight?" she asked.

Seth grinned. "Sure, why not. You can tell me all about that sorry arse that left you standing."

"Please, I do not wish to talk about Tate— I don't want to talk about that. How about, you tell me more about you."

He lay back down chewing on the bread. "Nothing to tell."

"I'll make you tell me," she said with a mischievous grin.

Seth opened his eyes. "How can you make me?"

In what happened to be the worst Russian accent she could muster Amelia said. "I have vays of making you talk."

Seth shook his head. "You're beginning to sound more like that detective every day, you spend far too much time with him."

"Why do you always deflect?" she asked with a frown.

He shrugged. "None of us is perfect."

She looked down at him, he was perfect to her, in every sense of the word, she wanted to jump on him and drink him in, kiss him all afternoon, all evening even, she wanted him too much it hurt. With his eyes still closed he smiled as though he had heard her thoughts.

"Lay down with me Amelia," he said.

Without her knowledge her body was doing just that. They lay side by side, their bodies barely touching.

"Listen," he said.

She closed her eyes and let her ears tell her the story. The faint noise of the ocean, the rustling of the trees, the birds squawking overhead and the bees that came close to the clover they lay upon.

"What do you hear?" he asked.

She lay silent for a moment listening to nature. She could hear herself breathing and if she concentrated hard enough she could hear her clothing rise and fall in time with her breath, then she heard it, his heartbeat, thum, thum; thum, thum, a steady low beat.

"Everything," she breathed.

She felt his hand entwine with hers; as they lay together under the sun her thoughts became clouded when she drifted into sleep.

*With no natural light from a window, she found it hard to take in her surroundings. The flames flickered from the torches on the walls and fire pit in the centre of the room, clanking of metal on metal reverberated around stonewalls. A tall man dressed in a white gown stepped towards someone kneeling on the floor, head bowed, sword in its sheath.*

*"Someone close to you has broken the seal, the true word." The tall man began. "But you won't give it up, is that correct?" he asked.*

*The warrior replied. "Yes, I am sorry Master Solomon."*

*As the warrior raised his head, his hood came away and she could just make out his features in the dim light. He looked like Seth, or was it that he was on her mind and he would be everywhere she looked.*

*"You know what has to be done," said the man in white.*

*The warrior stood, his armour glistening in the torchlight. "It will be done."*

*Watching him walk away, the old man called out to him. "Don't let me down... Son."*

*He stopped in the doorway, head lowered. "I will not, Father."*

When she opened her eyes, Seth was leaning over her blocking out the sun, the glow around his head halo-esque, though she was sure he was no angel.

"I'm sorry, I must have drifted off," she said half rising.

"You must have been dreaming," he said with a smile.

"Oh god, was I mumbling?" she was mortified.

Seth laughed. "So you talk in your sleep do you?"

"So I've been told," she muttered bringing herself to sitting. She arched her back to get rid of the stiffness and turned to Seth, "What time is it?"

"A little after six."

"Really? I must have been out a while."

"It's okay, I like spending time with you."

"Even when I'm comatose?"

He chuckled. "Even when you're comatose."

"Mmm, I'm starving, what time does the restaurant open?" she asked.

"Seven."

"Could you run me back home while I get changed?"

"You look fine as you are," he said.

"I feel grubby," Amelia said pulling at her top, "Besides, won't take me two minutes."

His grin widened watching her pack away the bottles, and throw the remaining croissants for the birds. Seth sat on the bike and revved it into life, as she sat behind him holding his waist she looked back at the flattened piece of grass they had been laid down upon and smiled to herself as two choughs flew down and began fighting over the pastry scraps.

It didn't take long for them to reach Lowe Cottage, he parked up behind her car and she slid off the bike saying she wouldn't take long, leaving the front door open as she ran up the stairs two at a time. Seth made his way into the lounge, listening to the steady run of water from upstairs. Continuing into the kitchen, he walked towards the back door and frowned. Holding the iron key in the lock he half turned it and then stopped while he ran his hand down the wooden door and closed his eyes.

"What's up?" asked Amelia walking into the kitchen.

He turned and faked a smile. "Nothing." Looking her up and down. "You look lovely."

She knew the simple black dress clung to her body in all the right places and knew it hadn't gone unnoticed by her companion for the evening. She began fidgeting with the leather bracelet around her wrist and changed the subject. "Thank you. Should we go?"

Seth slowly walked around the kitchen table, the look on his face suggested he was going to kiss her again, and if he did, they both knew it was unlikely they would make it to the restaurant. She was both surprised and disappointed when he linked his arm with hers and walked her to the front door. "We'll walk into the village I think, don't want your dress getting messed up."

She locked the front door and he relinked her arm with his. As they took a leisurely stroll, he told her about the various trees and the birds they passed on their way, that the woodland where he lived was classed as ancient woodland and the beach a site of special scientific interest. He went on to tell her if she wanted any work done on Lowe Cottage that she would need special permission because bats are roosting in the eaves. She loved the fact that he was knowledgeable about the area, and now he was beginning to open up to her, maybe now she would get some answers where Lois had left off. The smell of garlic wafted towards them as they neared the restaurant, her stomach growled under the expectation it would soon be fed. Seth opened the door for her and waved her through, leading her by the elbow towards the bar.

The young waitress greeted him enthusiastically, kissing both of his cheeks. She was a petite young lady with long raven hair, olive skin and had a thick Italian accent. "Solomon, wonderful to see you again."

Seth smiled warmly to her. "You look radiant Caterina. The place looks great after the refurb," he said looking around. "Did you go to Italy while they were working on the restaurant? I was looking forward to catching up with you all."

The young girl giggled. "Mamma e Papa send their love Solomon, they asked when they would be seeing you again."

"Are they not here?" he asked looking over her shoulder.

She shook her head. "Nonna is not well. Papa will not leave until she is feeling better. Come, come," she said ushering them both into the restaurant. "I have a special table for you both."

Amelia nodded and smiled at the pretty woman who led them to a booth set in a secluded corner with drapes hanging down the wall. She lit the large candle in the middle of the table and then turned the glasses right way up as Amelia and Seth both slid into the booth.

"Would you see the wine menu Solomon?"

He looked at Amelia, and then turned to the waitress. "That's okay Caterina. Do you have the Altesino 2013 Brunello Di Montalcino Montosoli?"

"Si, specialmente per te."

As she left to collect the wine from the bar, Amelia leaned towards Seth and whispered, "I've no idea what wine you just ordered, I hope it isn't expensive."

"I know you like your red wine, and, well, this is one of my favourites, I hope you like it too."

Caterina returned, uncorked the bottle and put it down beside the candle in the middle of the table.

"Here are your menus," she said handing them both the black leather-bound list. She smiled widely at Amelia. "Tornerò presto." The waitress left with a skip in her step.

Amelia looked at Seth with raised eyebrow.

"She said she'd be back."

"You speak Italian?"

"I've picked up a few things along the way."

After a few moments, the waitress returned holding a tray with jug of iced water, two glasses, a bowl of olives and rustic bread. "Complimenti della casa godono."

"Grazie, Caterina, puoi darci cinque minuti, quindi saremo pronti per ordinare."

"Grazie."

Amelia wished she had taken modern languages as an option at school instead of Latin. "All I got was five minutes."

"Sorry." He put down his menu and poured them both a glass of water. "She said compliments of the house and I said we'll be ready to order in five minutes. I'll keep it to English if you prefer."

"No, no, that's okay. I just like to know what's going on. It's my own fault for being so English about it."

"What do you mean?" he asked laughing.

She shrugged. "You know, that everyone understands or speaks English so why bother. Not that I take that view you understand," she quickly added. "I just didn't have the opportunity to learn. Well, that's a fib, I did have the opportunity, it's just that it came at the wrong time for me."

His eyes glowed in the candlelight. "Then there is no time like the present." He moved closer to her and whispered in her ear, "Amelia Scott, sembri affascinante stasera e non vorrei altro che baciarti."

Her skin exploded into goosebumps when his hot breath tickled her ear, she was certain he wasn't ordering steak.

"Erm, thank you?"

He pulled away from her with a cheeky grin that faded when he looked across towards the bar. Noticing his disappointment, Amelia turned to look in the same direction to see Detective Inspector Cooke sat on one of the bar stools raising a glass in acknowledgement of his presence.

"We can go somewhere else if you like," Amelia suggested.

"No. We're not going to let him spoil our evening." He poured her a glass of wine. "Here, try the wine, it is most excellent."

"Amelia lifted the glass, the aroma wafted as she brought it closer to her nose, smells of rich herbs filled her senses. "Mmm, smells divine."

"Tell me what you smell," he asked.

"The herbs hit you straight away." She inhaled deeply. "And something like, oh, I don't know, something familiar." She took another whiff. "Is that leather?"

Seth chuckled. "Are you a wine expert?"

"Why?" she asked innocently, hoping that she hadn't just insulted the merchants vineyard.

"You are quite correct. Drink, tell me what you taste."

She slowly took a sip and licked her lips. "Mmm, tastes like cherries, sweet cherries."

He raised his glass. "Saluti."

"Saluti," she said as they both clinked their glasses together.

The booth was private from the rest of the dining area. The drapes hid them from prying eyes and they managed to position themselves to avoid eye contact with the detective who was stubbornly watching them despite their efforts. They shared a large plate of mussels to start and both opted for steak as their main dish. When Amelia started to cut into her steak, Seth sat back watching her, feeling self-conscious, she stopped.

"What's wrong?" she asked.

"Nothing. I'm surprised you opted for rare."

She finished cutting a strip and put it in her mouth. The juices were tantalizing. "It's the only way to eat steak," she said with a shrug. "Are you not hungry?" she asked when he hadn't started his meal.

He looked down at the plate, "Yes, I am. But I would rather watch you."

She stopped chewing. "I'd rather you ate."

He smiled again, picked up his cutlery and cut into the bloodied meat.

"There was something I wanted to ask you," she said as he started chewing. "Something about Lois." She took a sip of her wine. "Did you know she wrote a book about this place?"

He finished chewing and swallowed. "I know." His tone was dangerously even but she continued nonetheless.

"She was telling me all about it, the day she… well, she was saying what had happened."

Seth put his knife and fork down and placed his hand on hers. "Amelia, do you mind if we talk about something else?"

"You're doing it again. Deflecting."

Caterina appeared at their table with two drinks, "Compliments of the gentleman at the bar," she said nodding back towards the detective.

Seth sighed. "He is no acquaintance of ours Caterina. Would you kindly take them back and tell him we are flattered by his generosity but respectfully decline."

"Of course Solomon."

She walked to the detective and put the two drinks down in front of him, and repeated the message. Stephen's expression turned steely when she walked away.

"Why does she call you Solomon?" asked Amelia, but Seth was too busy watching the detective to hear her. When she realized he was preoccupied, she touched his hand.

"Sorry?" he asked.

"Why does she call you by your surname?"

"She always has. She told me once that I don't look like a Seth." He picked up his drink, eyes still focused on the detective.

"I would have to concur. I don't think you look like a Seth either."

What she really wanted to say was that he looked more like a Setali, but given his demeanour and that he was not prepared to talk about the book, she thought better of it. Maybe reading the book had impacted on her more than she thought possible. Seth remained distant as they ate in silence.

"Are you not enjoying your meal?" he asked when she started moving food around her plate.

"Oh, its lovely, I'm just—" She paused trying to explain how she felt. She felt wonderful around him, but it appeared he had lost interest. "It's just, you don't seem to be enjoying yourself, is there something wrong?"

"Goodness no, Amelia, whatever gave you that impression?"

"You've been quiet ever since we had our main course delivered."

"I'm sorry. It just feels a little…" He looked over to the detective. "Crowded in here. Would you mind awfully if we finish early? I can't stand that man peering at us."

Amelia looked back to the bar. Detective Inspector Cooke was sat with drink in his hand and vacant expression.

"I see what you mean. Yes, I don't mind."

He picked up the half bottle of wine, "We can take this back to yours if you like, you can tell me the rest of your story, about Lois."

Her chest tightened. Seth, back at her cottage, and finally getting answers, this was too good to miss. "Of course, we can do that."

Seth waved over the waitress speaking to her in Italian. Caterina looked over her shoulder at the man sitting next to the bar then whispered something to him to which he nodded. She replied in Italian before taking the two plates away and disappeared into the kitchen. Amelia looked at Seth for explanation.

"She is going to ask the chef to prepare the meal to go, and apparently we are getting another bottle on the house. Come on," he said gathering their coats. "We'll collect it from the reception."

As they passed the detective Amelia shook her head. "Stephen. Really, I thought you were above this."

He took a swig of his drink and gave a sideways glance to Seth. "Like I said, doing my job."

Seth pulled Amelia away by the elbow and led her to the front door; the night air was cool and refreshing. They turned when Caterina's voice floated their way.

"Here you go Solomon, Miss Amelia. I hope you both enjoy the rest of your evening."

Seth took the bag of food and wine from Caterina.

"Grazie," he kissed the waitress on both cheeks and turned linking Amelia's arm.

Walking down the lane, she turned to him. "It'll be cold by the time we get to mine, is it really worth it?" she asked.

"Tsk! Amelia Scott. I hold in my hand the best steak you'll ever eat and most excellent wine to accompany it. Why would you turn away the opportunity to indulge yourself?"

"Well, if you put it like that."

They neared the top of the lane, leaving the distant lights of the village behind them. It was hard to see where they were going with the large hedges on both sides of the road.

"Aren't we out past curfew or something?" she asked avoiding a pothole.

Seth chuckled. "Are you worried you're out in the dark with a strange man, maybe wondering if you should be heeding the detective's advice?"

She patted his arm. "No, silly. I don't know, what with those bloody kids banging around my place, poor Valerie, Julia's disappearance, not to mention Lois, it's all a bit bonkers."

"Arh, so you think you've moved to crazy town or something."

She smiled, remembering her own thoughts when she first arrived in the village. "Maybe."

"Well," he said stopping and turning her to face him, "this is no Stepford, I can assure you."

"Are you sure about that?" she asked pulling away from him.

Seth stopped. "Amelia?" She turned around to face him. "Are you scared to be alone with me?" he asked innocently.

She scoffed. "Me? Alone with you?" She made a noise she wasn't sure she was capable of and shook her head. "I'm not scared to be walking the streets at night with you, that I am sure of. But there is a perfectly good bottle of wine in that bag going to waste. I think we do it injustice not to be drinking it right now." She turned picking up her pace.

He shook his head and spurted after her.

The warm glow from the living room gave them ample light as they approached the doorstep. "Keep them on timer, just in case," she said when she saw Seth looking at the windows with a frown.

Seth nodded. "Commendable."

While Amelia began fiddling in her pocket for the key, Seth turned around watching the tree line in the distance and sighed.

"Something wrong?" she asked turning to look in the same direction, for what she wasn't certain. It was apparent something out there had caught his attention, that he had seen something. Squinting she tried to make out shapes in the distance almost certain there was movement, but the wind had started to pick up and she convinced herself it was just the shadows playing tricks on her eyes.

"Nothing," he said interrupting her concentration. "Shall we go in?"

The door lock creaked under pressure as she turned the key and opened the door. "Finally," she said opening the door wider for Seth.

"I'll take these through to the kitchen," he said brushing past her.

Amelia closed and bolted the door behind him; the last thing she saw outside was his bike leaning close to her car, a sight she could get used to if only she would allow herself.

"I'll be down in a tick," she called out as she ran up stairs. Amelia rushed to the bathroom to refresh, made sure her minimal make-up had stayed in place, windswept hair was tamed and looked presentable. She kicked off her shoes and opted for the ballerina slippers for comfort; what she really wanted to do was get undressed and into her robe, but feared that would give him the wrong impression, she snapped out of the thought when her mobile phone began to ring.

"Hello?"

"You never logged on. What is the point in asking me to log on, all mysterious, when you forget to do it."

"Mum, god, I'm sorry, I was out and completely forgot."

"I still don't understand why you would have me log on, what aren't you telling me?" her mother asked out of concern.

"Amelia, where are the glasses?" Seth shouted from downstairs.

Her heart stopped certain her mother heard him.

"Who was that?" her mother asked.

She bit her lip, and whispered, "A friend, and I've got to go, sorry mum. I'll text you later, okay?"

"You'd better. Love you."

"Love you too." She hung up the phone and turned around to see Seth stood in the doorway to her bedroom.

"Sorry, I thought I heard voices," he said concerned.

Amelia tucked a strand of hair behind her ear, "Only Mum, she was worried. We have an agreement that I let her know everything is okay, but I missed our check-in," she said tossing her phone on the bed.

"You were after glasses?" she asked walking out of the room.

Seth joined her in the kitchen as she fished out the glasses; the bag of food lay on the kitchen counter.

"I wasn't sure if you wanted the food reheated or not," he said moving to the side of the kitchen table.

Amelia looked at the bag of food; reheating was more hassle than it was worth, and she was used to cold left-overs, it had become her staple diet lately, something she wasn't proud of, but it was convenient. It also meant they could finish the food and get down to talking about the history. "I'm fine with how it comes, if you are."

Seth nodded and pulled out the two large silver containers. They both took a meal and served it onto a plate, before taking them into the lounge.

"Wow, you got the fire going quickly," she said taking a seat opposite the hearth, marvelling at his technique.

He shrugged. "What can I say I have a magic touch."

She took a bite of her steak grateful it hadn't dried out and still retained most of its juices.

"So, Lois." He said as he sat drinking his wine.

"Lois." Amelia put her cutlery down and picked up the wine glass from the small table. "I still can't believe it you know. Stephen... I mean Detective Inspector Cooke," she corrected herself. "He said that she was fit as a fiddle and not under the care of any doctor, so he felt it odd that she would suddenly die from a heart attack."

"Looking for answers where there are none."

"Well, that's what I thought. You know he has this whole theory about everyone being guilty till proven innocent," she said. "You see, I wonder though, if there was something odd about that day."

Seth narrowed his eyes, "What do you mean?"

Amelia took another piece of steak. "There was just something that worried me, like I had left the back door open, or a window. That an opportunist could just happen by. But that's stupid, right? There would be no way that anyone could have made it past me and up the stairs to Lois and back down again without me or anyone else in the bookshop even noticing. That's just not possible."

Seth looked into his glass thoughtfully. "No one in, no one out?" he said quietly under his breath.

"Pretty much everyone I saw kept to the lower floor. There was no way..." she drifted for a second.

"Amelia? Do you remember something?"

"Yes. William. He came to the back door, but disappeared, and I didn't see him again."

She could see his jaw tighten when she mentioned his name. "Was that before or after?" he asked.

"Before," she whispered meekly, whenever she mentioned his name Seth got serious.

"And you're sure you didn't see him again?"

Should she tell him about seeing him at Creek Bay? She wasn't sure it was a good idea.

"Amelia. Did you see him again?" His eyes narrowed, she couldn't look away and she couldn't lie to him.

"I saw him later at Creek Bay."

Seth stood. "Son of a bitch." He began pacing the length of the sofa, running his hand through his hair.

"What is it with you two? Why would it matter when I saw William?"

Seth continued pacing muttering to himself. Putting her glass and plate down on the table she slowly walked over to him, placing her hand on his shoulder. He turned, eyes wide with horror.

"Tell me what the deal is between you and William, Setali?"

His eyes widened and face paled. "What?" he whispered.

"I read the book, did some research. You're both named after relatives from the two major families here in the village, the Solomon's and Malloy's. What kind of family dispute could last so long?"

Seth began to shake. "You don't know what you're saying."

He walked away into the kitchen leaning on the kitchen table with both hands, his head bowed.

"Then tell me. If there is an issue, I need to know about it. Besides, I don't think he's that bad."

A sharp laugh came from Seth then he went to brooding again. "Amelia," he said quietly lifting his head and turning around to face her. "Do me one small favour. Do not speak to William again."

"Not without an explanation I won't."

"He's bad news."

"That isn't an explanation. You're deflecting again," she shrieked.

Exasperated he flung his arms in the air above his head, "What is it with you? Why do you test me?"

He stormed past her towards the front door and stopped when she grabbed his arm, "I'm sorry Seth, I don't mean to—"

"You have no idea," he whispered.

She pulled his arm towards her, saw the hurt in his eyes, his face full of sorrow, standing on her tiptoes she leant in and kissed his cheek. His body felt tense when he wrapped his arms around her shoulders pulling her in to him, his grip tightening; she rested her head on his chest, listening to his heartbeat. The once steady thrum was quickening, and the heat radiating from him was becoming increasingly hotter.

"I am so sorry Seth, please forgive me. Come and sit down, please."

He sighed into her hair. "No more talk of him, please."

"I won't," she whispered. Pulling herself free, Amelia returned to the sofa and picked up both glasses. "A refill?"

Seth nodded. Amelia put both glasses down on the kitchen table and turned to get the wine from the cupboard when Seth appeared by her side at the kitchen sink with the dishes of food. She didn't feel like eating now either and it appeared his appetite had also waned.

"I'll sort these out," she said taking the plates. "You see to the wine."

When she had finished bagging up the food scraps, Amelia joined Seth on the sofa. He was laying back into the seat, his thoughts elsewhere.

"So," she said loudly in a bid to break the atmosphere. "What can you tell me about Fortune? I am excited to hear them play."

A smile tugged at the corner of his mouth. "They're okay I guess."

Picking up her glass she sat down and took a large gulp. "Well, I am excited anyway. They play next Friday right?"

"Yeah." He picked up his wine and moved closer to her, then placed it next to hers on the table. "Earlier today, did you regret kissing me?"

"Yes and no."

"Then you wouldn't mind if I kissed you again."

She felt her chest tighten again and her temperature rising, finding it hard to breathe. Kiss him again, here, tonight, god yes, and by the dilating of his pupils, she could tell he wanted to. As he leant in closer, his thumb traced her bottom lip and then down her jaw line to her neck, he wetted his lips in readiness, pulling her head to his he gently kissed her, she opened to him, slowly at first and then wanting more, but her head became hazy as she felt herself succumb to the darkness.

Seth placed her head gently on the cushion. Standing, he slid his hands under her thighs and picked her up, she gave a gentle moan and then rested her head on his shoulder. He carried her to the bedroom and laid her down on the bed, straightening her clothes. The distant muffled voices she heard sounded familiar to her.

"Valerian root compound?" asked Sonny.

The drug had the desired affect, he knew it would take a matter of seconds to work; it was a tried and tested recipe that has been in the family for years.

Seth turned to Sonny and Daniel stood in the doorway to the bedroom and nodded. "I used some of the compound."

"Gotta love that stuff." Daniel said as he came into the room, passing by the dresser he picked up a few objects and smelled them before stopping beside Seth. "What did she say?"

He looked down at Amelia deep in sleep, looking every bit the angel he had etched in his mind. "She has made the connection, but she thinks we are named after our ancestors."

"If only she knew how old you actually are," Sonny said taking a seat at the foot of the bed. "So what do we do now fearless leader?"

"William has been taking an interest and we need to make sure he doesn't get close."

Daniel leant against the large wooden headboard and crossed his arms. "What about the detective? If she has been talking to him, then he could make the connection too, maybe he already has, maybe that's why he's got a holiday room down at the station with your name on it. Listen, he's already causing us issues."

Seth looked up. "Such as?"

"I was moving a carcass that had been left on the grounds, it was a big buck too, he almost caught me moving it, and with the Wildlife Unit trawling the woods last couple of days it could have been difficult to explain. Pity he found that scarf though."

"Leave the detective to me," said Sonny.

"What about you Solomon?" asked Daniel.

He gritted his teeth. "I'm going to see to our old friend William."

"What about Amelia?" Sonny asked.

"I'll look after her if you like," offered Daniel.

Seth smiled. "I'm sure you would. Dan, I want you to keep the rest of them away from William. The longer they spend apart, the weaker they are, which means he will be defenseless."

"No problem." Daniel walked to the doorway and then turned. "You think she's the one?"

Seth looked down at her pale face, and brushed a strand of hair from her cheek, she rolled into his touch. "I'm sure she's the one."

"Come on," Sonny said pushing Daniel further into the doorway. "Let's leave the love birds to it."

*Amelia dreamt of a young couple sat in the clearing enjoying a picnic. The sun was high and no cloud in the sky, it was a perfect setting for the young lovers. Lois wore a light pink dress with little white flowers, hair styled in a ponytail, no makeup; while Charles opted for white shirt and dark trousers, his hair was slicked back as was fashionable for the time. They picked food out of the rattan basket and laid it on the checkered rug, giggling and laughing with one another, carefree and happy. The sun disappeared behind dark clouds and they ran for shelter under the trees when the sudden downpour began. Charles pulled the blanket over their heads to keep them dry, though they were soaked through. He bent down and kissed her, dropping the blanket he pulled her closer as she wrapped her arms around him.*

*The two lovers lay on the blanket in each other's arms, when Lois woke the sun had long since gone, and darkness surrounded them. They walked through the woodland trying to find a way out, their spirits not dampened, happy to be with one another when they came upon a lone white cottage. They ran towards the building, thankful for civilization. Noticing a light in the cellar Charles knelt down to announce their arrival, but when he saw the occupant he quickly scrambled back. Lois tried to console him, but he was in shock, he tried to stop her from looking, but she managed to pull free of him. What she saw made her gasp in horror, stumbling backwards Lois bumped into the metal railings alerting their arrival. Charles pulled her away and they ran as fast as they could from that place.*

# *chaptra peswardhek*

A melia slowly opened her heavy eyelids. Feeling the duvet underneath, she did not remember going upstairs or know why she was still fully clothed. When she sat up, her head began to throb, putting it down to drinking too much wine she mentally told herself to take some aspirin the first chance she got. The dial on the bedside clock read eight-thirty, which meant she wouldn't be late opening the store today. After a leisurely shower, Amelia donned her black combat clothes before heading out to the village.

Opting to walk, Amelia felt herself sway as though her legs were not her own, taking all of her energy to stay upright. She told herself she couldn't still be drunk, it had never affected her like this before and she didn't recall the percentage being particularly high; what she needed was caffeine and quick. When she got to the store the door was open, thinking Seth must have come down earlier, she quickened her pace, but her smile faded when she saw Sonny filling the coffee machine.

"Cripes, do I look that bad?" he said jokingly.

"I was looking for Seth."

"Not here. Asked me to open up for him."

Amelia felt herself sway again, her head felt light but foggy all at the same time. Sonny rushed to her side.

"You not feeling well?" he asked moving her to the nearest sofa.

She held her head. "I really don't know what has come over me. I just feel really vague, if that makes any sense."

Sonny pulled Amelia's hair back from her face; her complexion had paled and her pupils were dilated.

"It's okay. I'll get you a strong coffee."

She nodded as her eyes started to close. Leaving her curled up on the sofa Sonny finished setting up the machine and preparing the shop before dampening a towel and placing it across her forehead.

"Here, this will help."

The cool rag felt refreshing against her clammy skin, she held it in place enjoying the feeling. When she opened her eyes again Sonny was sat next to her with a hot mug of strong coffee, the aroma wafting towards her.

"It will do you good, drink up."

Holding the mug was like holding a five-pound weight, hell, even keeping her head upright was a struggle. Amelia took a sip of the thick dark liquid.

"Where is Seth?" she asked leaning against the sofa.

"Dunno. He just asked me to open up, didn't think you would be here either to be honest."

"Oh?" she asked.

"You're Monday to Friday, right? Just assumed you'd both be off today."

She raised her eyebrows but still couldn't open her eyes. "It's Saturday already?" she mumbled into her mug as she took another sip of coffee.

"Nice clothes by the way," he said with a smile. She knew he was smiling without seeing him because it was in his voice.

"Thanks. It's my 'Lara Croft' look."

"Well I think it's very sexy." He patted her knee and rose from the sofa. "I've got everything sorted here if you want to go home, you don't look like you're in any fit state to be up and about anyway."

"I'll just rest my eyes for five minutes then I'll be fine."

Sonny returned to his duties. Amelia could hear him in the back room moving some boxes when the doorbell chimed. The sofa seat dipped next to her and she opened her eyes to see Detective Inspector Cooke.

"Hey," she greeted.

"Long night?" he asked, looking like he had not slept much either.

"Something like that."

"Sorry." Stephen picked up her coffee mug and handed it to her.

She took the offering. "So you should be."

"Do you want any tablets?"

"It's not a headache, I'm just tired." She rubbed her eyes and drank some more of the coffee.

When the detective didn't speak she looked at him, "Well?"

"I am deeply sorry for the other night." He looked around the shop.

"He's not here," she said into her mug then turned to Stephen. "Seth. He isn't here."

"Morning your holiness," Sonny shouted from the corridor. "Nice of you to grace us with your presence so early in the morning." He emerged with a large box and placed it on the counter.

The detective slowly stood. "Sonny."

"Would you like a drink Detective Inspector?" offered Sonny.

Stephen walked to the counter and sat down on one of the bar stools. "Actually I will." He glanced at the wall chart behind him written in chalk. "I'll have one of those tall lattes please."

As Sonny worked the coffee machine the detective swiveled in his chair for a better view of Amelia. Her head was back against the rest; eyes closed and frown on her forehead.

"What's wrong with her?" he whispered to Sonny.

The young man put the detective's drink in front of him, "She and Seth had a late night."

"What's with the outfit?"

Sonny smiled. "Don't you like it? It's totally hot."

He turned to the young man with large grin, oversized tie-dye tee and dreads flowing free. "Mmm."

After ten minutes Sonny picked up the mug Amelia had left on the table by the sofa. "Wakey, wakey, sleepy head," he said nudging her knee.

Her eyes slowly opened. "What?" she whispered.

"You've been asleep." He sat on the table, his legs straddling hers, hands holding both of her knees. "Hey, why don't you sneak off while our friendly neighbourhood policeman is outback in the men's room?"

"No, I have to wait for Seth," she said groggily.

"I'll tell him you're looking if he turns up. Besides, looks like you need some fresh air, why don't you go down to the beach and clear your head, will do you more good than staying in here with me and the geek parade." He nodded to the two youngsters on the computers.

Looking over her shoulder she checked to make sure the detective was still occupied and scrunched her nose feeling guilty for bailing. "I guess I could make my escape now couldn't I?"

Sonny chuckled, "And I promise I won't tell him where you are." He put his hand on his heart, "Scout's honour."

"You did it wrong, but thank you," she said and quickly made her exit before Stephen emerged.

The sun seemed especially bright, so bright she could have done with wearing her sunglasses today. Avoiding people in the street she headed straight for the village gardens behind the Kings Arms pub and sat down on one of the benches beside the large shrubs. Fragrant lavender was in full bloom, a pretty cascade of blue purple foliage arched over the short bedding wall. She closed her eyes and listened to the bees as they busied themselves to collect pollen. Bending down she picked a stem and rubbed the flowers between her palms inhaling deeply, the delicate scent filled her senses and the foggy feeling in her head seemed to be lifting, she took another lungful.

"Told you I would see you again."

Without looking, she knew who it was. Amelia smiled at him sweetly. "I'm not allowed to talk to you," she said playfully.

He took the seat next to her, his arm resting on the top edge of the bench behind her back. "Oh? Why?" he asked innocently.

She shrugged. "You're a bad boy."

He threw his head back and laughed. "Really?"

Amelia felt his fingers on her back, making small circles just between her shoulder blades. Closing her eyes she was imagining his caress were it privately just the two of them.

"Where are you heading today?" he asked.

"Just needed some fresh air." Her eyes remained closed as she concentrated on his touch.

He looked at his bike propped up against the stone walling. "How about I take you for a ride, help you clear your head, maybe take in some retail therapy along the way?"

That made her smile. Why people assumed women liked to shop was unfathomable, if anything she found it tiresome. However, the night spent in the woods searching for Julia made her very much aware she was sadly lacking outdoor gear, and she did spy a couple of decent shops in town.

"Actually," she said turning to William. "That is exactly what I need right now."

"How about that," he said standing.

She tried to avoid looking at him; looking at him would make her want to hold him and that won't lead to anything good. Amelia stood too quickly, and started to sway. William steadied her, grabbing hold of her waist tightly and gently placed his hand on her forehead, the familiar smell from her pores made him recoil.

"Are you feeling well?" he asked, concerned.

"Yes, why does everyone keep asking me that?" She looked around over his shoulder. "Now where is that bike of yours?"

Detective Inspector Cooke walked back to the counter and sat on the barstool. Noticing she wasn't sat at the sofa, he looked around the store and started to worry when he couldn't locate Amelia. Hearing banging upstairs he walked to the bottom of the stairs to see Sonny putting books on the shelves when one of the youngsters called out asking for help with his computer.

"Did you see where Amelia went?" Stephen asked when Sonny reached the bottom step.

"Just a sec," Sonny replied, carrying on towards the teenager deliberately taking his time disabling the encryption protection. The detective tapped his foot impatiently until Sonny finally returned to the counter and pulled out two bottles of water.

"Well?" the detective asked.

"Well what?"

"Where did Amelia go?"

Sonny slowly poured one of the bottles into a tall glass, watching the water cascade over the ice and lemon slice.

"For gods sake." Stephen ran to the door in time to see Amelia sat on the back of a motorbike heading out of the village, the driver however, he didn't recognize. "Shit!"

The detective ran out to his car and fumbled for his car keys, by the time he got them out of his pocket the bike was long gone, he banged on his steering wheel and cursed. A gentle tapping on the passenger side window broke his concentration.

Sonny peered into the car. "Everything okay Detective?"

The journey was just what she needed to blow the cobwebs away. William took the long road into town, staying away from populated areas and off the beaten path. His leathers and musk had a whole new dimension where Seth's didn't; William was forbidden, that's what Seth had more or less told her. She was not to speak to him and she was not to be in his company, so why was she drawn to him? Everything about him made her want him, his smell, his touch, everything.

William parked the bike by the clock tower, as she slid off the back of the seat she was disappointed to have both feet on the ground again. William turned to her, his grin promised so much more than he would ever say.

"Where to first?" he asked.

Amelia turned around 180 degrees when she spied the first outdoor and camping shop. "Over there, I realise it's about time I need to get some Gortex gear if I am to survive in this climate during the winter months."

William held the base of her back as he gently guided her across the street. "What are you after?" he asked.

"You know… waterproofs, decent pair of walking boots, and some emergency stuff; torch, first aid kit, compass, oh and a Swiss army knife would be handy."

"You sound like you're planning a hiking trip." He bent down and whispered, "do you like to hike Amelia Scott?"

She smiled. "I do, yes. But I found out the other night, just spending a night out in this place means you need to be prepared."

"If you are not self-prepared, yes, I guess you're right," he said walking her along. "May I say something?"

"Sure."

"Why are you dressed for combat?"

She laughed heartedly. "Is that your one question?"

He flashed her his wicked grin. "Do I have one question? And one question only?"

Looking through her eyelashes at him, she was tempted to say anything at all, but she couldn't let him off that easily. "One question."

"Why are you dressed for combat?" he said more seriously.

"That's really your question?" She carried on walking to the shop. "Well, I totally love the comfort, and black *is* my colour, and… I have to confess to not having a lot of clothing choices these days, so this was my tried and tested comfort choice."

William acknowledged her response with a nod and followed her towards the outdoor and camping shop, his eyes wandering down to her derrière watching her soft flesh bounce as she walked.

"Are you coming in?" she asked when she realised he had slowed his pace.

He looked up to the sign and the top floor window with a frown. "It should be okay."

Amelia found that to be an odd answer, but decided to ignore it. They went up to the first floor for clothing and footwear, and she began looking through the racks of women's clothing, mainly pale blue or dusky pink; she wrinkled her nose.

"This is not you," William said walking around the rack with a look of distaste.

"Can I help you?" the pretty young girl asked of William as she appeared from behind the desk. He ignored her and carried on looking around the room with a look of displeasure.

Amelia thought that was exceptionally rude of him to ignore the sales assistant so answered for him. "No, thank you. I'm just looking."

The sales assistant looked her up and down, and gave a look which said what they had for sale was not going to be what this woman wanted. The young lady disappeared to harass another customer, one that looked like they had money.

"Why don't you try over here Amelia?" William suggested nodding to the section in the rear. It was mostly darks, whites and yellows.

When she started going through the rails she paused. "William, this is the boys' rail."

He shrugged. "But the colours suit you much better. Society likes to put people into neat little packages to conform to the norm. And my love," he said gently touching her cheek, "you are anything but the norm."

She didn't know whether to hug him or hit him. It was true, she didn't conform, she dressed for comfort and wore whatever she liked, regardless of the reception she might attract.

"Okay, Romeo," she said sarcastically. "Riddle me this. I have fifty pounds and require a top and bottom to complete my outfit, but the sale is not here in the boys' section. What do I do?"

A wicked smile pulled at his lips before she even finished her sentence. "Why, you ask me to take over the negotiations with the sales assistant."

He disappeared through to the other room before she could say anything, after a few moments he returned with the young girl who appeared flustered and more than eager to help where she could. Amelia felt awkward with the overly attentive nature she was now receiving, but William encouraged her to indulge. After ten minutes of close scrutiny, she came away with a padded gilet and padded trousers, both black.

"This, Amelia Scott, is most befitting," he said as she held up her new purchases. "Now, where would you wish to go?"

"I need torches, first aid kit and a knife."

"I'll take you downstairs," interrupted the sales assistant. Whatever William had said to her, had certainly done the trick, they even gave her a discount on new stock items, anything it seemed, to get them out of the store quicker.

William insisted on carrying her bags, although she was determined that she could cope, he would not hear of it. It became increasingly obvious to her that William was old school.

"Do you have any evening wear Amelia Scott?"

The question came out of the blue and she found herself answering before wondering why. "Not really, no."

He looked across the road to a boutique shop with delicate hanging baskets either side of the large bay windows. "I think we need to make a stop over there."

Amelia frowned. "It's really not my kind of thing to be honest, can we just—"

"Indulge me," he said taking her by the waist.

Standing outside the shop, Amelia looked in the window at the fancy dresses and exquisite laced underwear, definitely a shop she would never dream of walking into, she couldn't even remember the last time she bought a matching underwear set.

"I can't afford these prices," she gasped.

"Then I shall pay for you," he said with a regal tone.

Amelia turned to him. "Why? Why would you do that? I cannot allow you to be so extravagant. You barely know me."

William bent down and whispered in her ear, "Indulge me, if you do not wish to indulge yourself."

His lips brushed lightly against her ear sending a shockwave of excitement and terror all at the same time. He was opening the door and ushering her in before she knew it. William spoke briefly to a sales assistant, who took them through to a private suite; a beautifully tasteful and opulently decorated room, in the centre were three comfortable looking sofas, and the walls were adorned with elaborate floor to ceiling mirrors, at one end of the room was a private curtained changing area.

"Black or purple I am undecided," he said looking at Amelia.

"I beg your pardon?"

"Your colour. Black or purple." He brushed the hair away from her shoulder to reveal her jaw and neck. His eyes trailed down at the pale skin and focused on her clavicle. "Or maybe deep red is more your colour?"

William spoke again to the sales assistant, while another member of staff arrived with two glasses of champagne on a silver salver. This was clearly an expensive boutique and by the attention the staff were giving them, they were obviously expecting a sizable sale. The sales assistant reappeared with a rolling rail filled with the most gorgeous dresses Amelia had ever seen.

Pulling a dress from the rail William held it out to her. "Go and try this on," he said.

Amelia cautiously took the garment from him and turned towards the changing room, the little voice in her head asked why was she obeying everything he said. It seemed the moment she was away from him, her brain started to work again.

She slipped out of her combats and pulled on the figure-hugging dress. He had guessed her size perfectly, and the fit showed off her figure in all the right places; he was somewhat of a genius.

"Do you have it on?" His voice was just the other side of the thin curtain material. She pulled the curtain aside and walked back out into the suite.

William stood in front of her, his eyes seeming to glow when she emerged. The dark red dress fitted at the bust and waist, gently flowing out to the ground.

"Astounding. Étourdissant," he said breathlessly.

William took her hand in his and twirled her around, so she could see herself in all of the mirrors. The dress was amazing, but she couldn't allow him to pay for it, she would let him have his fun and then tell him she couldn't possibly accept.

"Amelia Scott. What a vision you are." He spun her around and then grabbed her waist pulling her in closer. Bending forward he dipped her, arching her back exposing more neckline and chest. His black curly hair tickled her bare flesh as he bent forward and breathed into her neck whispering, "longus moratus sum ad te in."

The blood began to rush to her head and the dizziness flooded back. "You waited for what?" she asked. It would seem the Latin classes hadn't been a waste of time after all.

He slowly brought her upright, the expression on his face unreadable, and then a smile crept from the corner of his mouth, but the sound of Amelia's mobile ringing made his smile quickly disappear.

"Sorry, I think I should get that." She dashed over to the crumpled pile of clothes in the dressing area and pulled out her phone, closing the curtain behind her. "Hello? Oh, hey, Sonny." She peered through the curtain to look for William but she couldn't see him. "Why? I'm in town. No. I am fine, the fresh air did me good. Yes, you were right. Just some bits and bobs. Anyway, everything okay down there? Have you left it in one piece? Cool, see you later."

She ended the call and stood looking at herself in the full-length mirror. This really wasn't her style; she wasn't the princess type to be swept away by the handsome stranger, things like that didn't happen to people like her. No, she had to stay grounded; she checked her phone, no missed calls from her mum, or from Seth.

"Something wrong Amelia?" asked William stood behind her. He had pulled the curtain aside without her realising. She looked at his reflection in the mirror; they looked an odd pair, her with the evening gown and he with his tight black shirt, black jeans and leathers. He was everything she wanted. His black curly hair cascaded down her shoulder when he bent down to kiss her exposed skin, a shudder of excitement raced through her.

"Are you getting changed, or do you wish to wear it now?" he asked.

"What?" she asked spinning around to face him.

"It is bought and paid for, so you can either let the assistant bag it for you, or you may wish to wear it."

"You can not, I will not allow—"

He held up his finger to her lips. "You should have the humility to accept a gift with the grace in which it is offered." His fingers traced her lips and her chin before she pulled back.

"Then I will graciously accept your gift, if you allow me to buy you dinner in return."

The smile was slow to spread across his lips as he raised his eyebrow, nodded and then turned away leaving her to get dressed in private.

Once she had changed back into her combats, Amelia felt much more comfortable. William was stood by the till watching the assistant delicately placing the dress into a box with tissue paper and carefully sprinkled scented petals over the top.

Amelia inwardly cringed. "Its ok," she said alerting them to her arrival. "I've got a bag," she said holding out her crinkled plastic camping store bag.

The sales assistant looked horrified and silently turned to William for instruction. When he nodded, the assistant carefully removed the petals, unfolded the paper and pulled out the garment while her colleague helped fold down the material so that it would fit into the bag offered.

William escorted Amelia to the town gardens linking her arm with his, for someone who dresses so young and hip, William was undoubtedly very old-fashioned, though he came across as rather forward at times. As they continued their walk she heard heavy footsteps pounding behind them and turned to see DI Cooke running their way. Amelia immediately unlinked her arm from William taking a few steps away from him, a look of displeasure flitted across his face.

"Stephen, what are you doing here?" she asked surprised.

He was out of breath when he finally said, "I wondered where you got to."

"Was there something you wanted?" she asked.

"I was following up on a lead in town when I saw you heading this way and wanted to check you were alright." The detective looked at William and eyeing him suspiciously asked, "and you are?"

"Entertaining a young lady. Who might *you* be?"

"DI Cooke."

Amelia attempted to quash the frosty exchanges. "Stephen, this is William Malloy."

"Figures, if it's not one, it's the other. Amelia, do you know where—"

"No," she said raising her voice. "I do not know where he is."

Stephen turned to William. "Then would you mind if I asked you a few questions about a couple of incidents that occurred down at Creek Bay, Mr Malloy?"

"Not now, you will note that I am otherwise engaged," he said taking a step closer to Amelia, his body language taking ownership of her.

"You're a hard man to get hold of, I thought while you were here, may as well kill two birds with one stone."

"Detective," William said stepping forward. "We have all the time in the world to discuss whatever 'incidents' you are referring to, but right now, I would like time alone with Miss Scott." He turned and winked at her, then returned his gaze to the detective, his expression hardening. "So, unless you are going to arrest me, I believe we are free to go." He didn't wait for a response, he simply relinked his arm through Amelia's and walked away.

Stephen stood fuming clenching his fists, when his phone rang. "What?" He barked into the receiver. "Excellent, keep a tail, I'll be there soon." He snapped the phone shut with a heavy sigh watching Amelia and William disappear out of sight.

The afternoon was glorious; spending time with William was like watching time itself fall away, she never felt like she needed to be anywhere but there. He was a drug, an addictive drug, and deep down she knew there was something to be afraid of, but she couldn't for the world figure out why she would think such a thing; he had been nothing but a kind and generous gentleman.

They walked down to the lake where a young boy was feeding the ducks with his mother. Amelia stood watching as the boy threw bread and giggled at the ducks as they came closer to grab a piece. It made her wonder if she would ever do the same with her own child. Children. The thought had never actually crossed her mind before, she had been focused on her studies, and then it all fell apart when Jude and her father left her. No, children never even came into play, not even in her future with Tatem. She knew she definitely didn't want children with him, perhaps that should have been an alarm bell, an alarm she was stupid to ignore.

"Where are you Amelia Scott?" He whispered in her ear, his breath was hot and sweet as it trickled across her cheek.

She looked at the young boy laughing when the ducks took bread from his hand, and then turned to William. "I remember feeding ducks with my dad, seems like a lifetime ago." She tried not to dwell on those painful memories and pulled her gaze from the young family. "Do you have any family William?"

"Lots." He smiled, motioning to the bench beside them. "Here, sit."

She did as instructed and watched the steady ripples of the lake made by the ducks as they came closer to the edge ready for a bite to eat.

"Lots of family? You're very lucky," she said lost in thought.

He threw his head back and laughed, his hair cascading over the bench, and his deep rich brown eyes almost a honey brown colour in the sunlight. "If you say so."

They sat in silence watching people walk by, a mix of young and old couples, families, joggers; the town gardens were a well-attended leisure facility it would appear.

"Do you like it here Amelia Scott?" he asked quietly.

Taken aback by his question she had to think about it, did she like it here? She liked being next to William, she liked how he made her feel, but she liked to be around Seth, she wanted to sit there with Seth, enjoying the sunshine and feeding the ducks. Her head felt foggy again as thoughts of Seth ebbed away.

"I do like it here," she whispered.

"But?"

"But, it feels like there is something missing."

The young mother and her son had walked away, leaving little breadcrumbs for the ducks to finish off, a young woman on roller blades glided past making them scatter before returning to fight over the last remaining crumbs. Amelia felt William's hand on her back again.

"You can grow to love it, if you let it," he said softly.

Passion descended down to her loins, and she wet her lips, no, she couldn't, she simply couldn't, this wasn't what she wanted, or was it? Amelia quickly stood wiping her clammy hands on her pants.

"I've had a lovely day today William, and thank you so much for the generous gift, but I really must be getting back," she said stepping away.

He stood slowly from the bench never taking his eyes off her; in the blink of an eye, he was standing beside her, pulling her close just in time to avoid a cyclist.

"I'm sorry," she said thankful he had seen the danger.

"Don't ever be sorry Amelia," he said returning to the bench and picking up her bags.

Watching him walk away, she was certain she had heard those words somewhere before, try as she may, she couldn't remember who had said them.

"Here." He held out the three bags. "These are yours I believe."

"Thank you," she said taking the bags from him.

They walked in relative closeness back to the bike, but she wouldn't touch him, she couldn't allow him to link his arm with hers. The black bike shone in the bright sun, two teenagers approached admiring the machine but quickened their pace when they saw William and Amelia.

"Back home, or to the shop?" he asked pulling the bike off the footrest.

Amelia watched him jump on the bike bringing it spluttering to life. She felt drained, what she needed more than anything right now was rest. "Home. Please."

Gathering the bags together she crammed everything into one and placed them between her and William, thankful for some distance between them, but she had to put her arms around him so she didn't fall off. Wrapping her arms around his waist, William placed his hand gently over hers, radiating a warmth she hadn't felt in a long time, clasping her other hand over his she gently squeezed and leant onto his back as he drove off. They arrived at the cottage far too quickly for her liking and when she slid off the back she felt a loss that she hadn't felt before. William watched as Amelia turned the key to unlock the door, once she was in the house he turned and drove away.

All in all it had been a funny old day, which she put down to being out of sorts, and not quite with it, her head still woozy. Amelia climbed the stairs, dropped the shopping bags onto the floor and threw herself onto the bed. Muscles finally relaxing she recounted her day with William. There was no denying that she had enjoyed spending time with him, so why did she feel like she was betraying Seth? He had told her to keep her distance, but wouldn't explain why, and he constantly disappeared leaving her in the lurch and for some reason the police are continuously on his case. Perhaps it was Seth that was the bad seed, not William.

She closed her weary eyes and tried to rest, letting thoughts of Seth enter her subconscious. Who was he, really? From the day she first met him he had been cagey about a lot of things, or perhaps that was the attraction. Did she really want to throw herself into another relationship so soon after Tatem? Not that she had seen him in that sense for the last three months of their relationship, she contemplated the use of the word relationship, it hadn't been one, not really.

Playing it safe with Tate, they were both a convenience to one another, that's all it was, that's all it ever was, and she should have left well alone. Maybe that's what she thought she needed now, someone totally different, a risk-taker, who didn't do things by the book. A bad boy who would have her mother shaking her head and worrying what she was up to. No, she would never do that to her mother, not intentionally anyway. Or was Seth a victim of circumstance, maybe she wouldn't be swooning over him if he hadn't of saved her life that day at the beach, thinking about it, it could quite easily have been Ned that got to her first. Would she have the same thoughts about him? But William was a true gentleman, and there was something about him that she was madly drawn to. So maybe it was Seth playing the jealous would-be boyfriend, or maybe he knew something about William she didn't.

The Solomon and Malloy families had a chequered history by all accounts, of that she were certain. Poor Lois, what had she and Charles seen in the cottage on that fateful day that had her running scared?

Exhausted, Amelia closed her eyes and tried to think about happier times, anything that didn't make her head swirl.

# *chaptra pymthek*

*T*he red-head ran as fast as her legs would carry her, but they were on
her heels, snarling and snapping their jaws at her ankles. Makeup
smeared her pretty young face; she was just a shadow of her former
'Miss High School' glory days. Tripping and falling onto the sodden ground
she wept into her hands praying for forgiveness, praying it would all be a
dream. "Bless me father for I have sinned."
Large canine teeth flashed before her, then all was silent.

Amelia awoke, her hand instinctively grabbing her neck. She had
never had a such a vivid dream like it before; *she* was Valerie, and she
was the one being attacked. Her fingers traced her neck, thankfully her
throat was intact and it had all been a dream, so lifelike, but a dream
nonetheless. She turned over and picked up her mobile, no missed calls,
no text messages. Sunday and the birds obviously didn't understand the
concept of a lie in, their songs spoke of a new day and no time to waste
it lying in bed, but she could quite happily stay in bed today. The week
had been a roller-coaster at best; a young girl dead, one missing and poor
Lois. What had happened to the quiet coastal life she had expected? The
birds were relentless in their song, and trying to block it out was useless,
Amelia decided it was time to peel herself off the bed and take a long
soak. As she stumbled by the bags on the floor, she picked up the camping
bag and pulled out the evening gown William had bought for her; she
wasn't entirely certain when he expected her to wear it. Holding the dress
against her body she absentmindedly felt the smooth material against her
body, remembering how it had looked on, how William bent down and
kissed her, closing her eyes she could feel him close to her, the dress smelt
of him, he was all around her. The landline phone rang with a relentless
loud piercing sound, laying the dress on the bed she leapt down the stairs
to answer the phone before it rang off.

"Hello?"

"Miss Amelia Scott?"

"Yes."

"My name is Derek Smythe, HR consultant at Langley Library. You
have an appointment tomorrow morning and I was just ringing to see if
you were still attending."

She had totally forgotten Tate had arranged an interview for her at
the central library, part of some relocation-type deal he had with the

contractors. "Right, sorry, Mr Smythe. Things have been a little hectic since I moved. What time was the appointment again?"

"Ten-thirty at the Regional Suite. Will you be joining us?"

Amelia pondered whether or not she should go now that she already had a job at the bookshop, one she was growing to love, and then she wondered if she would still like working there if Seth wasn't around as much as she hoped. Her father would not have been best pleased about her holding on to a job because of a boy.

"Sure. I'll be there. Would you be able to email me the directions again, I'm afraid I have still not unpacked and I couldn't find my personnel files."

It was a total lie, Tatem had arranged the meeting, he had all the information and paperwork relating to the interview. If she were to go through with it, would it seem as though he was still active in her life and that she owed him a great debt for getting her the job; or was she just reaching?

"Of course, what is your email address?"

As she rhymed off the address, he promised to send through the details of the library and a location map. Amelia couldn't believe she was really going through with it. She wanted to speak to Seth in person rather than a phone call or text about having time off, and knowing the shop opened slightly later on Sundays she took the opportunity to catch up on some TV programmes she had recorded that week.

By the time she arrived at the store the lights were on inside and she could just make out some movement in the rear. Opening the door, she prayed it would be Seth.

"You're an early bird," said Daniel from the mezzanine floor.

He was replacing the covers and cushions on the loveseat. Seth's comment about he and Sonny not being domesticated resonated with her.

"Hey," she called up to him, craning her neck to see who had disappeared into the back room. "Is Seth with you?"

Daniel whistled, and when she heard someone banging around in the back room and footsteps approach, her heart quickened with the anticipation of Seth coming around the corner. Her smile faded when Sonny approached.

"Mornin me bewty, what can I do for you?" He was carrying a tray of mugs fresh from the dishwasher, the steam and lemon fragrance filled the room.

"I'm looking for Seth, have you seen him?"

Sonny continued to the counter putting the tray of crockery on the top, and began unloading the contents.

"Nope. He was supposed to see us last night, but—" There was a loud cough from above making Sonny stop mid sentence.

Amelia frowned. "Well, if you see him, I need to ask a huge favour."

"Oh?" Sonny leaned forward, his dreadlocks touching the counter. "What favour would that be?"

"I need to take some time off on Monday."

"Sure that's fine. We'll sort out the store." When the last mug had been put away he picked up the tray and walked back towards the storeroom.

Amelia followed him. "Don't you need to ask Seth first? I mean, he is—"

Sonny turned around. "Amelia, it's fine, really."

"Then it's okay for me to take time off?" she asked.

Sonny carried on walking to the back room leaving the tray next to the sink. "Sure. Dan and I are happy to cover for you."

"I heard that!" shouted Daniel.

"He didn't say where he was going then?" she whispered.

Sonny shrugged and started to walk back to the counter, but stopped when she touched his arm.

"Is he in trouble?" she asked.

His smile was like sunshine, perfect golden complexion framing his youthful face. "Whatever gave you that idea?"

She let her hand drop. "Just that Detective Cooke has this idea that he is somehow involved, with Valerie and Julia, and when I asked Seth he was distant about it."

"If the police were sniffing around you, everyone pointing the finger, wouldn't you want to get away for some peace and quiet?"

"Well, yeah, but I wouldn't run if I was innocent."

Sonny came closer to her, his eyes losing their sparkle. "What makes you think he's guilty?"

"I don't, it's just… he wouldn't have to stay away if he had nothing to hide."

He was bearing down on her now, making her back up to the sink.

"That's enough Sonny." Daniel stood in the doorway, his arms folded and stern expression gave him an air of authority over the younger man. "You're welcome to your time off on Monday, Amelia. Why don't you go and spend your day off doing something leisurely?"

She slid away from the sink, eyeing Sonny warily. "I'll do that."

As she left the bookshop she overheard Sonny say to Daniel, "She reeks of him."

Amelia left the store in what could only be described as a foul mood. Sonny wasn't supposed to be the grumpy one, that position was reserved for Daniel. Her frown creased deeper as she found herself annoyed and frustrated when she bumped into Mr Bateman sweeping the path outside his shop.

"Morning Amelia. Everything okay?" he asked pleasantly.

She mumbled a good morning and then continued on her way, wandering aimlessly around the village green and finally sat on a bench watching the birds pick berries from the ground. A white light drew her attention to the backrest, the sun reflecting upon a piece of shiny metal embedded in the wooden bench, she hadn't noticed the plaque before and turned to read the inscription, '*In honour of our fallen WHM.*' Lost in thought, she heard raised voices and turned to see Daniel in the street talking to a man with platinum-blonde hair; he was tall, matching Daniel in height but appeared much stockier. She couldn't quite hear what they were arguing about and curiosity getting the better of her, she stood to get a better look. The sound of sirens in the distance became louder and the two men stopped arguing and departed. The 4x4 that flew past belonged to Stephen, he pulled up outside the bookshop wound down his window and began talking to Daniel, the conversation was brief before he sped off down the road. Mr Bateman continued his sweeping, eyeing Daniel as he went back inside the bookshop, just as two teenagers raced towards the middle-aged shopkeeper.

"There you are, you were supposed to start your paper-round fifteen minutes ago," Mr Bateman scolded. Amelia made her way across the road to the shop, hoping Mr Bateman had overheard the detective's conversation. "Come on, you can start now before I decide to dock your wages." As he turned to go inside the shop one of the young boys nudged the other. "What's wrong now?" he asked.

"Haven't you heard?" one of the boys began.

"Heard what?" asked Amelia as she approached.

The young boys eyes almost bulged out of his head. "They've found Julia."

"Where?"

"Old Man Malloy's place."

She ran off before either of the boys could finish their story. Old Man Malloy's held pieces to a mystery that the police just weren't putting together. She recalled it was also a connection to Seth, and not just to Seth, but also William. As she ran past the bookshop Daniel stood watching from inside.

The sirens sounded as though they were heading away from the village. Amelia wondered if Stephen would tell her what was going on if she asked, or would it land her in trouble for interfering with a police investigation? She had to get to Seth's cottage and find out more about her boss. Amelia quickened her pace, hoping Stephen wasn't heading that way.

The ground was relatively dry, apart from the morning dew, which wetted the bottoms of her trousers, she continued down the long winding lane to Holly Cottage, stopping when she could make out the distinctive white colour of the building. No police cars, no sirens, no Seth; his camper van was parked outside, which meant he wasn't down at the surf. Amelia took a couple of deep breaths proceeding down the lane. A large pile of wood was stacked high against the lean-to garage and beside that was his bike. Walking to the side of the building she could see a faint light, she continued to the front of the cottage and knocked on the door, which opened with little contact. Gently pushing the door open wider, she called out his name but there was no answer. The house was silent and she felt like an intruder wandering around his home without him, she called out his name again, waiting for his response; but there was no answer. She peered into the kitchen, spotlessly clean but for the small milk pan on the stove with half a tin of baked beans simmering away. She turned the hob off and when she called out again she heard a thud coming from below. Amelia stopped to listen, slowly walking towards the area the sound came from and waited for another sound. She opened the pantry door revealing nothing but shelves on all three walls with produce ranging from tinned and packet food to fresh vegetables. With a heavy sigh Amelia began to close the door when a faint strip of light at the bottom of the skirting board caught her attention. She tried to pull the shelves towards her in a bid to open the hidden door, but it was solid. Footsteps pounded echoing around the empty house, a shadow flitted across the light as the person approached. She was trapped with no way out, not knowing how she could explain being there. The shelving moved towards her and she found herself pinned against the opposite wall. Seth stepped out of the darkness, his brow wetted and face dirty.

"Amelia," he said breathlessly.

Fear and dread filled her core, she knew she shouldn't be there, and whatever was hidden beyond that wall was not for her to see.

"What are you—" she tried to see beyond him, but it was too dark.

"Nothing for you to worry about." Seth started walking towards her, making her step further backwards, but there was nowhere else for her to go, the shelving dug into her back.

"I've been looking for you," she started to say, but her mouth became unexpectedly dry.

"You found me."

"What were you doing down there?" she asked. A strange smell wafted from him, of damp woods and earth; a smell she remembered from the night of the search party. Sirens sounded in the distance. "Oh my god, its Julia, isn't it?" Amelia tried to push past him, "Julia!" she cried out.

Seth grabbed her arm. "What are you doing?" he growled.

Her eyes went wide with fear, worried she had let her judgment get clouded, hating that she was sucked in by his charm.

Seth glanced back into the room and then at Amelia. "What did you want?" he asked hurriedly.

"I wanted to know you were okay. I heard about Julia, wanted to make sure Stephen wasn't giving you a hard time." She felt the shelf dig further into her back as she tried to move away from him. Looking down at his shirt she saw red smears, her eyes widened. "Is that blood?"

His nostrils flared with annoyance as he stepped closer still. "You better leave," he said dryly.

Seth had taken on a whole different persona, he wasn't the carefree happy young man she first met, he had become tense and secretive and it worried her.

There was a loud banging on the front door. "Seth Solomon."

Amelia turned to the sound of salvation; there was no doubting that was Detective Inspector Cooke's voice.

Closing the hidden door, Seth grabbed her arm and moved Amelia out of the pantry and into the kitchen. "Go, now, you'll only make things worse if he finds you here." His fingers were digging into her flesh as he tried to get her to leave quickly.

"You know I can help you, if you just let me," she whispered.

"Seth Solomon, we have a warrant for your arrest." His voice was louder this time as he stepped into the lounge.

Seth let go of her arm and walked to the front door, three officers forced Seth to his knees, and cuffed his hands behind his back. The detective moved towards him, and once restrained, cautioned him for Julia's murder.

Stephen stepped closer to Seth, "You're going down Solomon."

Seth balled his fists to stop himself from lashing out.

"Take him away," Stephen nodded to the officers.

With his prisoner safely escorted out of the cottage and into the van, the detective stood with hands on hips looking around the living room. Pulling crime scene gloves from his pocket he slowly put them on as he walked around the room looking for evidence of Julia and Valerie, anything that would prove his involvement beyond doubt. He opened and closed drawers, slamming them shut, picked up books and shook them for loose pages to fall out, so far he was drawing a blank.

Amelia watched from behind the old log store at the side of the house, as she stretched to see inside a log fell off the top. She ducked down before he saw her; footsteps drew near as the detective walked into the kitchen towards the sound. She hoped he wouldn't look outside, not before she could make her getaway, and she really didn't want to explain to him what she was doing at Seth's cottage or that she saw the arrest. If she weren't careful he would be trying to pin the murders on her as well. Detective Inspector Cooke turned and opened the pantry door, Amelia held her hand over her mouth and waited as he picked up a few packets of foodstuff, sniffed them and then closed the door. Amelia began to relax back down behind the logs and continued to watch him through the window. When the detective disappeared from view she decided to run for cover amongst the trees.

From behind a large oak tree she watched the cottage; lights went on in various rooms as the detective moved about the cottage, his shadow betraying his location behind the closed curtains.

She crouched behind the tree peering around the trunk when he opened a set of curtains at the top floor window, hands on hips and a puzzled expression. When he turned away from the window and the light went out, she realized this was her opportunity to get away.

Amelia headed due West from the cottage into dense forest. With no track to keep to, she would have to remember how far she had come before starting to head towards the road over the pasture land which she hoped would lead her to the village. The night of the search party seemed a long time ago, but she was certain she recalled parts of open areas; it was then she remembered the map Ned had handed to the detective. She had been given it being the only one unfamiliar with the area. The map was crinkled having been stuffed in her combats all this time, but she managed to flatten it out and pin point Holly Cottage. She remembered Ned telling her Old Man Malloy's was just further down, between Holly Cottage and The Mansion. Turning the map around placing Holly

Cottage at the bottom she could make out the lane she needed to get onto which would take her back home. But it didn't seem that far to Old Man Malloy's from her current location and with everyone talking about it, curiosity got the better of her.

That decision was fast becoming a nightmare; the terrain was boggy in parts, even though there had been little rain during the week, the soft ground was treacherous as she struggled to keep her footing. A crow flew overhead squawking loudly making her jump and drop the map. As she bent to retrieve the map, something sparkling on the ground caught her attention. She pulled the thin chain attached to a pendant from the forest debris; if she wasn't mistaken it was a St. Christopher. The chain was lightweight, possibly for a child or a woman, she turned over the pendant to look for an inscription, but found none and so put it into her pocket to show Stephen later in case it had belonged to either of the girls.

She continued walking in the direction of Old Man Malloy's when the clearing in front of her looked familiar. It was where they ended up the night they were looking for Julia. The teenagers thought Valerie had been found on Trembleath Moor, but it was Stephen that mentioned Old Man Malloy's, and now, Julia's body had been found here, and Seth was under arrest for her murder. She wondered if her decision to be out there alone was a wise one after all.

In the distance she heard voices, faint at first until she quietly made her way around the outcrop and down behind the dense shrubs. Two men in white CSI coveralls and masks were bent over a mound of earth, a uniformed police officer stood next to them taking notes. One of the men in white was taking photographs while the other took measurements; and to think this is where they had been standing only days ago, not knowing that a few days later it would become the young girl's shallow grave. The police officer pulled out a blue and white roll of tape from his bag and walked to the edge of the clearing. He tied the crime scene warning tape around the nearest tree and proceeded to encircle the area. Distracted by the two men next to the body Amelia moved further down to get a better look.

"These are much older," one of the men said.

The other man stopped taking pictures. "We'll take these down to the lab and get an analysis of age and sex, see if we can ID them from dental records."

"Not for this poor sod," said the young man bent down holding up a skull. Amelia gasped. "Teeth have been removed, or taken by scavengers. We've no idea how long these have been here, anything could have had a go and taken them away."

The second man stood back looking at the pictures he had taken on the camera screen. "Hang on a minute."

He pointed to the area behind the man crouched down. "That's where we found the first one right?" The young man nodded. "And over there," he said pointing to the left, "there were three more. Yes?" He started to walk north of the digging area. "I wonder." He bent down and started to pull back the dirt with his hands. "I thought so."

"What is it?" asked the young man.

"I think we need to get the whole team up here," he said standing. "We've got ourselves a mass grave dating back centuries."

Amelia gasped.

"What are you doing here young lady?" asked the policeman standing over her.

Amelia had forgotten about the officer putting up the tape and went for the little girl lost look. "I was out for a run, and got lost, heard voices and—"

"You're hardly dressed for a run." He said looking down at her outfit and lack of running shoes.

"Spur of the moment thing," she said smiling.

"Come on," he said holding out his hand. "I'll give you a lift back to the main road, this is no place to be out on your own."

She had seen him before, maybe outside the bookshop when Lois was taken away, and she was grateful that she didn't have to make sense of that stupid map again. Amelia gave one last look at the site where the forensic team were busy putting markers out over the spots where they had found remains, there seemed far too many of those little yellow pegs.

The police officer escorted her back to Holly Cottage where a frustrated DI Cooke was pacing the driveway, when he saw his officer with Amelia he folded his arms.

"Found this one wandering near Malloy's," the officer said as they approached the tree line.

Amelia stepped forward. "Actually, I was out for a run and found myself at the mercy of nature." The detective looked at her footwear with raised eyebrow. Okay, maybe running in Doc Martens wasn't everyone's first choice of suitable footwear. "It was a spur of the moment thing, you know, nice day, loose end and all that."

"Amelia," Stephen said holding out his arm, she went to him as he put his arm around her shoulder. "Can you tell me something? Something truthful."

She nodded. "Of course."

"Did you see Seth today?"

His eyes did that intense police thing again, the type of look that made her mouth go dry and worry he could actually read minds.

"I think I saw him," she said meekly.

"Where did you see him? Out there?" Stephen pointed to the trees referring to the woods.

"No. I think he was in the back of a police car."

Stephen let his arm drop off her shoulder. "Really? You saw that from all the way back there?" His tone suggested he did not believe her.

"Well, it was from quite a distance, I couldn't be certain. You see, I started my walk over the pasture, you know, from the lane, and when I saw the lights, I turned to see the car fly past and was sure it was him in the back." Now it was her turn to give him the stare. "Have you arrested him?"

The uniformed officer's radio crackled, he turned away holding the radio to his ear listening to his colleagues.

"Seth Solomon has been arrested," he said.

"For?"

"The murder of Julia Bent."

Amelia had to pretend she didn't know, and hoped her surprised voice didn't give her away. "You found Julia? Where?"

"Miss Scott, I have no time for your games, you know exactly where we found that poor girl, in fact, I would like you to come down to the station and give me your statement of events over the last week. It seems death has a funny way of following you around."

"What?" Amelia shrieked. "Are you serious?" He escorted her to his vehicle, opening the door and motioning her to get inside. "You can't believe I had anything to do with what has been going on in this village. I've only just got here."

"And things have only just started to happen, funny coincidence don't you think. Get in." His face was stern and unforgiving.

She put one foot on the footrest and then turned. "Are you arresting me?"

"You are helping us with our investigation. And I may remind you that if you fail to—"

"Yeah, yeah," she said climbing in.

# chaptra hwetek

T he duty officer finished booking Seth as two officers escorted him down towards the cells awaiting interview when the detective walked into the reception with Amelia.

Seth turned sharply catching sight of her before turning the corner and struggled to free himself. "Amelia, what are you doing—"

The officers fought to restrain him while they pushed him along towards the cell. She could hear Seth shouting her name as he disappeared through a set of doors.

"Interview Room 2 free Charlie?" asked Stephen.

The duty officer nodded. "Sure, who should I put in the book?"

DI Cooke took Amelia by her elbow and led her through to the corridor. "Miss Amelia Scott will be helping us with our enquiries."

The three-meter-square room felt claustrophobic with the table and two chairs occupying most of the space, adding people made the room feel even smaller. There was a digital device for recording interrogations attached to the wall with an omni directional microphone set in the middle of the table. The inspector checked the device before sitting down opposite her.

"Amelia."

"Stephen."

Amelia and Stephen sat staring at one another, one desperate for knowledge, the other waiting for a piece of information to nail the bad guy. She kept telling herself not to let him get to her.

"Are you ready to tell me the truth Amelia?" Stephen asked sitting back in his chair, arms folded, looking so bored he didn't seem to have the strength to talk anymore.

"Always," she said with raised brow.

The detective leant forward and clicked on the machine. "DI Cooke interview with Miss Amelia Scott thirteenth of June at eleven fifteen."

The ticking of the office style clock on the wall seemed fade as the interview started, she watched the hands moving painfully slow around the face, counting the hours, minutes and seconds of her incarceration.

The detective pulled out a buff coloured file and placed it in front of him on the table, reams of paper lay loose inside, she could make out writing and diagrams and maps, even some pictures, some pictures she didn't want to see. The detective sifted through some pages and finally spoke.

"Amelia Scott, you have willingly accepted this interview to help us in our investigation into the murders of Miss Valerie Temple and Miss Julia Bent."

She nodded.

"For the recording."

Clearing her throat, Amelia leant forward towards the microphone on the desk. "Yes."

The voice that came out was not a confidant voice, not Amelia's voice, it was someone else speaking for her.

"You arrived in Creek Bay on Sunday evening, that was the… sixth of June, is that correct?" he asked.

"Yes."

"Is that when you first met Seth Solomon?"

"Yes."

So far so good, she was answering his questions truthfully, and she wasn't giving anything away, even started to sound a little like herself again. Amelia began to relax back into her chair when there was a knock at the door. A uniformed officer walked in with two cups of coffee, fresh from the vending machine.

"PC Ellis has entered the room with refreshments for Detective Inspector Cooke and Miss Amelia Scott."

She assumed the running commentary was for the benefit of the recording, and gratefully accepted the hot beverage handed to her. The officer then left the room.

"PC Ellis has left the room. Tell me Amelia, what was your first impression of Seth Solomon?"

That was a question she felt she could almost certainly answer truthfully. "He saved my life. I certainly couldn't think anything bad of him."

"Some might say that has clouded your judgment of him."

"People like you perhaps Detective Inspector?" she took a sip of the syrupy hot drink, the sharp undertone flavours making her recoil.

"He is also your boss at The Bay Book Shop, is that correct?"

She gave him a knowing smile. "Yes. Yes, Seth is my boss, he saved me from the quicksand, I find him attractive, some may say that has clouded my judgment, but I ask you this," she said leaning forward over the table. "If you ask anyone here in the village, they will all say the same, Seth is a good man. He helps out at the coastguard, he works with the local community, helps the school children—"

"Arh, thank you for bringing that up." He interrupted. "That leads me onto my next question. Were you aware that Seth was tutoring both Valerie and Julia?"

"Not until you told me."

"Don't you find that a bit odd?" he asked sarcastically.

"Not really, no. I've only been here a week, why would he give me his life story?"

The detective leaned forward almost touching her arm. "Don't you think it odd that he was tutoring straight-A students?"

Amelia shrugged. "Depends what he was teaching!"

The detective fell back into his chair. "Music."

Amelia laughed. "Music? You've arrested him for teaching them music? Are you insane?"

Stephen sat forward and pulled out a couple of pictures from the file, both graphically told the story of how the girls met their untimely demise and it was not pretty.

Amelia closed her eyes unable to look at the pictures. "Whatever happened to these poor girls was not at the hand of Seth Solomon."

"How can you be so sure?"

"I don't know, I just know." She raised her voice in an attempt to make him understand. "All I can say is this, those two girls were involved in something, something that Lois knew about, and you know what happened to her."

The detective narrowed his eyes. "Pathologist said it was a heart attack."

"Oh? Brought on by what?" She started to tap the table top, "Valerie and Julia found out a secret, something the villagers are desperate to keep under wraps, something that sent Lois bonkers way back when, turning her into a paranoid old woman, and I don't know why, but I know for sure it was nothing to do with Seth."

The detective looked down at the two pictures rubbing the days old stubble on his chin. "The relationship between you and Seth, would you call it a work relationship?"

Amelia sighed. "In that he is my boss and I am his employee."

The questions were becoming tiresome for Amelia, and the god-awful coffee was not helping, nor the florescent lights that stung her tired eyes.

"What would you say your relationship is with William Malloy?"

"William?" she whispered. "What has he got to do with this?"

"What is your relationship with Mr Malloy?"

"That is none of your goddamn business. I thought you wanted to talk about Valerie and Julia."

"Indeed. What were you doing at Old Man Malloy's today?"

"I told you, I was taking some fresh air, came across the crime scene."

"And you often take walks out there alone do you?"

"Actually, you were the first person to take me there Stephen, and today is the second time I have been out there, so no, I do not make a habit of it."

There was banging outside in the corridor and shuffle of feet as a struggle ensued with a new detainee.

"Are we done here?" she asked taking a gulp of her coffee.

"One more thing. Lois Chandler. What was it that you two last spoke about before she passed away?"

Amelia looked down at the chipped table top, Lois' face came into her mind, how happy she looked when she was talking about Charles, then how sad and worried she was talking about the cottage and what they both saw.

"Lois was talking about her past, you know how old people do, she was telling me about the love of her life."

The detective pulled out a piece of paper from his file. "Mr Charles Lane, born 1914 died 1940."

She nodded. "I believe so."

"They spent as little as two years together. Do you really think he was the love of her life?"

"Where is your sense of romance Stephen? It was long enough for them to enjoy one another, and she has never forgotten him, hell, she even wrote that book in his name, how much more can that tell you?"

"And there was nothing else, nothing at all that she said before you left her alone upstairs?"

Amelia closed her eyes. "Nothing."

She heard the movement of paper again. "Because I have my notes here that say you mentioned something about what she saw that terrified her."

Her stomach flinched, she had forgotten telling him about that. "Yes, but I got called away downstairs, so never did find out what she meant. Part of me thought it was just kooky old Lois Chandler, you know. I wonder if whatever terrified her, actually came back."

"What do you mean?" he whispered.

Raised voices and thuds outside the room got the attention of the detective who decided to cut the interview short. "Interview terminated at eleven forty-five morning of the thirteenth of June."

He switched off the machine and gathered his papers, when the noise outside started to become raucous. "Excuse me Amelia," he said stepping out of the room.

The room was silent without the two of them talking. The file in front of her was far too tempting not to take a peek, opening the buff folder she saw the white papers sketched in black ink and pulled them aside to reveal the two case profile pictures of Valerie Temple and Julia Bent, the ones they use for press shots. Amelia frowned sliding the file closer, she turned it right way up and looked down at the two girls. She had seen both of them, so clearly in fact, but not on the street, not in the bookshops, but in her dreams, and they had been petrified. How could she be dreaming about these two girls when she had never even met them, not even once, not even their pictures on the news. The interview room door opened and Stephen shouted an order to his officers, Amelia quickly moved the file back where she had found it before he walked back into the room and took the seat opposite her.

"Sorry about that. Your boyfriend's causing my officers some trouble."

"He's not my boyfriend," she said, though she wished she could call him such. "What has he done now?"

"Nothing for you to worry about." He pulled the file towards him. "Now, about Lois."

"Don't you need to switch that on?" she asked nodding to the machine.

Stephen smiled. "I'm not trying to catch you out Amelia. You offered to look through that book for me and found a couple of interesting facts about Solomon and Malloy but something you said about Lois being terrified has got me thinking."

"What?"

"I don't know, I need to have a look at the book for myself. Do you still have it?"

"Yes, it's at home."

"Good." He stood putting the paperwork under his arm. "Then I will give you a lift back and have a look at that book if you don't mind."

Amelia slowly stood. There was nothing in that book that mentioned Seth had anything to do with it, she was certain, as she thought about it some more she couldn't remember what it was she had been researching. Charles Lane, yes, but Solomon and Malloy, what was it that she had found?

"Sure, you can have my notes too if you like."

If she showed him she had nothing to hide, then she wouldn't end up in a cell next to Seth.

Amelia sat in reception waiting for Stephen to emerge from his room. Inside, the duty sergeant stood beside his superior.

"Let me know if Mr Solomon gets a call from his lawyer."

The Sergeant nodded. "And Miss Scott?"

Stephen stood from his desk, car keys in his hand. "I think she knows something she's not letting on."

"Seems pleasant enough to me boss."

"The boyfriend abandoning her and the new job the second she rolls into the village. I'm not buying it. Find out what you can about the boyfriend, maybe he can shed some light on all of this."

The Sergeant nodded, opened the door and watched him walk out of the station with Amelia.

Detective Inspector Cooke pulled up outside Lowe Cottage and sat looking out to the empty lane. The movement of the car jerking when Amelia slammed the door shut broke his concentration.

"Come in," she called opening the front door. A cold chill filled the air; she told herself she really needed an engineer to look at that heater. "Go through to the lounge, the book is in my bedroom."

Amelia ran up the stairs tripping over the last step into the bedroom and frantically began searching for the book, trying to remember where she had it last. She checked the usual places; it wasn't on her bed so she pulled the bed covers back, it hadn't slipped underneath, and it wasn't under her pillow or on the nightstand. Turning around she went to the dressing table and stopped when she noticed her trinket box had been moved. She always kept it closed and the clasp had been partially opened. She lifted the lid, all seemed to be present and correct. Amelia went back to her search and knelt down looking under the bed to see if the book had fallen onto the floor, but it was not there either, the only other place she could think she left it was the lounge.

"Did you find it?" he asked as she darted past him.

"No. I swear I put it in the bedroom," she said moving cushions from the sofa and sliding her hand between the seats. Walking into the kitchen she stopped mid-stride, a ring of daisies had been left on the tabletop, the sight of which made her blood run cold.

"Something wrong Amelia?" he asked.

The last person in the cottage was Seth but she couldn't tell Stephen, he would charge him with unlawful entry on top of murder, she tried to compose herself.

"Everything is fine. I must have left it at the bookshop."

"That's not a problem. I will pop round there now. Who is looking after the store today?"

"Sonny," she answered, lost in thought.

"Great. Well at least it isn't the other one." He started to walk back through the lounge and called out. "I'll see myself out."

She heard the opening and closing of the front door and engine of his car as he drove away. Picking up the daisy-chain she looked at the fresh flowers which hadn't long been picked. She wondered who had access to Lowe Cottage other than herself and although it sounded far-fetched, she considered her ex might be playing mind games. Checking the back door was locked and the window hadn't been forced she went into the lounge and checked the front window, but all seemed perfectly normal. She felt dirty in her own home, someone had been inside, moving and touching her belongings and it had tainted her sanctuary; she had to get out.

Picking up her bag she opted for a walk to the village and by the time she arrived at the bookshop DI Cooke was leaving, making her wonder if he managed to find the book after all.

"You're back." Daniel greeted her, moving the large box from the counter.

"Yeah, went for a walk, feel better for it."

"And I take it you've heard?" he put a beer on the counter and opened the cap.

She took the beer and sat on the barstool. "About Julia?" she whispered trying to avoid the other customers overhearing.

"Seth."

"Yeah. I heard," she said mournfully. "I saw."

Daniel stopped wiping the glass and placed it down on the counter. "Really? When? Where?"

"You know," she took a sip of the beer. "At his place."

"You were…" he looked up at the mezzanine floor. "Today?"

"Yes, today, just before he was arrested."

"Interesting," he muttered. Picking up the glass he continued rubbing it dry with the towel. "And did you speak with the detective?"

Amelia put the beer down. "I went for a walk, didn't want to get involved, but that was short-lived when I saw—"

She knew she had his attention when he leaned towards her over the counter and whispered, "What? What did you see?"

"Nothing. I headed back to Holly Cottage, that's when I bumped into the detective and he invited me to the station to answer a few questions."

"About?"

"Oh, you know, the usual." She took a long gulp of beer this time. "Seth, Lois, Valerie, Julia… William."

"William?" it was almost a growl, making Amelia pause when she turned in her seat.

"Yes, William." The look he gave her suggested he knew him, and he wasn't a fan either. "Seth doesn't much care for him either. What is it with you guys? Weren't you once friends?"

"Who told you that? William?" Daniel was giving her the steely look, the one where she felt he could see all the way through her brain.

"No, just an observation," she said avoiding eye contact.

Sonny peered over the banister above them, "Daniel, could you come here a sec?"

Daniel walked slowly up the stairs keeping his gaze focused on Amelia. She decided that he was odd, really odd. One minute he was okay and she could find herself enjoying being around him, and the next he totally blew it with his arrogant, surly manner. She could hear Sonny and Daniel conversing, Sonny obviously trying to make Daniel control his temper. All three of them acted weird at times, yet for some reason, she felt quite at ease in their company. Her phone vibrated in her pocket, pulling it out she read the incoming text, 'Malcolm taking me out for dinner, text if you need me.' At least someone was having a good time. She closed the message and put the phone back in her pocket when she saw Sonny looking over the banister, his blonde dreads flowing over his face.

"Hey, Amelia. Would you mind popping up for a minute?" His smile was the usual sweet smile and he showed no signs of his previous outburst. Amelia nodded and took the stairs one at a time keeping her gaze on both Sonny and Daniel, who was now sitting on the arm of the loveseat.

"Please, take a seat," Daniel gestured to the seat next to him.

She sat down in the furthest corner possible to avoid being too close to either of them.

"You saw Seth earlier?" Sonny asked.

Amelia nodded. "Yes, before he was arrested."

Daniel and Sonny looked at one another. "And he didn't mention anything, anything at all?" Sonny was doing his best not to frown she could tell by the slight crease at the bridge of his nose.

"No, he was taken before we could really talk, he was down the basement and…" She stopped talking when she saw their expressions.

"And then what happened?" asked Daniel.

"Then the police came and took him away."

"Did you see William today?" Sonny's nose was flaring as he spoke, bearing his teeth as though he could smell the man.

"Not today, no." Amelia shifted uncomfortably on the seat.

"But you *have* spent time with him?" Daniel said leaning towards her.

The frown she gave them both was reactive to his body language, but her tone was pure annoyance, "What if I have?" Her gaze flitted between both men. Standing, she wiped her pants free of lint from the newly washed covers and started towards the stairs. "I have to get off now. I'll be opening the store as usual tomorrow."

"What about your day off?" asked Sonny.

Amelia stopped at the top step. "Oh yes, I forgot about that. I'll be back mid-afternoon for Book Worm Club, with Seth not—" She couldn't finish that sentence. "Besides, there is no reason why the children go without."

She continued walking down the stairs waiting for one or both of them to shout after her, but they didn't, so she quickened her pace and left the store before they changed their minds.

It was plain to see that none of them liked William, which meant she would have to look for that bloody book and her notes to remember what it was that caught her attention in the first place; they were all connected somehow. Walking down the lane she passed Mr Bateman who told her about Julia being found and that the police were doing more investigation work at Old Man Malloy's, nothing she didn't already know, but when he mentioned Brendan and Shaun hadn't turned up for their shift at the corner shop that got her wondering whether they were running scared, or maybe they too had fallen foul of whatever was going on. They were, after all, the only other people she knew who were connected to Valerie, Julia and that book.

She hurried along to Lowe Cottage and slammed the door shut bolting it tightly. The feel of the place was still strange after someone had been in, but telling DI Cooke would just make matters worse. Checking the back door and noting it bolted and secure she went up stairs and started looking for the book again, pulling boxes out from under her bed, paperwork fell to the floor in a heap. She pulled off the duvet and covers underneath, exhausted and frustrated Amelia threw the box of paperwork to one side and ran herself a hot bath. As she waited for the bath to fill, she sat on the rattan chair pulling the t-shirt over her head and letting it drop to the floor, as she bent down to pull off her socks something caught her eye, a piece of paper lay underneath the roll-top bath. Kneeling on all fours she pulled out the paper and unfolded it. It was written in her hand. In bigger letters at the bottom were the words 'Seth = Setali Setali = Seth' followed by a question mark. It was coming back to her, she was sure Seth was named after Setali Solomon, and was certain she had mentioned that to him the other night. The evening was still hazy in parts, that wine had done a number on her all right, whatever it was, she would have to speak to him about it. She bent down looking for more of her notes, wondering why she would have left them in the bathroom in the first place for she was certain they were tucked within the inside of the book for safe keeping. Had someone been in the house and taken the book deliberately, wanting to make sure no one else read its contents? The only other person who had talked about the book, apart from DI Cooke was Brendan, the one who had been playing a prank on poor Julia; perhaps now the prank was on him. If he was running scared there was no way she would be able to get in touch with him, unless she asked Justin when he was working at the pub. Looking down at the bath she noticed the water had reached the overflow, turning off the taps she stripped the rest of her clothing and stepped slowly into the tub.

Amelia closed her eyes, thoughts racing of what was happening at Old

Man Malloy's place, wondering how many bodies had been discovered up there, and how far back they dated. She was certain the forensic guys mentioned one of the bodies was really old, so why are they only now being discovered? Or was that something that Lois had written about? She had to try and remember where she put that book. Fleeting visions of her last couple of days spread out before her; time with Seth, time with William, walking past Old Man Malloy's, seeing the bones unearthed, then her vision went back to the meal with Seth. She had enjoyed spending time with him outside of the bookshop and even more so when she thought he was beginning to open up to her. She recalled coming back to the cottage with him, pouring away the remains of their meal while Seth poured their wine. She remembered sitting on the sofa talking with him, being close to one another, his touch, and his kiss after she had said the name Setali, then there was a feeling of being light, the smell of him was close as she felt the heat from him, then she felt softness beneath her. Muted voices in the background rousing her, but the darkness pulled her back and then nothing.

Amelia opened her eyes with a start. She had confronted Seth about the name Setali, maybe that's why he was being cagey at Holly Cottage before he was arrested. Whatever it was, she was regaining her memory and she had to keep picking at it to put the pieces back together.

# chaptra seytek

The following morning, as she stood looking down at the scribbles on the note pad next to the phone, Amelia was reminded she had an interview at the library today. She tapped her fingers on the receiver deliberating whether or not to make the call, asking herself whether she should go through with the interview? What if she liked it, what would Seth say? He had told her from the outset that it was a gesture of goodwill, that she could leave if and when she found something else. But it hadn't been that long and she felt guilty for drawing on his good nature, though he had said it was her choice. Amelia sighed and picked up the phone, looking at the numbers she had written on the message pad and then slammed the phone back into its cradle. She couldn't mess Seth around like that, he had been nothing but helpful to her since she arrived in Creek Bay, but there was something about the Bay that had taken a dark turn; the murders, the bodies, the accusations Seth had been through, why DI Cooke had taken such a dislike to him. Then again, she was new to the village and maybe she was blind where Seth was concerned.

"Damn it!" she said between gritted teeth picking up the receiver.

When the person on the other end answered she confirmed her appointment and quickly hung up. Decision made, she picked up her car keys and like it or not, she was on her way to that interview, cute boy be damned.

The traffic was surprisingly clear for a Monday morning and having printed off directions from the website she found it easily enough. The building was imposingly grand, with the entrance surrounded by pillars, a mountain of steps and the inherent gothic styling and steeple, it was clearly beautiful standing out in the town square. The entrance was cavernous, hushed voices echoing off mosaic flooring and walls, walking through the metal detectors she passed through security at a snail's pace behind a few visitors and then stood in the middle of the reception area, looking up at the large dome skylight. Hurried footsteps drew her attention to a little old woman in blue blazer and pencil skirt shuffling towards her, face tight and eyes peering over her half-rim glasses.

"Ms Scott I presume?"

Amelia looked the old lady over, dark blue conservative clothing, well spoken. "Yes."

"Edith Burns, curator of Langley Library. Would you care to follow me through to the Regional Suite."

The lady turned and set off at a surprisingly fast pace, Amelia had to almost jog to keep up. Several uniformed staff nodded as the lady passed by and then she came to an abrupt stop beside a large door, clicked her fingers, and one of the security team came over and unlocked the door with a swipe card holding it open for them before it closed again with a bleeping sound. The room they now occupied had decorative thick rugs on the wooden floor, leather chesterfields, two large chandeliers at each end of the room and portrait paintings lining the wooden panelled walls. Amelia slowed her pace while she took in her new surroundings.

"You will note that we have tight security here Ms Scott. Please," she turned and pointed to one of the chairs by the desk. "Take a seat."

Amelia slowly sat down. The curator stood by the desk, watching the door they had just entered.

Feeling uncomfortable Amelia finally said, "So would you like to—"

The door behind them opened and a young man entered, tall, dark and elegantly dressed.

"Sorry I am late." He nodded to Edith and then sat in the leather Captain's chair behind the antique walnut desk.

Amelia stood. "William!" Not able to hide the surprise in her voice for he had never mentioned anything to her about the library before now.

The old woman sneered looking down her nose at Amelia referring to him on first name basis.

"Miss Scott, how lovely of you to join us, please," he motioned to the chair, "take a seat."

Her frown deepened as she sat down, watching him curiously and before she could say anything William turned to the old woman. "Thank you Edith, that will be all."

"Master Malloy." The old lady bowed before taking a quick exit leaving the two alone.

"Why didn't you—"

William held up his hand. "First of all, welcome to Langley Library and secondly," he turned and pulled out a decanter. "Would you care for a drink Miss Scott?"

Amelia shook her head. "I'm confused."

"About the drink? Bourbon, something to calm the nerves, I believe interviews are rather harrowing."

She continued to shake her head in disbelief. "No, not the drink, I mean, what are you doing here?"

William stood smoothing the creases from his jacket and walked around the side of the desk, sitting on the edge when he reached her side. "The Library was a… let's say, an acquisition."

"You own this place?"

"In a manner of, yes. Malloy have but a few homely possessions and this," he gestured around the room, "is one of them."

"And the others?"

"A few small holdings in the village. Most of our holdings are in land ownership, the majority of woodland here in fact."

"I think I'll take that drink now," she whispered.

His smile was warm when he turned and picked up a glass tumbler filling it with the golden liquid. "I trust you are here for the interview, yes?"

"Well, actually, it was made through a—"

He pulled a file from his desk, "One Mr Tatem London. Yes, I have his details. I believe the contractors did some work through an agency as part of the Water Springs development and he contacted us following a relocation enquiry. And you know him how?"

"Tate—" she coughed. "Mr London was an acquaintance." Amelia looked at him through her eyelashes in an attempt not to meet his stare.

He placed the papers down. "Was? I see. And Mr London is no longer part of your acquaintance is he not?"

Amelia shook her head and took a gulp of whisky to steady her nerves. The heat hit the back of her throat making her cough. "No."

He folded his arms. "I wouldn't want you to think this job has any bearing on your past life. Whether you got the job or not Miss Scott, it would be on your own merit, you do realize that don't you." She nodded. "Amelia, are you happy at the bookshop?"

She nodded enthusiastically, "Oh yes. I am."

Pushing himself forward he tilted his head to one side, "Then do you mind me asking why you are here today."

"Is this part of the interview?" she asked.

He threw his head back and laughed, a wonderful sound as it bounced around the room, his white teeth gleaming from the morning sun bursting through the lead lined window. "If you like." William walked to the window and looked outside. "You see, I have seen something in you Miss Scott."

"Oh?"

"Yes." His voice drifted off as he stared outside then turned back to her. She was a vision sitting by his desk, her dark brown hair tumbling over her shoulders, resting below her breasts.

"Can you tell me more about the job?" she asked getting back to the point.

"Arh yes," he chuckled, "the job."

The phone on the desk buzzed and a voice came through the speaker. "Master Malloy. We have a situation in the private parking area."

William bent over the desk and pushed the illuminated red button. "Then deal with it Miss Burns, I am somewhat tied up at the moment."

There was a pause before she continued. "Begging your pardon Master Malloy, but I'm afraid this needs *your* attention."

William scowled. "Very well." Looking up at Amelia he smiled. "Amelia, please forgive me for the intrusion, but I am afraid something has come up."

"Not at all." She stood and placed the empty tumbler on the desk.

When he walked her to the door she paused looking at one of the portraits depicting a young man in colonial dress looking every bit like William. She looked at William and then the painting. "Is that?"

"A relative. Like I said, the library was an acquisition many, many years ago." Pulling the door open he held her hand, warmth radiated through her. "With regards to the job, it is always here for you, no matter what the circumstances."

"But I…"

He bent down and kissed her cheek. "No regrets Amelia Scott. Ring my office should you decide otherwise."

One of the security team approached and ushered her along to the exit. William spoke with the second security team member and they quickly departed through another door with 'private' written in golden letters.

Sitting in her car, Amelia pondered what just happened. The offer of a job with undisclosed duties, from a man she hardly knew, who had bought her a gown, and seemed to turn up at the right time. It was just too surreal, flattering, but surreal. As she started the ignition, her phone rang in her bag. Fishing out the handset the display said Bookshop, hoping it would be Seth to answer, she found herself talking to Daniel and could hear raised voices in the background.

"Do you know where the manifest is for the last shipment?"

"Yeah, it's in the black file by the counter."

"Looked there, can't find it." The background voices became louder.

Amelia sighed. "I'm thirty minutes away, can you hold on 'til then?"

"Sure."

She put the phone down and pulled out of the parking area. When she turned the corner she saw two bikes outside the security gates and was certain one of them had a yellow stripe just like Sonny's bike. She slowed trying to see past the two guards when the impatient driver behind her beeped his horn. Putting her foot down on the accelerator she waved an apology to the other driver and continued to the store.

Pulling up behind the shop she parked beside Seth's camper van and quickly made her way inside where she was confronted by five customers yelling at Daniel, who was doing his best to keep everyone calm. An elderly woman noticed her arrival and turned to her.

"Amelia. Will you tell this man that my back catalogue is due in and I have already paid for it!"

Amelia nodded. "Mrs Holden has paid for her back catalogue. She paid three weeks ago."

Daniel shook his head. "Not according to these records you've not."

Dropping her bag she pulled the black file from under the counter and presented it to Daniel.

"Where did you…?" Daniel started.

"You did the man-look right? You looked with your eyes instead of your hands." The comment was met with a few giggles from the female customers.

In a bid to regain his pride, he used his authoritative voice and asked people to take a seat while they went through the manifest.

"Mrs Holden has paid, see," she said pointing to the entry.

Daniel shook his head as he scrolled through the computer version. "Then why is it not logged on the system?"

"I don't know Daniel, I wasn't here three weeks ago." Murmurs started again around the shop. "I'll ring the supplier," said Amelia.

When she got off the phone she called the attention of the crowd. "I'm sorry ladies and gentlemen, but there seems to have been a mix up at the suppliers. They have your orders, all accounted for, but unfortunately the shipment has been sent to Cardiff." More murmurs continued. "Please, ladies and gentlemen, it is solvable, and I am deeply sorry for any inconvenience."

"But that was a birthday present for my sister Jean. It'll never get here in time," said Mrs Holden.

Amelia looked at Daniel, he knew what she was asking of him, he inwardly cringed and then nodded knowing Seth wouldn't be best pleased if he lost customers.

"Daniel will go and pick up the shipment from Cardiff now, which means it will be with us later this evening."

Mrs Holden stepped forward. "Would it be possible to arrange a home delivery for my order?"

Daniel took a deep breath as Amelia spoke for him, "Of course Mrs Holden. You have been nothing but sympathetic to our predicament. In fact," she addressed the rest of the customers, "all of your packages will be delivered to your homes." She heard Daniel sigh behind her.

"Better take the van then," he muttered as he picked up the keys from behind the counter.

"Wait!" She called after him. "You'll need this." She handed him the piece of paper with orders and addresses of the customers along with the details of the store who had received the order by mistake. "I'll ring ahead, let them know you are coming." Daniel started to walk away. "Thank you," she whispered. He nodded and then disappeared out of the back door.

She enjoyed working at the bookshop, and she would miss dealing with these enquiries if she were to take that job at the library, whatever the job was, William never did elaborate on the details.

Crisis averted, Amelia sat down on the stool looking through the computer records and noticed that a few details were missing compared to the hard copy. She went back five months to catalogue all the orders and log them onto the system to avoid any further mishaps. A few hours later and she had completed all forms she set out to do when there was a knock at the door. Looking up from the laptop she saw a young lady carrying a child with blonde pig-tales and immediately recognized the little girl from Monday evening. Amelia opened the door and let them in.

"Hello? Can I help you?"

"Is Book Worm Club still on today, only," she looked behind Amelia into the store, "I heard Seth was… unavailable."

Amelia smiled. "Of course the club is still on today, how can we go without it." She smiled at the little girl who pouted in return.

"Mummy, I want Seth to read."

The lady patted the little girls back. "Lydia honey, it is not polite to say that when the nice lady is giving her time for you."

Lydia turned to face Amelia, pout still in place. "I bet she can't do the voices like Seth."

"I'll try my best." Amelia said smiling to both the little girl and her mother when another lady appeared with twin boys. "Come on in, can I get you all a drink?" she said motioning the parents and children to the sofas.

"Juice for the children, and we will both have red wine please," said one of the mothers.

She started to prepare the drinks as she watched the mothers gather the scatter cushions and seat their children. After giving the children their juice she handed the glasses of wine to the women.

"I'm Amelia, and you are?"

The tall attractive lady sighed while the other lady spoke for them. "I'm Hattie, and this is Mina. She's not always a," she whispered behind her hand so the children couldn't hear, "b-i-t-c-h."

"I heard that!" said Mina.

"You were meant to, the little ones weren't."

Mina turned to Amelia, "I'm sorry. It's just we only have this one night a week where we can ogle over the sexiest man in the village, and we seem to have been somewhat short-changed this evening."

"Didn't you hear?" asked Hattie. "Seth has been—"

Amelia stepped in before the gossip had chance to take over. "Seth is unavailable this evening, so I'm afraid you're stuck with me, but I assure you I will try my very best to keep them entertained."

Hattie leaned forward. "I hear Colleen won't be bringing her two tonight, she said Tom had told her not to."

"God, that man is a Neanderthal!" said Mina.

Turning to switch off the main lights and computers, Amelia lit some candles and locked the front door. "I'll give them until quarter to and then we will start."

The two ladies nodded and then asked their children if they needed the toilet. All three children jumped up and down claiming they had to go, so Amelia left the duty to the respective mothers. Preparing herself for the story, she dragged a stool from the counter and put it against the computer table in front of the cushions, where she remembered Seth had sat last week. Leaving the bottle of wine on the counter top for the ladies to take their own refill, she had an idea that they would need more alcohol with Seth not being there. When the children had settled Amelia turned to the first page of *The False Collar by Hans Christian Anderson*. No more arrivals made her sad that village gossip had affected the children's entertainment and while she tried to be as animated as Seth would have been, she saw from their expressions that she obviously didn't have the same impact on the youngsters. Finishing the last sentence and closing the book she looked at each face adorned with quizzical expressions.

"That's stupid." Lydia said, arms crossed.

"Lydia, don't be so rude," her mother chastised. "Apologise to Amelia."

The little girl huffed and made a point of holding her arms tighter to her chest. "I don't get it, it was stupid."

"Now, now, Lydia, Amelia did a very good job of the reading. I think you owe her an apology." His soothing voice was welcoming. The children cheered as they ran to Seth grabbing hold of his legs. Lydia held back as she looked up at him and when he smiled at her she hugged him too.

"Sorry Amelia," said Lydia, her face buried in the side of his knee.

The two ladies also showed their approval of his timely arrival. "Well," whispered Mina, "this was worth coming after all."

Seth's unkempt appearance only added to his pulchritude. Amelia stood and put the book down on the counter. "Welcome back, I didn't expect to see you today."

Seth walked to the counter with all three children clinging to his legs, giggling and screaming their joy.

"Mr Solomon, looking devilishly handsome as usual," said Mina licking the rim of her wine glass.

Seth smiled. "Thank you Mina."

The children let go of his legs when Hattie presented chocolates while Amelia took the glasses into the kitchenette. From the back room she heard them talking, it was great to have Seth back. When she returned Seth was behind the counter and Mina was propped up opposite him with her cleavage on show. Lydia and her mother were already standing by the door waiting for Mina to organise her children but she showed no signs of moving. Hattie dressed the twin boys in their coats and had them by her side when she made a loud coughing sound.

Mina turned to her friend. "Well, guess that's my cue to go and be the dutiful wife," she said.

Seth waved the children goodbye. "OK gang, what do we say to Amelia for the story?"

The children walked through the door one at a time each one monotone in their reply, "Thank you Amelia."

When Hattie closed the door behind her, Amelia turned the sign to read closed and bolted the lock. "Tough crowd." she muttered.

"Hey, what can I say, they're kids and fickle as you like."

Amelia smiled. "Thanks for coming in when you did, I thought I had a lynch mob on my hands."

He shook his head. "Anytime, and I do think you did a great job."

"You heard that?" she asked. She wondered why she hadn't seen or heard him enter the store, certain he wasn't there when she started. "How long had you been listening?"

He shrugged as he pulled two beers out of the fridge, "Heard it all."

"You sly dog, and you never let on!" she said taking the beer.

"Hey, I had to see how you would cope under pressure, and I'm happy to report you passed."

She turned to collect the cushions from the floor when Seth came from behind the counter. "Leave those, we'll deal with them in the morning."

She sighed when she felt him close to her. "Where have you been?"

"You know where I have been." He turned to face her. "They had no evidence to keep me, so I have been released."

Desperate to know if it was he and Sonny at the library today she wondered if he would answer her question. "Were you in town today?"

"What makes you say that?" he laughed as he turned his back to her, so she didn't get to see his expression.

"I thought I… never mind."

He took a seat on the sofa next to the window. "Back where we started," he said patting the sofa next to him.

"Well technically we met at the beach remember," she said sitting.

He smiled as he took a large swig of beer. "Granted." Looking around the store he nodded. "Like what you did with the place, the candles add that touch of elegance."

"Don't be coy," she said nudging his arm. They sat in silence drinking and looking out to the store when she finally said, "Good to have you back."

# chaptra etek

Amelia had a skip in her stride and for the first time in her life actually whistled on her way to work. The postman handed her a bunch of letters as she opened the shop. Turning the sign to read 'open' she left the post on top of the counter and switched on the power. The computers immediately booted into life while she pulled out the water jugs, she was in the back room when she heard the front door chime and raising her voice she told them she would be with them in a minute and continued to fill the jugs with water. The door chime went again and she quickly walked into the main room to find no one there.

"Hello?"

There was no reply.

She poured fresh coffee beans in the machine and flicked the switch to warm up when she noticed the post on the counter top had been moved. She distinctly remembered leaving them by the cloche, but they were now on the other side and not in the neat pile she had left them. Sifting through the letters she tried to remember how many there had been. The sound of the door chime immediately stopped her thinking about the post and onto a bigger problem - the old couple. They came into the store, sat down, unfolded papers and announced their drink order. Amelia mumbled a good morning under her breath while she started to make the coffee.

"Good morning Roy, Mary." Seth bellowed from the corridor. He was carrying a large crate of papers, which he placed on the table by the unoccupied sofa.

The old lady positively beamed when she saw him. "Seth, lovely to see you, did you enjoy your camping trip?"

"I did thank you Mary. And how are things with your niece in Australia? Have they recovered after the bush fires?"

Mary continued to retell the tale of the unfortunate bush fires her niece had encountered in northern Australia. It wasn't something Amelia had heard about, but Seth was very attentive while she spoke. Her husband on the other hand looked as though he had heard the story a thousand times and had decided to switch off from the conversation and read his newspaper. Ten minutes later Seth emerged at her side.

"Did they give you any bother last week?" he whispered.

"Oh nothing I can't handle," Amelia said. "What happened to her niece?"

He half-turned watching the old couple sit in silence while they both drank their coffees reading the news. "She is a veterinary nurse, went to Australia to help out at the shelter, met a bloke over there and decided to stay. They own a large farm way out in the middle of nowhere, which meant they were at the mercy of nature when the fires began. They had to let all the animals loose and hope for the best before the smoke got them. Mary was just saying they were still locating a few strays."

"Gosh, I hope they manage to get them all back home safe."

Seth turned to her and smiled. "You an animal lover Amelia?"

"Yeah, who isn't?" she pulled out the laptop from underneath the counter and switched on the machine.

"But you don't have any at the moment?" he asked watching her.

She frowned when the light flickered from the monitor. "No, when Mr Chips died I couldn't bring myself to get another cat."

Seth frowned. "Mr Chips?"

"I know, I know, it wasn't my choice of name, believe me," she said typing in the password. "He arrived shortly before Jude's birthday, so she had the pleasure of naming him, he was a stray we took in, tried him on commercial cat food, but all he would eat was chips," she smiled as she remembered the little fur ball, "until we got him the gourmet cat food."

"Sounds like you were had," he said, making sure the sticky buns under the cloche were still edible.

"Mmm. Anyway, tell me what you have planned for today." She needed to take her mind off Jude and Mr Chips before she started getting upset about the losses in her life.

"Well, I've decided that I'm staying here today seeming as I have neglected my number one employee." When she frowned Seth continued, "Daniel told me what happened with the mix up, and I am grateful that you managed to sort it out without causing a scene."

Amelia blushed, "Oh that, it was nothing. It was Daniel who did the recovery and distribution." When Seth just looked at her she quietly said, "He did *do* the deliveries right?"

Seth chuckled. "Yes, he did, and he also mentioned he would not be coming again in the future."

Amelia pulled out the order book and placed it by the laptop, "Oh?"

Seth leaned closer so the old couple couldn't hear. "He said one of the customers got a bit fresh with him. I can't start to imagine who that was."

A smile tugged at her lip when she looked up at him. "Oh, I think I can imagine who it was. Anyway, I've made sure the hard-copies and computer file tally, so it hopefully won't happen again."

Seth pulled the screen towards him. "You did!" He looked at the spreadsheet and noticed there were detailed notes as well. "I don't know what to say."

Pouring a glass of water she added cheekily, "You could give me a raise." She looked at his expression and laughed, "How about the rest of the week off." Seth raised an eyebrow, "Okay, then how about the quiz tonight."

He took the glass and drank half, "Deal. Been ages since we went anyway. You don't mind the guys coming too do you?"

Turning the laptop towards her she began scrolling down, "Why would I mind?" she said with only the slightest hint of disappointment in her voice.

"You don't look very happy that's all."

"I am. It's just," she looked over the screen at him, "I don't think I'm Daniel's favourite person at the moment considering I made him do that trip and home deliveries."

Seth laughed. "Forget about it. Besides, if you hadn't of told him to do it, I would have, so we're even." When she didn't look convinced he leaned over to her and pushed the laptop lid so it almost closed. "He isn't bothered. Besides," he leant back onto his stool. "He is great on the history section, and Sonny, well he has the music down."

"Tea please." Detective Inspector Cooke stood beside the counter with a young man at his side. "Two teas."

Seth smiled at Amelia before turning to him. "DI Cooke, lovely to see you again. If you'll excuse me, I have some business to attend to in the store room, but my lovely assistant would be only too pleased to serve you."

As Seth slid off the stool the detective and his colleague watched him disappear into the corridor and out of sight.

"Two teas," Amelia said bringing their attention back to her. "Take a seat, I'll be over with them shortly." She watched the two men take the sofa next to the old couple chatting to them as they approached. It was one thing being hounded by the police but another to have them in your establishment all the time; if they weren't already, people would start to talk. She left the mugs and teapot on the table beside them then walked away, only to be called back by the inspector, she turned and put on her fake smile.

"Would you mind awfully if we had a few moments of your time? At your convenience of course." His smile was equally fake; the circles under his eyes, crow's feet and general haggard expression said he was no longer forthcoming with pleasantries. Obviously he was having as hard a time of the investigation as they were, only they didn't have full knowledge of the facts that he did, and lately, he wasn't for giving her any.

"Of course, when I've got a spare moment, I'll give you a shout."

Amelia made herself busy by going through the sales figures. The mundane task alone would make her concentrate on anything but the two policemen sat in the store, avoiding his eye contact to avert attention away from his questioning.

An hour later and Seth appeared from the back room. "Amelia, have you got a moment?" he asked of her.

Looking around, everyone seemed occupied searching through the bookshelves, sitting at the computers or sat reading on the sofa. She felt the two police officers watch her walk away and when she neared the back room Seth pulled her in by her hand taking her by surprise.

"What is it? What's wrong?" she asked.

The room was overly crowded with the new delivery from yesterday, seemed more than just the orders had been sent to Cardiff, it made standing in the store room even more difficult, and she was forced to push up against his thighs.

Seth turned to whisper, "Are they still here?"

Amelia caught her breath. "Roy and Mary?"

Still holding on to her hand he frowned and shook his head. "No, I meant the filth."

"Oh," she tried to push her head back to the wall; his fringe tickled her cheeks and she could feel the muscles in his thighs tensing as they rubbed against hers. "Yes, they are still here."

"Any chance they'll be leaving soon?"

She shook her head. "Looks like they are here for the long haul."

Seth breathed heavily, moving her hair from her shoulder, the heat prickled her skin, sending waves of vibrations through her core. Gently letting go of her he moved his hand to the wall blocking her in. His expression was hard, then softened as he looked down at his legs between hers. Leaning in she could feel his breath on her lips and anticipated his touch when they heard the door to the bathroom open and close. Reminding herself it was neither the time nor the place she slid from underneath him.

"I'll get back to the shop," she said moving away.

The glance she gave him on the way out of the storeroom made his loins buckle. Punching the wall he turned back to the boxes and tore the top off one of them.

Walking down the corridor Amelia moved to one side as the bathroom door opened and the inspector walked out.

"Glad I caught you," he said wiping the stubble on his chin.

Amelia turned to him, leaning against the wall, waiting for him to bombard her with mundane routine questioning, when he paused and looked over her shoulder. Frowning she turned to see what had caught his attention. The wall of photographs paid tribute to the life of the bookshop: its memories in pictorial form.

The detective stepped forward standing by her side looking over the faces then he stopped searching and concentrated on one photograph in particular; Amelia followed his gaze and gasped. The picture he was looking at was dimly lit and its subjects were Valerie, Julia, Seth and Lois. The two girls were playing guitar while Seth sat beside them with a book in his lap, Lois standing behind them with a stern expression, her eyes trained on Seth.

"I never saw that before," Amelia whispered.

"You see now why I connected the dots," he said wearily. Pulling the picture from the wall he continued down the corridor to the store, Amelia close behind.

"But that doesn't prove anything," she said when they approached the corner to the store.

The detective slowly turned. "I'd say this picture speaks a thousand words." He turned the photograph towards her. "You see anything familiar here?" he asked. Amelia frowned in concentration looking over their faces. The two girls looked happy as they played the instruments, but it was Lois' expression that concerned her and she wondered when the picture had been taken. When she didn't say anything the detective answered for her. "They are all dead, except Seth. I think that makes him a person of interest, don't you."

Turning away he left Amelia standing with her mouth open. Noises coming from the storeroom suggested Seth was still unpacking the delivery. Looking back to the store she saw the detective bend down and whisper something to his colleague before he walked out of the shop.

She was just about to go and speak to Seth when the old couple stood, Roy started rattling change in his pocket ready to pay for their drinks. Amelia begrudgingly proceeded to serve the couple, her questions would have to wait.

A fairly quiet day in the shop meant she had nothing to do but mull over the photograph. When she checked on Seth around lunchtime he had disappeared from the storeroom, leaving some boxes unpacked, the contents strewn across the floor. She carefully avoided the piles of books as she steered her way towards the sink to refill the water container and replenish milk. The plain-clothed police officer still sat where he had been earlier, and was now looking through one of the Books of the Month. The door chimed, a middle-aged man entered and went straight to one of the computers and attempted to log on. He was ruggedly handsome, with short hair, olive skin and casually dressed. She wandered over to give him the Internet access code.

"Afternoon, are you stopping long?" she asked.

Pulling out a leather-bound book with too many pages he turned to her. "Couple of hours should do it." His eyes trailed from her feet and slowly finished at eye level and it was then that she noticed his striking green eyes.

When he smiled she felt a burning sensation behind her ears that spread to her cheeks. "The code for the net is Trojan. Can I get you a drink?"

Turning his attention back to the computer he entered the password. "What you got?"

Amelia hated it when people asked her that, and wondered if she was supposed to reel off the entire list, it was a long list that she could never really remember off by heart. Looking him over she didn't think him the type for designer coffee so condensed the list. "Hot, cold, alcohol."

That got his attention; he slowly turned on the swivel chair to meet her stare, "Yeah?"

"Beer do you?" she asked thankful for small mercies.

Turning back to the screen he opened up the search engine, "Beer would be excellent."

Returning with the opened bottle of beer she placed it next to the computer and glanced over to his book opened to a page adorned with hand written scrawl and sketches of symbols and flowers, obviously a notebook rather than print. She squinted trying to get a better look but he leant over obscuring her view. He was also quick to minimise the screen so that she couldn't see which site he had logged on to. The store implemented certain restrictions for online use, so she was certain that it wasn't anything dodgy, but it was intriguing nonetheless to know what he was up to. She smiled politely and then went back to the counter to pour herself a glass of water.

Amelia watched the man from a distance, her thoughts running wild with theories as to what he was looking at. From the brief glance of his book she did make out a sketch, symbols and something that resembled a list of ingredients, not bad memory recollection considering it was fleeting. The police officer ordered more tea and sticky buns to keep the boredom at bay while he made his notes and observations of who came into the store when two teenagers appeared at the counter.

"Is Seth here?" one of them asked.

She had completely forgotten that he disappeared earlier and wondered if he had sneaked back in again. "I think he's out the back, just a moment." Making her way to the corridor she almost collided with him when he came rushing towards her. "Hey, some students to see you," she said pointing to the youngsters. He nodded and walked over to them.

The man at the computer screen turned briefly, then carried on with his business. Noticing his bottle was empty Amelia approached him. "Would you like another?" she asked catching a glimpse of the website before he minimised the screen again.

He turned quickly on his seat and smiled; perfect skin, perfect teeth and those eyes were certainly a winner in her book. "Please." When Amelia turned he put out his hand to stop her. "Don't suppose you have any... rare books?"

Amelia leant against the desk. "What kind of rare books?"

The man looked over his shoulder to make sure no one was listening then leaned towards her and whispered, "Reference books about," he coughed when he said, "demonology."

Amelia frowned wondering whether he was a nut just like the young teenagers. Sighing she pulled herself away from the desk and pointed to the mezzanine floor making her way back to the counter. "You might find something up there."

He gathered up his belongings and logged out of the computer. As he passed the counter he picked up the bottle of beer and started up the stairs. Seth and the stranger exchanged frosty glances, which didn't go unnoticed by Amelia. The two teenagers appeared rather enthusiastic as they asked him about Friday night when Fortune would be playing. Leaving them to their conversation she opened up the laptop and continued checking through the bookshop accounts.

When the two youngsters left, Seth leant against the counter and whispered, "Who's that?"

Amelia followed his gaze to the police officer sat at the sofa. "One of Stephen's goons. Where were you earlier?, I popped into the storeroom but you'd disappeared."

Seth stood upright and sighed. "An errand." Looking up at the railings he noticed the guy looking through books. "Who's that?"

Not taking her eyes off the laptop she said, "A customer, looking for a book. It *is* a bookshop." She could feel his stare on her. "What is with you today?"

He walked to the side of the counter and put his hand on hers so she couldn't scroll down the spreadsheet. "All work and no play makes Amelia very cranky."

Raising her eyebrows she sighed. "I'm at work, and the boss will get pissed with me if I slack off, he's a bit of a tyrant you know."

Sliding to the back of the counter so he was next to her he whispered in her ear, "Then let me have words with him and you and I can get off early."

Blushing, she smiled at him. Bunking off and spending time with Seth sounded divine, but it wouldn't look good if the shop kept closing early, and then she worried how it would look to the police who would most certainly keep a tail on them wherever they went. There was a bang upstairs and an apology as several books were dropped. Amelia and Seth looked up through the railings to see the man picking up a couple of books from the floor and replacing them on the shelves and then sit on the loveseat with one.

"Just an hour to go, and then we can close," she said moving her hand away from his and carrying on with her scrutiny of the spreadsheet. "Besides, you've got some work to do in the storeroom. It's a mess in there. I nearly fell over the bloody things earlier."

The policeman looked up from his book and scribbled something down in his notebook.

"Careful, or our friend here will have a bestseller on his hands." In a mocking tone he continued, "Police officer takes credit for bestselling autobiography, a day in the life of the dull bookshop owner who can't keep a tidy storeroom."

Slapping him playfully on the arm she narrowed her eyes, "Go and sort out the order and bring in these for me." She handed him a piece of paper with four books listed. "It's the books for little Lydia."

Taking the sheet from her he smiled. "Arh, yes, adorable Lydia." As he began to walk away, Seth looked down at the list. "Little Red Hood?" he said out loud and stopped.

"She loved it so much she just had to have it." Seth turned to her and Amelia shrugged. "That's what her mum said anyway." He carried on walking through the corridor when Amelia shouted, "She's coming in before closing so make sure you dig them out." The policeman looked up from his notes with a frown.

Clock-watching was painful, as she watched the minute hand move slowly round to quarter-to. She sighed and then smiled when the door chimed and Lydia ran straight to the counter, her mother followed closing the door behind her.

"Did it come, did it come?" she asked excitedly.

Amelia smiled at the little girl's enthusiasm, Seth approached with four books tucked under his arm. Lydia ran towards him, putting the books down he picked her up holding her aloft, she squealed with pleasure as only a giddy child can.

Her mother stood by the bottom of the stairs and smiled. "She's been waiting for those, driving me mad." Turning to Amelia she pulled out a piece of paper, and then stuffed it back in her pocket before pulling out her purse. "Twenty-five wasn't it?" she asked.

Amelia minimised the screen and opened up the manifest scrolling down to the order number. "It says here twenty."

Seth put the little girl down and walked to the counter, "Any books bought in the Reading Month are half price, so Little Red Hood is half."

Lydia's mother looked down at her daughter. "Bonus." Handing over the money Amelia tapped the amount into the till and presented her with the receipt.

The little girl was pulling at Seth's shirt. "Will you read it again Seth? Pleeeeeeease."

He bent down and playfully tugged at her pigtails, "Well, now, that wouldn't be fair, not without the rest of the gang here."

She shook her head and whispered, "I won't tell."

Standing he rubbed her head. "I'm sure you wouldn't."

"Come on Lydia, we need to get back and make tea for daddy." Her mother said pulling her away. The young girl pouted.

Seth pulled a bun from under the cloche and handed it to Lydia. "Here, this is for dessert, but you can only have it if you eat everything on your plate." The pout immediately dissolved as she took the bun from him and smiled. "And that includes your greens."

Her mother mouthed a 'thank you' to Seth and then walked her daughter to the door as the little girl sang thank you to Seth before skipping through the door and down the street, her mother walking fast to keep up.

"You're great with her," said Amelia.

Seth shrugged. "What can I say, she's my number one fan."

She looked up at the clock, thankful that the minute hand was now at two minutes to closing time. She looked around the store, only the policeman remained, until the sound of pages turning from the mezzanine reminded her of the guy still up there. She started up the stairs when her phone rang. "Hey, what's up?" she said, slowing her pace.

"Does something have to be up for me to ring?" her mother said, sarcastically. "I was ringing to see how the interview went."

Amelia stopped and turned to look at Seth. "Went okay, tell you about it later."

"Did you get it?" she asked.

"Mum, I'll talk later." She switched her phone off and continued walking up the stairs. The customer was sitting on the edge of the seat, two books on the floor, one on the seat and was frowning as he read the one he held.

"Find what you were looking for?" she asked.

He looked up from the book, appearing startled that she was there.

"Sort of," his voice gruff. When he looked down at the page again she stepped forward.

"It's just that we are closing."

He looked at his watch. "Crap." Closing the book shut he collected the one from the seat and the two on the floor and left them on the table. "Thanks." He stuffed his own book into his backpack and then walked past her and down the stairs.

As she approached the table where he had left the books and money for the beers, she heard the door chime and a few clinking noises from downstairs. Looking at the titles she picked up the one on top, *Lore of the British Isles*. Turning it over she began to read the sleeve to find out more about the book when the door slammed shut downstairs. Putting the book down she walked to the edge of the balcony to see the commotion. Seth was bent over the table collecting crockery, the young policeman noticeably absent, he looked up at her and smiled.

"I take it he left of his own accord," she said walking down the steps.

Seth shrugged as he walked through to the back room. "Man needed reminding we were closed."

Amelia followed him through to the storeroom. "It's behaviour like this, that got you thrown in a cell in the first place."

She stopped at the entrance to the storeroom, noticing that he had unpacked and the boxes were neatly stacked at the side underneath his waterproofs. Putting the crockery into the dishwasher he rinsed his hands in the sink and shook them dry. Turning back to Amelia he grabbed her waist with cold, wet hands making her shriek.

"It's being around *you* that got me thrown in a cell."

"How do you figure that?" she asked watching his pupils dilate and eyes grow darker.

He leaned in to her neck, hot breath trickling down her chest warming her inside, she closed her eyes in anticipation waiting for him to make the first move; as soon as he would she would melt into him, make sure he knew what she wanted. When she felt coldness on her waist she opened her eyes seeing that he had pulled away from her, a perplexed expression formed on his features, his hands now by his side.

"Quiz starts at seven and I need to sort out a few errands before then," his tone was even as he turned and picked up his leather jacket. "I can drop you off on my way."

Amelia inwardly sighed. "That's fine, I'll walk."

He turned with the smile, if only she had made the first move. Seth opened the back door and set the alarm while Amelia collected her belongings. When she returned he had punched in the numbers and the alarm was emitting bleeps before arming. While he locked up she stood looking at the shiny black bike with chrome highlights. It was a fast machine for sure and she remembered how good it felt to be holding onto him that first day he rode them to his cottage, but the face of the rider was not Seth in her memory, it was William. Seth sat on the bike and switched on the ignition.

"Actually, would you mind dropping me off?"

Nodding over his shoulder she slipped on the back secured her bag over her shoulder and leant in to hold him. Leather, ocean and musk, flooded her senses, she closed her eyes as she let her head rest on his back, when he didn't set off she looked up.

"Something wrong?" she asked.

Feeling his shoulders bunch and stomach tighten she pulled back trying to see his face, his stern expression and tight lips told her he was on edge about something.

"I can walk, it's no problem," she offered.

Holding her arm across his waist he shook his head. "No, it's fine, I thought I heard something." He kicked the footrest back and revved the engine before leaving the parking area.

His actions made her tense, that and the extreme speed. They arrived at Lowe Cottage in a heartbeat; she slid off and watched him ride away down the lane leaving her wondering what errands he had before they met tonight. A cold draft hit her as she walked inside, cursing the heater she went up the stairs and into the spare bedroom; the room felt warmer than she expected, opening the cupboard the boiler's warm air floated towards her, she reached out to the metal cylinder, warm to the touch. The dial indicated it came on half an hour ago, plenty of time to get the whole house adequately warmed. She ran down the stairs, feeling radiators, they were all lukewarm which didn't explain why the house felt so cold, when she turned into the kitchen she stood still, her heart stopped beating when she saw the back door wide open. Her whole body convulsed frozen with fear making the hairs all over her body stand on end. She couldn't look away from the gap through to the garden and noticed the axe was still propped up by the woodpile. As she edged slowly towards the doorway, Amelia reached out for the axe, picking up the heavy object she quickly closed the door locking it shut with the large key. She pulled the axe closer to her body; if anyone was to come in, she would start swinging and god help them.

Rushing through to the lounge she picked up her bag and pulled out her mobile phone scrolling down the list of names until she reached the one person she felt would be able to get to the bottom of her problem. When it went through to answer phone her gut tightened waiting for the beep to sound before leaving her message.

"Hi Stephen, it's Amelia. Amelia Scott. I wondered if you could ring me back. It appears the kids are getting a little adventurous in their games and it's beginning to freak me out. I'd really appreciate it if you could give me a ring tonight on this number. I'll be at the pub."

# *chaptra nownsek*

Seth, Sonny and Daniel arrived by quarter to seven. Their arrival on foot surprised her considering the distance they had walked from Holly Cottage. Sonny and Daniel walked ahead engrossed in a heated debate about music that made no sense to her, which meant she could take a more leisurely stroll chatting with Seth, who was in high spirits talking about his plans for a book club that he wanted to start geared towards adults. By the time they reached the pub she could hear the quizmaster making an announcement about the curfew now being earlier. There were some moans around the room when he continued to address the congregation.

"So that means we will be missing out a couple of speciality rounds and last orders will be at nine-thirty." More groans and whistles sounded, no more so than the two people stood at the bar.

"Godsake. What the hell are they playing at?" asked Daniel. "I had that round in the bag."

Amelia shook her head. "So you're not bothered about the wellbeing of your fellow villagers. You wanted to win the quiz tonight?"

Daniel held out a pint for her. "And the problem with that is?"

"Come on," Sonny said patting him on the back. "Let's grab that table in the corner and enjoy what little evening we do have."

Daniel and Sonny walked over to the corner booth leaving Seth and Amelia at the bar. She shook her head and looked over to Seth with a look of exasperation, he smiled at her sympathetically as he picked up his pint from the bar and nodded over to the booth.

Collette left quiz papers and pens on tables before the quizmaster made his final announcement for starting. Amelia and Seth joined their companions, Daniel and Seth sitting at opposite ends of the semi-circular booth. Taking charge of the answer sheet, Sonny started to write a name at the top right corner where it asked for team name.

Looking down at the sheet Amelia frowned. "Fortune?"

Sonny stopped writing and looked over at Seth. "Yeah. Fortune. Didn't Seth tell you?"

Amelia looked at Seth then back at Sonny her mouth agape.

"*We* are Fortune." Daniel said with a gleefully smug expression.

Seth leant forward. "I wasn't sure how you'd react, but yeah, Daniel, Sonny and I are Fortune."

"How many more secrets do you have Seth Solomon?" she asked

eyeing him suspiciously.

Lucky for Seth the quiz had started and he didn't have to answer her. The general knowledge round kicked off with a standard question, 'how high is Snowdon?' Sonny was quick to write down the answer without conferring, for which she was grateful. Daniel and Sonny worked together whispering and nodding to each other while Sonny wrote down the answers.

Amelia leant back. "I don't feel I am contributing much tonight."

"Give it time," he said patting her knee. "These are just the warm up questions, the speciality questions come after."

"That's what I'm worried about, to be honest, I don't think I'll be any good at those either."

Ned walked up to the bar and gave his order to Collette while he sat down on the barstool. When he looked around the room he waved to Seth and then his smile dropped when he saw Amelia.

"He's upset you didn't ask him tonight," said Daniel.

"Me?" she said raising her voice. "I doubt he would want me as a quiz companion again, I only answered a few and then they were on movies."

"Cool," Sonny said lifting his pint. "That means we can concentrate on the music questions." He downed the rest of his pint and nodded to Daniel who made his way over to the bar.

Seth waved to Ned, who approached, giving Daniel a wide berth. Pulling a chair to one side of the booth he sat down.

"Didn't know you'd be in tonight," he said to Seth.

"Spur of the moment thing."

Amelia avoided eye contact with Ned, worried about Daniel's comment. When Seth rubbed her leg, he leant over the quiz sheet noticing Sonny had left one blank. "Ned, what is the term for someone who fears clowns?"

Amelia flinched involuntarily, the three men turned to her, and Seth smiled. "You don't like clowns Amelia?" he asked.

She closed her eyes. "Not my favourite thing, no."

"Coulrophobia," Ned whispered.

"I don't care what it's called they freak me out too, I'm with you on that one Millie," Sonny said, writing the answer down.

The only person who ever called her Millie was Jude, with a glazed expression she sat staring at the table ignoring the conversation going on around her, the heat on her arm was the only thing bringing her to the here and now.

"Are you okay Amelia?" asked Seth concerned, his hand on her arm.

"Sorry, I must have zoned out there."

"She really doesn't like clowns," laughed Sonny, his gaze still on the sheet before him. Daniel came back putting the drinks down on the table.

Saving face, Amelia smiled and took a large gulp of her beer. Shuffling closer to Seth she motioned to the seat. "Do you mind, I need to make a trip to the ladies."

Seth slid out from the booth allowing her to pass.

From the toilets she could hear the muted voice of the quizmaster rhyming off the questions and the clinking of glasses as the punters enjoyed their Tuesday evening. Splashing cold water over her face she looked in the mirror, her complexion had paled, as always did when she thought of Jude, her hands began to tremble and she felt nauseous as she bent over the sink. A sudden banging noise against the window above one of the stalls made her look up. The door to the bar opened letting in louder sounds before dying away again when it slammed shut behind the woman who entered. She must have been early forties, possibly one of the women from Book Worm Club, but wasn't certain; wiping her face, Amelia quickly left. When she got to the corner of the bar she saw DI Cooke stood watching her.

"Thought I saw you go in," he said leaning against the bar. "Did you want me earlier?"

Sitting down on a stool Amelia exhaled. "Yes, I did."

"Everything okay?" he asked quietly. "You don't look so good."

"Just tired." She closed her eyes, seeing Jude, remembering her smile, her laugh, dancing with the boy, the loud bang and then Jude's blood all over her hands. She breathed deeply and the images faded.

"You said something about the kids. Has it escalated? Are they doing more than just banging?"

Taking another deep breath she looked up at him. "Yeah. I should have told you earlier, but someone was in my house, they—"

Stephen moved closer and gently held her arm. "Someone was in your home and you didn't say anything. Why didn't you report it?"

"I wasn't sure, what I mean is, I didn't know if Seth had left the—"

The detective huffed. "You know, you really should keep better company."

"Let me finish," she said. "I thought Seth left me the ring of daisies, but he couldn't have, he wasn't around, and then there were trinkets on my bedside table that had been moved, but nothing taken, apart from a book, I think. I can't be certain, I may have misplaced it. But today, when I got home from work the back door was wide open. That wasn't the first time either. Then, I thought it must have been me, not locking it properly when I first moved in, not knowing how the lock works, but when I got home tonight, the door was wide open again."

She felt better for getting it off her chest, if only his expression was more calming. He held her hand and gently squeezed. "If you want me to come back with you, I'll get the forensic guys to do a dusting, see if we can pull any prints." It felt so reassuring when he said it, like a weight had been lifted.

Daniel nodded over to Seth. "Don't look now, but your girl seems to have eyes for someone else."

When Seth turned in the direction Daniel was looking he pulled his lip back, a growl rumbled in his chest.

"Play nice," Sonny said watching the policeman holding Amelia's hand and rubbing her back. "We don't want a scene."

"Do you want me to—" Daniel started but stopped when Seth glared at him. "I'm just saying. It would be my honour to give the police officer a taste of true justice."

Seth's eyes narrowed as he focussed on DI Cooke's hand on Amelia's back. He stood from the booth, fists balling and knuckles turning white when the quizmaster announced a ten-minute break before continuing with the next round.

Amelia turned towards the booth and noticed Seth watching her, his chest rising and falling in quick succession. She smiled at Stephen and slid off the stool. "If you could come by tomorrow with the forensic guys that would be a huge help," she said before quickly returning to the group.

When she reached Seth she held his hand. "I'm not feeling very well, do you mind walking me back home?" she asked.

He ran his free hand over her forehead and down her cheek. "You're flushed, is everything okay?" he asked.

"Must be coming down with something," she looked down at the two men sat in the booth, the chair opposite empty, "Where did Ned go?"

"Had to dash, something about a flute." Daniel said with a shrug.

"Jessica," she muttered taking her coat from Seth when he offered it to her. "Sorry to leave you to it."

Sonny laughed. "And we were doing so well with you."

Seth pulled her tight towards his body as they walked up the lane. Her head felt dizzy and hazy, like she had been in a sauna for too long, she had no recollection of the journey and they arrived at her front door quicker than they had previously. Amelia leant against the doorframe as he turned the key in the lock, when the door opened she slid down. Seth caught her before she hit the ground and carried her into the house. He gently set her down on the sofa while he went back to the door and checked it was locked, when he returned she was attempting to stand.

"Hey, steady," he said trying to get her to lay back down, "You're not well Amelia, you need to stay off your feet."

She closed her eyes feeling the softness of the cushions beneath her. Seth pulled the throw from the back of the sofa and gently placed it across her body leaving just her head exposed.

"There, you'll feel better soon, I'll get you a drink of water."

"Don't go," she said reaching out. He knelt down next to her, bringing the throw tighter around her. "I want you to stay," she said opening her eyes and staring into his. "Please."

"I'm not going anywhere," he whispered. Leaning forward he brushed the hair from her face and then felt her forehead again. No signs of a fever but her cheeks were visibly flushed. "Just now, at the bar, what did he—"

Amelia silenced him with a kiss. This time she was making the first move and he wasn't getting away. She pushed the throw back freeing her arms and was wrapping them around his back, pulling him closer; he was warmer than she remembered and getting warmer. Pulling himself upright, he sat on the edge of the sofa and leant closer, his body and lips crushing hers. As he deepened the kiss she allowed herself to relax under his weight, feeling his excitement grow between his legs.

He pulled back breathless. "Amelia, we shouldn't."

But he had been the instigator, he was the one who kissed her first, and now he was pulling away. She looked into his eyes, almost black in colour, a thin line had formed between his eyebrows, and worry consumed her, wondering if she had imagined his advances.

"I'm sorry, I thought you wanted—"

He bowed his head. "I do, trust me I do."

"Then what's stopping you?" she asked.

He brought his head level with hers, the glow of her eyes, her porcelain white skin, dark hair and ruby lips were all the enticement he needed. Slowly bending down, he kissed her bottom lip. Amelia closed her eyes and raised her chest, allowing him to reach her breasts. She felt herself slipping into exultation waiting to be carried away to the depths of rapture when there was a knock at the front door. Seth pulled away, his expression stern then softened, he stood up and straightened his shirt.

"Leave it," she purred, pulling him back.

"Believe me, I wish I could." Bending down he kissed her forehead before going to answer the door.

She heard familiar voices and wondered what was so important that would make them stop by.

"They were all over it, tracked 'em back here, wondered if you had gotten into any trouble."

"What trouble?" asked Amelia now standing behind Seth.

Sonny stopped talking and turned to Daniel. "We hit a bit of bother with our bikes, gotta borrow lover boy, sorry."

"Do you have to go?" she asked of Seth.

He held her waist kissing her hard. "I'm sorry Amelia. Keep that thought."

Seth was out of the door before she could blink. Every time they got together something drove them apart, it just wasn't fair. Bolting the door Amelia made her way upstairs and threw herself on the bed, exhaustion taking control, the power completely drained from her core. Letting out a deep breath she pulled the duvet to one side and crawled underneath.

She concluded that her time spent alone with Seth was always brief in nature and whatever it was that kept pulling him away was always linked to Sonny and Daniel, or DI Cooke, and whatever so called 'bother' they had come across with their bikes just didn't ring true with her. They were all hiding something and that bothered her. It was making her question whether her mothers' thoughts on dating in the modern world, allowing yourself to become invested in another individual, was just not all it was cracked up to be. She had let herself drift allowing another man to dominate her thoughts and feelings and this had to be a fresh start, as an independent woman, as someone who can make it on her own. She put a note in her phone diary to speak to her mum about coming down to Creek Bay, so she could see for herself how she was building a new life, minus the dodgy ex. As she looked at the growing pile of clothes on top of a cardboard box, she also made a note to start unpacking her belongings. When she was finished typing Amelia frowned.

"But they weren't on their bikes tonight."

# *chaptra ugens*

She woke to the noise of her mobile phone bleeping and a message from Seth informing her that he was at the surf early today and would see her later. With a sigh she pulled back the duvet, so much for leaving off where they started.

It was uncommonly cold for summer today, Amelia opted for the combat trousers and oversized cardigan wrapping it tight across her chest as she walked into the village. There was little activity today, no old couple outside the shop waiting for her and no postman to chat to on her way. Outside the corner shop Mr Bateman was sweeping away blossom that had fallen from the creeping honeysuckle arching to the first floor window, the sweet aroma wafted towards her as she approached the bookshop. She entered the shop leaving her bag on one of the tables and automatically made her way through to the back door and then stopped. The absence of the alarm bleeps made her wonder if she had forgotten to set it again, but remembered it was Seth who had set it last night. She looked at the control panel, the system had been deactivated, with a frown she checked the back door was locked and then opened the door to the storeroom hoping to find either Daniel or Sonny, but it was devoid of anyone. Walking back through the shop Amelia started up the stairs to the mezzanine, but that too was silent and still. Shaking her head she made her way downstairs and started going through the motions; switching on the power to the coffee machine, till, lamps and computers, emptying the water and milk containers. When she returned she almost dropped both when she saw the detective standing by the bottom step.

"Jesus Christ, you gave me a start!" Putting down the containers she grabbed her chest waiting for the shock to subside.

His expression was sincere when he said, "I didn't mean to. I wanted to come by and make sure you were okay after last night."

Walking to the coffee machine she shook her head. "I am, thank you. Really don't know what came over me."

"It's just that you were so upset and I wondered if…" his voice trailed off as he spoke drawing her attention to his demeanour.

"A good night's sleep sorted me out, something I think you're in need of Stephen." She put her hand atop his and gently squeezed. "Stop thinking of others and take care of yourself for once."

He looked down at her pale hand on his. "Chance would be a fine thing. What with the investigation and the new evidence."

She slowly withdrew her hand and put the containers into the machine and pushed the on switch. "Go and sit down. I'll bring you a coffee and you can either let off some steam or just relax. If anyone asks I'll tell them you are chasing a lead."

"A coffee would be great."

"Seth is down the surf." She pulled out a large mug and gave it a quick wipe. "So you can relax."

He sat on the sofa nearest the window, his eyes closed and fingers pinching the bridge of his nose. As Amelia approached he quickly released his hand and smiled when she handed him the mug of steaming coffee and sat down next to him.

"Don't you have things to be getting on with?" he asked blowing on the hot beverage before taking a sip.

She looked around the shop. "As you can see I am rushed off my feet, but I can always spare some time for you."

He smiled as he put the mug on the table. "Any more activity at the cottage?" he asked.

"No, thank god," she said leaning back. "But it is really creepy. How did they get in without even breaking the lock or a window? There's just something not right about it."

"And you don't think it's the ex?" he asked.

"Tatem? Nah." She thought about the idea; would Tatem be doing this to her to make her pick up the phone and ask him back? Amelia frowned. "Why would he do that?"

The detective shrugged. "People do the strangest things Amelia, I thought you'd know that by now." Leaning forward he picked up the mug and sipped the hot liquid, savouring the feeling as it wet his mouth. "Do you know where he is?"

"Actually, no I don't. The last I heard from him was the day I moved here and he made it quite obvious he wanted nothing more to do with me."

"Some people get off on mind games. You'd be surprised how many of those are close relatives, someone you know, the last person you thought would do something like that."

"I remember you saying," she whispered then shook her head. "No. I definitely don't think its him, it isn't Tate, it's not his style. He'd rather have an affair as a way of—" she stopped herself having given too much away already.

Stephen looked at her with a perplexed expression. "He cheated on you?"

Picking at the loose cotton on her trousers she shook her head, wondering why she ignored the signs. "More than once."

"He's a fool."

She watched him drink the coffee and considered whether he had a significant other in his life, whether he too had been hurt before, when the door chime sounded and the man from yesterday walked in and went straight to the computers. She excused herself leaving the detective to his coffee and approached the man as he started typing in the password.

"I see you remembered," she said over his shoulder.

"What can I say," he said not taking his eyes off the screen. "I'm a devil for remembering stuff like that."

She watched him open up the search engine and his fingers poised over the keyboard, he looked at her from the corner of his eye.

"Anything I can do for you?" she asked.

"To be left alone would be great."

The harsh words didn't go with his handsome face. Amelia stammered when she spoke, "I only…"

"The lady asked you a question, the least you could do is be courteous," Stephen bellowed from where he sat.

The man glanced over his shoulder; he knew what the law looked like. Turning back to Amelia he smiled. "I'm sorry, rough night. Please accept my apology. It was rude of me to take it out on you." Scanning the menu board he replied. "A coffee and toast, please."

Turning away, Amelia whispered 'thank you' to the detective and set about preparing the order. The smell of toast made Stephen's stomach growl. "Could you put a couple on for me as well Amelia? I can't remember the last time I ate," he shouted.

After serving the man at the computer she left a plate of toast with the detective and replenished his coffee before setting down a mug of tea for herself. "Did you say you would be bringing the forensic guys round to the cottage?" she asked taking a sip of her drink.

He nodded. "I checked the diary, what with all the activity up at Old Man Malloy's we're pretty thin on the ground, but I can get someone round tomorrow first thing, that's the earliest I can do unfortunately."

Her heart sank, she wanted to be assured the culprit would be caught sooner rather than later. "Sure. That's fine. I'll ask Seth if I can come in later tomorrow. How are things going up there?"

He took a bite of toast and began chewing. "You know I can't answer that. Mmm what bread is this?"

Amelia shrugged, "Granary I think, Seth makes it himself." He stopped chewing. "Don't worry, its harmless. He is a very good cook."

The detective carried on chewing. "You know I can't go into details, but you were there and you saw more than most, so what I can tell you is that we are in the middle of an investigation that goes back years. I've got experts for this and that coming out of my ears."

Images of the two men in white digging up skulls flashed before her. "And Seth, is he?" She couldn't even bring herself to ask.

"I'm sorry Amelia, you know I can't."

She picked up her mug and walked around the side of the table. "Worth a try." Seeing that the man had pushed his plate and mug to one side she went to clear them away; two bites had been taken and the rest left. "Was there something wrong with your toast?" she asked.

He looked down at the sorrowful article. "Lost my appetite."

Stephen left at midday when the teenagers came en masse. He managed to close his eyes for half an hour and with only him and the stranger in the store Amelia left him to it. The atmosphere changed considerably with the loud chatter of the youngsters, much to the annoyance of the young man at the computer. They were excited about Fortune playing at the store and the girls were quick to add their opinion on who was the best looking. It wasn't until she remembered what Daniel had said that she felt awkward listening to the young girls swoon over the man she had been lip-tied to last night. Leaving the jug of juice and four glasses for the group she retreated to the counter and opened her laptop; ten past one, and still no sign of Seth. Noticing her mother was logged onto Skype, Amelia clicked on conversation and started to type when someone grabbed her waist. She gave out a loud shriek that alerted everyone in the store.

Seth chuckled into her neck. "Did I startle you?"

"Are you trying to give me a heart attack?" she said elbowing him in the gut.

Seth pulled back before the impact winded him. The teenage girls gave Amelia dirty looks before returning their attention to the group of friends. He smelt of the ocean, and something more fragrant.

"Mmm, what's that smell?" she asked sniffing his t-shirt.

"Sex wax." He leant against the counter on one arm with a mischievous grin.

"I beg your pardon?"

"Mr Zog's sex wax, the wax I use for the board," he chuckled. "What did you think I meant?"

She shook her head. "With you, anything's possible." Leaning towards him again she let her senses take in his redolent aroma. Ocean, leather, and… "Coconut."

When the chime sounded she saw the door closing, glancing around the store she looked to see who had come in or out when she noticed the seat at the computer was empty and money left by the side of the monitor.

"Something wrong?" he asked.

"No. Nothing. Slow day today."

Grabbing her waist he slid forward, pushing her legs aside his. "Then let me make it up to you."

The chatter had died down from the youngsters who were obviously eavesdropping. "Later," she whispered pushing him away.

Stepping backwards he sighed. "Spoil sport."

Leaving Amelia to finish off the conversation with her mother, Seth spoke to the children about the geography project they were researching, but they were more interested in hearing about band rehearsals. After a few messages back and forth, Amelia had to ask the one question that was niggling her, had her mother heard from Tatem? The conversation light was blinking and she wondered if her mother would reply, or phone and demand an explanation. Seeing Seth deep in conversation with the teenagers, Amelia looked down at her screen, still no answer from her mother. She started to panic and wondered if a phone call would be more appropriate, thinking perhaps Tatem had been in touch, and her mother didn't want to upset her. She tapped the keyboard in frustration and then closed down the lid. When the minute hand on the wall clock hit thirty, Amelia shoved the laptop into her bag and slid from the stool making her way to the door, pausing when Seth shouted her name.

"That's my shift done, I'll see you later." When she turned and opened the door she remembered the appointment with the forensic team. "Oh, I need to do something first thing, okay if I start later?"

Seth nodded with a frown, the youngsters nudging one another as they watched Amelia leave.

The fast-paced walk to Creek Bay brought on a sweat. Removing her cardigan she linked it through the bag handle and pulled out her phone. No new message from her mother. When she reached the bench Amelia sat down and entered her mother's number. It took a while before she answered.

"Where have you been?" she asked out of breath.

"Amelia? What's wrong?" her mother asked.

Catching her breath she sat back against the bench. "You didn't reply to my last message and I was worried something happened."

Her mother tutted. "I was making soup when you sent the messages, got carried away and nearly burnt the batch."

Amelia sighed, thankful that it was nothing more than a near cookery catastrophe. She remembered the smell of the house when her mother made soup, the freezer would be crammed full of different flavours and she would never label them so it was a surprise every time she chose one. "Sorry, I was getting a bit nervous."

"What about?"

"Nothing. Hey, which soup did you make?"

"Potato and leek, and don't change the subject!" her mother scolded.

"Sorry Mum. I was going to ask." She stopped herself before she opened the can of worms that really should be bird food. Would the message have been deleted when she severed the connection? She wasn't sure. "I've forgotten, what did my last message say?"

Her mother went silent; the sound of footsteps as she made her way to the computer desk from the kitchen. "Let's see, oh, you're offline. Erm, the message is greyed out." As she heard a couple of clicks and then her mother swear under her breath Amelia hoped the message had been deleted. "Bugger," her mother finally said. "It disappeared, I must have deleted it."

Relieved, she let out a long sigh. "It was probably nothing important anyway mum."

Not one for letting things go her mother pressed. "Are you sure poppet? You sounded quite insistent earlier."

"Really. If I remember, I'll give you a ring. Give my love to Malcolm."

Closing the phone Amelia placed it into her leg pocket and released a long breath as she narrowly averted a heated conversation, when she felt the presence of someone close to her.

"I have forgotten what it was like to have a mother," he said not taking his eyes off the waters. "Do you love her?"

She thought that an odd question. "Of course I love her."

"Would you do anything for her?" he asked.

She shifted uncomfortably on the seat. "Of course."

His gaze slid to her knee, up her thigh, lingering on her chest and finally to her face. If she didn't know any better she would have said he had been crying. "You are blessed."

"I'm sorry for the other day, at the library," she said trying to pull the conversation back to something she could manage. "I'm sure it is a really lovely job, but I am happy where I am for now."

"For now," he repeated.

Her conversations with William were always cryptic, but today his attention was elsewhere. Although he looked at her, he didn't seem to see her. "Aren't you working today?" he asked.

"My shift ends at two-thirty. Thought I'd get some fresh air."

"You don't always finish at two-thirty." He said looking back at the ocean.

For someone who seemed to know her whereabouts, she didn't find it particularly creepy. "No, sometimes I stay later."

"I see." He frowned watching the gulls squabble over rotten fish on the beach. "Are you hungry?" he asked.

"Actually, I haven't eaten today."

"Would you like a bite to eat?" he asked, the velvety smooth voice returning like a purr from a kitten.

Without thinking, without going through the motions, she answered before her brain had time to compute. "Yes."

# chaptra onan warn ugens

The Manor was impressive, there was no other word for it, with its imposing stature set amongst a foray of green abundance, the architectural genius was simply divine. William's bike looked out of place amongst the expensive cars on the gravel car park but it didn't stop him from walking with his head held high as he always did, with dignity and gentility. Holding out his arm, he linked his with Amelia as he walked her through to the lobby.

"I'm really not dressed for fine dining," she said pulling at her oversized cardigan.

Looking down at his black t-shirt, jeans and boots he smiled. "And I do I suppose?" he said putting her at ease.

The concierge welcomed his newest guests with a bow. "Welcome. Master Malloy, and…"

"Miss Amelia Scott," William announced, possessively.

"Miss Scott, please come through to the dining room." He gestured to the room off the main hallway.

The chatter from diners and clinking of cutlery could be heard as they made their way through the dining room. Women with furs and large jewels smiled adoringly at William, but did not extend the same courtesy to his guest making her feel self-conscious; people like her didn't belong in places like this. Amelia quickened her pace trying to avert their stares by hiding behind William.

The concierge stopped when he reached a table set in the large bay window that stretched from floor to ceiling, leading out onto the veranda. "Sir, your table is ready." Pulling out the seat nearest Amelia, William nodded for her to sit as the waiter did the same for William.

The Sommelier approached the table, as with all the restaurant staff he had a pristine white waiters cloth draped over his arm. "Would you like to see the wine list, Sir?"

"The usual please."

"Of course Sir." He left the table clicking his fingers to two of the waiters who hurried along to the service table. Diners nodded to William as he met their glances.

"You have your own table?" she whispered.

William pulled a napkin from the table and set it down on his knee. "I do."

"Then you're a regular here."

He laughed softly, straightening the knife before him. "You could say that."

The Sommelier returned with the bottle of champagne and presented it to William, who nodded. He uncorked the bottle with a gentle fizz and placed the cork on a small silver tray on the table and paused. William touched the glasses to check they were the right temperature, then checked the condition of the cork and the year it was corked, he lifted it to his nose taking in its aroma before nodding to the Sommelier who poured the first glass. William lifted the glass to check the clarity, colour and bubble density, then breathed in the champagne's bouquet before finally tasting it. After William gave his approval, the Sommelier poured a glass for Amelia before leaving the bottle in the ice bucket.

"You really didn't have to order champagne William," she said taking the glass.

He picked up his glass and nodded. "To absent friends."

Amelia repeated the toast; thoughts of Tatem sprang immediately to mind. If he were to blame for her recent problems at Lowe Cottage, then she would be more than happy for DI Cooke to throw the book at him.

Looking at her over the rim of his glass he took a large sip and then smiled. "Tell me," he said with an assured tone. "Why is it that you chose the bookshop over the library?"

Amelia put the glass down without drinking.

"You said no pressure, remember?"

He absentmindedly moved the knife again. "I did. I'm sorry. It's just that I don't understand. Both have books, but what the store doesn't have is a thirst for knowledge. All those people under one roof searching for answers." He clucked his tongue. "And we have the biggest collection of mammals and archaeological findings in the UK."

Amelia frowned. "Really? I didn't know you had—"

"There is a lot you do not know Amelia."

The waiter returned with the menus, Amelia took the one offered to her and looked down the list.

William held his hand to the waiter, "Pheasant, red snapper, lobster."

Amelia quickly looked down the menu at the fancy names and delicate sounding dishes, half of which she did not understand nor know what they were. The only thing she did recognise was terrine of pheasant, and not to feel out of place she smiled sweetly. "Why that sounds delicious William, I think I will have the same."

Handing the menu to the waiter she took the glass and gulped the champagne to steady her nerves. "Oh my goodness that's really good," she said licking her lips. Turning the bottle around to read the label 'Louis Roederer Cristal 2008' she tried to memorize the name so she could look it up later, though she was certain it wouldn't be anything like the price tag of the sparkling cava she was accustomed to.

"They can be a little pretentious with the menu explanations, they have to keep up appearances for them," he said nodding to the rest of the dining room.

Amelia looked around the large room, the white linen tables, each one occupied by the super rich and pillars of society. With everyone wearing light colours, they stood out amongst the crowd, and she was thankful their table was set aside from the other diners.

It wasn't long before the waiter returned with two plates. Looking down at her meal she didn't know whether to eat it or frame it. The three pieces of meat were carefully cut into the same size and placed on some greenery, with a red sauce delicately drizzled around the edge, the terrine was served separately with melba toast. When William picked up his cutlery she did the same.

The concierge approached the table. "I am very sorry to interrupt Sir, but would you be able to sign the release for the wedding request?" He handed William a piece of paper. The ivory textured letterhead looked expensive and the writing had been crafted in calligraphy. William looked over the letter and then signed the bottom.

When the concierge left Amelia leant forward and whispered, "Why did you have to sign for a wedding request? Are you getting married?"

He laughed. "Heavens no. But we don't allow just anyone to get married here you know."

She choked on the piece of meat she had been chewing. "You own this place too?" Her raised voice made the woman on the nearest table turn with a horrified expression for she thought Amelia a heathen, not worthy of his company.

"One of those acquisitions I mentioned," he said taking a sip of his drink. "I hope you don't think any differently of me."

"No, of course not." She watched him cut into the meat and wondered what sort of life he had, and to think she was worried about him spending money on a dress for her.

"Ever wondered what it would be like to just run away?" he asked twirling the glass by its stem with his thumb and forefinger, sounding more like a statement.

"Do you?"

He smiled. "Responsibility." When he looked up his expression was jaded. "Gets to us all."

There was so much more to William than just the guy who always turned up when she needed him. He was lonely, like she was and with all that he had, it seemed as though he had nothing.

"Don't you have someone? Someone to share all of this with?" she asked.

He had a crooked smile and glint in his eyes when he said, "I'm working on it."

The rest of the meal was delightful, she had never eaten lobster before, and the meaty texture was surprisingly flavoursome. Conversing with William was effortless, he was revealing more about his life, something she hoped Seth would do one day, and when she looked out to the rest of the dining room she noticed that everyone had left and the waiters were busy clearing tables.

"What time is it?" she asked looking around for a clock.

William looked out of the window to the sky. "About six-thirty I would imagine."

She pulled out her phone and pressed a button to illuminate the homescreen, the clock read six-fifteen. "Gosh, I had no idea it was that time."

"Somewhere you need to be?" he asked taking another sip of his drink.

The truth was she didn't have anywhere to be, and there was no one she had to be nowhere with. "No. I was just shocked we've been here so long."

He smiled. "Time flies when you're—"

"Having fun," she said finishing his sentence.

William laughed. "I was going to say when you're in the company of a beautiful woman."

He was charming, knowing exactly what to say and when to say it. "I suppose I really should be making a move."

"Of course." He nodded as she started to rise from the table and quickly reached out for her arm. "Would you do me the honour of one last thing before you leave Amelia Scott."

With William nothing was simple and she wondered if she should agree to something without hearing what it was first. "What would that be?"

"I need your opinion. A woman's opinion," he said pulling his hand away and sipping more of his wine.

Amelia looked around, he had plenty of female staff, what made her opinion any more special? "About?"

He slowly stood and walked to her side, gesturing to the patio doors, "I wanted to know what to do about the wedding."

Amelia gulped. "Wedding?"

Opening the bay window he stepped onto the veranda and helped her through, guiding her by the waist. "Of course. I wanted to do something different, something that hadn't been done before, what do you think to an outdoor service in Autumn?"

"Outdoor services are lovely," she whispered following him down the large stone steps to the expansive grassed area.

"There is a wonderful willow crop just beyond the trees, it's beautiful, would you mind taking a look with me?"

His smile was tempting and without knowing why, she let him lead her into the dense woodland leaving behind the opulent dining room, a million miles away from her new surroundings. The raw natural foliage was beautiful; willow branches twirled and entwined acting as a natural canopy above their heads. Blossom fell from the nearby trees flowing like confetti. Amelia gasped as she looked above.

"It's beautiful," she said. Spinning around she watched the blossom fall to the ground amidst the fallen leaves readying themselves for change. Berries would soon adorn the branches of the trees teeming with birds joyfully chattering for their bountiful horde. "I have never seen trees blossoming and shedding their leaves at the same time. Are they supposed to do that?"

"An unexpected issue," he said solemnly.

"I thought I had green fingers, but nearly all my potted plants have wilted since I moved here."

"A few years ago we encountered a false Autumn following a really dry Spring, maybe related to that? I couldn't say."

"All the same. You should probably get someone to check them out, although they will look stunning for the wedding."

"I'll do that," he said distantly.

They walked a little further when he stopped and looked upwards. "I come out here when I need to think," he said sitting on a large rock underneath the hawthorn tree. "It's one of the places that I can actually relax, not everyone knows about it."

She looked down at him, the expression he held earlier when he spoke of running away didn't suit him, and she wanted to strip it away and have her William back.

Kneeling down beside him she whispered, "Thank you."

He gave a short laugh. "For?"

"Bringing me to your special place. I can understand why you like being here." She looked up to the blossom falling and held out her hand to catch a few strays and then closed her eyes. "I feel like I've been here before, like I belong." Realising how stupid that must have sounded, she quickly added, "not that I could have you understand."

William slid off the rock and sat on the floor next to her. "I can and do understand Amelia. This place holds a lot dear to me, loves won and loves lost. I pray the sorrow will fade as joy enters here once more."

Looking into his eyes she wondered what hell he must have been through to want to leave everything behind, to forget it all and keep running. He quickly pulled away and stood looking back towards the Mansion. "I think I hear someone calling."

Try as she might, Amelia didn't hear anything, but stood and followed him back through to the reception area.

One of his staff whispered something to him as they approached, William nodded to his servant and then turned to Amelia. "Please forgive me Amelia, but I'm afraid I need to tend to some business. Nigel here will give you a lift back to the cottage." She looked at the man stood in grey and maroon, and then back at William. "He'll make sure you get home safely." He wrote his number on a piece of card, and handed it to Amelia, "Here, I want you to ring, or text me so I know you got home safe."

She took the card and smiled as she followed his concierge to the large black car with tinted windows parked beside the Mansion.

The driver didn't speak to Amelia on the journey back home, though he seemed to look in the rear view mirror at her more than the road. Thankful to be back home she quickly got out of the car and darted to the door as she heard the car pull away. Fishing out her keys she was startled when Seth appeared from underneath the lychgate.

"Shit. You're determined to give me a heart attack," she shouted.

"Where have you been?" he asked in stern voice.

Finally getting the keys in the lock she opened the door a crack and then stopped, "Where have I? What?" She turned to him, hands on hips. "Why?"

"I was waiting for you," he said pacing the front garden.

"Did we have an appointment?"

Seth laughed. "I need an appointment now do I? I see how very busy you are these days, perhaps it was a mistake." He turned to walk away.

"Perhaps you should," she shouted back after him. "Besides, I didn't ask for a keeper, I asked for an employer, something you seem very hazy about."

Seth stopped in his tracks, his shoulders rising and falling quickly. She regretted every word, not knowing why she had said them, only knowing that she was angry about being spied upon.

"You've been with him, haven't you?" he said accusingly.

"By *him*, you mean William. Yes."

He spun around so fast, he was pressing against her before she could open her mouth. "I told you to stay away from him." The door started to give way behind her as he pressed into her chest, his skin becoming hot to the touch. "Why won't you ever listen!"

She looked into his black fire eyes. "Give me a reason to."

"I can't."

She wondered what was so important that he couldn't tell her, why he was evasive when it came to William, she wanted him to explain everything. But there was something stopping him, something that he wasn't saying, or maybe couldn't say. Pushing him back she stood on the top step defiantly. "Then I think you better leave before I say something I'll regret."

Seth started to turn and stopped when he reached the road. "He's not what he seems you know."

As she watched him walk away she shouted after him, "Yeah? Who is?!"

Slamming the door and throwing her bag down on the floor, Amelia stormed over to the kitchen and poured herself a large whisky, muttering to herself how frustrating Seth had been. He was overly protective when it came to William, but he would never tell her why. Pulling out the mobile phone and card from her pocket she typed a message to William saying she had arrived home and thanked him for a lovely afternoon. He responded straight away with a polite message saying their time together had been wonderful and he was looking forward to their next meeting. How awful could one man be to have Seth, Daniel and Sonny so wound up? If anything he was a total gentleman, something she had started to see wane in all three of them lately. Pouring herself another whisky she downed the bittersweet liquid and slammed the glass down before retiring to bed.

# chaptra dew warn ugens

The willow arches above creaked in the wind, their bony fingers entwined, desperate to stay together. A cloaked figure took Amelia's hand and led her down the path stopping when they reached the large oak tree. Features blocked by the heavy hood, she reached out to pull the garment aside, her hand immediately blocked by the owner. The silver ring on his little finger drawing her attention, she momentarily froze, she had seen William wear the same metal band. A howl pierced the night engulfing her with fear hearing the animal calling out to its pack. She held him tight for protection, hoping he would be able to keep the animal at bay, his fingers tightened on her arm reassuringly, but when he didn't let go and his grip became painful she looked up at him, trying to see beyond the hood, reaching out she pulled the material to reveal the figures' identity and screamed in terror as she exposed a wolfs head snarling back at her.

Amelia sat upright, the dreams were becoming more and more vivid lately, shaking her head she pulled the covers back and walked to the bathroom, splashing cold water over her face she looked at her reflection in the mirror. Walking back to her bed she stopped when she passed the window and looked outside; the street lamp on the corner illuminated her car, but the rest of the lane and the fields opposite were in darkness. Squinting, she focused on the dense woodland beyond, she was convinced she saw something move in the field, moving closer to the window, her breath condensing the glass. Amelia squinted again, dogs, in the field, it had to be, they hunkered down, rolling in the meadow; a howl echoed in the darkness making her jump. Dropping the curtain she ran to her bed and pulled the covers up to her chin. The lonely voice of the dogs outside made her shiver, she wondered if they were what Ned saw the night he stopped by, or maybe the culprits of the so-called animal attack; whichever it was, she hoped they would keep their distance.

A knock at the front door woke her at seven-thirty. Running down the stairs in her dressing gown she opened the door to a female police officer.

"I'm sorry Miss Scott, Detective Inspector Cooke asked us to come by and do a dusting."

Behind the uniformed officer was a man in plain clothes carrying a large brief case. She stood aside and let them enter, showing them through to the kitchen where the majority of activity took place. Once she had given them her prints, Amelia left them to dust the door and window frames and her bedside cabinet while she got ready for work, thankful that finally she would soon have answers about whoever had been in her home.

It was of no surprise to her Seth wasn't there when she opened the store, their parting words had not been pleasant and she hated herself for it. The plain-clothes policeman made himself comfortable in the same seat as yesterday and ordered a large pot of tea and a scone. Her mind was elsewhere while she did the stock take, numbers and names bled into one another, the screen flickered to screensaver after being untouched for so long and she watched transfixed as the colourful swirls bounced effortlessly across the screen. She wondered if she imagined last night, reality and dream had started to become hazy of late, her trance was broken when the laptop lid moved. William stood behind the counter looking at her with a confused expression.

"I said are you okay?"

If he had been talking to her, she hadn't heard a word. "Sorry, I was just…" Smiling she closed the lid completely. "What can I get for you?"

William smiled, his perfect teeth flashing in the dim light. "I asked if you would join me for a drink tonight."

The thrill of seeing him again was overwhelming, spending time with William seemed to pass all too quickly, but what would Seth say?

"We're having a get together," he continued. "You remember the wedding reception at The Manor the other week?" Amelia nodded. Of course she remembered, she was stuck in the store cupboard waiting for the speeches to end so she could slip out unnoticed. "They are back from honeymoon and we are having drinks to celebrate. I wondered if you would come, as my guest."

As his guest, not his girlfriend, or a date, but as a guest; she could handle that, surely Seth would be able to handle that. Besides, she was intrigued, she had to know more about William, and maybe it would stop her being freaked out every time she found him staring.

"It's a Masquerade Ball," he concluded.

"Sounds exciting."

William smiled. "It is." As he turned to leave he stopped and looked over his shoulder. "And Amelia."

Her stomach fluttered. "Yes?"

"Be sure to wear that dress." His smile was wickedly handsome, thoughts of him ripping the material from her flesh made her giddy.

The policeman watched William leave and wrote the occasion in his notebook before returning to the newspaper opened on the table. Things were starting to become interesting in Creek Bay.

Opening the laptop she minimised the spreadsheet and clicked on the search engine looking at images for Masquerade Ball masks. Scrolling through the range of masks, Amelia was finding it hard to choose between the highly decorated and feathered to the metal-framed masks, but she found the Venetian leather masks to be wonderfully expressive although subtle in their design. Opting for a decorative Colombina style mask she searched for local suppliers and found one a few miles out of town.

With plans of the evening swirling around in her mind, Amelia was lost to thoughts of what to expect at the ball. She had never been to one before, but imagined it would be exquisitely opulent just like everything else William did. The setting at the Manor was a perfect choice with high ceiling mouldings, full-length bay windows and large chandeliers, she could imagine the crowds of people laughing and dancing to the music.

"You can get off now if you like."

Looking up from the laptop she saw Sonny leaning over the counter, his hair tied back and wet, the salty sweet smell of the ocean almost making her gag which she quickly disguised as a cough. Looking at the clock she wondered why she had been given a reprieve at one-thirty with an hour left on her shift, but she wasn't one for looking a gift horse in the mouth, besides, she had put in enough hours of late.

"Great," she said closing down the laptop and placing it under the counter. "I have a few things I need to sort." Amelia picked up her bag and left the store as quick as she could before he changed his mind.

The directions to the shop were simple enough, as she pulled up outside Amelia looked up at the sign swinging on the side of the building. It was a traditional costume for hire shop, but this one was certainly of the up-market variety. Opening the door the chime rang out, she found herself amongst racks of clothing adorned with silks and cottons the likes of which she had never seen before. Walking through the tunnel of clothing the store opened out where she found an old man busy strapping metal armour to a customer.

"There," he said patting him on the shoulder. "I am sure the clan of Akran will be most pleased with this one."

The young man turned looking down at his breastplate, the red and gold engraving intricately worked into the metal. Amelia stood watching as he nodded in appreciation at the handy work. "Excellent. And the bracers?"

"Already packed and ready for you. I took the liberty of including the drinking horn."

"The one with the rabbit fur?"

The old man nodded with a smile watching his customer admiring his armour in the mirror. When he turned, the old man noticed Amelia and put the leather straps on the counter. "May I help you young lady?"

"I'm looking for a mask."

"Anything in particular?" he asked with tilt of head.

Amelia coughed when she saw the young man turn with his hands on hips watching her closely. "Something to wear for a Masquerade ball."

The old man walked towards her with a pleased expression. "Arh, then you will be looking for something along the lines of the feathered Arabian mask," he said gesturing for her to follow him through to the back room.

"Actually, I was wondering if you had any of those Venetian soft leather masks."

The old man stopped and slowly turned. "You know your masks."

Amelia sheepishly replied, "Internet, did a search before I came out."
The old man continued walking. "Do you have any?" Her question was
answered when they entered a room full of colourful masks adorning
walls, and mannequins, the shelving awash with the various styles
ranging from the outrageously decadent to the modestly simple. "Wow,
this is a collection," she said breathlessly.

The old man stood to the side, "Perhaps you will find something here
that will suit your taste." He watched her take in the display and smiled
to himself. "Are you sure about the Arabian mask?"

She had almost forgotten about the old man until he spoke, "Yes, I
think so."

Now that she saw them in the flesh, she wasn't entirely sure about her
choice. Her reflection in the mirror made her stop, probably should have
made sure her hair wasn't all over the place before coming in. The old
man approached with something in his hand.

"Here," he said presenting her with the delicate mask.

"No, really, I don't think I should."

"Please," he said holding the mask out further. "I insist."

Amelia smiled politely, turned to face the mirror and then lifted the
mask up to her face. It was so delicate and fragile she worried about
breaking it.

"Here," the old man said taking the silk ribbons. "Let me." He tied the
ribbons around the back of her head to secure the mask and stood back
admiring his handiwork.

Amelia looked at the tall feathers and then to her reflection, the mask
was certainly beautiful, but she wasn't sure she could pull it off. "Thank
you, but I think I will go for something a little less…"

"Extravagant?" he questioned.

Turning back to the mirror she looked at the mask one last time
and untied the ribbon. "Yes. If you don't mind." Handing the mask
back to the old man. "It is beautiful though." Amelia wished she had
the confidence to pull off the look; she inwardly sighed thinking she had
made the wrong decision to accept his invitation after all.

"Thank you. All hand-made."

"You made these?" she asked looking around the room taking in the
extraordinary craftsmanship.

"Yes," he turned to place the mask on the wall and then looked at
the floor with a puzzled expression. "Leather masks you say?" Amelia
nodded. "I have several over here," he said pointing to the furthest wall.

She followed him towards the mask display, all individually carved and
crafted from fine soft leather. The shelves and wall space presenting an
array of differing styles, including a medieval medical mask that instantly
brought a shiver; invisible eyes staring back from behind tinted glasses.

"Here." He picked out a reddish-brown mask with thin copper wire
designs intricately embedded on the front. Amelia nodded. When she

placed the mask over her eyes it moulded to her cheekbones and eye sockets perfectly, the smell of leather overpowering her senses.

"Do you have a dress?" he asked looking at her from the mirror.

"Yes, a friend bought me a ball gown the other day." She frowned when she said it; had William known he was going to invite her to the ball, had the chance meeting been a ruse all along?

The old man motioned her to look at the mask in the mirror. "Gown colour?"

She stopped breathing when she saw her reflection, understated and subtle, yet amazing. It framed her face perfectly. "Red," she looked at the deep red textured colour of the mask, it would go without saying the mask would be a perfect choice.

"And cloak?"

She spun around. "Cloak?"

"Yes." The old man put a finger in the air requesting she wait while he disappeared into the main shop. He returned with a piece of deep red material draped over his arm. "Here, try this."

Amelia received the heavy garment constructed of a deep woollen felted material velvety smooth to the touch. She wrapped it around her shoulders and tied the string, the length was perfect, just half an inch from the floor.

"Will you be wearing heel?" he asked.

"Not if I can help it," she laughed. But it was no laughing matter; Amelia in heels was a disaster waiting to happen, there would be a slight chance she would remain upright walking in heels, but never dancing.

"Then I do not need to let the hem out."

He patted down her shoulders looking at her reflection, moving the material over her arms and then tugged at something behind her head. She didn't realise what he was doing until the material surrounded her ears. The cloak had a large hood flowing gently over her head and down past her shoulders. The combination of mask and cloak was quite befitting, and she couldn't wait to see how it looked with the dress to complete the ensemble. The person looking back at her in the mirror was not the Amelia she knew, it was someone daring, someone dark, and someone she wouldn't mind meeting more often.

"I'll take both," she said without hesitation.

It was the longest bath she had ever taken, the water now lukewarm and her fingers starting to prune, but that didn't matter, Amelia was looking forward to her social outing in more ways than one. Finally, maybe she would find out more about William and as thoughts to the evening played out in her mind, her day dream was interrupted when her mobile buzzed snapping her back to reality. Lifting herself up from the water she turned the trip lever to release the bath water and carefully stepped out of the tub reaching for a towel from the heated rail. One new message from William stating he was sending his driver to pick her up in an hour, she quickly made her way to the bedroom and looked at the dress carefully laid on the bed in all its glory, she ran her fingers over the smooth material and sighed.

When Amelia heard the car horn outside, she downed the whisky, shrugged into the cloak and picked up the mask. As she locked the door she heard the roar of motorcycles in the distance and thought of Seth, he hadn't contacted her since last night and he would not be happy to know where she was heading. Amelia quickly slid into the back of the car waiting outside. Noticing it was the same driver who had dropped her off yesterday, she gave a quick nod and smile of recognition and then pulled out her phone to distract herself from the monotonous journey ahead. When he didn't pull away she looked up to the rear view mirror where she could see his eyes focussed on her.

"You need to put your mask on before we arrive," he said dryly.

She looked down at the mask on her knee and frowned then looked up once more and nodded to the driver; he slowly pulled away flicking on the headlights. Blowing out a slow breath Amelia put the mask in place and tied the leather strap underneath her hair before pulling the hood up and over which made her feel safe and protected. Motorcycles roared past the car, the flash of yellow made her take a second look, there was no mistake it was Sonny's bike, and she was certain the other two riders would be Seth and Daniel, but she had to forget about them tonight, tonight she would enjoy her time with William.

The car pulled up to the manor and the nervous tension came back with a vengeance. She closed her eyes and counted to ten, by the time she reached five the driver had opened the rear door and was waiting for her to exit. Amelia gathered her cloak and dress so as not to trip over the vast amount of material and slowly stepped out of the car, a hand appeared before her for assistance, which she gratefully accepted. When she looked up, the person stood beside her wore black cloak and black mask, but there was no mistaking his smell. Her smile widened as she drank him in, oblivious to the flurry of activity around them as people arrived and chatted to one another.

"You look ravishing," he said.

His silky smooth words made her glow, she was grateful for the mask to hide her reaction. "And you look handsome as ever."

She allowed him to lead her towards the reception area where a waiter offered champagne from his tray. William picked two glasses handing one to Amelia. She felt his warm touch on her lower back as he escorted her into the dimly lit ballroom.

The room was adorned with candles and fruit garlands, people mingled laughing and chatting, all faces hidden behind exquisite accessories. The ladies wore brightly coloured masks with feathers while the men's were more muted. As they approached, the men bowed and women curtsied while William nodded acknowledgement, she felt as though she was walking with royalty. Taking a sip of the champagne, Amelia watched as the crowd parted when they came to the centre of the room. A waiter took their glasses when William turned to her holding out his hand

and bowed. Looking around the room she was grateful no one would recognise her, she wasn't the dancing type, not ballroom dancing at any rate, she took his hand hoping that he would lead and she would simply just sway to his rhythm. As he pulled her tight to his chest, she was close enough now to see his eyes through the mask, his beautiful sparkling eyes; his lip turned upwards into a smile as the orchestra started playing The Masquerade Suite by Khachaturian. William started to move to the music holding her close, Amelia prayed that her feet stayed in contact with the floor and used all her concentration not to stand on his feet as he led her around the room.

A low chuckle came from underneath his hood. "I don't need to see your face to know you are scowling," he said quietly.

She looked up at him; his smile all the more wicked underneath his hood. "I forgot to tell you I can't dance," she whispered.

William pulled away and twirled her around, images of those around her fused into one with an array of colours and then she was looking at him again. "Nonsense Amelia Scott. There is no such word as can't."

She shook her head. "You sound like my mother."

He pulled away again and then brought her closer, his musk filling her senses. "Then she is a wise woman is she not?"

Amelia smiled. "Well, she would love to hear you say that."

After a few moments the other guests joined the dance-floor, keeping a respectable distance from them. Amelia couldn't fathom why they kept nodding whenever William looked their way.

"You're treated like royalty. I'm not surprised you like it here."

She felt his body tense when he momentarily stopped, and then his body heat started to rise as he began to sway once again.

"I never said I liked it here," he said forlornly.

Looking up to catch a glimpse of his eyes she pulled away and squinted. His mouth was tight and his eyes dull; she was an idiot. "I am so sorry if I offended you William. I forget to engage my brain before I speak sometimes."

He stopped and looked at her, the guests nearest to them looking over with concern. She waited for him to react, hoping she hadn't made a mess of the evening when he threw his head back and started laughing, relieved, she breathed once more.

William's hood fell down to his shoulders revealing his mask. "Amelia Scott you truly are magnificent." Grabbing her arm he pulled her towards the patio doors. "Would you care for a stroll?"

She looked back to the room full of guests, each one laughing and twirling in time to the music; no one appeared to be watching, they could sneak away unnoticed and at least being outside meant she didn't have to make a fool of herself when she fell over or stepped on his toes. Then she turned to William, his lips looked fuller with his face obscured by the mask, kissable and soft. Amelia moistened her lips. "If you like."

He led her down past the ornamental garden and through to the large oak trees when she stopped. It all seemed so familiar, walking through the garden towards the woods, the cloaks, the masks.

"Something wrong Amelia?" he asked.

She studied her surroundings closely, her heartbeat quickening as she started to remember fragments of the dream. "I've been here before."

"Yes. We were here yesterday."

"No." She pulled the cloak tighter around her body taking away the night chill. "Not yesterday. We were standing here, wearing these clothes. I don't know, I am having serious case of deja vu."

William stepped closer to her, his mask almost touching hers. "Deja vu?" Amelia nodded as he leant towards her ear and whispered, "Then tell me Amelia, what happens next?"

The hairs on the back of her neck slowly rising the moment his breath tickled her lobe when he spoke, he moved his mouth dangerously close to hers. As his lips came closer to her own, Amelia wondered what he would taste like and then he tilted his head and kissed her gently. She closed her eyes as his soft warm lips connected with her own allowing the kiss to linger. Parting her lips she kissed him back thankful he reciprocated, he brought his hands around her back and gently pulled her closer, the heat from his hands radiating through her body bringing a tingling sensation along her skin. She kissed him urgently, a sensual fever taking control, tangling her hands in his soft dark curly hair wanting to devour him, take all of him, when he pulled back.

His smile widened as he watched her and that's when it came to her — the dream she had about the man in the cloak, but it was no man, not any man that she could recall. She looked closely at his mask, the detailing, the engravings, the shape; wolf. Amelia shook her head and started to step backwards, she could see his lips move but heard no sound, the buzzing in her head pounding so fiercely she was sure her skull would crack, limbs went numb from underneath her and then there was darkness.

Opening her eyes, the blanket of stars in the night sky welcomed her and then he appeared.

"Thank goodness. You had me worried. Are you okay?" he asked.

His expression was one of worry and concern and she was grateful to see all of him, minus mask. His porcelain good looks and dark hair framed his features, then she focused on his plump lips and without warning, kissed him.

Holding her shoulders he pushed her away. "Amelia, you took a tumble, are you hurt?"

She shook her head. "Of course not." Amelia wondered why he asked such silly questions when all she wanted was to be kissing him again, she advanced on him but he held her firm.

"Amelia, please, you're bleeding." He stroked her hair above the temple parting strands to reveal a lump and small cut.

Her hand immediately shot up to the area he examined and when she made contact with the lump it sent a shock-wave of pain through her cranium making her wince. He moved closer to her and parting her hair again, bent down and kissed the cut gently. Heat radiated through as the pain ebbed away, he licked her wound and then looked at her. His eyes black as the night, her blood stained his lips, but all she wanted was for him to take her. He licked his lips and held her upright.

Fearing her clumsiness had put a kibosh on the evening she mentally berated herself. "I feel fine, really. Why don't we go back to the party? Have some more of that delicious champagne."

William chuckled. "I'm afraid the party has finished."

Amelia sat up of her own accord. "What time is it? How long was I out?"

He reached to brush aside a strand of hair from her face. "You were out for a while, I asked everyone to leave." The words didn't make any sense to her. "You see now why I was worried. I would like to take you to the hospital, just to be sure."

Her hand traced the area across the lump again, filled with remorse for ruining their evening. "I am so sorry William to have pulled you away from your friends to look after clumsy comatose me."

William stood and looked down at her. "Whether awake or asleep, I like spending time with you Amelia Scott." The foggy feeling returned and she felt her eyelids become heavy. "I think perhaps I should take you home," he said forlornly.

He bent down and picked her up in his arms, her legs dangling over his forearm; she wrapped her arms around his neck and rested her head on his shoulder. His warmth radiated through her chilled skin, his gentle motion rocked her like a baby in lullaby as she fought to keep her eyes open, but she couldn't resist resting them for just two seconds.

# chaptra trí warn ugens

The sound of sirens woke her from slumber. She stared at the blank wall and through the haze realised that she was home and in her own bed. Pulling back the covers she looked down at her nightdress, with no recollection of how she got home or getting changed and into bed. Her phone buzzed atop the nightstand; one new message from William. As she read the text a smile crept across her face; ever the gentleman he had sent her home after the party with a female member of staff who made sure she was safe and in bed before leaving, the last sentence however confused her. '*I hope your lumpy head feels better.*' Her hand instinctively went to her head, as she felt around she didn't feel any lumps or bumps. Making her way to the en-suite she switched on the lights and leaning over the sink took a closer look in the mirror. Above her left ear dried blood had congealed bonding strands of hair together. She pulled the hair apart and looked at the skin underneath; no sign of injury, nothing to suggest she had hurt herself. Frowning, she picked away at the dried blood and made her way back into the bedroom, her dress and cloak were hanging on the wardrobe door looking like a deflated version of herself from last night.

Memories began to resurface, the ball, dancing, William, and the taste of his lips. She traced her lips with her finger and smiled remembering his soft warm touch. Picking up her phone she read the text from him again, but the time in the top corner of the homescreen brought her back to earth when she realised she was going to be late for work.

Entering the bookshop through the back door, Amelia keyed in the code to disarm the alarm and made her way down the corridor switching on the lamps as she went by when she saw a Fortune flyer on the coffee table. She picked up the flyer and was lost to thoughts of how Friday had come by so quickly when a tapping on the front door made her jump. The postman stood outside waving a small parcel and couple of letters, unbolting the door she let him in.

"Parcel for you Miss Scott and this letter needs to be signed for."

She took the items offered while he pulled out the small device from his bag and scanned the consignment number. Turning over the parcel she saw no date stamp or indication of the sender, just a small icon of some description in the top right corner printed onto the cardboard.

"If you could sign here please," he said holding out the machine and plastic pen. Amelia put the items down so she could scrawl on the small screen and then handed it back to the young man. "Looking forward to tonight?" he asked.

"Yes and no," she said looking down at the parcel on the table.

"Highlight of the month for most of us round 'ere," he said putting the device into his bag and fishing out more letters.

As she turned to answer him, Seth walked into the store.

"Hey Seth, just saying, looking forward to tonight." When Seth offered a nod he noted the silent exchange between Seth and Amelia and made a quick exit.

The door banged shut echoing around the empty store, she watched Seth disappear down the corridor and heard the back door open and close in his wake. Amelia shook her head at his lack of social graces and turned the sign on the door to display 'open' before switching on the computers, finally making her way to the coffee machine. More banging from the rear of the store and footsteps ensued, she braced herself for a showdown but was surprised when Sonny walked past carrying a bass drum.

"Morning." His greeting pleasant as always. Placing the drum down by one of the sofas Sonny pulled the table out and hoisted it over his shoulder.

"Christ, you need a hand?" Amelia asked wide-eyed, she knew only too well how heavy those tables were from trying to move them a few inches to clean underneath.

Daniel walked in carrying an amp and cast Sonny a look of disappointment, but when he saw the look on Amelia's face he shook his head and grimaced. "Showing off to the lady Sonny?"

Sonny stopped and looked back to Amelia. "You were taking forever to unload the van, thought I'd get a head start." He continued past Daniel and down the corridor.

"What's going on?" Amelia asked looking at the empty space created.

Daniel put the amp down beside her. "Making room. We won't be long. How 'bout you put some coffee on."

Picking up the letters and parcel from the remaining table Amelia put them next to the cloche and pulled out the water container from the machine. "Was just about to before you guys came in," she said brushing past him.

Daniel watched her walk away, his eyes flitting to her firm rump when Sonny arrived with more drums and placed them in the space he had created.

"What the hell are you doing carrying shit like that in front of people man?" Daniel said hurriedly.

Sonny shrugged. "I forgot. Besides, she's not going to think anything of it, relax."

"Sonny. She's a regular Miss fucking Marple. I wouldn't like to presume anything."

"You're reaching," Sonny said dragging a sofa to one side making an L-shape with the other. "Besides, I like her."

Daniel huffed. "She's not *yours* to like."

"Nor yours," he said squaring up to him.

"Guys, what's the hold up?" asked Seth as he came through carrying another amp and a guitar.

Daniel looked at Sonny with a dead expression.

"Am I missing something?" Seth asked of his two companions. "Because if I need to set this straight, we will."

The two men replied 'no' in unison and left to collect more equipment passing Amelia who was returning with the full water container.

Seth waited for her to install before making his approach. "I'm sorry about—"

"Forget about it," she interrupted him.

"It was stupid of me to think you would be home." He watched her click the cover back into place and pull out the grinder compartment. When she didn't offer eye contact he waited for her to turn towards him and gently touched her hand. "Amelia." She looked down at his hand on hers. "Truly, I am sorry."

She closed her eyes and sighed. "I forgot the milk." Pulling away from him she drew out the drawer and left to refill from the kitchenette.

Seth noticed the priority letter, then glanced at the parcel addressed to Amelia; the crest on the packaging filled him with sorrow.

"Can we draw a line under it?" she asked walking back to the counter placing the milk down and pulling out the coffee beans. "Every time we see one another these days either you or I are apologising for something or another. It's exhausting."

He looked up at her, his eyes moist. "Of course."

When he turned to leave she looked down at the letter. "Oh, this came for you special delivery, signed for it this morning." He nodded stuffing the letter into his back pocket. "Do you want me to put some toast on?" she shouted after him.

He didn't stop when he answered. "We ate well this morning."

Sonny and Daniel sat inside the rear of the camper van smoking and chatting, their earlier argument a thing of the past. Their banter died down when Seth approached.

"Did she mention anything about last night?" asked Daniel.

Seth shook his head. "I haven't asked."

Daniel jumped out of the van and leant against the sliding door. "Don't you think you should? He's stepping up and you're playing it cool. You're going to lose her."

Sonny shuddered. "Hate those gatherings, they make my skin crawl."

"Too swanky for me too," said Daniel handing Sonny the cigarette. "You'd think after all these years they'd do something a little more…"

"Modern?" offered Sonny handing the cigarette back.

Daniel sucked hard on the vervain. "Yeah."

"Ours is not to question why," Seth said taking the cigarette from Daniel. "But Amelia was there, and he made a quick exit with her."

"I hate that shit," Daniel said wincing at the taste in his mouth. "I'm going to go to the apothecary and get something else one of these days."

"It is unpleasant," Seth replied examining the roll up in his hand. "You have my permission to seek an alternative remedy. Speak to Grace next time you go, she's not as—"

"Uptight," offered Daniel.

Seth nodded agreement.

All three were quiet lost in thought to last night, how to broach the subject with Amelia, wondering if she had been taken. Sonny slid to the edge of the van and laid back, his legs dangling over the metal frame, looking up at the ceiling he laughed.

Daniel turned to his friend. "What's so funny?"

"Patricia."

Daniel began to chuckle, and after a while Seth joined in. It wasn't long until all three were laughing loudly when the back door banged shut and they turned to see Amelia walking towards them struggling to carry four drinks. Seth immediately went to her aid.

"What's so funny?" she asked.

Seth took two of the drinks from her. "Guys being guys."

Amelia looked at each one of them searching for answers where there were none and handed the last drink to Sonny. "So are you all set for tonight?" she asked enthusiastically.

"In spirit, yes, in body, no," answered Sonny with a grin as he took a sip of his beverage, grateful to be taking the vervain taste away.

"Late night last night?" she asked eying each of them over the rim of her mug. She watched the three men look at one another and realised none of them was about to disclose the truth.

"We were out with old friends. How about you? Did you have a nice evening?" asked Seth.

She looked at Sonny and Daniel who eyed her expectantly. "I did as it happens, thank you." In answer to Seth's raised eyebrow she continued. "Must have been a good one too because I can't remember much."

Seth took a step towards her, his frown deepening. "How are you feeling? Dizzy, nauseous, weak?"

Amelia wrinkled her nose. "What?"

"Anybody serving?" Ned called from the back door.

Leaving to tend to her customer the three men huddled together.

"He knows the rules. He couldn't use that on her, she has to go willingly," whispered Sonny.

Seth shook his head. "We don't know that he did use it, she seems perfectly fine in herself."

Daniel threw the cigarette away. "I'm telling you, he's not giving up. You need to do some—"

"Silence." Seth turned to Sonny and Daniel. "There is nothing we can do if she has chosen, we deal with whatever comes our way."

"And if he doesn't play by the rules?" asked Daniel.

Seth watched the door slowly close and then narrowed his eyes. "Then we deal with him… and the pack."

Ned sat on the bar stool nursing his drink watching Amelia fill the cloche with sticky buns. "Are you going to be here all day and evening?" he asked.

"Not sure, need to speak to Seth about that. Would be nice to go home and change. What time do they usually start?"

Ned turned in his seat, watching Sonny assemble the drum apparatus. "They usually let some kids jam with them before they start, around five. Is quite popular. Valerie and..." he stopped himself before he realised what he had said.

Valerie and Julia were both keen to learn guitar and Seth was teaching them when he could. She remembered the photograph of Valerie, Julia and Seth and old woman Chandler looking on, she will never forget the expression on the old lady's face. Lois never seemed to have any issues with Seth as far as she could remember, and so couldn't understand why she looked so upset in that photo.

Amelia watched Ned play with the mug staring off into the distance. "Yeah, I heard they enjoyed playing," she whispered.

"All done here," shouted Daniel.

"Great you can help me with that angle," Sonny said pointing to the metal construction as he slid a cymbal into the top.

Amelia sat behind the counter watching the men put the equipment together. When Daniel leaned over the bass drum to assist Sonny, his buttocks and strong muscles strained against his tight pants, lost to thoughts of how hard he felt, she was mortified when Ned coughed having caught her staring and gave her a knowing smile.

"Well, I'm off. I have time with my little one before she goes to her mum's tonight."

Ned had never eluded to his personal circumstances before, but piecing together their conversations and his demeanor of late, she was beginning to realise he was finding being a single dad a struggle at times. Ned pulled out his wallet to pay but she shook her head, answering her with a smile he slid off the barstool. "So I'll see you later then?"

Amelia nodded.

Listening to the men putting the equipment together she looked down at the parcel. She wanted to open it, but there was something about the mark on the packaging that made her want to open it alone. Amelia picked it up and put it away in her bag, when she straightened, Seth was beside the till.

"Do you have a moment?" he asked.

Amelia nodded and followed Seth to the mezzanine balcony. He was pacing by the time she got to the top step and she began to panic wondering if he heard she had been for an interview and was going to sack her before she had chance to explain.

When he saw her approach he stopped pacing. "Amelia."

Something about his tone concerned her. "Is there something wrong Seth?" she asked walking tentatively to his side.

"I wanted to know you were okay."

"Of course, why wouldn't I be?"

"Its just what you said earlier—"

"Oh that," she said waving her hand and sitting on the edge of the loveseat, thankful it was nothing to do with the job. "I got a bump on the head, was out cold apparently, but I'm all fine now."

Seth turned to her, holding his hand to her head. "Where, where did you bump your head, are you sure you're okay?"

Amelia leaned away. "Yes, quite sure. Mustn't have been much, there was only a little bit of blood, but can't see any scratches."

Seth pulled her hair to the side, when Amelia tried swatting him away he held her gaze. "A bump on the head is not to be messed with, especially if you bled. Where was it?"

His stern expression and tone of voice left her pointing at the spot where she found the dried blood. Seth gently parted her hair to one side examining her scalp where he found the tiniest of bruising not visible to the human eye. He knew what had happened for the wound to heal so fast and gritted his teeth.

"Well, can you see anything?" she asked expectantly.

Letting go of her hair he sighed. "You're fine, nothing major."

"See, I told you," she said standing.

He was radiating a warmth that made her want to hold him, his gentle musk intoxicating and his sad eyes made her want to kiss him and make him happy again. When he didn't move she stepped closer to him, their hands touching, he gently slid his fingers through her own and leant forward resting his forehead on hers. She enjoyed the secure feeling of his touch, closing her eyes she sighed, just being near him again made everything disappear. Amelia rose on her tiptoes and kissed his lips, thankful that he kissed her back. Pulling her arms around his waist she was as close to him as she could possibly be, the warmth from his hands on her back sent a wave of excitement as her body reacted to his touch, longing for his hands to be touching her bare flesh. His kiss was slow and gentle until he brought his hands to her head tangling his fingers through her hair kissing her urgently. She pulled away to catch her breath and they held one another, eyes locked.

"Close your eyes," he whispered. Amelia slowly closed her eyes. Bending down to her ear he asked, "What do you hear?"

"My heart beat."

"What do you feel?"

"Your heat."

"What can you taste?"

"You," she answered breathlessly, rising to her tiptoes and kissing him passionately.

The two lovers lay embraced on the loveseat staring into each other's eyes, stealing kisses. Repositioning the cushion under her back, Amelia glanced at the wall clock above them and was horrified when she realised the time.

"Holy crap!" She exclaimed pulling herself upright, adjusting her t-shirt.

Seth idly rose from the loveseat. "What's wrong?"

"Seth, It's one o'clock and we've been up here while the store has been open," she whispered.

He strolled to the banister and looked down. The store was in darkness and the sign on the door had been turned to read 'closed'. He turned back to her with a grin. "The guys shut up shop."

Amelia pulled the belt round her waistband and dusted down her pants. "Good god, you mean they…" Running her fingers through her hair she turned a light dusky pink and inwardly groaned. She had never made out while at work before, but gathered if she was going to do it, why not with the boss. "Seth, I am so sorry, I didn't realise." She walked towards the stairs.

"Are you sorry it happened?" he asked.

"No, god no. I would have rather we didn't…" She looked back at the small sofa. "I would have rather we weren't on show is all." Her eyes grew darker recalling his touch.

Pulling her in tight he brushed the hair from her face. "Relax, they left before anything was on show."

Amelia pulled back. "How do you know?"

"Solomon." Daniel shouted from beyond the corridor.

Amelia shrank away from the banister as Seth turned to address his friend. "Brother?"

The young man coughed. "We were going to do a sound check."

"Pur dha!" He turned to Amelia sat on the edge of the seat her head in her hands. "You can finish early if you can't face them just yet."

She let her hands fall to her knees. "Do you mind? It's just that I can't face Daniel and his 'I know what you've been doing' expression."

"I wasn't aware he had that."

Amelia stood and walked to his side. "Oh yes, along with the 'I can't believe I have to talk to you' expression."

Shaking his head he smiled, aware that his friend was somewhat socially awkward by most standards, if only people knew that deep down he was a good-hearted man.

"Coast is clear." He announced.

Amelia quickly ran down the stairs, grabbed her bag and exited the store as quickly as she could. The door chimed on her way out as Sonny and Daniel emerged from the back room, the knowing smile on their faces exactly what Amelia had been afraid of.

Seth joined them. "Thank you for your discretion."

"Hey," Sonny declared opening a beer. "What are brothers for?" He handed the bottle to Seth opening two more, passing one to Daniel.

Daniel leant against the staircase railings sipping his drink. "So I gather everything is okay? She didn't?" Seth shook his head. "Then why the parcel?"

"I don't know, maybe we are wrong about his intentions."

Daniel spat out some of his beer. "That's bullshit and you know it."

"I have to believe he is better than that," Seth whispered.

Sonny slammed his bottle of beer on the counter, a cloud of foam forming at the ridge. "After all these years, you're going to give him the benefit of the doubt. Don't forget what he is capable of, what they are all capable of, *and* what he did to us." His youthful eyes became dead remembering the horror the three of them had been dragged through.

"I haven't forgotten. I will never forget."

Daniel's scowl deepened. "If this goes against us, we are screwed. You know that don't you."

"If what goes against you?" asked the detective by the open door. The three men each turned watching him approach.

"What can we do for you DI Cooke?" asked Seth. As Daniel stiffened Seth held out his hand across his chest and gave him a stern look. "We were discussing the sound check. If it doesn't go according to plan, we won't sound our usual."

Sonny made his way to the makeshift stage they had created, turning on the power at the main switch.

DI Cooke looked at the equipment and then back to Seth. "Oh I forgot it was tonight. Never been to one of your shindigs. Think I might make an exception this once."

"You are most welcome to join us Detective, and please bring as many colleagues as you like." Seth answered courteously.

Sonny shook his head as he banged the bass drum adjusting the microphone by the cymbal. "As long as they are hot police chicks, we don't mind who you bring," he shouted.

"Quite." The detective looked to the mezzanine floor. "No Amelia today?"

Daniel folded his arms across his chest and smirked at the police officer. "Just missed her, she left after her and Seth got—"

"I let Amelia go early because of the... shindig, as you call it," Seth interrupted.

The detective looked at Daniel with narrowed eyes and then to Seth. "I'll be back later then. Or maybe I will pay her a visit at home." He turned to leave.

"You do that," Seth shouted after him.

When he had left the store Daniel turned to Seth. "You're quite happy for him to be making house calls on your woman?"

"She isn't mine," he turned towards the nearest amp picking up his guitar. "Not yet."

# chaptra pedar warn ugens

Amelia sat at the kitchen table looking at the parcel contemplating opening it when there was a knock at the front door. "Stephen?" she asked surprised, "to what do I owe the pleasure?"

"May I come in?" he asked.

She motioned for him to enter. Making her way back to the lounge she sat on the sofa waiting for him to follow, he closed the front door and stood by the fireplace.

"Any news on the fingerprints?" she asked.

"That's what I wanted to talk to you about."

"Oh?" Her gut tightened when she heard his tone, whatever he was about to say did not bode well.

"I'm afraid we were unable to pull any prints that match the database."

"That just means they haven't been caught before."

"Let me finish," he said holding up both hands. "What they found was," he paused and shook his head, "unexplainable."

She moved to the edge of her seat. "What do you mean unexplainable?"

"The only prints we found were your own of course, but there was something else."

"What?" The look on his face made her stand. "What did you find?"

"Hair."

"Hair?"

"Animal hair. Canis Lupus to be precise." He said matter of fact pulling out the small clear packet from his jacket.

"Dog?" she asked taking the evidence slip.

"Wolf."

Amelia walked to the window and held the packet up to the natural light. "Out there," she said looking towards the tree line. "I saw some wild dogs last night, in the meadow. Could they be scavenging? Coming closer to the village maybe?" she asked.

"That is a possibility. I assume they'd act like foxes, take whatever was easiest for them. Can't know for sure without asking an expert."

Amelia sat down and frowned. "It can't be wolves though, that's just not feasible. William said the library has the biggest mammal collection in the country. Maybe there is a professor at the library who could explain why the wild dogs are coming close."

"If you want to take the sample with you, you're more than welcome, but don't lose it, it is evidence after all. Could be that our guys got it wrong, maybe it is just feral dogs."

"I'll do that," she whispered lost in thought looking at the hair.

"But we both know dogs can't open doors, so you need to make sure you lock up at night before we get to the bottom of it. I'll make some house calls on our usual suspects, see if they have heard anything. I've not seen Wilbur St. Clemins in a few months, it's about time we had a catch up."

Amelia hummed while she continued examining the hair sample.

"So," the detective said. "You'll be at the bookshop tonight I presume."

"What? Oh, yes, I'll be there."

He noticed her demeanour and tried to reassure her best he could. "At least we know it's not the crazy ex, right?"

The Unison workers demonstration over a year ago resulted in his prints being added to the police database when things got out of hand, Tatem never did elaborate on the details, but that presented more unanswered questions.

Amelia tutted. "Reassuring."

"You may want to think about getting a guard dog. Young woman living on her own."

She followed him to the hallway and held the door open for him. "Actually, I'm more of a cat person."

The detective laughed. "Then get a really big mean cat." He waved her goodbye and went on his way.

Amelia observed the bookshop filling with youngsters eager to play with the band; Daniel was quietly tuning his bass guitar while Sonny engaged in playful banter with two girls sat nearest the drums, giggling to one another. Amongst the chatter Lydia entered and ran towards Seth.

"Seth, Seth, will you play for me?" she squealed.

Her mother came running through the door trying to grab her daughter by the hood on her coat. "Lydia, what did I tell you about running off like that?" she said trying to catch her breath.

Seth looked down at the little girl whose eyes were wide with excitement. "Lydia, what did I tell you about listening to your mother?"

The little girl looked at her guardian. "Sorry Mummy." Turning back to Seth she started to sway as the excitement built. "Will you play my favourite?" she asked.

Seth nodded to her mother as he picked up the little girl and sat her on his knee. "I will play your favourite munchkin, if you promise me you'll never run off like that again."

Lydia held up her little finger, "Pinky swear."

Seth linked his little finger with hers, "Pinky swear."

Amelia made her way past the youngsters congregated around the band chatting to the would-be musicians, waving her arrival she went to the counter and placed her bag underneath. Hattie approached with a wry expression.

"Got you working tonight I see."

Amelia smiled as she checked the coffee beans. "I offered really. My first music night, so wanted to get to know everyone, what better way than to be serving."

Seth approached carrying Lydia in his arms. "She flaked out bless her," he said stroking her hair.

Hattie smiled at her daughter who held on tight to Seth.

"There you are," the little girls father said taking her from Seth. Lydia groaned but still didn't open her eyes when her father took her into his arms. "I was wondering where you got to," he said to his wife.

Hattie stroked her daughter's cheek. "Calm down Paul, she only wanted to listen to one song, and now you can take her home, don't forget Gregg's guitar, he'll not be happy if you do."

He quickly kissed his wife goodbye and greeted his son who was in deep conversation with Sonny. Mina burst through the door, and made straight for Seth who moved around the side of the counter towards Amelia.

"Everything okay?" he whispered to Amelia stroking her arm out of view of others. Amelia nodded with a smile while she poured a jug of iced water. Happy she agreed to come along, Seth returned to his band mates managing to bypass the vixen.

Mina glanced at Amelia. "I see you didn't waste much time," she said leaning over the counter in her low-cut dress.

"Mina," Hattie chastised. "It's not your place to question. Besides, she is single and you are not."

Mina clucked her tongue. "Red wine," she requested. "And make it a large one."

Amelia turned to Hattie. "Can I get you anything Hattie?"

"I'll have the same," she answered with a slow release of breath.

As Amelia poured the ladies their beverages Mina asked, "So have you and Seth sealed the deal yet or are you just fooling around?"

"Mina!" exclaimed her friend.

"What? I can ask." Picking up the glass she took a large gulp. "He must be a hot lover, I've watched him down the surf in his wetsuit; those bulging muscles, firm torso, thighs that could crack a walnut, pert backside… I've sneaked a peek too at his—"

"Will that be all?" asked Amelia ignoring the taunts.

Mina's voice was even. "Better leave me with the bottle."

Amelia put the cork in the bottleneck, which was swiftly taken by the young mother making her way to the nearest sofa.

"I'm sorry about Mina," apologised Hattie.

"Don't be," Amelia said with a smile. "She's had her fun."

"I thought she'd given up on Seth to be honest, seemed quite taken with a tall black man she had seen around the village a few times."

"Oh? What's his name?" Amelia was expecting Hattie to say the name she wanted to forget. If Mina had presented herself to Tate, she was most certain, given his past record, he would have obliged.

"I don't know. Mina said she never saw him again. Just vanished. I'm sure Mr Bateman said he was staying at your cottage." Hattie quickly joined her friend, furious for the embarrassment.

Amelia considered speaking to Mr Bateman about the paper deliveries, try and piece together when he actually left, there were no newspapers piled up behind the front door when she arrived; did she even want to know what he was doing now, convincing herself he could be dead in a ditch for all she cared.

A few beats of the drum and the crowd started to settle. Seth and Daniel sat on stools either side of the drum-kit, Sonny twirled his drumsticks and beat the bass drum while Seth picked up his guitar. Four taps of the drumsticks and Daniel started to play the first bars on the bass, the undisputed riff to the beginning of 'Dusted' by Belly went down well as an opening number which was quickly followed by Garbage's 'I Think I'm Paranoid'. As the song progressed some of the youngsters danced in what little room they could find, while some sat on the steps. She caught a young couple heading up to the mezzanine floor and quickly followed after Seth had mentioned the youngsters try to sneak out of sight. Making sure no one else tried to head in the same direction, Amelia pulled out a floor cushion and sat down on the top step watching the band perform, the height giving her a birds-eye view of the whole store in case anyone needed a refill. When the fourth song rang out she felt a cold breeze and the hairs on the back of her neck rising, turning she saw William on the loveseat looking at her with a wicked grin.

"How did you get up here?" she asked. "I didn't see you come in."

He smiled at her and patted the seat beside him. With Seth, Daniel and Sonny preoccupied she slid from the step and approached.

"Well?" she asked again.

William shrugged. "I have been here a while. Please, sit with me."

She looked back at the band again and to the people around the store. "I can't. I need to keep an eye on the cash register."

He pulled two cold beers from the side table and handed one to Amelia. "Then I shall join you at the step while you perform your duty," he said gallantly.

Amelia returned to the floor cushion and pulled another alongside for William. She sat watching the band sipping her cold beer, William however was watching her.

"Why do you do that?" she asked.

"Do what?"

"Stare at me like that."

He took a sip of his drink. "You fascinate me. Is that so wrong?"

"You are so strange." With all eyes focused on the band she turned to William, leaning closer so he could hear her over the music. "I wanted to ask you something about the library."

"You've decided to join us?" he asked enthusiastically.

She shook her head. "Sorry to disappoint. I wanted to know if you had any resident experts."

William's eyes burned a darkness she had not seen before. "Oh? What kind of expert?"

She pulled out the small clear plastic packet from her pocket and turned it over in her lap, smoothing out the creases. "Someone who could tell me what this is."

As he looked down at the packet his nostrils flared. "I believe you would be seeking Professor Armand's knowledge. He is quite excellent when it comes to mammals."

"And does he reside at the library?"

William nodded. "He will be leading a conference tomorrow as it happens, of which you are most welcome to attend." His eyes did not move from the packet. "May I ask where the sample is from?"

She quickly put it back in her pocket. "Just something that was found at the cottage."

The crowd applauded and some teenagers showed their approval with whistles, noticing Mina at the counter she excused herself. Another bottle of red for the alluring young mother and a pitcher of iced water for the youngsters, she finished serving refills before the band started again, this time with a slow number. Dropping some change, Amelia bent down to pick up the copper pieces when she noted her parcel peeking through her opened bag, taunting her with its contents; she held it in her hands tracing the symbol with her finger. Pulling two more beers from the fridge she made her way back to the mezzanine and sat down at the top step, William was lying down resting his head on his hands, his shirt revealing hair below his navel. She averted her stare as he pulled himself upright.

"Here," she said handing him the beer. "This has been bugging me." Amelia held the parcel in her hands. "It's from you isn't it," she said searching his reaction.

He nodded. "Yes. Why have you not opened it yet?"

"I think I was waiting to do it with you," she said frowning. "I have no idea why though."

William smiled. "I am here now. Why don't you open it with me." Amelia turned the parcel around and looked at the symbol. "My family crest," he said answering her silent question. "But I think you know that."

"Yes, and I don't know how I would know that. Have I seen it before? Maybe at the Mansion or library?"

"It is a possibility," he said watching her play with the brown parcel. "Open it."

Amelia pulled the tab and lifted the lid. A black velvet pouch lay inside, holding the pouch she felt the hairs on her arms rise. Pulling the cord Amelia tilted the pouch and emptied the contents into her palm where a pendant lay motionless and cold to the touch. Turning over the stone she examined it closely, black as the night and delicately set within a wire encasement on a silver chain.

"It's beautiful," she breathed.

"Let me," he said taking the pendant.

When Amelia pulled her hair to one side he knelt closer to secure the pendant around her neck. Once it touched her skin she felt a wave of cold through her body and let her hair fall down. William gently kissed the exposed skin on her shoulder.

"I was right, it suits you perfectly," he whispered.

Clasping her hand over the stone she sighed. "I can't accept this William."

"You already have," he reminded her, looking at the black stone against her pale chest.

"Why?" she asked.

"Why not?"

Amelia hadn't realised the music had stopped until one of the youngsters sat on the step below her coughed to get her attention.

"Sorry, could I ask for another orange juice please," he said holding up his empty glass.

Amelia pulled herself away from William and followed the boy to the counter to refill the glass where a few more people had lined up expecting refreshments; murmurs around the bookshop became louder as she continued to serve the revellers.

"That's gorgeous Amelia, where ever did you get it?" asked Hattie admiring her necklace. "I don't remember seeing it earlier."

Her hand immediately went to the pendant. "Oh, it was a gift."

She finished serving the last person and looked over to Seth, Sonny and Daniel who were noticeably absent. Locking the till she looked up towards the railings, where there was no sign of William. Knowing how much they hated her new friend, she wondered if they had seen her talking to him, or worse still, made him leave.

Making her way to the back door she saw it was left ajar, pulling it open she stepped out into the car park. The side door to the camper van was open but there was no sign of the band. Walking around the side of the building she caught sight of Sonny.

"Hey. Where did you guys disappear to?" she asked.

"Just having a break." His smile disappeared when he noticed the pendant. Sonny's voice was even was he said, "You saw William today?" Amelia nodded. He looked down at the ground, kicking a pebble and nodded to himself. "Would you care for a smoke?" he said offering his cigarette.

"No, thank you. I don't smoke."

"Wise choice, these things will kill you," he said walking away.

She followed him back to the van where Seth and Daniel were talking in hushed voices and abruptly stopped when Amelia approached.

"You guys sound amazing."

Both men turned with the same expression Sonny had presented, she couldn't fathom why they were sad, as a band they sounded awesome.

Seth forced a smile. "Thank you Amelia."

The awkward silence was enough for Amelia to excuse herself and head back to the shop leaving the three of them at the van.

Sonny gritted his teeth. "Did you…"

"Yes," interrupted Seth.

"Then we know his intentions." Daniel said leaning against the van. "And we know he won't give up any time soon."

"Amelia has to make that decision for herself. There is nothing more we can do."

By the time she returned there was no sign of William. The music took a sombre turn as they churned out a few well-known hits combined with their own material; Amelia sat listening to the songs, her heart filled with sorrow. Seth didn't look up from his microphone and they all wore the same unhappy expression, whatever happened had affected all of them. Scanning the crowd she spotted the detective stood by the door with another officer taking notes and wondered whether his presence there had made them tense, but it couldn't have been the detective; she was certain whatever had happened, happened because of William. It was always about William.

Seth thanked his audience for attending and left quickly before anyone could talk to him. Sonny and Daniel both followed him through to the back door with Mina hot on their heels. Given their demeanour, she was certain a run-in with the temptress would not be welcomed, Amelia quickly ran down the steps and blocked the corridor.

"Can I help you Mina?"

If looks could kill she would have been a pile of dust on the floor. "I wanted to thank them for a wonderful evening."

"I'll be sure to let them know," Amelia said meeting her stare. The young mother continued to look down her nose at Amelia. There was something about Mina that concerned her, though she couldn't quite understand why.

The young mother started to laugh. "Calm down, I'm not after your man. I was heading to the bathroom." She nodded at the door to her right.

When she noticed the sign on the door Amelia breathed a sigh of relief. "Of course. Make it quick, I'll be locking up soon."

She waited by the door for Mina while the store emptied, from her vantage point she could see Hattie stood by the front door chatting to Ned and the policemen, but there was no sign of the band. When Mina had finished she left the store with her friend leaving just the two police officers.

"Did you enjoy the music tonight?" asked the detective.

"Yes, thank you Stephen, did you?"

He shrugged. "So, so. Where did the band disappear to?"

"Just getting some fresh air."

"I see. You'll pass on my regards won't you?" he said smirking.

Amelia returned his smile. "Of course."

When the policemen left she proceeded to switch off the coffee machine, till and lights. After waiting ten minutes she rang Seth's mobile but there was no answer, sending him a text message she explained she was locking up and hoped he had a key if he needed to get back in.

Amelia was thankful that she had driven that day, she didn't fancy walking back home alone in the dark. There was something about that lane at night that had taken a sinister turn. Every dream she had lately featured that lane, and her mothers' words of reading about wild dog attacks in the area made her more vigilant.

The light she had left on in the lounge lighted her way as she pulled her car into her parking space. Shutting the door behind her she exhaled relief, relief to be back, to rest and to contemplate. Whatever had Seth, Sonny and Daniel acting strange had happened during the interval break to have affected each of them, and it was no coincidence that William had disappeared at the same time. Pouring herself a large glass of wine she lay on the sofa and pulled out her phone; no new message from Seth. She typed a message to William hoping he was okay and that she was sorry he left before she could thank him properly for the pendant. Her fingers idly caressed the pendant, rolling her fingers around the stone she felt the surge of ice cold upon touching it. It was beautiful, and she really didn't know why he kept offering her gifts - first the dress, and now this. It had her wondering what it was he would expect from her in return. A text message came into her inbox from William thanking her for company with a reminder about the conference Professor Armand would be leading tomorrow, and that he would leave an access pass for her at reception. Amelia decided William was a thoughtful man, kind and generous, not to mention hot as hell, her thoughts drifting to why he hadn't been snapped up by now.

# *chaptra pymp warn ugens*

The drive into town was peaceful. Amelia tuned into a local radio station playing the recent chart hits when a weather bulletin interrupted the last song warning of fog along the west coast. Looking out of the window to sunshine and blue sky, Amelia ignored the warning knowing how unpredictable weather forecasts can be, it couldn't possibly affect Creek Bay on a day like today.

When she arrived at the library's reception Amelia was handed a pass and directions to the conference. Following the map she made her way through the maze of doors and collections towards the auditorium. The room was packed out, on stage a tall man dressed in tweed with beard and long hair addressed his audience, the screen behind him displaying pictures of large cats and their kill; he spoke eloquently and with passion. After ten minutes he announced there would be a break for half an hour; the collective noise of the flip-up seats banging against back rests sounded around the auditorium as the room started to empty. Amelia passed the last few stragglers making her way down to the stage.

"Miss Scott, I presume." He announced in booming voice. "Master Malloy informed me you would be coming to see me today." Making his way down the steps he held out his hand and smiled at her. His unkempt hair fell just to his shoulders and his scruffy beard made him look like a vagrant.

She held her hand out for pleasantries. "Nice to meet you."

His hand was warm and soft, and his manner was inviting, he motioned for her to sit at the front seat next to him when a young woman came into the auditorium and handed the Professor a drink.

"Would you care for a beverage Miss Scott?" he asked taking the drink offered to him.

"Amelia," she said hoping he would call her by her first name. Being referred to as Miss Scott made her feel twelve again. "Water would be lovely."

The young woman nodded and quickly left. Amelia sat down next to him distracted by the Predators display on stage.

"Magnificent aren't they." He said smiling at the current slide. The Professor turned to Amelia. "Master Malloy said you had something to show me."

"I do." She pulled out the clear plastic wallet from her back pocket and presented it to the professor. "I was told this was wolf hair, but I wanted an expert opinion. William tells me—"

The professor started to laugh. "William?"

Thinking she had made a terrible mistake Amelia shrank back in her seat when the young woman approached with a bottle of spring water and made another quick exit. Sipping the water she watched the Professor examine the hair through the packet.

"May I?" he asked. Amelia nodded. Opening the packet the Professor inhaled and then pulled the strands out between his thumb and forefinger. "I see."

"Well? It's just dog hair isn't it. I told the police it couldn't be wolf."

"The police?" he asked.

Amelia nodded as she took another sip of water. "Yes, they found this at my cottage. Strange things have been happening there lately."

"Oh?" said the Professor putting the hair back into the packet. "What kind of strange things?"

"Banging mainly. I thought it was kids picking on the new person, but it looks like these wild dogs have been foraging for food or something. Mr Bateman at the local shop said he's had a few posters for missing pets lately. Is that a possibility?"

The Professor handed the packet to Amelia. "When a carnivorous animal such as the wolf makes his way into the human world, one should be curious as to why."

"So it is wolf?" Amelia looked at the packet before putting it in her pocket. "But why, and how? Shouldn't we be notifying someone? And what do they want at Lowe Cottage?"

"Lowe Cottage?"

"My home." Amelia shifted in her seat as she tried to fathom the probability of wolves prowling outside her home at night. "I see them, at night, across the meadow watching. Always watching. Like they are waiting for something. I just assumed they were feral dogs."

The Professor took a sip of his tea. "Miss Scott. Can you tell me anything more about their behaviour? Do they venture close to the property when you are there? Is it just in the twilight hours or have you seen them during the day? Have you seen any discarded food at all?" He looked at Amelia, her eyes wide with horror. "I'm sorry, I am asking too many questions. You see." He put his tea down. "I am very passionate about my work, and this would be a perfect opportunity to study the animals in close proximity. Do you see them every night?"

"Questions I can handle. If I don't see them, I certainly hear them. They have been sniffing around the property while I have been there, and it has always been late evening early morning, never during the day and I have never seen any evidence of food. Oh, we did find something of a pit out in the woods, smelt like a sewer, could that be anything?"

"Wolves defending an area will sometimes use one particular area for eating their kill. This is most fascinating. Where exactly in the woods did you find this so called pit?" he asked leaning towards her.

There was a murmur of voices behind them as a few delegates started to filter back into the auditorium and take their seats.

"It was near Old Man Malloy's place. Do you know it?"

"I have heard of the place, yes." He drank the remainder of his tea. "Have you seen any of them up close?"

Amelia shook her head. "No. Oh, hang on. I think maybe yes. One was hanging around the front of the house when a friend popped round. It ran away very fast we didn't get a good enough look really."

The professor nodded. "I see."

"There is one thing though." Amelia said quietly. "The noise. Awful piercing noise."

"Oh?" he asked expectantly. "What does it sound like?"

"It is the worst noise I have ever heard, sends shivers down my spine. Painful and raw, like it is taunting me."

The professor pulled out his mobile phone from his jacket and clicked a few buttons before holding it up to her ear. "Does it sound like this?"

When he clicked the play button the noise resonated with her, forming a lump in her throat.

"Yes, that's it." The words strangled. The professor clicked the phone to stop the recording and put it away in his jacket. "Well? What can we do?" she asked.

"Nothing," he replied, matter of fact. Standing the professor brushed down his trousers.

"Nothing?" Amelia all but squealed. A couple of the delegates looked up from their notes. "Nothing?" she said again in hushed voice. "I have wolves prowling around my home at night and you say we do nothing?"

"Yes. I say you leave them alone and they will leave you alone." He walked to the edge of the stage and looked up at the seats all but filled waiting for the last remaining few to return from break. "I believe they are within their territory, and any threat to that would increase your chances of a confrontation, so I say you leave them well alone and they will do the same."

Amelia tugged at his sleeve. "Easy for you to say. You haven't been in that house while they are outside banging on the doors screeching like banshees."

The professor looked down at her hand on his sleeve and then held her stare. "Miss Scott. These predators are not to be messed with. If they feel threatened, they will try to take out the threat to maintain the health of the pack. I suggest you look at what you have been doing to make them act this way."

"What I've been—"

"Professor Armand. We are ready to start when you are." The young lady beside the stage interrupted.

The professor nodded and pulled his arm free from Amelia. "You are welcome to stay for the remainder of the conference, but I suggest you go home and think about what I have said." He turned climbing the steps onto the stage and addressed his audience.

Amelia felt wounded; if one person could help sort her wild dog problem it was supposed to be this guy. She watched him on the stage, animated and passionate about the subject of big cats and their kill while his audience lapped it up. She walked away deflated.

Passing security outside the auditorium she noticed a sign pointing to the museum. William had mentioned they had the largest mammal collection, and that meant they must have wolves, and if so, she had to see what she was up against for herself. Walking down the long corridor she came to an area that was roped across. Security stood either side of the large double doors.

"Can I help you?" One of them asked.

She flashed her access card. "I wanted to visit the mammal collection."

The guard took her card and swiped it in his hand held machine. The machine beeped displaying her name and access code. "Of course Miss Scott. Enjoy your stay." He stood to one side allowing her to pass.

The room was enormous, stretching as far as she could see, three floors with various animals in poses befitting their station in life. As she looked up, she saw the blue whale stretching across the ceiling, with various marine mammals posed beside the gentle giant as though in motion. Making her way to the big cat section she stood next to the lion; the undisputed king of the jungle. His mane was impressive and his paws enormous, but as she walked beside the tiger it was then she realised how much larger the tiger was in comparison. The most revealing element that always struck her when looking at stuffed animals was their dead eyes, taxidermists could never capture the life essence of the animal it once was. The lioness and cubs made her stomach flinch, the fact they were babies made her sad for them to be stuffed and put on display. She held out her hand and stroked the little cub nearest to her, its coarse hair and solid form shocked her under the expectation it should be soft.

Moving along she looked at the jaguar draped on a large tree trunk, his nose scrunched into a snarl and mouth open wide flashing large canine teeth. A tear ran down her cheek as she looked at the beautiful creature, memories of her black cat never far away. She carried on walking past the hyenas and foxes and then came to a halt. Beside the large tree a brown bear stood on hind legs at full stretch, she looked up at the enormous beast, snout turned to side and teeth exposed. The form of its claws fascinated her, how dull and blunt they looked compared to the large cats, though just as deadly she assumed. Then she saw the fluffy white tail of another creature peeking through from the next display, she hurried along to the next section and stood back.

The large rocks each displayed the wolf family; Arctic wolves on the lower level surrounded by fake snow showing them pouncing on their prey, the grey wolf on the upper levels looking down at his brothers and one with head tilted back in howl. There was a card in front of the display explaining the history of the wolf, and its origins with native lore, Amelia read with intrigue. Out of the corner of her eye she was sure something moved, suddenly being alone surrounded by all the animals was starting to become disturbing, as she looked around the room their dead eyes stared back, she felt her skin prickle under her clothing.

The black wolf on the second rock stood out amongst the others, she glanced around the room making sure there was no one around, and climbed onto the rock. Sitting next to the black wolf she held out her hand and touched its fur, velvety soft to the touch releasing a delicate scent. Amelia looked at the eyes, moist and welcoming. She noticed that all of the wolves had eyes like that, stepping down onto the next rock she stroked the grey wolf from snout to tail, she wasn't certain, but it looked as though the fur sprang back like the skin underneath reacted to her touch.

"Miss Scott." The voice rang out in the empty room.

Amelia quickly jumped down from the display, her heart pounding.

The security guard was standing by the big cat section. "I'm afraid this area is due to be cleaned and I must ask that you vacate."

She quickly made her way towards the security man, feeling eyes on her back as she did so.

Handing her access pass to the receptionist she felt a sudden loss. Touching her fingertips with her thumb she recalled the feel of the wolves fur, electrifying to the touch. She would have to come back and look at the display more closely.

# chaptra seyth warn ugens

The drive back home was filled with questions from her conversation with Professor Armand; why he didn't seem to think they should call the authorities, that she should think about what it was that *she* has done to make them come close. Getting out of the car Amelia rummaged through her bag pulling out the David Eddings book she was currently enjoying, a day at the beach reading was something she could do with, something to take her mind off recent events. Finding a peaceful spot away from tourists she sat down on the soft sand and pulled out the book. She still had some water left in the bottle given to her at the library and took a long sip, refreshingly good on a beautiful day. As she looked at the words on the page she couldn't stop thinking about the wolf display; the feel of the fur, the eyes, the smell; so unlike the other displays, so lifelike, so real. She closed her eyes from the bright sun reflected upon the page and let her head drop onto her bag.

"And you're sure you haven't seen her today?" asked Seth.

"No, she hasn't been down today, is there something wrong Seth?" asked Mr Bateman.

He shook his head. "No, nothing wrong." He tried to fake a smile. "Thank you for your time." He walked back to the store shaking his head when Sonny and Daniel approached. "I've looked everywhere."

"Not everywhere," said Daniel.

"I'll try the cottage again." Seth took the mobile phone out of his pocket checking for messages. "Could you two do a sweep again, if she is on foot then maybe she is walking back from somewhere."

Sonny and Daniel both nodded and left the bookshop, the roar of motorbikes echoed in the darkness. Seth locked up the store, setting the alarm as he left, he sat on his bike and sighed; Amelia's absence did not bode well, revving the machine to life he sped off to Lowe Cottage.

The cottage was in darkness except for the lamp in the window. He felt the bonnet of her car with the back of his hand, stone cold. He sniffed the air searching for clues and then flinched, climbing onto his bike Seth pulled out his phone.

"Meet me at Old Man Malloy's, she has to be with him."

The cool breeze on her face brought her out of slumber, but it was the greyness that had her confused. She looked around at the deserted beach;

the sun had long since set and the ocean was black. The wind began to rise, shivering she pulled her cardigan tighter to her body to conserve heat. Picking up her book and water bottle she placed them in her bag and made her way towards the rocky outcrop aided by what little light was left. When she got to the top Amelia looked down at the winding lane surrounded by high hedges. Walking in the dark again, she shook her head, however did she get herself into these situations, picking up her pace she prayed she would be home soon.

Amelia focussed on the lane ahead, the night calls of the owl rang out in the distance, she tried to think of a happy place, and started to hum a tune that had no rhythm, but gave her the company she desperately needed. The tall hedges seemed to close in as she neared the bend, and then there was a noticeable silence, the call of the night animals could no longer be heard. She felt her stomach tighten. The hedges to her left rustled, a cat she thought, but it was too large to be a domestic feline. Thudding steps on undergrowth grew louder; she broke into a fast walk desperate to reach home when she heard heavy breathing. Whatever was in the hedge was keeping pace with her, a scraping guttural noise sounded and she stopped. Trying to recall the notes on wolves from the museum, she panicked, was she supposed to play dead, or run, or was she supposed to make a lot of noise, she wasn't sure, maybe that was bear encounters. Instinct took over and she grabbed her bag and ran. The pounding of the heavy steps echoed to her right; she was surrounded.

Amelia started to panic, taking in quick breaths she could taste metal in the back of her dry throat, her breathing became laboured and chest tightened. The grey road ahead bent to the left, shadows formed on chimney tops when she neared one of her neighbours' cottages, she let out a long breath hoping they would be home. In the distance she heard motorcycles and the thought of Seth made her run faster. The bushes rustled as they came closer still, but the roar of the bike seemed to be closing in. She ran as fast as she could towards the noise when she saw a blur of grey pounce from the hedge behind her. Amelia shrieked. Her feet pounded the hardened tarmac surface, the soles of her feet numb from impact. Nearing the corner she darted out of the way to avoid colliding with the motorbike hurtling towards her.

Amelia fell to the floor, her hands stopping her body from hitting the ground, but her knees were not so lucky. The rider skidded towards the hedge and rolled to safety, the bike carried on down the lane, sparks flying in its wake, as the metal ground against the road. Amelia looked up to see Sonny run towards the hedge; he looked back and yelled something to her then took off towards the meadow; two blurs of grey followed him. Having dropped her bag in the commotion, the contents strewn across the ground, she watched the water bottle roll down the hill and then stopped when it hit something soft. The animal crunched down on the bottle popping the plastic and emptying the remaining contents, the bottle fell to the ground with a hollow sound. The large wolf looked up at her and growled; her eyes widened watching it walk slowly towards her. The only sound she could hear was the sound of her blood thumping in her head, she almost didn't hear the other bikes when they screeched to a halt behind the beast.

"Amelia," Seth shouted. "Run."

The wolf turned and snarled, snapping his jaws at Seth and Daniel, its head lowered and lips pulled back to reveal canines as it put itself between the men and Amelia. Seth scrunched his face at the beast revealing his human set of teeth and growled, finding her footing, she felt a surge of pain in her knee when she stood. Daniel walked to the other side of the animal trying to distract it giving her a chance to get away. All it took was another bellow from Seth to get out of there and she did, as fast as her legs would carry her.

She heard Daniel and Seth yelling at the animal behind her and carried on down the lane when a blur of grey burst from the hedge ahead. The wolf snarled and snapped its jaws at her, looking around she noticed the gap in the hedge it had made and dashed through towards the meadow in the direction Sonny had fled. She ran through the long grass whipping at her ankles, stinging and numbing her cold flesh, but she had to keep moving, she heard the animal behind her panting and pounding, glancing to her right she saw two figures running in tandem. Seth and Daniel must have gotten away but were also being pursued by more wolves. The small wall ahead looked easy enough to scale, glancing behind she saw the wolves advance and knew it would be no obstacle for them. The trees beyond the wall were tall, and the lowest branches were not within her reach, she knew once she got over the wall she had to look for a tree she could climb.

Scrambling over the stone wall she lost her footing and scraped her leg down the sharp edges of protruding stone, she winced with a sharp intake of breath, but knew she had to keep moving. More shouting in the darkness made her think of Seth and the others, they wouldn't abandon her, it was all that kept her from giving up.

The ground became softer under foot, a welcomed change from the hard tarmac and long grass; weaving between the trees she almost burst into tears when she saw a light up ahead. A small cottage appeared through the darkness, chimney was smoking and there was a light coming from a room on the ground floor. A burst of energy propelled her forward towards salvation, with little time to think, she had to get their attention before she arrived at the house. Amelia called out but there was no reply, when she approached the front door she banged as hard as she could. The wolves were closing in, she saw two at the tree line slowly padding the perimeter, their eyes fixed on her. Amelia ran to the side of the house and saw a wood store propped against the wall; looking up to the rear of the house she saw a faint light through thin curtains in the top room. Climbing on top of the pile of wood she pulled herself onto the lower single storey roof just as the black wolf jumped forward, Amelia pulled her leg up quickly. The other wolves prowled around the bottom of the wood store snarling at her, she knew it wouldn't be long until they realised it wasn't too high for them to try. Ignoring the throbbing pain in her leg she pulled herself up onto the sloping roof and frantically banged on the window with the palm of her hand.

"Is anyone there? Please, let me in."

A clatter below told her the wolves were getting adventurous, claws scraped the wall sounding like nails down a black board she held up her hands to cover her ears and closed her eyes, whatever was to come she didn't want to see it. As she waited for the end, she suddenly felt arms around her waist and was being pulled backwards. Punching her arms and legs she began to scream and then she was on the floor again. Above her she saw a tall man looking out to the darkness, he slowly closed the window and drew the curtains before turning to her.

"William? What are you doing here?"

He was stood in just a pair of black jeans, no shirt, and no shoes or socks. His chest rising and falling quickly. "Are you hurt?" he asked quietly.

Amelia looked down at her arms, scrapes from the fall in the lane no doubt and the climb up the wall.

"You're bleeding," he said kneeling down next to her.

"Just surface scrapes nothing major," she said shrugging holding up her elbow.

He shook his head and moved her right leg. "No, you are bleeding."

When she looked down at her leg caked in blood she wondered what colour that was. "So I am." Amelia fainted.

William laid her gently on the bed brushing her hair from her face. He stood looking at her and sighed. "It was not meant to be this way."

Raised voices roused her from sleep, when she opened her eyes she looked around the room, modestly decorated, but not without its extravagant additions. The four-poster bed was comfortable, and from where she lay she could make out what looked like a luxury en-suite. A small dresser by the bed had a jug of water and tumbler, which she quickly reached for. The tightness of skin on her leg stopped her from over-reaching, when she pulled back the covers she had been undressed and was now wearing just her t-shirt and knickers, her trousers noticeably absent. Looking around the room she saw them draped over the edge of the chair at the bottom of the bed. Pulling her leg towards her she ran her fingers down her calf, where a bandage was neatly wrapped around her right ankle. The voices became louder from somewhere else in the house, and she could make out a few of the words. Standing, she hobbled to the door and slowly opened it a crack to better hear.

"It happened and we deal with this."

"This is not how it was supposed to be. You have made a mockery of our ancestry."

"I am well aware of protocol Eldrich, I did write it after all." His voice sounded strained, but still held its velvety quality, there was no mistaking it was William.

She took a step out of the room to see who he was talking to, from the top of the stairs she saw William and four men in the hallway, one of them she recognised as the guy with bright white hair who had been arguing with Daniel outside the bookshop.

"Then I suggest you get back to the drawing board and make some new ones before all our heads roll. Onen hag oll."

A crack sounded out and there was silence.

"May I remind you what happened to the last brother that questioned my authority," said William.

"Running a bookshop is not a punishment," sneered Eldrich.

The sound of sliding metal echoed around the house as William unsheathed a vicious looking medieval sword, it's design to ensure the most damage against soft tissue. Amelia held her breath.

"You forget your place." William held the sword to Eldrichs' throat, the edge of the blade dug into his skin, blood trickled down the blade towards the hilt. His brother knelt down before him, arms outstretched. "If you wish for a life of servitude then all you need do is ask." He clenched his jaw. "She comes willingly that is the rule. Circumstance has merely brought the decision quicker."

"How do you know she will?"

"She will."

"But Setali—"

Amelia gasped stepping away from the top step, the floorboard underfoot creaked alerting the men downstairs.

William looked up the flight of stairs and then turned to his brothers. "Leave us."

She heard footsteps and the front door open. Peering around the corner she watched William pull the sword away and place it back in its sheath. The remaining men each nodded and turned to leave, the white haired man kneeling slowly stood, bowed to William, then turned to join his brethren.

Amelia quickly returned to the room and jumped into the bed, lowering herself under the covers. William entered smiling to himself.

"I have brought you a snack," he said placing the tray on the nightstand. "Toast and honey, and a mug of tea."

Amelia turned over to face him and yawned. "Mmm. Sounds lovely," she said sitting upright.

"My housemaid tended to your trousers, did a very good job of stitching them back together." He walked to the bottom of the bed and held up her trousers inspecting the lower leg. "Really remarkable, you wouldn't know."

He sat on the edge of the bed and passed her the tray of food. Amelia took a bite of the toast and let the flavour roll over her tongue. "You must thank her for me."

"Of course." He watched her eat and smiled sweetly. "May I take a look at your bandage?"

Nodding she pulled back the covers and let him hold her leg, placing it on his knee he slowly began to unravel the gauze.

"I heard voices," she said watching him closely.

"It was nothing."

When he got to the skin he ran his finger over the pink flesh.

"Well?" she asked. His expression worried her when his brow knitted together. "How does it look?" When he didn't answer her she became anxious. "William?"

"I am so sorry," he whispered.

"What?" She asked, unsure she heard him correctly.

Putting the toast down on the plate Amelia tucked her leg to her chest so she could inspect it for herself. There were three horizontal lines on her ankle, which didn't look that horrendous, if anything, they were healing well. "I can't believe I fainted at the sight of my own blood. I have never done that before."

"Perhaps it was the adrenaline," he offered.

The memories started to come back to her. Walking down the lane, the strange noises in the hedges, the feel of her feet on the tarmac and then falling when Sonny almost rode into her.

"Sonny," she said trying to get out of bed. "My god, William, you have to go check on Sonny, he fell off his bike."

William held her shoulders. "It is alright, Amelia, calm down."

She had been running, running from the wild dogs, but they weren't dogs, they were, "Wolves," she whispered. "William, did you see the wolves? They chased me here. Chased Sonny, Seth and Daniel. You have to see if they are okay."

"Amelia." William gently squeezing her arm, his touch warm and soothing. "I have sent some people out looking for them, if there is anything wrong, they will let me know."

Her stomach growled, taking another bite of the toast she started to feel more relaxed.

He looked away unable to maintain eye contact. "I need to talk to you about something."

"But you said they would—"

"Not about them, about..." He closed his eyes.

"About what William?" She edged closer to him pushing the food away and placed her hand on his knee. "What do you need to talk to me about?"

He stood and walked to the window leaving her sat on the bed. "I am glad you are okay."

Amelia huffed. "Takes more than a pack of wolves to see me off," she said sarcastically, if only to calm her own nerves. Last night had been intense and happening upon the cottage was a godsend. When he didn't turn around she began to show concern. "What is it, what did you want to talk about? Is it the Library job?"

He slowly turned to face her. "I am so sorry."

She had never seen him that way; he looked so lost, like he had no one else in the world. Walking over to him she held his hand, forcing him to look at her. "Tell me. What's happened?"

"The wolves. They are not like other wolves."

"Lupus something or other, the professor said. He also said if we leave them be, they wouldn't bother us." She rolled her eyes. "Wait 'til I see him."

"They are not like other wolves you have ever known," he whispered. "They carry a genetic makeup never seen before and I am afraid your wound is…" He closed his eyes.

"My wound? What do you mean?" She looked down at her leg. "You mean one of them bit me? I'm infected? Is it rabies?" Her voice gradually rising.

"Shh, no Amelia," he said trying to calm her down. "It is not rabies."

"Good, I thought I was going to die there for a minute."

"That is the point."

"You mean I *am* going to die?" A lump forming in her throat.

"You are not going to die."

She shook her head. "William you are not making any sense." She turned to sit on the edge of the bed, the scar on her ankle burning and itching she began rubbing it to ease the ache. "Everyone dies William, eventually."

"No, I mean you are not going to die. Not ever."

"Have you been smoking something?"

He sat by her side. "Amelia. The wolves."

She looked at him waiting for him to continue when his eyes turned black and then flashed amber in colour. She moved away from him. "What the hell." Jumping off the bed to the other side she slammed into the wardrobe. "Stay the hell away from me."

He stood holding out his hand. "Amelia, please."

The scar on her ankle started to burn with an intensity she had never known. Pain shot up her leg making her knees buckle, crying out in pain she fell to the floor. William leapt to her side to hold her upright. "Stay away from me," she shouted.

"Amelia, please let me explain."

"Explain what?"

"I am sorry."

"Sorry for scaring the shit out of me."

He sat her on the edge of the bed and knelt down before her. "I am truly sorry for biting you."

She stopped breathing. "You said the wolf…" Her thoughts raced, he spoke of belonging, of responsibilities, of his brothers, of longing. Then the dreams filtered into her subconscious, the ball, the cloak, the wolf mask. It all started to make sense. "Oh my god, are you saying you're a…" she couldn't bring herself to say it.

"Humans call us werewolves or lycans."

"Phfft." She restrained a laugh. "This is all a dream, a dream. It's got to be, and any minute now I'm going to wake up. Please I just want to wake up now," she said shaking her head.

"I didn't want it to be this way."

"Oh, right, because the first thing you say to a person you like is, 'hey, wanna be a werewolf like me?'"

"Amelia. Don't be facetious."

"No, you wait. You're saying there are beings the human world would have us think are myth and you're expecting me to just accept it?"

"I was hoping—"

"You were hoping what? I would be some sort of groupie that couldn't wait for some vampire or werewolf to bite her, make her immortal, take her to be his bride." He lowered his head. "Oh my god. Is that what I am to you? This is some sort of cult thing?"

William growled. "We are not a cult."

"I've got to get out of here." She jumped from the bed, picked up her trousers and ran to the door. When her hand touched the handle William slammed the door shut.

"You cannot go."

"Am I a prisoner?" she asked dangerously.

"Of course not."

"Then let me go."

He shook his head. "I cannot do that."

"So I *am* a prisoner."

"Amelia, you make this very difficult for me."

"For you." She folded her arms in defiance. "I'm sorry, did you just have your whole world ripped apart from under you? No. Are you being held against your will? No."

"You need to stay here for your own protection."

Amelia threw her trousers on the bed. "Oh, this just gets better! For my own protection? So tell me," she said turning to face him. "Who, or what do I need protection from?"

He walked slowly towards her stopping within an inch, Amelia's body relaxed, the tension easing away. "From yourself."

# about the author

Ruth Shedwick graduated from Liverpool John Moores University with a degree in Environmental Planning. Her passion for the natural environment and love for creatures great and small is evident in her writing. She currently lives in Northern England on rural moorland on the edge of ancient woodland and shares her home with three mini-panthers (*felis silvestris catus*).

Since an early age, Ruth has been intrigued by the ancient world, folklore, myths and legends and explores the unknown. She started writing following a series of recurring dreams and has not looked back since. She has contributed to several projects including 'The Dark Carnival: An Anthology of Horror' which became Amazon number one best seller 'horror anthology'.

Ruth has a passion for creative design and has worked with animal charities, environmental programmes and heritage groups, including South Lancashire Bat Group. She is also the creative backbone for Bríd's Cross Brewing.

For further information visit her website at
www.ruthshedwick.com
Social media channels can be found @ruthshedwick
Twitter, Facebook and Instagram

# *acknowledgements*

As this is my first novel, I have a lot of acknowledgements to make, not only for pushing this through to publication, but also for those who have helped me grow as an individual and as an author.

To all those who gave me life lessons - thank you for planting the seeds. Thank you to Danielle, Gemma and Alexandra for falling in love with my work and engaging with the characters - you guys have really helped me face my fears and given me the inspiration to continue.

Thank you to my parents, sister and niece for smiling through my eccentricities and to my personal cheerleader, Meg, for believing in me, I cannot thank you enough. To my love, Sean, you give me inspiration every day to fall deeply into this world and entrust my passion, you are without doubt, my driving force.

To my extensive family and friends, I'm truly blessed to have you in my life. For all the losses (and there have been plenty) both personally and professionally, you've been my therapy.

Thank you Alex for trusting my judgement and seeing this through to the end. Massive thanks to Stuart and the team at Chiselbury for taking on Trembleath and believing in my work, and to David for introductions.

A big big shout out to the hugely talented Vivian for the beautiful watercolour cover artwork, the original of which is proudly on display in my home.

And lastly, but by no means least - thank you to YOU for picking up this novel and reading, I'm truly honoured.

*next in series*

# Gourvleydh

Printed in Great Britain
by Amazon

36682934R00128